The DINOSAUR Lords

VICTOR MILÁN

A TOM DOHERTY ASSOCIATES BOOK | NEW YORK

THE DINOSAUR LORDS

Interior illustrations by Richard Anderson

Maps by Rhys Davies

A Tor Book
Published by Tom Doherty Associates, LLC
175 Fifth Avenue
New York, NY 10010

www.tor-forge.com

Tor® is a registered trademark of Tom Doherty Associates, LLC.

ISBN 978-0-7653-8211-5

Our books may be purchased in bulk for promotional, educational, or business use. Please contact your local bookseller or the Macmillan Corporate and Premium Sales Department at 1-800-221-7945, extension 5442, or by e-mail at MacmillanSpecialMarkets@macmillan.com.

First Edition: July 2015
First Mass Market Edition: June 2016

Printed in the United States of America

0 9 8 7 6

To my friends whose astonishing generosity and sacrifice made possible not just this book but my continued survival.

I can't name you all—I don't even know who all of you are—so I'll name none. You know who you are.

Neither words nor riches can ever repay what I owe you. My awe, humility, and gratitude will live so long as I. As will my love.

Thank you.

ACKNOWLEDGMENTS

My deepest thanks to my fellow writers of Critical Mass, whose kind wisdom taught me how to write this novel: Daniel Abraham, Yvonne Coats, Terry England, Ty Franck, Sally Gwylan, Ed Khmara, George R. R. Martin, John J. Miller, Matt Reiten, Melinda Snodgrass, Jan Stirling, Steve "S. M." Stirling, Emily Mah "E. M." Tippetts, Lauren Teffeau, Ian Tregillis, Sage Walker, and Walter Jon Williams.

I believe there is no other resource like you in the world. (And please forgive me if I overlooked you!)

Special thanks to my old friend Mike Weaver, who told me how Grey Angels Emerged.

To my Dinosaur Army, who helped me spread the word.

And to Wanda Day, who crocheted me a Triceratops head. And for whom Rob's axe is decidedly not named.

AUTHOR'S NOTE

One thing you should know.
This world—Paradise—isn't Earth.
It wasn't Earth. It won't ever be Earth.
It is no alternative Earth.
All else is possible . . .

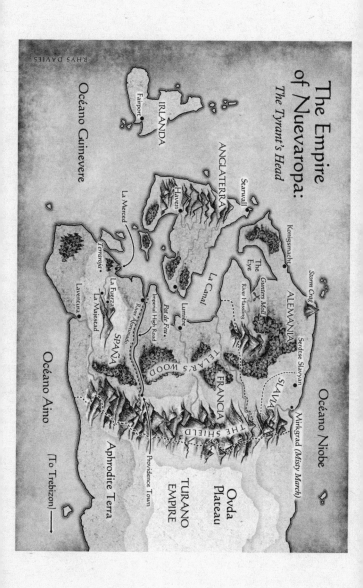

The Empire of Nuevaropa:
The Tyrant's Head

RHYS DAVIES

IRLANDA
Fairport

ANGLATERRA
Starwall
Haven
La Merced
Terranja
Laventura
La Fuerza
La Majestad
SPAÑA
Imperial High Road
River Montañada
Por de Feu
Lumière
La Canal
Königsmacht
The Eye
Gunters Mill
River Hassling
ALEMANIA
Storm Crag
Sardtse Slavyan
Minkgrad (Missy March)
SLAVIA
TEARS' WOOD
FRANCIA
THE SHIELD
Providence Town
Aphrodite Terra
TURANO EMPIRE
Ovda Plateau

Océano Guinevere
Océano Niobe
Océano Aino

(To Trebizon) ⟶

La Merced

Los Altos

Lance's Castle

④

⑦

Creators'
House

Hadrosaur
River

El Abrazo

Bahia
Alegre

Maris' Shield

1 The Three Sisters
2 City Palace
3 The Market
4 Coast Road
5 Commerce Way
6 Firefly Palace
7 Creation Square

Adelina's Road

The Horns

Adelina's Frown

La Canal

RHYS DAVIES

Wars begin when you will,

but they do not end when you please.

—NICCOLÒ MACHIAVELLI,
FLORENTINE HISTORIES, BOOK III, CHAPTER 2

Prologue

Pastoral/Aparecimiento
(Pastorale/Emergence)

Dragón, **Dragon**—*Azhdarchid*. The family to which
the largest of the furred, flying reptiles called fliers or
pterosaurs belong; wingspan 11 meters, stands over 5
meters high. Lands to prey on smaller dinosaurs and
occasionally humans.

—THE BOOK OF TRUE NAMES

THE EMPIRE OF NUEVAROPA, FRANCIA, DUCHY OF
HAUT-PAYS, COUNTY PROVIDENCE

Toothed beaks sunk in low green and purple
vegetation, the herd of plump, brown, four-
legged dinosaurs grazed placidly, oblivious to
the death that kited beside sheer white cliffs high above.

Though he lay on a limestone slab with hands
laced behind his head, their herd-boy was less complacent. He had put aside his broad straw hat and
green feather sun-yoke, intending to doze away the

morning. His small Blue Herder dog, lying in the grass beside him, would alert him if danger from the ground threatened the three dozen fatties in his charge. But then he spotted the dark form wheeling hopefully against the perpetual daytime overcast, and all hope of relaxation fled.

He didn't believe stories about monstrous flying reptiles like this great-crested dragon swooping down on short-furred ten-meter wings to carry off beasts or men. Nobody he knew had seen any such thing. What dragons *could* do was land and, tall as houses, stalk prey on wing-knuckles and short hind legs.

I'm not scared, the boy told himself. It was mostly even true. Like land-bound predators from little vexers to Nuevaropa's greatest predator, the matador, a dragon preferred easy meat. It wouldn't like stones cast from the boy's sling, nor the yapping and nipping of a dog far too clever and nimble for it to stab with its sword beak.

The dog hopped up and began to bark excitedly. The boy sat up, feeling bouncer-bumps rise on his bare arms. That meant danger closer to hand.

He sat up to look for it. It wasn't lurking in the meadow splashed with blue and white wildflowers. That didn't offer enough cover even for a notoriously stealthy matador.

To his right rose the white cliffs, and beyond them the Shield Mountains, distance-blued, a few higher peaks silver-capped in snow despite the advent of spring. Away to the southwest the land shrugged brush-dotted foothills, then sloped and smoothed away into the fertile green plains of his home county of Providence, interrupted by the darker greens of forested ridges and stream-courses.

Several fatties, still munching, raised frilled heads to peer in the same direction the dog did. Though members of the mighty hornface tribe of dinosaurs, they lacked horns, and might. Meek, dumpy beasts, they grew to the length of a tall man and the height of a tall dog.

They were staring at a dozen or so plate-back dinosaurs that swayed into view in the meadow not forty meters downslope. The beasts' bodies looked like capital Ds lying down. The herd bull was especially impressive, four meters tall to the tips of the double row of yellow spade-shaped plates that topped his high-arched back, his scaled hide shading from russet sides to yellow belly.

His tail spikes, nearly as long as the herd-boy was tall, could tear the guts out of a king tyrant. The fatties began switching their thick tails, spilling half-ground greenery from their beaks to bleat distress. Plate-backs were placid, but also nearsighted. They tended to lash out with their tails at anything that startled them. Which meant almost anything that got close to them.

The herd-boy was on his feet, dancing from foot to foot, sandals flapping against his soles. His best course was to stay put and hope the intruders went away on their own. If they didn't, he'd have to chuck rocks at them with his sling. If that didn't work, he'd be forced to run at them hollering and waving his arms. He *really* didn't want to do that.

He looked urgently around for some alternative. And so he saw something far worse than a herd of lumbering Stegosaurus. His dog began to growl.

It strode from the cliff fully formed, Emerging from white stone in one great stride. Two and a half meters tall it loomed, gaunt past the point of emaciation, grey. It lacked skin; its flesh appeared to have dried, cracked, and eroded like the High Ovdan badlands the caravanners described.

He knew it, though he had never seen one. No one had seen one in living memory. Or so far as anyone knew—because most of those who laid eyes on a Grey Angel, one of the Creators' seven personal servants and avengers, didn't live to talk about it.

The Angel stopped. It turned its terrible wasted face directly toward the herd-boy. Eyes like iron marbles nestled deep in the sockets. Their gaze struck him like hammers.

I'm dead, he thought. He fell facedown into pungent weeds at the base of his rock and lay trying to weep without making noise.

Through a drumroll of heartbeats he heard his dog barking furiously by his head, where, both prudent and courageous, she had withdrawn while still shielding her master from the intruder. The acid sound of fatties whining their fear penetrated his whiteout terror and kicked awake the boy's duty-reflex: *My flock! In danger!*

Realizing he was somehow *not* dead—yet—he raised his head. His fatties were loping away down the valley, tails high. Then fear struck through him like an iron stinger dart.

The Angel was looking at him.

"Forget," the creature said in a dry and whistling voice. "Remember when you are called to do so."

White light burst behind the boy's eyes. When it went out, so did he.

———

He woke to his dog licking his face. Bees buzzed gently amidst the smell of wildflowers. A fern tickled his ear.

What am I doing dozing on the job? he wondered. *I'll get a licking for sure.*

Sitting up, he saw with sinking heart that his flock was strewn out downhill across low brush-flecked foothills for a good half kilometer.

For a just a moment his soul and body rang, somehow, as if he stood too close to the great bronze bell in All Creators' Temple in Providence town when it tolled. He tasted fear like copper on his tongue.

The feeling passed. *I must have had a bad dream,* he thought.

He stood. Cursing himself for a lazybones, he began trotting down toward his vagrant flock.

He prayed to Mother Maia he could get them rounded up again before anyone noticed. It was his greatest concern in life right now.

Part One

La Batalla Última

(The Last Battle)

Chapter 1

Tricornio, **Three-horn, Trike**—*Triceratops horridus.* Largest of the widespread hornface (ceratopsian) family of herbivorous, four-legged dinosaurs with horns, bony neck-frills, and toothed beaks; 10 tonnes, 10 meters long, 3 meters at the shoulder. Non-native to Nuevaropa. Feared for the lethality of their long brow-horns as well as their belligerent eagerness to use them.

—THE BOOK OF TRUE NAMES

THE EMPIRE OF NUEVAROPA, ALEMANIA, COUNTY AUGENFELSEN

They appeared across the river like a range of shadow mountains, resolving to terrible solidity through a gauze of early-morning mist and rain. Great horned heads swung side to side. Strapped to their backs behind shieldlike neck-frills swayed wicker fighting-castles filled with archers.

"That tears it!" Rob Korrigan had to shout to be heard, though his companion stood at arm's length on high ground behind the Hassling's south bank. Battle raged east along the river for a full kilometer. "Voyvod Karyl's brought his pet Triceratops to dance with our master the Count."

Despite the chill rain that streamed down his face and tickled in his short beard, his heart soared. No dinosaur master could help being stirred by sight of these beasts, unique in the Empire of Nuevaropa: the fifty living fortresses of Karyl Bogomirskiy's notorious White River Legion.

Even if they fought for the enemy.

"Impressive," the Princes' Party axeman who stood beside Rob yelled back. Like Rob he worked for the local Count Augenfelsen—"Eye Cliffs" in a decent tongue—who commanded the army's right wing. "And so what? Our dinosaur knights will put paid to 'em quick enough."

"Are you out of your tiny *mind*?" Rob said.

He knew his Alemán was beastly, worse even than his Spañol, the Empire's common speech. As if he cared. He'd had this job but a handful of months, and suspected it wouldn't last much longer.

"The Princes' Party had the war all its own way until the Emperor hired in these Slavos and their trikes," he said. "Three times the Princes have fought Karyl. Three times they've lost. Nobody's defeated the White River Legion. *Ever*."

The air was as thick with the screams of men and monsters, and a clangor like the biggest smithy on the world called Paradise, as it was with rain and the stench of spilled blood and bowels. Rob's own guts still roiled and his nape prickled from the side effects of a distant terremoto: the war-hadrosaurs' terrible, inaudible battle cry, pitched too low for the human ear to hear, but potentially as damaging as a body blow from a battering ram.

An Alemán Elector, one of eleven who voted to confirm each new Emperor on the Fangèd Throne, had inconsiderately died without issue or named heir. Against precedent the current Emperor, Felipe, had named a close relative as new Elector, which gave the Fangèd Throne and the Imperial family, the Delgao, unprecedented power. The Princes' Party, a stew of Alemán magnates with a few Francés ones thrown in for spice, took up arms in opposition.

The upshot of this little squabble was war, currently raging on both banks and hip-deep in a river turning slowly from runoff-brown to red. As usual, masses of infantry strove and swore in the center, while knights riding dinosaurs and armored horses fought on either side. Missile troops and sundry engines were strung along the front, exchanging distant grief.

Rob Korrigan worked for the Princes' side. That was as much as he knew about the matter, and more than he cared.

"You forget," the house-soldier shouted. "We out-number the Impies."

"Gone are the days, my friend, when all King Jo-hann could throw at us was a gaggle of bickering grandes and a mob of unhappy serfs," Rob said. "The Empire's best have come to the party now, not just Karyl's money-troopers."

The axeman sneered through his moustache. "Pike-pushers are pike-pushers, no matter how you tart 'em up in browned-iron hats and shirts. Or are you talking about that pack of spoiled pretty boys across the river from us, and their Captain-General, the Emperor's pet nephew?"

"The Companions are *legend*," Rob said. "All Nuevaropa sings of their exploits. And most of all, of their Count Jaume!"

As I should know, he thought, *since I've made up as many ballads of the Conde dels Flors' deeds as Karyl's*.

The Augenfelsener ran a thumb inside the springer-leather strap of his helmet where it chafed his chin. "I hear tell they spend their camp time doing art, music, and each other."

"True enough," Rob said. "But immaterial."

"Anyway, there's just a dozen or two of them, dinosaur knights or not."

"That's leaving aside the small matter of five hundred heavy-horse gendarmes who back them up."

The house-shield waved that away with a scarred and crack-nailed hand.

Standing in formation across the river, the three-horns sent up a peevish, nervous squalling. A rain squall opened to reveal what now stalked out in front of their ranks: *terror*, long and lean, body held level, whiplike tail swaying to the strides of powerful hind legs. In Rob's home isles of Anglaterra they called the monster "slayer"; in Spañol, "matador," which meant the same. In *The Book of True Names*, they were Allosaurus fragilis. By whatever name, they were terrifying meat-eaters, and delighted in preying on men.

A man rode a saddle strapped to the predator's shoulders, two and a half meters up. He looked barely larger than a child, and not just in contrast to his mount's sinuous dark brown and yellow-striped length. For armor he wore only an open-faced morion helmet, a dinosaur-leather jerkin, and thigh-high boots.

Thrusting its head forward, his matador—matadora—roared a challenge at the dinosaur knights and men-at-arms waiting on the southern bank: "*Shi-raa!*"

The axeman cringed and made a sign holy to the Queen Creator. "Mother Maia preserve us!"

Rob mirrored the other's gesture. Maia wasn't his patroness. But a man could never be too sure.

"Never doubt the true threat's not the monster, but the man," he said. He scratched the back of his own head, where drizzle had inevitably filtered beneath the brim of his slouch hat and begun to trickle down his neck. "Though Shiraa's no trifle either."

"Shiraa?"

"The Allosaurus. His mount. It's her name. Karyl gave it to her when she hatched and saw him first of living creatures in the world, and him a beardless stripling not even twenty and lying broken against the tree where her mother's tail had knocked him in her dying agony. It's the only thing she says, still."

No potential prey could remain indifferent to the nearness of such a monster. That was why even the mighty three-horns muttered nervously, and they were used to her. But the house-shield did rally enough to turn Rob a look of disbelief.

"You know that abomination's *name*?" he demanded. "How do you know these things?"

"I'm a dinosaur master," Rob said smugly. Part of that was false front, to cover instinctive dread of a creature that could bite even his beer-keg body in half with a snap, and part excitement at seeing the fabled creature in the flesh. And not just because meat-eating dinosaurs used as war-mounts were as rare as honest priests. "It's my business to know. Don't you? Don't you ever go to taverns, man? 'The Ballad of Karyl and Shiraa' is beloved the length and breadth of Nuevaropa. Not to mention that I wrote it."

The axeman tossed Shiraa a nervous glance, then glared back at Rob. "Whose side are you on, anyway?"

"Why, money's," answered Rob. "The same as you. And Count Eye Cliffs, who pays the both of us."

The axeman grabbed the short sleeve of the linen blouse Rob wore beneath his jerkin of nosehorn-back hide. Rob scowled at the familiarity and made ready to bat the offending hand away. Then he saw the soldier was goggling and pointing across the river.

"They're coming!"

Shiraa's eponymous scream had signaled the advance. The trikes waded into the river like a slow-motion avalanche with horns. Before them sloshed the matadora and Karyl.

From the river's edge to Rob's right came a multiple *twang* and *thump*. A company of Brabantés crossbowmen, the brave orange and blue of their brigandine armor turned sad and drab by rain, had loosed a volley of quarrels.

Rob shook his head and clucked as the bolts kicked up small spouts a hundred meters short of the White River dinosaurs.

"It's going to be a long day," he said. "The kind of day that Mother warned me I'd see Maris's own plenty of."

The axeman shook himself. Water flew from his steel cap and leather aventail.

"It doesn't matter," he said, all bravado. "Even riding those horned freaks, those Slavo peasant scum can't withstand *real* knights. Young Duke Falk's already chased the Impy knights back up the north bank on our left flank. Soon enough our rabble will over-run their pikes. And there's our victory, clean across."

Glaring outrage that the man should forget that both of *them* were peasant scum, Rob said, "You think shit-foot serf conscripts can defeat the Brown Nodosaurs? Even at a three to one advantage? Man, you're crazier than if you imagine our fat Count's duckbills can beat Karyl's trikes."

"He never faced *us* before."

"You really think that matters, then?"

"Five pesos say I do."

I thought you'd never say that, Rob thought, smirking into his beard.

Downriver to their right, trumpets squealed, summoning the Count's dinosaur knights to mount. Which meant they summoned Rob.

He held faint hope his scheme, which to himself he admitted was daft enough on the face of it, would win his employer's last-minute approval. But of faint hopes was such a life as Rob Korrigan's made.

A cloud of arrows rose from the three-horns' fighting-castles, moaning like souls trapped by wiles of the Fae. Voyvod Karyl, that many-faceted madman, had famously commissioned artisans in his Misty March to discover treatments to keep bowstrings taut in rain such as this, and to prevent the wicked-powerful hornbows from the arid Ovdan uplands from splitting and becoming useless.

"Shit!" Rob yelled. He was almost out of time.

A-boil with conflicting emotions, he turned and ran as best a run as his bandy legs could muster. He clung to the haft of Wanda, the bearded axe slung across his back, to keep her from banging into his kidneys.

"You're on!" he shouted back at the house-shield. "And make it ten, by Maris!"

Arrows stormed down on the mercenary crossbowmen on the Hassling's southern bank. Men shrieked as steel chisel points pinned soft iron caps to their heads and pierced their coats of cloth and metal plates. Rob saw the sad little splashes the return volley made, still fifty meters shy of the trikes. Recurved White River bows sorely outranged the Princes' arbalests.

The three-horns' inexorable approach had unnerved the Brabanters. Shiraa's roar knotted their nutsacks, if the state of Rob's own was any guide. Getting shot to shit now, with no chance on Paradise of hitting back, was simply more than flesh could stand.

Throwing away their slow-to-reload weapons, the front ranks whipped 'round and bolted—right into the faces of their comrades behind. Who pushed back.

The four stingers the Count had emplaced in pairs to the mercenaries' either side might have helped them. The light, wheeled ballistas outranged even barbarian hornbows. Their iron bolts could drop even a ten-tonne Triceratops.

But the engines lay broken and impotent in the shallows with their horsehair cords cut. An Eye Cliffs under-groom who'd watched it all had told Rob how a palmful of Companions had emerged from the river Maia-naked in the gloom before dawn. As he yelled his lungs out to raise the alarm in camp, the knight-monks daggered the engineers and the sentries guarding the stingers as they tried to struggle out of sleep. Then with the axes strapped to their bare backs, they'd had their way with the stingers and dragged the wrecks out into the Hassling with the artillery-men's own nosehorn teams. Before the dozing Augen-felseners could respond, they dove back in the water, laughing like schoolboys, and swam home, having lost not a man.

The under-groom, who for reward had gotten a clout across the chops for not raising the alarm ear-lier and louder, had seemed equal parts disgusted and amused by the whole fiasco. To Rob, it was a classic piece of Companion derring-do. In the back of his mind he was already composing a song.

But now he was in among the war-mounts—Rob's own charges—and needed all his wits about him. He dodged sideways to avoid the sweep of a tall green and white tail, vaulted a still-steaming turd the size of his head, sprinted briefly with a little pirouette at the end to avoid being knocked sprawling by the breastbone of a yellow-streaked purple duckbill that lurched forward as it thrust itself up off its belly.

The last he suspected was no accident. Invaluable as their skilled services were, dinosaur masters were commoners. Nobles who employed them, as the Count did Rob, generally suffered them as necessary evils. Their knights didn't always appreciate them as more than uppity serfs who wanted knocking down.

Or squashing beneath the feet of a three-tonne monster.

But Rob was born sly. His mother had sold him as a mere tad of fifteen to a one-legged Scocés dino-saur master. If he hadn't made that up; at this re-move he had trouble remembering. He'd been forced to come up wise in the ways of war-duckbills. And their owners.

Men shouted. Hadrosaurs belled or piped, each at

ear-crushing volume. Down by the river, the Princes'
luckless arbalesters screamed as White River arrows
butchered them.

Uncrushed, Rob reached the high ground where
the Count had pitched his pavilion. When the Augenfelsen contingent arrived at yesterday's dusk, this
whole stretch of riverbank was all green grass as tall
as Rob's head. Their monsters had chomped it low
and trampled the remnants into the yellow mud.

Rob's head swam from unfamiliar exertion and the
concentrated reek of dinosaur piss and farts. That
was familiar, surely, but he wasn't accustomed to
forcibly pumping his head full of it like this.

Hapless arming-squires grunted to boost the Count
of the Eye Cliffs' steel-cased bulk into the saddle.
Though the cerulean-dappled scarlet duckbill bull
squatted in the muck, it was a nearly two-meter climb.

The Count rode a long-crested sackbut—or Parasaurolophus, as *The Book of True Names* had it. Like
most hadrosaurs, it usually walked on its huge hind
legs, and dropped to all fours to gallop. It had a great
triangle of a head, with a broad, toothed beak and a
backward-arcing tubular crest. The crest gave its voice
a range and striking tones like the slide-operated brass
musical instrument called a sackbut, thus the name.

With a great groan of effort, the Count flung his leg
over. Middle-aged at eighty, his lordship tended to
spend far more time straddling a banquet stool than a
war-mount. It showed in the way his chins overflowed
onto his breast-and-back without apparent intervention of a neck. Unlike their lesser brethren who rode
warhorses, dinosaur knights didn't need to keep themselves in trim. Their real weapon was their mount.

Snorting from both ends, the sackbut heaved him-

self to his feet. A rain-soaked cloth caparison clung
to his sides, molding the pebbly scales beneath. Rob
counted it a blessing that clouds and downpour muted
both the dinosaur's hide and the Count's armor, enameled all over in swirls of blue and gold and green—a
pattern that the Anglysh, usually without affection,
called "paisley." Unlike most dinosaur knights, the
Count had neither picked nor bred his mount to sport
his heraldic colors. They clashed something dreadful.

Rob sucked in a deep breath through his mouth.
As dinosaur master it was his job to keep his lord's
monsters fit, trained, and ready for war. But it was
also his duty to advise his employer on how best to
use his eye-poppingly expensive dinosaurs in battle.
Duty to his craft now summoned Rob to do just that,
and he wasn't happy about it.

He'd have been tending the Count's sackbut this
very instant had his employer not curtly ordered Rob
and his lowborn dinosaur grooms to clear out and
leave final preparations to the squires. In their wisdom, the Creators had seen fit to endow the nobles
who ruled Nuevaropa with courage and strength instead of wit. Or even sense.

"My lord!" Rob shouted. He clutched at a stirrup.
Then he danced back with a nimbleness that belied
his thick body and short legs as the Count slashed at
his face with a riding crop.

"Shit-eating peasant! You dare manhandle me?"

"Please, Graf!" Rob shouted, ignoring what he
deemed an unproductive question whose answer his
employer wouldn't like anyway. "Let me try my plan
while there's still time."

"Plan? To rob me and my knights of glory, you
mean? I spit on your dishonorable schemes!" And

he did. The gob caught Rob full on the cheek. "My knights will scatter these brutes like the overgrown fatties they are."

"But your splendid dinosaurs, lord!" Rob cried, hopping from foot to foot in agitation. "They'll impale themselves on those monsters' horns!"

Slamming shut the visor of his fatty-snout bascinet—which Rob found oddly appropriate—the Count waved a steel gauntlet at his herald, who blew *advance* on his trumpet. Rob winced. The herald couldn't hit his notes any better than the Count's mercenary crossbowmen could hit the White River archers.

Rob sprang back to avoid getting stepped on as the Count spurred his sackbut forward. His knights sent their beasts lurching at a two-legged trot down the gentle slope to the water.

"You'll just disorder your knights when you ride down your own crossbows, you stupid son of a bitch!" Rob shouted after his employer. Whom he was sure couldn't actually hear him. Fairly.

We don't just call them 'bucketheads,' he thought, wiping spit and snot from his face, *because they go into battle wearing pails.*

Despite the urgency drumming his ribs from inside, Rob could only stand and watch the drama play out. Even rain-draggled, the feather crests, banners, and lurid caparisons of fifty dinosaur knights made a brave and gorgeous display.

The mercenary arbalesters had stopped shooting. To Rob their only sensible course now was to run away at speed. He knew, as dinosaur master and minstrel both, how little *pay* means to those too dead to spend it.

Instead, insanely, the rear ranks now battled outright with their fleeing fellows. The Brabanters were among the Empire's ethnic odds and sods, swept together into a single Torre Menor, or Lesser Tower, that claimed to serve all their interests. Even at that it was inferior to the other Towers: the great families that ruled Nuevaropa and its five component Kingdoms. The Brabanters made up for insignificance with lapdog pugnacity. Which won them a name as right pricks.

The White River archers had stopped loosing too. Their monsters now stood just out of crossbow range. Evidently Karyl was content to observe events.

These happened quickly. At last the Brabanters got their minds right. They quit fighting each other and, as one, turned tail. To see bearing down on them the whole enormous weight of their own employers' right wing.

As hadrosaurs squashed the mercenaries into screams and squelches and puffs of condensation, the Legion's walking forts waded forward again. From their howdahs the hornbowmen and -women released a fresh smoke of arrows.

With a pulsing bass hum, the volley struck the Count's dinosaur knights. Arrows bounced off knightly plate. But duckbills screamed as missiles stung thick hides. Rob guessed the archers had switched to iron broadhead arrows.

Already slowed by riding down the crossbowmen, the dinosaur knights lost all momentum in a chaos of thrashing tails and rearing bodies. Wounded monsters bugled and fluted, drowning the shrieks of riders pitched from saddles and smashed underfoot.

Rob held up his right fist to salute the Count, a

single digit upraised. It was, he told himself, an ancient sign, and holy to his patron goddess, Maris, after all.

Then he turned and scuttled east. His employer was a spent quarrel. Now he'd carry out his plan himself.

Chapter 2

Morión, Morion—*Corythosaurus casuarius*. A high-backed hadrosaur; 9 meters long, 3 meters high at shoulder, 3 tonnes. A favored Nuevaropan war-mount, named for the resemblance between its round crest and that of a morion helmet.

—THE BOOK OF TRUE NAMES

Racing across a wasteland of slick, piss-stinking mud proved almost as challenging as evading skittish three-tonne hadrosaurs, if not half so hair-raising. Rob tripped once and slipped once, getting well coated in reeking brown ooze before reaching ground where enough grass survived to stabilize the soil.

Even before he mounted a low hummock to see the log pen he had built to hold his pets, he heard grunts and evil muttering compounded by the odd squeal of annoyance. Upslope by the woods his blue-dappled grey hook-horn, Little Nell, had her snout with its short, thick, forward-curving nasal horn stuck happily in a flowering berry-bush. A stout strider-leather rope secured a hind leg to a tree nearby.

On the palisade perched four local youths. Rain plastered threadbare smocks dyed by the dirt and flora of every place they'd ever been to washboard bodies. They craned frantically up- and downriver in an effort to take in the whole terrific spectacle at once.

Rob had felled the trees for the enclosure in the woods behind the Princes' camp. His Einiosaurus had dragged them into place. Any dinosaur master worth his silver was a capable jackleg pioneer.

He had built the pen strong. Its two dozen occupants were nearly blind, with brains as weak as their eyes. Like most dinosaurs they wouldn't customarily challenge a barrier that *looked* solid. But they might blunder into it.

Renewed trumpeting and banging brought Rob's head up. The Count's dinosaur knights finally blundered through into the river, raising big rust-shot wakes. They left most of the Brabanter mercenaries and half a dozen knights on the bank as reddish highlights in mud and the odd steel crumple.

Duckbills stampeded by White River arrows had smashed through the Eye Cliffs riders like boulders tossed by improbably vast trebuchets. Instead of a solid mass the dinosaurry were a straggling herd. But still that invincible buckethead aggression carried the survivors forward.

Straight onto the horns of Karyl's Triceratops.

Splendid morions and gaudy sackbuts shrieked agony as file-sharpened steel horn-caps impaled chests and throats. Some hadrosaurs reared away from the awful spikes, only to have unarmored bellies ripped open. Never shy about fighting, the trikes put their gigantic heads down to gore and toss with savage joy. Stricken hadrosaurs fell squealing, raising splashes higher than the fighting-castles strapped to their destroyers' backs.

Meanwhile the archers in those lath and wicker howdahs, hung with slabs of nosehorn hide for armor, kept up their high-intensity arrow storm. At this range the missiles penetrated even plate.

Hornbowmen and -women aimed for helmet eye-slits and the weak points at joints. Some took up lances as targets offered to the sides where their mounts couldn't engage. The Struthio Lancers, mercenary skirmishers mounted on lithe striders, swarmed around the Princes' Party flanks, stinging like hornface-flies with arrows, darts, and javelins.

Voyvod Karyl rode his terrible mount in among the foe. Rob saw Shiraa rip an armored sword arm right off a knight, and toss it away like a dog playing with a bone. Karyl's arming-sword flickered like silver flame. Where it struck, nobles fell.

Rob shook his head. Rain and mud flew from his hair. "I told you so, you great git," he muttered to his employer. Who was too far to hear, not to mention preoccupied. And wouldn't have listened anyway.

Rob now found himself facing the dinosaur master's classic dilemma: above all things he loved dinosaurs, the greatest and most majestic of all the Creators' works. Yet it was his fate to set them to destroy each other. As always when watching a battle he had helped to make, Rob Korrigan both exulted and despaired.

Worse—far worse—was soon to come. He knew because he would bring it.

Running a hand over his face to clear his eyes of

muck, Rob turned and yelled for his helpers to fetch the reed torches he'd laid by in tarred, covered baskets to keep dry, and the cheap tin horns he'd bought from a camp-following sutler's cart.

"My turn, laddy bucks," he said.

"Do you really find it beautiful, Jaumet?" Pere asked. His slight build showed despite full white-enameled plate armor. His eyes were large and dark in a gamin face, the lashes long. He wore his jet-black hair shorter than his captain's, finger-length. Rain stuck it fetchingly to his forehead.

Jaume Llobregat, Count of the Flowers and Captain-General of the Order of the Companions of Our Lady of the Mirror, raised his face to the warm rain. He ran both hands up his face and back through his orange, shoulder-length hair. He relished it all—the feel of skin on skin, the sodden hair's texture and the flow of water through it. Even the smells of a score of nervous hadrosaurs: all.

Sensuousness was, for him, religious duty.

He sighed.

"I really do," he said. Standing apart from the other Companions and their giant mounts mustered halfway down the face of the ridge called Gunters Moll, the pair spoke català, the language of their homeland. "The Lady Bella forgive me, I do. We all know how ugly war is up close. But at this remove"—he gestured at the abattoir river—"yes. A terrible beauty. But beauty withal."

Pere shook his head. "You're better at finding beauty amidst ugliness than I."

Though Pere carefully tried to keep his inflection

conversational, Jaume heard the sullen undertone. They had grown up together, best friends long before they became lovers.

He smiled, hoping to lighten Pere's mood. "Perhaps. After all, isn't life always a matter of picking out the beautiful from the hideous?"

"If only all things were beautiful," Pere said.

"What then, dear friend? We strive to increase beauty in this world of ours. But we'll never eliminate the ugly. Should we even hope to? You're a master painter. Isn't the figure meaningless without ground? Without ugliness for contrast, how can we perceive beauty? Isn't it ugliness that gives beauty meaning?"

Pere gave his head a peevish little shake. "You're always right."

Jaume put a hand on the pauldron that protected his friend's left shoulder, enjoying the feel of curved steel and the raindrops beading on its smooth surface.

"Don't I wish that were true? And anyway, when I'm lucky enough to be right, it doesn't mean you're wrong, does it?"

Pere looked away. He always brooded before combat. He had no taste for battle. He was merely very good at it.

But Jaume knew something more was undermining his friend's composure.

"How I love this rain!" a sardonic voice called from behind. He turned to see Mor Florian approaching, looking only slightly awkward as he negotiated the slanting mud and wet grass-covered slope in his metal shoes, or *sabatons*. His blond hair, normally kinked, hung like a wet banner past his shoulders.

"How can you like this rain?" demanded red-haired

Manfredo, who stood nearby talking with his lover, Mor Fernão. A former law student from far Talia in the Basileia of Trebizon, Manfredo loved Order as much as Beauty. As such he mistrusted Florian, who seemed to him to represent its opposite.

Florian grinned. "Consider the alternative: boiling alive in our portable steel ovens."

The others laughed. Even Pere relaxed. His hand at last sought Jaume's and was happily received. Although delicate in appearance, it had the strength of steel wire, and the telltale calluses left by the tools of his three excellences: brush, *guitarra*, and the blade.

I know what troubles you, old friend, Jaume thought. *You dread our return to the Imperial Court at La Merced. But if Uncle accepts my suit, and I marry my Melodía, things needn't change between us.*

He shook his head. That was fatuous. The problem wasn't with the Princesa Imperial, his other best friend and lover—quick-witted and spirited, with her cinnamon skin and laughing dark-hazel eyes and wine-red hair.

Jealousy was considered a vice on Nuevaropa, particularly in the cosmopolitan South. But it had always gnawed Pere. Now it threatened to consume their friendship.

"Dispatch for my lord Count Jaume!"

Down the flank of Gunters Moll, past the plate-and-chain-armored ranks of Brother-Ordinary men-at-arms standing by their coursers, rode a young page in von Rundstedt livery. His blue-feathered great strider seemed to fly across slick grass.

"Give way! I bring a change in plans to the worshipful Captain-General!"

"It's time," said Jaume. "Bartomeu, if you please?"

He walked toward his own mount, the beautiful white and butterscotch morion Camellia. She stood tipped forward onto her forelimbs, plucking daintily at weeds with her narrow muzzle. Hers was an oddly graceful breed, despite the way their low-set necks emphasized their bodies' bulk. She had carried Jaume through many desperate adventures; he loved her like a daughter.

Blond Bartomeu, his arming-squire, trotted up to strap Jaume's bevor shut at the nape of his neck to protect his lower face and throat. Then he urged Camellia to her belly with soft words and pressure on her reins to allow Jaume to mount.

"What could this mean, Jaumet?" asked Pere as his own arming-squire brought his strikingly patterned white-on-black sackbut Teodora to the ground.

"A change of battle plan?" said Florian. "How? It seems pretty straightforward: wait until the White River three-horns break the Princes' knights, then chase the survivors into the hills. Easy, thank the Lady. What's there to change?"

"Whatever our marshal commands, we must obey," intoned Manfredo. His beauty was marred by a somewhat over-square chin, and a tendency to sententiousness.

The strider's long-toed hind feet scrabbled to a halt near Jaume. Its young rider, with blue eyes and a peaches-and-cream Northern complexion beneath near-white hair, simpered at Jaume as he handed over a wax-sealed scroll.

"If you think you're going to seduce your way into the Companions," Florian called, "think again." The boy blushed furiously.

"Florian, be kind," said Jaume. "Well done, lad. Thank you."

The courier stammered thanks and rode back up-hill as fast as his steed's two strong legs could carry him. Jaume frowned at the Imperial commander Prinz-Marschall Eugen's signet stamped into indigo wax. He wondered the same thing as Florian. With a curious apprehension creeping up his neck and into his cheeks he broke the seal, unrolled the scroll, and read.

A chill swept over him like the winter wind that blew down from the Shields into his homeland. He read the few lines of obsessively neat penmanship three times over, blinking at the rain. The letters did not rearrange themselves into a more pleasing order.

Crumpling the parchment, he threw it to the ground. He felt startled gazes. It was an uncharacteristic gesture.

"What is it?" Pere cried.

Not trusting himself to speak, Jaume turned and vaulted into Camellia's saddle. Clucking gently, he got her to her feet. She raised her head with its great round orange-dappled crest and sniffed the air eagerly. Like any good war-hadrosaur, Camellia welcomed battle.

Jaume leaned down to accept his sweep-tailed sallet helmet from Bartomeu. A page stood by holding Jaume's shield and lance. He took them.

Cradling his helmet in the crook of his arm, he faced his knights. *So few, so brave, so beautiful*, he thought. They were only sixteen, out of the twenty-four their Church charter allowed his order. So many more Companions than that had passed through their ranks, to invalid retirement or the Wheel's next turn.

Who'll join them today? he wondered. *If it's my time to be reunited with my Lady, I won't regret it. I have lived my life in beauty.*

"Brothers," he called, pitching his voice to carry. "Whatever I do, follow my lead."

The others stared. "What else would we do?" Florian asked in disbelief.

Jaume shook his head. "I've never asked you to perform such a mission before. And I pray our Lady, never again!"

"Come on, girl! That's the way!"

Whacking Little Nell's flank with a willow withe—which didn't hurt her; that would've taken an axe handle, or better, an axe—Rob drove the two-tonne hook-horn into the river. The chains he'd yoked her with clattered taut. With a groan the wall section tipped outward, then fell with a splash and a slam.

The penned dinosaurs raised bleats of alarmed annoyance. Moving up to grasp the halter strapped to Nell's snout behind the horn, Rob led her far enough upstream to clear the logs from the opening. Then he unhooked the chains and let them fall into the water.

He slapped the hook-horn's broad fanny. Snorting and tossing her head, she trotted twenty meters, splashing maroon water, then turned and hightailed it up the bank. She would wander into the woods a short ways and graze; Rob knew his beloved mount well.

"All right!" he yelled to his young helpers. "Chase 'em out!"

On the inland wall, the four Eye Cliffs youths blew enthusiastically on toy horns and waved torches that

popped and smoked and sparked in the now-sparse
rain. Despite the circumstances, the discord made Rob
wince.

Can't the little blighters try *to find the pitch, even
on such lousy instruments?* But now was no time to
play the artiste. He pulled a tin horn from his belt
and blew it as thoughtlessly as they.

The herd of wild lesser mace-tails he'd spent the
past week catching and gingerly herding along behind the Princes' army streamed out the gate. *The
Book of True Names* dubbed them Pinacosaurus. A
smallish breed of ankylosaur, no more than five meters long, with rounded bony-armored backs as high
as Rob's shoulder, they carried really terrifying two-
lobed bone maces at the tips of their tails.

Which they swung ominously from side to side.
The brutes were well and truly pissed. In that state their
first reaction was to smash something. Also their
second and third.

Above all, the mace-tails feared two things: fire
and noise. By means of both, the urchins drove them
into the river. Rob hoped his terrible tootling, plus
the keen sense of when to jump and which way that
was a vital part of any dinosaur master's repertoire,
would keep the monsters from venting their rage on
him.

Blunt armored heads held low, the mace-tails
churned across the Hassling. Hoping the youths would
remember what he'd told them to do—and actually
do it—Rob ran alongside the herd, honking like a mad
thing.

A cry of many voices but one single note—droning
despair—rose from the Princes' left. Men-at-arms,
dismounted and helmetless, sloshed up the near bank.

On a silken banner stretched between them, its once-glorious colors smirched unrecognizably, they carried the limp form of the Count.

The black shaft, fletched with the White River Legion's two grey feathers and one white, jutting from the right eye-slit of his bascinet told all.

The handful of rebel dinosaur knights who had survived the three-horns were in full retreat. A hundred meters from the river, a thousand men-at-arms sat warhorses that fidgeted and rolled their eyes as the musically bellowing monsters stampeded past to the west of them. Poised to chase and butcher foes fleeing the Count's war-hadrosaurs, they now found themselves facing the full jubilant wrath of the White River Legion trikes.

Karyl rode Shiraa along the front rank, reordering the monsters into a compact horn-bristling bloc. Though some of the fighting-castles had lost crewfolk, so far as Rob could see not a single three-horn had fallen.

Legion trumpets blew. The Triceratops came inexorably on again.

The mace-tails were loping now, breaking water powerfully if not fast. Rob and his yokel helpers stopped knee-deep in water to watch. They didn't want to be close to what was about to happen.

Colossal three-horned heads tossed and bellowed. The trikes' eyesight wasn't keen. But they smelled ancient enemies. And the mace-tails smelled *them*.

Paranoid, bellicose, rivals for the same graze, mace-tails and three-horns were uniquely suited to do each other harm. Trikes could flip the low-slung monsters on their backs with their horns to gash open tender bellies. But in close, the ankylosaurs could smash

Triceratops knees with their eponymous tail-clubs. They could even scuttle under a three-horn to bash the vulnerable insides of its legs.

These things began to happen. In an eyeblink the Legion's iron discipline shattered. Eyes rolling in terror, Triceratops bolted from those terrible tails. Fighting-castles broke away from tall backs to topple into the water, carrying passengers to mostly horrible fates.

Laughing and weeping, Rob Korrigan danced in bloody water. What he felt was beyond even his jongleur's tongue to describe.

He despised all nobles with a fine lack of discrimination. With one exception: Voyvod Karyl Bogomirskiy, the lord who was his own dinosaur master, the age's unequaled artist in the use of dinosaurs in war. The hero who had fulfilled his legendary quest.

Now, with one frightful stratagem, Rob was bringing down Karyl's invincible White River Legion. And crippling and killing the things Rob loved most on Paradise. It was triumph and profanation all in one.

"What are you waiting for, you tin-plated cowards!" he shouted at the immobile ranks of Princes' Party cavalry, who assuredly couldn't hear him. "I've given you victory on a golden plate. Take it! Take it, and *eat*, damn you!"

Choking on sobs, he fell to his knees. Snot streamed from his nostrils.

To his right the fighting had died down. Rob saw the Princes' peasant infantry flowing back south out of the Hassling, but without a rout's mad urgency. The Brown Nodosaur ranks inexplicably continued to stand on the northern bank, wall-solid behind a berm of corpses. They showed no signs of indulging in their customary pursuit plus slaughter.

Down the now-clear river rode several score dinosaur knights. Rob blinked in amazement. Leading them came the Princes' Party hotspur, young Duke Falk von Hornberg. His mount, Snowflake, was the most dreaded flesh-eating dinosaur in all of Aphrodite Terra, a king tyrant—Tyrannosaurus rex, an import to Nuevaropa. An albino, Snowflake was small for his race, no longer than Shiraa, though burlier. Whether dwarf or merely adolescent, Rob didn't know.

Waving above the hadrosaurs that trudged nervously behind the big white meat-eater, Imperial banners mingled implausibly with those of the rebel Princes.

"What in the name of the Fae is going on here?" Rob demanded. He sat back on his heels in the bottom muck to watch.

From the north bank pealed a mighty fanfare. White-enameled armor gleaming even in the paltry sun, the Companions trotted to the aid of Karyl's Legion. *That* roused Rob's soul: if he could admire another noble than Karyl, it was Count Jaume.

Of course, that intervention by a handful of dinosaur knights, with five hundred heavy horse behind, could spoil the grand and perfidious success of Rob's scheme. But he'd shot his bolt. Now he prepared to watch events unfold with a connoisseur's eye—and happy anticipation of the clink of silver in his cup from the songs he'd sing about *this*.

Jaume, his face obscured by sallet and bevor but whose famous mount, Camellia, was unmistakable, couched his lance and charged. After what seemed a moment's hesitation, his Companions did likewise. As one, their hadrosaurs opened their beaks to bellow.

No sound came out—that any human could hear. Rob rocked back with eyes slamming shut as the terremoto's side blast struck him like an unseen fist.

When he opened them again, he refused at first to believe them.

It wasn't the approaching dinosaur knights reeling and clutching heads streaming blood from ruptured orifices. It was Karyl's fighting-castle crews.

Armored from the front against the hadrosaurs' silent war cry by bony frills and faces, almost all the three-horns had their backs to the Companions. They too suffered the terremoto's full effects: fear, burst eardrums, even lesions in the lungs. A Triceratops bull reared high, pawing the air and bleating like a gut-speared springer. Its howdah broke loose, spilling men and women flailing into the river.

The Companions charged straight over them.

Rob boiled to his feet. "What's this?" he screamed. "Treachery?" He hardly knew what else to call it.

The surprise attack caught the already-disordered mercenaries utterly helpless. Even though by now the mace-tails had bulled their way clear to scramble up the north bank and make for the woods, the Legion stood no chance. Formidable as Triceratops' horns were, they were effective only against an enemy in front of them. Even the Companions' Ordinaries worked wicked execution, their horses looking like toys as they hamstrung horned colossi with sword and axe.

Karyl rode Shiraa at a spraddling, splashing run,

trying desperately to herd his surviving three-horns west. That way offered their sole hope of escape.

His matadora came flank to flank with a Companion halberd. The white-and-green brindled hadrosaur was bigger; Shiraa had teeth. Though his eyes rolled in fear beneath a crest with rounded blade to the front and a spike angled to the rear, the Lambeosaurus bull didn't give way. The Companions trained their mounts to overcome even their marrow terror of big meat-eaters. Indeed, the halberd could easily knock the war-galley-slim Shiraa down.

But Karyl's blade slid unerringly through the eye-slit of the Companion's close helmet. The white knight fell. His mount fled, trumpeting despair.

Falk and Snowflake fell on the mercenary lord from his blind spot. For Rob it was a surfeit of wonder: since carnivorous war-mounts were so rare, they almost never faced each other in battle.

Somehow sensing danger, Karyl wheeled Shiraa clockwise. Snowflake struck first. His huge jaws tore a strip of flesh from Shiraa's right shoulder.

The matadora screamed. Her raw wound steamed in the rain, which had begun to come down heavily again.

Falk's battle-axe swung down to smash in the crested crown of Karyl's helmet. Rag-limp, Karyl Bogomirskiy fell into the rising, frothing torrent and vanished.

For a moment Rob thought Shiraa would stand above her master. She and Snowflake darted fanged mouths at each other, roaring rage.

Dinosaur knights, Princely and Imperial alike, closed in. Reluctantly Shiraa backed away. With a sorrowing wail she turned and fled downstream.

The rain closed in, obscuring Rob's sight. Or was it tears?

Rob Korrigan rocked on his knees in the unforgiving river. He mourned beautiful and mighty beasts, and greatness's fall. And cursed himself for the part he'd played in all.

"What have I done?" he sobbed. "What have I sold?"

He raised fists to a leaden Heaven. *"And what has it* bought *me?"*

Chapter 3

Horror, Chaser—*Deinonychus antirrhopus*. Nuevaropa's largest pack-hunting raptor; 3 meters, 70 kilograms. Plumage distinguishes different breeds: scarlet, blue, green, and similar horrors. Smart and wicked, as favored as domestic beasts for hunting and war as wild ones are feared. Some say a Deinonychus pack is deadlier than a full-grown Allosaurus.

—THE BOOK OF TRUE NAMES

The first thing he knew was pain.

Agony beat from his left hand like the pounding of a drum. Blind, he pulled. A cold, rubbery grip resisted.

He became aware of a chill enveloping his whole being, which leached away whatever strength remained within him. A stench, vast as a slow sea surge, of decay. A more concentrated stink, like wind-driven chop, of filth and feces and stale grease.

Cadenced grunting, as of effort. The pain resolved to the root of his finger.

Last came light on sealed lids, red through. He tried

to open his eyes. They refused. The pain in his hand came rhythmic, insistent. His head hurt.

Still without knowing who did so, he willed his eyes to open. Hard. Eyelids parted with a tearing like a wound reopened. He realized dried blood had stuck them together. A crumb caught in the lower lid rasped his left eyeball.

The clouds hung darker and lower than usual. He lay among reeds, half-submerged in cool water. Indistinct against slate sky, a haggard, filthy figure squatted in the river, sawing at his ring finger with a knife. Its blade was apparently none too keen.

He tried to pull his hand away. Squalling like a vexer, the looter yanked back. Dark eyes widened in fury and alarm behind kelp-streamer hair. The knife flashed toward his face.

He fell onto his back in the water, still joined to the looter by his wrist. He put his right hand down to brace. His fingers encountered something hard, cruciform. Before he consciously knew it was a sword hilt, he had it grasped and was lashing back.

Impact shivered up his arm. Blood slashed his face in a hot, hard spray. The looter screeched again and fell back, thrashing and splashing green water that gradually turned the color of rust.

Absently the man wiped at nose and cheeks, discovering in the process a stubble of beard. It felt unfamiliar.

The looter's sloshing subsided. The man glanced down at the sword in his hand and grunted. The blade was snapped off half a meter from its ornate hilt. It had sufficed.

Now still, the looter's body floated on its back with arms extended and forehead tipped back in the water, surrounded by hair like a water-weed halo. From the long skinny breasts tied across its belly with a rawhide thong the man realized he had killed an old woman.

The knowledge evoked little response, beyond detestation for those who preyed on the helpless. Nuevaropa abounded so fantastically in plant and animal life that starving took effort. To be sure, foraging had its risks—like everything else. But no hunger of the belly had driven this creature to attempt to mutilate him. Or kill him when he had the temerity to wake.

That she looked old struck him strange. He did not know why.

He examined his wounded hand. His third finger bore a heavy gold ring that showed a three-horn's head in bold relief. A line of blood encircled its base. Looking closer he realized the wound was shallow but ragged. As he'd suspected, the looter's knife was blunt.

Likely she had a bag of small stolen treasures, now sunk with her in shallow water. That brought complete indifference. He was beyond any desire for gold now.

Survival was another matter. Maybe. He felt vague stirrings of alarm.

The ache throbbing in his head was even more persistent and powerful than that in his hand. He reached up gingerly.

Fingertips found close-cropped hair. The right side of his skull felt moist, mushy; he wondered if it might actually be dented. The pain that shot behind his eyes clear down to his stomach didn't encourage him to probe further.

He felt his first stab of true emotion: dread that he might feel the exposed surface of his brain.

He knew where he was, in general. He remembered facts about his surroundings, the natural world, the structure and functions of his body. And how to wield a sword, clearly, natural as breathing; he transferred it to his left hand without conscious thought. But what he was *doing* here, naked in the shallows of a broad river beneath storm-threatening skies, was a mystery to him.

So was just exactly who he might be.

Urgency began to churn his belly. Life wasn't exactly proving attractive, now he'd been restored to it. But the animal within, once wakened, desired desperately to cling to it.

He rose from the water. Unsteady on quivering blue-white legs, he looked around. The world resolved about him as though summoned into being by the act of observation: a riverbank fenced with a green riot of weeds. The mud beyond, churned by the feet of many men and monstrous beasts. A slope covered in low vegetation climbing to a forest. The air lay cool on his skin.

The stench of rotting flesh was profound.

A tearing noise made him turn, splashing, sword-stub ready. Fifteen meters out in the river and a bit downstream lay a dead duckbill. In the wet warmth the gases of decomposition were already ballooning its vast body. A once-glorious hide of scarlet, orange, and gold had faded to greyish pink, ochre, and mud. A small tailless flier with drab brown fur perched atop it, ripping up a strip of skin with its beak.

Everywhere sprawled or floated the rotting corpses of men, horses, and dinosaurs. Not twenty meters from him a Triceratops lay on its side in mud, its eyes picked empty. Beside it lay a fighting-castle, wickerwork sides and wooden frame broken by the monster's fall. Inexplicably, the sight of the great dead dinosaur twisted his heart and stung moisture from his eyes.

Who am I, he wondered, *to wear a ring worth finishing me off for, and to grieve so for a dinosaur?*

It scarcely mattered now. Now he was no one, mother-naked and stinking with a dent in his skull, lost.

It was morning, he observed from the feel and color of the sun's diffuse light and the way the faint shadows leaned east. Neck muscles creaking and bones crackling protest as if they'd expected never to be used again, he turned to look upstream.

Carnage lay thicker there. Indistinct with distance and mist wisping from the river, men moved about the banks, singly or in small groups. Most were afoot; a few rode horses or striders. He saw no living warhadrosaurs. Nor any big meat-eaters drawn to the feast.

Oddly, that saddened rather than relieved him.

Fear stabbed him through: *I mustn't be found!* he thought.

Whoever he was, he felt a sick certainty that those men would do him harm if they learned he still lived. Painfully he climbed onto land and began to stagger downstream through tatters of mist.

Returning circulation first pricked his legs like needles, then stuck like knives. As he forced himself to a jarring trot, his pulse kept stride. The hammers beating at his temples did likewise.

From thicker fog before him a figure appeared, dark, compact, hooded. He stumbled to a halt, though limbs and body cried out together that once he lost momentum he might never get it back. For three heavy heartbeats, each of which threatened to burst his skull, he stood watching, head tipped to one side, breath wheezing through open mouth.

The figure stood unmoving. Waiting.

What have I left to lose? the man asked himself bitterly. He approached. He couldn't really walk, but only engage in a more-or-less controlled forward fall.

He knew he wasn't a large man. The waiting figure was smaller still. Despite the looseness of its coarse brown robe, its carriage told him it was female.

The apparition's voice confirmed it: "A moment, Voyvod Karyl," it said, feminine and low.

"Voyvod Karyl," he repeated slowly. The words seemed to echo through the clangor in his skull.

He touched his head. "He's dead, I think."

The cowl nodded. "I know. It's why I speak to you. I speak only to the dead."

"You're . . . the Witness?" he asked. Childhood stories, half-remembered and less believed, clamored in his memory, like faint contending voices overheard down a long corridor.

"I am. I try to watch all of this world's great events."

"And never intervene," the man said.

He felt no sense of identification with the name she had given him, had scarcely any sense of that man or his past. His memories were too troublesome, too painful, to try to bring into focus.

"Just so," she said.

"Not possible. The Witness can't be real. I've known of people living as much as three centuries. No longer."

"The Creators made me different," she said.

He uttered a corpse-tearer croak. It was as close to a laugh as he could come.

"The Creators don't exist either. My wounds are making me delirious. Well then, myth. What do you want from me?"

"Knowledge," she said.

"You must have a surfeit of that. If you're the Witness, you're as old as the world."

He spoke bluntly, for dead men have small need of tact. He recalled that the man he had been spoke little and to the point as well.

"Older," she said. "Seven centuries isn't long, for the subject I study. Barely a beginning."

"What can I teach you?"

"I want to know what it means to be human."

"Compared to what?"

"Dead or not," she said, "that I cannot tell you."

"I am cold and naked," he said. "My mouth is as parched as the rest of me is soaked. I'd drink, and no doubt I'd be famished, if my stomach weren't in total rebellion. My head feels ready to split apart. Someone hunts me, I don't know who. I doubt I've time to tell you much."

"You've no time at all, Lord Karyl," she said. "But each conversation with the doomed, however brief, expands my knowledge."

"We're born in pain and trepidation. It seems we die the same way, although for some unfathomable reason I've yet to learn for sure. We like to imagine we can live in some different state. Whether that's illusion, I know no more than you."

"You're eloquent for a man in your condition. The tales told of you seem true."

He waved dismissal with the broken sword. "Whatever they say, they're all lies now."

She floated toward him, her legs not stirring the

hem of her robe. A white blanket of mist hid her feet. The cowl tilted up toward his face.

Inside he could see nothing but blackness.

"Ah, Karyl Vladevich," she said. "You have done deeds that shook the Tyrant's Head, and may yet reverberate across Aphrodite Terra and all the wide world. I had such hopes for you."

"No doubt I've disappointed many people," he said. "I fear I've gotten many killed. I don't think I want my memories back. Even if you offered me something for sharing them."

"I can give you nothing. It would disturb Equilibrium."

"The sacred Order of the World," he recited like a catechism. It *was*, he realized. His lips twisted in a savage smile. "We can't have that."

She raised sleeve-shrouded arms as if to touch his face. Irrationally he recoiled.

"There's something about you—" She stopped, shook her head: an oddly peevish gesture for a mythical being. "No. It can't be. You will soon be dead to stay, and so will end the saga of Karyl of the Misty March."

It was only then he realized she'd spoken his Slavo all along, not Spañol, his native tongue, though her accent was that of a Rus, rather than his Češi people.

From the thickening mists came a chilling sound: a drawn-out ululation.

"They come with dogs to smell you out, Lord Karyl," she said. He thought he heard a note of sadness in her voice. Or maybe wistfulness. "And horrors to take you."

"Who?"

"Your murderers."

He looked over his shoulder. Panic boiled up inside him as a second hound gave tongue. Beneath it he detected the chirps and snarling of the real killers, the raptor-pack who followed the dogs.

"Now I find that, though I thought my life already forfeit," he said bitterly, "my body still doesn't want to let it go. Am I to be spared nothing?"

She said nothing, just slowly backed away.

"Help me."

She spread sleeves that still hid her hands. "I cannot."

Left and right he whipped his head, seeking some road to safety. His heart fluttered like a netted bug-chaser. He vibrated with the need to flee. He hated the fear. Yet he couldn't still it.

He glared at her. "Cannot or will not?"

"They are the same. Good-bye, Lord Karyl. May your death be swift and painless."

"Doubtful," he said through peeled-back lips. "Can't you see the future?"

"If I could, would I have troubled you? Now run, my lord. Or die here. Whatever will ease your final moments, do."

She turned and glided up the slope to the broad-leaf trees thronging the ridgeline that paralleled the river. He knew their tantalizing shelter was a lie: his pursuers would be on him before he could hide among them.

Driven as hard now by defiance as dread, he fled east. He ran without hope, and only pain for a companion. His brain bubbled with images: of childhood, lost friends, long travel in exotic lands.

And *war*. Always war.

They caught him as he ran out of world.

Two kilometers east of the battlefield the ground simply dropped away. Three hundred sheer meters below, the inland sea called the Tyrant's Eye lay hidden beneath a rumpled grey-white plain of clouds that seemed to extend from the Cliffs of the Eye.

He mastered the temptation to keep running.

Panting from his flight, sword-stub upraised in his left hand, he turned at bay beside a clump of scrub oak. A whistle caused the pair of grey-brown dogs with wrinkled faces and great dangling dewlaps streaming froth that loped in close pursuit to veer aside. Dark eyes rimmed with scarlet veins burned with resentment at being denied the kill.

But they did as they were trained. The brightly feathered death that ran behind would rend them as eagerly as their prey. When their hunters' blood blazed with the hot joy of the chase, the raptors could only just be restrained from turning on one another.

Eight green horrors trotted into view on strong hind legs, the big killing-claws on their feet daintily upraised. Deinonychus: the biggest and worst of Nuevaropa's pack-predators. Thus beloved of the nobility, who kept them to hunt men as well as beasts.

Pampered in some lord's kennel, the three-meter-long killers had gotten their spring plumage early. Their upper feathers were a brilliant green with yellow highlights, their breasts buff streaked with brown. The crests on their narrow skulls were shiny black, as were brow-stripes above staring yellow eyes. Their muzzles were likewise yellow.

A pair of riders followed the pack. A brown-bearded man whose blue, silver, and black tabard, well freighted with belly, proclaimed him a knight straddled a russet great strider with a dainty white feather ruff and silly yellow plume on its small head. It high-stepped in obvious terror of the hunting-pack.

The other man rode a white mule. Taller and leaner than the knight, he wore a ratty cloth yoke to shade his shoulders, greasy loincloth, and beggar's buskins. His bare legs and wasteland torso were smeared with grime. Beneath greased-back blond hair his face was round yet sparely fleshed, with a brutal beak of a nose.

As they closed in on their quarry, the horrors slowed and began to hiss and sidle. They were as notorious for their cunning as for their cruelty. The sheer cliff at the man's back helped him: the monsters couldn't get behind him.

A horror stepped forward and reared to almost the man's own height, erecting its crest and spreading feathered forelegs wide. Their undersides were shocking scarlet, loud as the challenge the raptor screamed. Its breath stank of death.

A second horror, circling to the man's right, sprang for him with talons forward and jaws agape. Undistracted by the first one's display, he sidestepped and hacked off black-clawed toes with a forehand cut. The return stroke gashed open the shrieking green face as the horror flew past. The blade-stump missed the glaring yellow eye, but flooded it in blood.

The creature put its maimed foot down and collapsed. Squalling, it lashed its long tail so violently that the man had to dodge to avoid being knocked off his feet, and possibly the cliff.

The other raptor pounced. The man flowed to meet the attack. Slipping right he sliced the horror's throat. With a blood-strangled squawk, it stumbled forward over the edge.

The pack chittered furiously. Two had turned to savage their maimed fellow. Behind them, not ten meters from the hunted man, the beak-nosed man sat applauding sardonically on his mule.

"Well done, Lord Karyl," he said in Alemán. "You bring your legend to its appropriate end. Too bad no one'll ever hear the tale of your valiant last stand."

The four horrors not engaged in murdering their injured pack mate hung back, dancing nervously from foot to yellow foot.

"Karyl's dead," the man said. The language came readily enough to his tongue. Its gutturals less so to his raw throat.

"That signet ring on your sword hand suggests otherwise. And like the allegedly late voyvod, you're left-handed, I see."

The knight's livery struck forth sudden memory: a midnight-blue helmet, nodding plumes of black, azure, and white. Beside them a curved axe-blade, fast descending.

Then a flash of light, and nothing.

"So the young Duke of Hornberg wants a trophy?" the fugitive rasped.

"No," the peasant said. "His mother. Or rather, a token that you're safely dead. It seems she fears you pose a threat to her ambitions for her baby boy. And perhaps she's right. She was surely wise to send us to make sure of you; you're as Creator-lost hard to kill as a handroach."

"Oh, dear," the fat knight said, as teeth through feathered throat bit off the injured horror's cries. "His Grace will be most displeased at losing such prime animals, Bergdahl."

"His Grace will have to buck up," the commoner

said. "Does he think there'll be no cost if he wants a man like this dead? Or the Dowager Duchess does. And don't think *she* gives a malformed hatchling what finishing off the Voyvod of the Misty March costs her dear son in playmates."

"I hate to kill a man's pets," the man said. "Call them off and come face me yourself, Mor Lard Tub."

"We have *explicit* instructions—" the knight gobbled.

"Not even this hedge knight's that big a fool," the commoner said. "Kill all you can. More will hatch."

More pain came, in the form of remembering.

"I've died once," the man said. "I can do it again. If your horrors take me my one regret is not avenging Count Jaume's treachery."

"Life's full of disappointments, my lord," the peasant said.

Lagging behind his swift-footed pack and mounted betters, a stout, balding huntsman with Duke Falk's black toothed-falcon insignia painted on his hornface-hide tunic came puffing up. He whipped the two horrors still squabbling over their comrade's corpse back to duty.

Joined by a third they rushed their prey. Two more swung wide to his left to catch him like a soldier-ant's pincers.

He charged them. His blade split one's skull. It grated free to chop almost through the forelimb the second reached with to grab him.

Midleap the horror twisted to snap at him. He dodged. The raptor fell among the three lunging from the right and bowled them into a spitting, tail-whipping tangle.

The man ran right at the two riders. Instead of

going for the sword hanging from his baldric, the fat knight froze, bearded chins trembling. The commoner merely laughed as if this were the world's finest joke, and would only be made sweeter were he cut down by a naked man with a broken sword.

But one pack-hunter had hung back. It leapt. Raptor hit man, chest to chest. Lightly built though it was, the horror was as heavy as he. Its momentum drove him back. He punched at it with both fists, trying to fend off the killing-claws slashing at his exposed belly and genitals.

The creature struck like an adder. Sharp teeth snapped shut on the man's sword arm just above the wrist, crunching through muscle and bone to meet with a clack. Pain shot through him like lightning.

Still gripping the broken sword, the man's hand flew as if propelled by a blood-jet to land on bare white soil half a meter from the edge. The voyvod's signet glinted mockery on a twitching finger.

"Well, that's more luck than we deserve," the commoner said.

Clutching his feathered assassin to him with his last hand, the man toppled backward into the void.

PART TWO

El Palacio de las Luciérnagas

(The Palace of the Fireflies)

Chapter 4

Troodón, Tröodon—*Troodon formosus*. Pack-predator raptor; 2.5 meters long, 50 kilograms. Sometimes imported to Nuevaropa as pets or hunting beasts. Like ferrets, tröodons are clever, loyal, and given to mischief. Vengeful if abused.

—THE BOOK OF TRUE NAMES

THE EMPIRE OF NUEVAROPA, SPAÑA, PRINCIPALITY OF THE TYRANT'S JAW, LA MERCED, PALACE OF THE FIREFLIES

"—*y con alma tuya, hermano*," the hooded man replied to a hushed greeting from an acolyte he encountered in the gallery that ran along the north wing of the Palacio de las Luciérnagas.

They went their opposite ways. Morning sunlight shone through piercings in fanciful floral shapes carved in the outer wall. On the practice-ground a story below, the Scarlet Tyrants—Imperial bodyguards—contended with a clatter of wooden swords and shields.

The man in the cowl had no name that mattered. He was consecrated to life as a *what*, not a *who*. He wasn't tall. He wasn't short. He was neither wide nor narrow. The skin on his hands and within his hood's recesses was sun-browned olive. His eyebrows were black laced with grey, his eyes dark. He looked like many men in Spaña, the southernmost realm of the Tyrant's Head.

He wore the brown robe of the Kindred of Torrey, with that Creator's trigram embroidered in yellow on the breast: a solid line with two broken lines beneath it. The current Emperor was well known for piety far beyond what his office required. Men and women of all sects' cloth were common here.

Altogether, the hooded friar was as unremarkable as craft could make him.

Leaving the loggia, he passed into cool interior and turned into a stairwell. To his right was a nook on whose back wall was painted a fading, peeling scene of black Lanza, the Creator most identified with war, defeating a swarm of misshapen hada during the High Holy War. It concealed a door that opened only in response to a knowing touch.

The cowled man supplied it. He slipped into a narrow way illuminated only by light that filtered from rooms and corridors to either side through slits made to look like ornamentation or even random cracks in the walls. It was part of a network of secret stairs and passageways meant for trusted servants, discreet errands, and persons of high station on low missions.

The Firefly Palace sprawled across a high headland that protected the southern side of Happy Bay, about which stood, leaned, and occasionally rioted La

Merced, the Empire's richest seaport. Yellow-white limestone walls as high as twenty meters and as thick as ten encompassed a square kilometer inside an approximate pentagon. Within lay yards, stables, shops, and barracks. The Palace proper dominated all: an enormous rambling structure well spiked with towers, and courtyard gardens and pools tucked away within.

By arrangement with its owner, Prince Heriberto, the palace currently housed the widowed Emperor, his two young daughters, and the usual gaggle of courtiers. Emperador Felipe liked his comforts, and equally disliked the intrigues and stuffy self-importance of court and Diet in the Imperial capital of La Majestad. Easygoing La Merced was far more to his liking.

But figurehead that he was, the man who sat the Fangèd Throne still attracted intrigue. Especially one who had roiled the waters of state as vigorously as the placid-seeming Felipe.

The hooded man climbed three dim stories. Though he had never been inside the palace in his life, he knew the way well. Nor had he been to the Principado de la Quijada de Tirán. His real order didn't even serve the Middle Son.

Under most circumstances, this assignment would have been carried out by someone already within the palace, preferably in the Imperial retinue. But none was available. And this commission was urgent as well as of the highest importance.

He peered into a sunlit room through a reaper-feather hanging to confirm it was vacant, then crossed to a door. He had to take great care: the Emperor's apartments occupied this floor. If he were spotted here, not even his clerical robes would save him from scrutiny he couldn't risk. The simple fact that he didn't belong would not escape the attention of men with gazes as sharp as their spears who guarded the Emperor.

He wasn't afraid of torture. His death would mean little; when he swore the oaths, he had accepted that he would die serving the Mother. The Brotherhood had blessed him with its confidence to carry out this task. He could endure anything but failure.

He slipped into a corridor with milky morning sunlight streaming through pointed-arched windows at either end. He saw no one, but heard prayers murmured behind closed doors. Incense thickened the air.

Silently he strode down the hallway. Despite fanatical training and years of meditation, his pulse raced. So much lay on this single cast. . . .

And here. The door.

Inside the room a figure garbed the Father's grey sat in gloom. His back was to the door, his hood bowed in contemplation.

The intruder slipped his right hand inside his capacious left sleeve. His fingers closed around the cool familiar hardness of his dagger hilt.

Carefully he extended his right foot, laid the whole sandaled sole at once on maroon tiles. He would have sworn he made no sound—he would have staked his life.

The grey hood turned. The man looked upon the visage within.

"Your Radiance!" he exclaimed, but softly, softly. He dropped to his knees. His hand slipped from his sleeve, holding his now-forgotten weapon.

"Forgive me," he said as the figure rose to towering height and approached. "Forgive me, Radiant One! I didn't know. How could I know?"

"You are forgiven, my son," replied a voice soft and dry and grey as ash. Its owner reached for him as if to confer benediction.

Naked and still damp from her afternoon bath, the Imperial Princess Melodía Estrella Delgao Llobregat sat on her stool while her maidservant brushed out her long hair, listening to the deep tones her best friend drew from the springer-gut strings of her *vihuela del arco*.

She enjoyed the way the music flowed, sweet and dark as Ruybrasil molasses, across the sitting room's blond-and-dark-wood parquetry floor. She also enjoyed how easy they made it to ignore the girl who sat sobbing in buttery sunset light beneath a window facing out on La Canal.

"You've finally got something big and hard between those white-bread thighs of yours, Fanny," said another of Melodía's five ladies-in-waiting, "and all you can do is sit there and scratch it."

Melodía's cousin Guadalupe was Princess of Spaña, lean, dark, and rather fierce-looking. Also rather fierce.

"Old joke," said Abigail Thélème. Only child of the Archduke-Elector of Sansamour, she was taller even than Melodía, slim and pale and cool as a blade.

Frances Martyn, Princess of Anglaterra, reddened to the roots of her curly gold hair. She kept on playing. Beautifully. She was used to jokes about her alleged prudery. Unlike the rest of Melodía's retinue, who wore silken loincloths and a few feathers in the late-autumn tropic heat, the short, well-rounded Princess was dressed demurely in a sleeveless blouse and skirt of foam-green silk that left only her belly bare between thigh and throat.

Melodía's dueña, Doña Carlota—stout, devout, and moustached like a bandit—sniffed loudly from the stool where she sat discreetly with her fellows beneath a wall hanging woven of bright dinosaur feathers. Following the general custom that older folk wore more clothes than young, the other dueñas had on light cloth gowns; Doña Carlota was so swaddled from chin to instep in heavy blouse, mantilla, and thick dark skirts that Melodía found it a wonder she didn't pass out.

"*Some* highborn young ladies don't know how to act according to their station," Doña Carlota said sternly. Her fellow dueñas sniggered subversively.

The sturdily built young woman on the *banco* stopped sniveling. A dark eye peeked over the handkerchief she held to her face. She offered a particularly soulful sob.

"All right, Fina," Melodía said, "what are you emoting about now?"

It came out sharper than she intended. Especially to the adored daughter of their host, or landlord, Heriberto, who liked to be called Prince Harry in Anglés style. The Principe was a good friend of Melodía's father, but there was no point in pushing things.

Besides, Josefina Serena was a good friend to Melodía, within her limits. She could be a fearful pill, what with her weeping and vapors and passions, as fierce as summer Channel squalls and usually as brief.

"It's terrible," Fina moaned, "how the nobles treat their peasants."

"And you're just now finding this out?" Abi Thélème said. "It's what they do, as dung beetles eat dung."

As usual, she held her long blue eyes half-closed. On another it would be silly affectation; Abi made it sinister. Melodía thought her quite the most striking girl in the room, with her finely chiseled features and silver-blond hair hanging to the small of her back.

Lupe scowled, which her single brow equipped her well to do. No one would call her pretty, exactly; she was handsome in an intense way, like a well-made quirt. Her skin was dark olive. Her blue-black hair, wound into tight pigtails that failed utterly to make her look innocent, came to a widow's peak. A purple and yellow tröodon-feather gorget partially obscured her small breasts.

"How can you talk that way?" she said. "You're highborn yourself."

"How keen of you to notice, Lupita," Abi said. Lupe's face turned the color of well-cured nosehorn leather.

Sensing *attention* slipping away, Fina sniffed more loudly than before.

"Oh, very well," Abi said. "Out with it, before you snort your face inside out."

Fina glared, but recounted a recent holiday upcountry with her father at his vassal barony of Lago Bravo.

"It was the way Baron Ludovico treated his peasants," she said. "He was most frightfully cruel. He had them whipped for the slightest misdeed. I even saw one poor young man—a handsome, strapping fellow—branded on both cheeks for impertinence!"

"You're right," Melodía said, wincing. "That *is*

awful. It's not right for lords to treat their people cruelly. Even serfs."

At least Fina's found something more interesting than palace gossip to cry about, she thought. She briefly thanked the Creators, in whom she didn't really believe, for distracting her companions from their earlier chatter about the latest fashions from Lumière, a subject that bored Melodía stupid.

"My father would've had them roasted alive over a slow fire," Abi said brightly.

"Which?" Fanny asked. "Lords or serfs?"

Abigail Thélème smiled.

"Why don't you do something, Día?" asked Llurdis.

That was another cousin: the Princess of Catalunya, which although subject to Spaña was nominally a kingdom. It was unlike Llurdis to be last into any conversation. Melodía guessed she'd just been waiting for a chance to stir things up.

"What on Paradise am I *supposed* to do?" Melodía snapped. At once she regretted letting her cousin get under her skin. It only encouraged her.

"*You're* the Emperor's daughter," Llurdis said. "Not me."

She was large and powerfully built, with breasts so large Melodía wondered she didn't have a constant backache. Her hair was black, as coarse and untamable as she. Her features were too emphatic to be considered pretty, any more than Lupe's could. Like the Spañola, Llurdis more than made up for it with flamboyant passions, and a tireless appetite for sex and other dramas.

Melodía tossed her head in irritation. Pilar was trying to tease out a recalcitrant snag. The movement made the captive lock yank painfully at Melodía's scalp. She grimaced and turned, slapping her maid's hand away.

"Be *careful*, Pilar! That hurt. What's the matter with you?"

Pilar's dark cheeks tightened, and her green eyes narrowed. She bowed her head. "I'm sorry, Highness. Please forgive my clumsiness."

Ignoring her, Melodía turned her glare back on her cousin where it belonged.

"What *good* does being Princess do me?" she demanded. "My father's position is mostly ceremonial, as you never tire of reminding me, Llurdi, thank you so much. And it's not as if he pays attention to me."

"He loves you, dear," Fanny said, switching to a lively galliard to lighten the mood.

"Yes, yes," said Melodía, not about to let herself be mollified, or otherwise deflected from a good rant. "He loves both his daughters. When he remembers he has them. But he never *listens* to me. 'Yes, dear,' he says, and nods. Then he goes back to what really interests him: plotting his next hunt or war, whatever. And then there's that creepy confessor of his. Fray Jerónimo. He's been with Father three years and I haven't even *seen* him."

"No one has," Fanny said. "I hear he's under a vow of seclusion."

"I hear he's hideously deformed," Fina said in a voice that quivered between titillation and sympathy.

"Imperial law says I can't inherit the Throne," Melodía said. "Fine. And my father's got the rest of the family so pissed off with his military adventures I'm never going to get elected on my own. Fine. Who wants to be Empress anyway? It's just a pain in the ass."

"Young lady!" Doña Carlota said briskly. "*Language.*"

"But can't I at least do *something* worthwhile? All the court and my family want to do is push me into the background like—like an ugly piece of furniture!"

"You could run away and become a mercenary," Abi Thélème suggested.

"Or a pirate," said Fanny. Anglaterra was still called Pirate Island, in commemoration of the national pastime that had gotten it conquered and annexed by the Imperio in the first place.

"Why not join your boyfriend's private army?" asked Lupe. "Oh, that's right. It's boys only."

"But such beautiful boys," Llurdis said.

"Who mostly like boys," said Lupe.

"That doesn't matter," Melodía said, thinking Lupe was a fine one to talk, given her open, if sporadic and occasionally violent, affair with Llurdis. "So long as Jaume likes *me* best. And he does. He loves me. I love him. I'll marry him, as soon as my father gives him enough breathing space from fighting to *ask* me."

"If I were you, Día, I'd worry about that black-haired lieutenant of his," Fina said earnestly. She said everything earnestly. Unless she sobbed it.

"He's a pretty one too," Lupe said.

"Jaume and Pere have been friends since childhood," Melodía said. "And he's Jaume's best knight."

"And Pere's been doing him since they were striplings," Llurdis said. "Haven't you noticed how Pere looks at you? *¡Ai, caray!* Daggers."

"Oh, don't be absurd. I've known him since I was a child! Anyway, he knows Jaume and I sleep together."

"Don't talk that way, Princess!" Doña Carlota said. *"¡Escandalosa!"*

"Oh, don't be a ninny," said Lupe's dueña. "Let girls be girls. If you weren't a superstitious old baggage, you'd do your duty and teach her how to have fun and not get pregnant."

"I already *know* that," Melodía said indignantly, to titters from her friends. Except for Fanny, who as always blushed when sex was discussed.

"It's the clear word of the Creators that we're meant to enjoy the bodies They gave us," Fanny's dueña told Melodía's, "despite the gabble of those crazy preachers you listen to."

"Poor Carlota never had many volunteer to help her enjoy hers," said Abi's dueña in her smoky Slava accent.

Doña Carlota scowled and muttered something about hada wickedness. Melodía rolled her eyes. She didn't believe in demons—in the Fae. Much less the bizarre asceticism of the Life-to-Come sect to which Doña Carlota so inconveniently belonged. She was always interfering in Melodía's love life.

Not that *that* had kept the woman busy of late.

As if reading her mind, Llurdis said, "See, that's your problem, Día. You just need to get fucked."

Melodía crossed her arms tightly beneath her breasts. "Don't I know it."

"It's nobody's fault but your own," said Lupe. "You won't so much as look at even the handsomest stableboy."

"I don't like *boys* at all."

"There are plenty of young knights and lords at court who'd be more than happy to take the edge off for you," Abi said.

"*Courtiers*." Melodía shook her head. She felt Pilar let go of her hair to avoid pulling it again. "Nosehorn-flies, the lot of them."

Lupe said, "You could always—"

"No. Not you, not Llurdi, not both of you at once. I don't have the energy for the dramas *that* would cause."

"Well, it's not as if Jaume's rushed back to you," Llurdis said. "The Princes' War ended four months ago. He's been cooling his heels in Alemania a whole half year!"

"He isn't 'cooling his heels.' He was making sure there was no more trouble up North. With peace secured he's coming back to La Merced to report."

"And that's why you're so testy," said Abi. "Horniness, plain and simple."

"You'll dry up like your dueña if all you do is read about war and politics," Lupe said.

"I'll make my mark on one or the other," Melodía said. "Someday."

"I wonder where your sister is, Princesa," Doña Carlota said pointedly. If she knitted her vegetable-wool any more furiously Melodía thought it would catch fire.

"No doubt she's down in the hornface stables," Llurdis said, "squatting on her heels and peering like a sea-skimmer at the grooms and monsters."

"Best watch her close, Doña Carlota," Lupe said with a crooked smirk, "or she'll wind up carrying a stable hand's chick."

Melodía's eyes narrowed. "That's *quite* uncalled-for, Princesa," she said. "She's just a little girl. She's *fourteen*."

And a half, she narrowly stopped herself from

adding—as Montserrat inevitably did, even though it wasn't even true yet.

A knock forestalled further sniping. Doña Carlota's imposing brows bunched, and her eyes flicked suspiciously to the door.

"Enter," Melodía called.

The door opened. An under-chamberlain in red and yellow Imperial livery stood there jittering.

He drew in a breath that seemed to double the size of his narrow young chest. *"His-Imperial-Majesty-the-Emperor-Felipe-respectfully-requests-the-presence-of-his-daughter-Her-Highness-the-Princess-Melodía-at-an-audience-in-the-Great-Hall-in-half-an-hour's-time!"* he declaimed in a rush.

Melodía's eyes widened. She waved Pilar away and stood. Fanny played a quick triumphant coda and set aside her bow, smiling.

"Tell my father I'll be there," Melodía said. The under-chamberlain nodded and fled.

"Guess who's finally home?" Lupe singsonged as the door closed.

"Hoo!" said Llurdis, fanning herself. "Did it suddenly get humid in here?"

Chapter 5

Matador, Slayer—*Allosaurus fragilis*. Large, bipedal, carnivorous dinosaur; grows to 10 meters long, 1.8 meters at shoulder, 2.3 tonnes. Nuevaropa's largest and most-feared native predator.

—THE BOOK OF TRUE NAMES

Shiraa opened her eyes.

She peered through a screen of fronds into the heart of a forest. Down here it was still dark, but dawn light glancing off the tops of trees across the little valley struck them alight with green fire. Around her the forest breathed with the sounds of a thousand small creatures, all fervently hoping she wouldn't notice them, and the rustle of ferns and flowering bushes in the morning breeze. She could almost see the prey-smell strands in the cool air.

Swinging her long balancing tail and powerful hips, Shiraa strode into the open. Fronds thrashed. Branches clashed. A flock of small tailless fliers exploded from the trees, azure and gold, raising raucous cries.

For a time Shiraa had known nothing but pain

and the blackness of loss. She hid. She was good at that.

Eventually hunger overcame the agony of the wound the white monster had given her. When she set out painfully from her hiding place, she found meat lying all around in dizzying abundance. Between gorgings, the smell of rotting flesh lulled her to sleep with its song of plenty.

The great feast ended as the meat turned to slime sucked down by the soil. Shiraa could easily eat the tailless two-legs who continued to roam the killing-grounds, small and slow and weak as they were. But she had been taught to respect them since she hatched and first laid eyes on her mother, who was herself a two-legs. Unless they attacked her, she must not harm them—not without her mother's permission.

So she limped away from the battlefield to forage, and heal, and await the strength to search for her lost mother.

Now she had recovered. It still hurt to move in certain ways. She endured.

Deep longing drove her now. She needed her mother's love to feel *fullness*. To belong.

Her mother had gone away. But she knew her mother would never abandon her.

Shiraa hungered. She would eat. Then, following some *knowing* it would never occur to her to question, she continued her journey south.

Somewhere that way, she knew, she would find her mother again.

Racing each other into the market square, a pair of laughing children jostled Rob Korrigan. They seemed too intent on the entertainment that had already attracted a sizable crowd to the middle of this central Francés town called Pot de Feu to notice.

Rob put a quick hand to his pouch. A bump like that was a common trick to cover a purse-slitting; he'd done it himself, as a tad. The strider-hide bag was still flat as a titan-trodden vexer, of course. It was the principle of the thing.

"Barbarous continentals," he muttered.

Folding his arms he leaned against the side of a victualer's covered wagon to watch the show. He kept his axe, its head cased in stout nosehorn leather, propped close at hand. He didn't think he had any enemies here. But he hadn't kept his head attached to his shoulders—almost literally, since he could boast but little by way of a neck—by taking things for granted.

The busker was good, Rob had to admit. No taller than Rob himself, built like twine-tied sticks bundled in a tatty brown cloak, he sat before a patch of wall where the whitewash had peeled away from grey mud brick. Dark hair, silver-shot, hung to his thrown-back hood. His eyes were dark in a face from which it seemed all nonessentials had been crushed. Their raptor intensity struck Rob to the spine when their gaze brushed his.

Though he laughed often, he didn't speak. He didn't need to; his antics were eloquent. He pulled a handkerchief from the nose of a stout market lady in a red head-rag, and discovered copper coins in delighted children's ears.

As merchants folded up their kiosks and crated their wares for the night, his audience grew. Sparrows and tiny tailed fliers hopped among sandaled feet foraging for scraps. A toothed raven and a similarly sized green-crested flier squabbled over a melon rind. A tame vexer perched on an onion cart cursed both in screeches.

Sunset came quickly, throwing light like fire-glow across the western faces of white stone towers and tall narrow buildings huddled close, and the slates of steep-pitched roofs. A rising breeze brought the rich damp smell of crops awaiting harvest, and the thicker scent of the woods that lurked beyond the constraints of axe and plow. In Nuevaropa the wild was never far away, and never more than held at bay.

The wind also brought an eye-watering whiff of sulfur from Vieux Charlot, the nearby volcano. They didn't call this dump Firepot for nothing.

The busker finished his sleights and began to juggle. *And now I'm impressed*, thought Rob. The man lacked a left hand.

And therein lay Rob's problem.

Splendid. The silly sod has gone and lost his bloody sword hand.

If a wound didn't kill you, it healed quickly and well. That was common to all the creatures of Paradise. But once a part was gone, it was lost for good.

I wonder if my principal will dock my pay for delivering damaged goods. If it really is him.

First the busker tossed fired-clay bowls borrowed from a merchant at a nearby booth with his right hand, to catch them upside down on his stump and flip them back in the air. Next, he juggled ninepins plundered by giggling urchins from the village green a few streets over.

Sadly, he also blew enthusiastically on a fatty-herder's reed pipes he'd stuffed in his mouth. *Once again I question whether my perfect pitch is a gift from the Creators, or a spite of the Fae,* thought Rob.

The busker's next trick almost made Rob forgive his noise: he juggled daggers. His stump flipped them by their blade-flats as they descended, back to his right hand. He worked up to five at a time. Then he pretended to let one slip. Catching it by the tip he tossed it high to twinkle like a yellow spark in the last slanting light, to a rush of delighted applause. He sent the others after in fast succession.

He looks *like him,* Rob thought, studying his target under the guise of watching, fascinated at his tricks. Though he was that too. *At least, he looks like the portraits I've seen, and the descriptions I've heard.*

Rob had never seen the man he'd been sent to retrieve from closer than sixty yards. And the bugger hadn't exactly been holding still at the time. . . .

The daggers fell to plant themselves in a line like daisies in the hard-packed soil before him. As the onlookers clapped and hooted, he took from his sack a shallow brass bowl and a stick about half a meter long. Laying the stick down before him, he placed the bowl on its tip. Then he sat back on skinny haunches, smiling beatifically through his beard.

Around Rob the villagers and passers-through speculated eagerly as to what the busker would do now. Some did so in Francés, which Rob understood passably well and spoke with a deliberately outlandish accent. Others used Spañol, which everyone in Nuevaropa theoretically knew. By order of the Creators, it was said, though Rob begged leave to doubt it.

Actually, Rob never begged leave to doubt. He seldom begged leave to do anything at all. *Doubting* was the very last thing on Paradise he'd ask permission for, except perhaps singing and playing his lute, laughing, drinking, wenching, and nursing sullen resentment against those who did him down.

A silver coin rang in the busker's bowl. It made a nice musical sound. *More musical than his playing, in any event,* Rob thought sourly.

Another followed quickly, then a very cascade of copper centimes and Imperial centavos, plus a silver peso or two, as onlookers took the hint to encourage the performer. Rob couldn't see which urchin had tossed in the first coin. He took for granted it was a shill, provided with two pesos and allowed to keep one. With perhaps the threat of a beating with the meter-and-a-half-long blackwood staff that lay beside the busker to keep him or her *committed.*

Once primed, the audience responded readily. The busker had a winning way about him, always smiling and laughing and getting others to join in. His deformity, and the ingenious use he made of it, aroused both sympathy and admiration.

To his left Rob noted three men who had appeared in an alley mouth. They stood watching the performance with folded arms and scowls. To his eye they looked like professional toughs. He'd encountered more than a few such in his travels.

What interest might they have in a poor street performer, and him kitten-harmless, so?

The busker's bowl was duly filled. He emptied it into his purse. Then with the tip of his stick he hoisted the bowl into the air. Still puffing furiously on his pipes he stood up, holding the stick upright and setting the bowl to twirl. He finished with stick balanced on chin, and the bowl spinning atop it. The crowd erupted in applause as urchins ran among them with more bowls.

"He seems to have quite the going concern here," Rob said as he straightened, to none but himself. He was always his best audience, after all. "Maybe he won't be interested in my proposition at all. And wouldn't that be my luck all over?"

The three hard men were no longer to be seen.

He caught up with the busker in a narrow, noisome alley toward the village outskirts nearest the volcano, whose eponymous crater stained red the sky above the rooftops, and whose bone-deep demon mutter never paused for breath. The street performer had a slouch hat, his sack shouldered, and carried his stick in his lone hand. Though not after the manner of a man who needed its help to walk.

"How are the mighty fallen," Rob Korrigan murmured to himself.

And maybe, *of* himself. His life had been no path of blossoms since he'd been sacked.

He followed his quarry across a street little wider than the alley, then stopped and looked around. He saw nothing but shuttered windows and a rat or two to overhear him calling the busker by a dead man's name.

"Ho, there, Voyvod Karyl," he called softly.

The man broke stride momentarily. Then he continued. He didn't look back.

Rob scowled at the cloaked back dissolving into the gloom.

"Wait, may the Fae curse you," he said more loudly.

Instantly repenting letting anger take the reins of

his tongue—as it did so often—he hastily added, "I've a proposition which might bring profit to the voyvod."

On the brink of disappearing the busker halted.

"Voyvod Karyl is dead," he said without turning. Like Rob he spoke Francés. His accent was unmistakably Slavo.

"You can speak?" Rob said.

The man walked on.

For a moment Rob stood scowling, with his big scarred hands folded over Wanda's head. "Ah," he said, "that I, a dinosaur master, should be reduced to chasing down alleys after madmen."

For gold, the ever-present voice at the back of his head reminded him. *With your purse as empty as your stomach soon will be.*

And it was a princely sum he was promised for such a petty errand: a gold trono, sufficient to buy a sword or suit of clothes, either worthy of a gentleman. Which Rob knew well he'd never be.

"Then again," he said, "as a minstrel, an *Ayrishmuhn*, and a Traveler, what's more natural to me than skulking down alleys?"

Tipping the oak axe haft back over his shoulder, he trudged after the man he called Karyl. He was still puzzling over how he might nail down the busker's attention long enough to make his pitch when three men stepped from the shadows in front of him.

Chapter 6

Chián, El Rey, The King, *Padre Cielo*, Father Sky—
King of the Creators: *Qian* ☰ (Heaven)—The Father.
Represents Fatherhood, rule (and misrule), power, and
the Sun. Also dinosaurs. Known for his majesty. Aspect: a sturdy, white-bearded man with gold-trimmed
scarlet robe and golden scepter, sitting on a throne.
Sacred Animal: Tyrannosaurus rex. Color: gold. Symbol: a golden crown.

—A PRIMER TO PARADISE FOR THE IMPROVEMENT
OF YOUNG MINDS

Uncomfortable as always in her elaborate
Imperial regalia of red ridiculous reaper
plumes and heavy gold baubles, Melodía
stood by the left arm of the Emperor's chair. She was
bored, as she always was when called upon to wear
that outfit.

She shut her ears to the drone of the stout priestess, who wore the grey robes with the eight-sided
symbol on the front that signified dedication to all

eight Creators without patron or favor. The Princess had long practice at that.

If she squinted through the gloom, Melodía could just see her father's Chief Minister, Mondragón, standing like a scarecrow on the other side of the Emperador's throne-away-from-home. The Great Hall of Firefly Palace devoured light. She knew that the alternating courses of sand and amber stone that vaulted upward over the Imperial heads constituted an architectural wonder. At the moment she had to take it on faith. It wasn't as if you could actually *see* it. Especially now, with no sunlight streaming in the courses of narrow arched windows to alleviate the darkness. A myriad of oil lamps and candles burning their little hearts out could barely scratch it.

She let her eyes slide over the gaggle of courtiers and local grandes standing about pretending to listen raptly to the convocation. There were times she almost envied the more prudish North, with its predisposition to more body covering despite its warmer clime. Parchment-skinned pots and sagging breasts were not complemented by loincloths and feather yokes, however resplendent.

Though she could, to her regret, put names to almost all the hangers-on, she had far less notion of what most of them *did*.

The priestess finished. Felipe smiled and nodded approvingly. She withdrew amidst a gaggle of acolytes, who waved censers enthusiastically about, surrounding her with dense aromatic clouds as if warding off mosquitoes.

Melodía's father had an infinite capacity for pious boredom. So, apparently, did the Creators themselves, who forbore to strike down even the longest-winded of Their servitors. It was another reason Melodía secretly doubted their existence. *She* would have slagged the marble beside the priestess' sandals with a lightning bolt, just to see her dance.

The Imperial Herald stepped forth and in tenor-trumpet tones began to introduce Felipe by his titles, real and fanciful: "*Behold his Imperial Majesty, Terror of the Evildoer—*"

Luckily Melodía also had experience keeping her face expressionless. Not even she thought of her father as *prepossessing*. Felipe Delgao was a man of middle age, middle height, and slightly more than middling paunchiness, wrapped in a gold-trimmed cloak of scarlet feathers. A simple crown with a single red reaper plume sat on short hair just on the red side of sandy. His slightly protuberant eyes were pale green this evening.

He looked, even to his daughter, who really did love him, like the personification of mediocrity. Which fact had much to do with his Election. All factions had agreed the stout Duque de los Almendros was far too inconsequential to upset any dung-carts.

And here he was, kicking them over right and left like a child pitching a tantrum among his toys. Melodía wished she could enjoy the dismay her father caused Nuevaropa's magnates. Unfortunately she deplored his methods as much as his sternest critic did.

"*—Defender of the Faith, Shield and Sword of the Holy Church, Upholder of Creators' Law—*"

Felipe looked amused by the hyperbole, knowing it accreted to the office, not the man. Sometimes in private he liked to remark they'd spout the same encomiums to Don Rodrigo, the fat, half-blind, and toothless old Tyrannosaurus rex that served as Imperial Executioner, should he somehow get elected. And the courtiers would suck up to him as eagerly.

Still, Felipe looked for all of Paradise as if he were enjoying this immensely.

"—*el Emperador del Imperio de Nuevaropa, Felipe!*" the Herald finished ecstatically. The mob of hangers-on erupted in applause, as if Felipe had just slain a legendary monster like his progenitor and predecessor, Manuel Delgao.

Melodía glanced down at her sister, fidgeting by her side. As Infanta, Montserrat got away with just a modest silver circlet confining her unruly dark-blond dreadlocks. She wore a simple white child's gown, which for a wonder was spotless. Its state meant some harried attendants had shrewdly waylaid the girl and wrestled her into it as she was on the utter threshold of the Great Hall. Her Imperial inveterate tomboy Highness Montserrat could notoriously get dirty walking across five meters of freshly scrubbed tile.

With nobody else paying attention, Montse stuck her tongue out at her sister. Melodía winked back. She felt a warm rush of closeness and love.

In some ways the siblings were as different as fur and feathers. Yet they loved each other with a fierce and almost conspiratorial devotion: allies against an indifferent, uncomprehending court and world. And, too often, father.

The guards flanking the entrance stamped their nosehorn-hide sandals ceremonially. Trumpets flourished. Conversation died as the tall ironwood doors groaned open. A herald entered between the stone-faced Scarlet Tyrants with their figured and gilded cuirasses, scarlet capes, golden red-crested barbute helmets, and altogether businesslike halberds. Felipe grinned.

And why not? His favorite kinsman and personal champion was about to walk through those doors.

That made Melodía smile as well. She held her breath as the new herald belted out, "His Grace—"

What? she thought. *Did father make Jaume a Duke and not tell me?*

"—Falk, Herzog von Hornberg."

A figure strode in, tall, wide, and astonishing in gleaming royal-blue plate armor. A black cape hung from impossibly broad shoulders. A black falcon displayed, wings elevated, screamed silent defiance from the silver shield painted on his breastplate. Blue and black plumes nodded from a helmet held in the crook of his arm. The head above all that splendid metal was wide, if no wider than the neck, the strong, square face fringed by black beard. The eyes pierced like naked sunlight through blue glass.

After a breathless moment, the courtiers swirled into excited whispers. Melodía realized she had been holding her own breath. She let it go.

"Von Hornberg?" she heard the Chief Minister exclaim. "Von Hornberg, the rebel?"

The newcomer looked down at Felipe, who sat gazing up at him wide-eyed as a hatchling raptor. He stopped the prescribed three meters from the throne.

"Your Majesty," he said in a voice like a great bass drum, "I have come to thank you for the most gracious pardon you have seen fit to bestow upon me, and pledge my sword to your service." He spoke in excellent but abominably Alemán-accented Spañol.

Voices cried out in alarm as he drew blade. The

Tyrants behind Felipe's throne stepped forward, ready to split that huge head like an orange with their halberds.

Falk tossed the meter-long weapon in the air. It turned over once. He caught it by the tip in a gauntleted hand, took two strides forward, and knelt with a *tunk* of steel kneecap on scarlet carpet, presenting the hilt to his Emperor on his low dais.

Shocked silence ensued, and lingered for many beats of Melodía's heart.

"Oh, bravo!" Felipe cried. He clapped his hands in delight. He reached out and briefly grasped the proffered silver pommel.

"I accept your service and gladly, my good Duke," he said. "Rise, and know that you have won my favor."

The courtiers clapped madly again as Falk rose once more to his imposing height, feeding his arming-sword back into his scabbard as he did so.

Father always was a sucker for cheap melodrama, Melodía thought.

Pages stepped forward to guide Duke Falk to the appropriate place to the Emperor's right. Mondragón's gaunt great-nosed face looked even more pinched than usual, as if he smelled someone who'd stepped in fresh horror dung.

From his side Melodía saw the Duke staring frankly at her. She frowned and looked quickly away.

Then she glanced back. *Why, he's so young!* she realized with a shock. *He can't be a dozen years older than I am.* His outlandish size and presence had masked his youth.

Trumpets skirled again. The herald seemed somehow revived when he stepped forward this time.

"Comes now," he cried, "the most worshipful Montador Jaume, Comte dels Flors, Knight-Commander of the Order of the Companions of Our Lady of the Mirror."

A waiting ensemble struck up a tune with brio: "Un Ball per la meva Noia Jove," "A Dance for My Young Girl." Melodía felt a flush rise hot up her cheeks: it was she for whom Jaume wrote the tune, years ago when she was a child and he a dashing youth who had already begun to make his name in the professions of both arts and arms.

Jaume entered the Great Hall as if he'd just conquered it, step lively, head high. He was tall, lean, and lithe, yet wide across the shoulders in his cream surcoat with the red Lady's Mirror emblem of his order on the chest. His dark-orange hair was tied back.

Long turquoise eyes met Melodía's. Thin lips smiled ever so slightly.

Things had *evolved* between them, since she was a child and he a lad. She thought now, as she always did, that he was the most beautiful man she had ever seen. Or would see.

His famous longsword, the Lady's Mirror, rode in a baldric of pale brown strider leather over his right shoulder. It had been a shocking gaffe on someone's part to allow Falk—a recent rebel as well as a stranger—near the Emperor armed. But to their bodyguards' despair, it had long been the custom for Emperors to allow those who bore arms in their names to carry them into their presence. What sense, Felipe argued, did it make to have a champion who couldn't actually defend you in person?

Jaume knelt before his sovereign. *No nonsense*

about him juggling his blade, Melodía noted with a spiteful glance at Falk.

Beaming, Felipe stood. "Arise, *mi Campeón Imperial*," he said, "and let me embrace my beloved nephew."

This time the hall rang with applause as Felipe hugged Jaume. Melodía knew most of it was unfeigned. As the foremost poet of the day, and perhaps its greatest knight, Jaume was popular throughout Nuevaropa, and nowhere more than here in the South.

Of course, there were a few less admiring looks turned his way as well. She chose not to notice them.

"You have brought me a great victory," Felipe said, stepping back with a last fond pat on Jaume's shoulder and resuming his seat.

"With respect, your Majesty, I had little enough to do with winning it. The Princes' War was almost over by the time my Companions and I arrived."

His eyes flicked left to Falk. Melodía thought he was a bit surprised to see his recent foeman standing there ahead of him.

"Your reports were admirably complete," Felipe said. "I hope to hear the whole story from your lips as soon as may be."

"At your service, Majesty."

He bowed again and turned to his right. Bowing once more, gravely, he said, "Infanta Montserrat. You've gotten taller since I saw you last."

"You don't need to bow to me, Jaume," she said. "You're my friend."

"Always, Infanta. But we're at court, now, where other concerns take precedence."

"How can anything be more important than being

friends?" Montserrat piped. One of her minders stepped forward to shush her.

"How, indeed?" Jaume murmured, smiling. He turned a few degrees more.

"Alteza," he said. "My lady Melodía. You've grown so beautiful I fear it surpasses my gifts to describe."

"I doubt that," she said.

She thought she saw a shadow flit behind his eyes and regretted teasing him. *Almost.* But she knew that if anything was bothering her friend and lover, it certainly wasn't that. They'd been teasing each other since almost the day they met.

She took his hands. As always their wiry strength thrilled her.

"I never flatter, Highness," he said. "You of all people should know that."

She blushed, feeling utterly naked in her gold-and-jewel encrustation of state. Although to be fair, it left a lot of her bare, as was common on formal occasions. Jaume raised her hands toward his lips.

Metal clashed on metal. Startled, Melodía and Jaume turned to look at the great door. A palace steward stood beyond Tyrant halberds crossed to bar his entry.

"Your Majesty!" he cried, face flushed and sweat-shiny in amber lamplight. "An intruder has been found in your apartments."

"He's been taken into custody, I trust," Felipe said.

"No, señor," the steward said. "He's been murdered!"

Chapter 7

Pájaro carraca, Carrack-bird—*Hesperornis*. A common type of flightless aquatic bird with a toothed lower beak; 1.5 meters long, 8 kilograms. Eats mostly fish, but also small amphibians and other animals. Elegant in water, clumsy on land; prone to truculence.

—THE BOOK OF TRUE NAMES

H old up there, mute," said one of the three. Their backs were to Rob. They showed no awareness he was in the alley behind them. They carried clubs. "We want a word with you."

"If he can hear it," a second said.

Evidently the busker could. He stopped and turned. By a yellow gleam straying out of window shutters Rob saw his face. It looked composed, almost serene.

Rob wondered at his sanity.

"We represent the Bonnechance County Entertainer's Guild," the first man said. He was long and lean, with a prominent Adam's apple. "You've been performing publicly without a Guild license."

The man Rob believed—hoped, anyway—to be

Karyl Bogomirskiy canted his head right. His brow was lightly furrowed as if in thought. Rob could see, even under his cloak, that his shoulders stayed relaxed.

"You're depriving good Guild members of pay! We can't have that. Our families will starve."

"Can we hit him now?" asked the second Guildsman. He was even slighter than Karyl and no taller. He cradled his arm-long truncheon as if it were a baby. Rob reckoned him much more interested in inflicting pain than alleviating that of starving Guild families.

The third man was a bulwark of shadow. Though he hadn't said anything, a slight sway betrayed uncertainty. Indeed, none of the three struck Rob as overly confident. The leader covered hesitancy with bravado, the second man with viciousness. Did they suspect their victim's identity?

No, Rob decided. *They've no way of knowing that. They're simply bullies. Their victim's failure to show deference or fear unnerves them.*

"Nothing to say for yourself?" the leader demanded. He squeezed out a brassy laugh. "But I forgot. You're mute!"

The cloaked man turned away. The volcano muttered evilly to itself. Brimstone spiked the warm, heavy air.

The chief bravo grabbed the busker's left shoulder and spun him around. As if by accident the cloaked man's staff rapped the bravo's left knee.

The Guildsman yelped and danced back, clutching his leg. The second bravo, the eager one, shouted "Hey!" and lunged.

The leader stumbled over a strew of junk and sat

down hard. The busker leaned forward as if concerned. His stick pivoted over his thigh to jut to his right.

Before he could stop, the second Guildsman ran his groin right onto it. He doubled over with a bellows wheeze.

"Bastard!" the lead bravo shouted. He scrambled up and swung his club.

The busker had straightened and stood holding the top of his staff. He wheeled away from the cudgel-stroke. His staff swung out. It tripped the Guildsman, who fell onto his doubled-over companion. Both went down.

The leader squawked like a wet vexer as the two rolled in alley muck reeking of mildew and decay. As if reluctantly the third man advanced on the busker. A cauldron belly overhung his strider-leather loin-cloth. Rob could make out little of his face, but it looked oddly shaped. Rob wondered just exactly what sort of public entertainment this one provided.

Taking hold of his staff again, the busker kicked its lower end. It pivoted quickly up to crack the other beneath a lantern jaw.

Dropping his cudgel, the bravo fell to his knees and began to weep, clutching a split and bleeding chin.

"I've had enough of you!" the lead Guild bravo yelled. He had disentangled himself from his cohort and regained his feet. A short sword glinted in yellow alley light.

He charged. The cloaked man leaned away, avoiding a forehand slash guided more by rage than skill. As he did he whipped his staff down and away from himself. Something flew away to land clattering in impenetrable dark.

The bravo had overbalanced. As he fought to recover, the busker stepped past his right side with his own right leg. Light scurried like a handroach along a meter of bright metal.

Rob heard a sound like tearing silk.

The bravo fell to his knees. Black spray fanned from his neck.

The busker turned to face the other Guildsmen. He had lost his hat. Where he had held a stick before, now he held a single-edged sword.

The surviving bravos had found their feet, and short swords of their own. They rushed their foe with desperate fervor.

Like a living shadow, the cloaked man slid left, toward the smaller attacker. Rob thought he had never seen a man move as quickly. Yet he didn't seem to *hurry*. Impossibly, there seemed an air of deliberation about his movements, as if each were planned carefully in advance and exactly executed.

The little bravo raised his short sword for an overhand hack. His opponent whipped past him, slicing open the belly thus exposed.

Gobbling a cry more of surprise than pain, the bravo tripped in slimily gleaming loops of his own intestines and pitched forward. As he went down, the cloaked man slashed him diagonally across the back of the neck. His piteous gurgles ended.

The lead bravo flopped on his face, bled dead.

Wheezing like a frightened morion, the big man rushed the busker. His opponent spun clockwise out of the way of a clumsy but powerful downward cut.

The short sword swept past a cloaked left shoulder. As he faced away from his opponent, the busker reversed grip on his own weapon. He laid his left forearm on its butt and thrust straight back beneath his right arm.

Rob saw the big bravo's eyes go wide as the sword-tip crunched through his sternum. He uttered a child's wail of pain.

The busker yanked his sword free as the last man fell.

Then he stabbed with it, straight down. The bravo kicked at foul-smelling mud and went still.

"You want to make sure your victims die?" Rob asked. Somehow his voice had grown hoarse in the last handful of seconds.

"He was dying anyway," the busker said. "He didn't need to suffer."

He glanced up and down the alley for further foes. Rob's announcement of his own presence made no visible impression.

The cloaked man flicked his blade. It shed dark droplets like a carrack-bird's back. Kneeling, he wiped the sword on the back of the lead bravo's vest. Then he walked to where the rest of the blackwood staff lay. He inserted the sword-tip in the scabbard mouth, angled it up, thrust it until it clicked home.

Rob applauded softly. And only half sardonically.

"This is a bad thing," the busker said, shaking his head. Though the night was warm, as most nights were, Rob couldn't make out the faintest sheen of sweat on his pale forehead. "If only they hadn't drawn blade. . . ."

He picked up his bag of props, which he had dropped when the Guild bravos braced him. Then he walked on his way.

"Why were you acting mute?" called Rob, who could barely imagine *voluntarily* not talking.

"To avoid misunderstanding," the other said. He neither paused nor turned his head.

Rob glanced at the bodies. "Hard to misunderstand *this*," he said to himself.

As dogged as a matador trailing a wounded thunder-titan, he followed.

The busker's hovel slumped at the village outskirts. Beyond it, fields of ripe grain and bean frames stretched pale to the ever-waiting woods. Apparently built for storage, the shack was a jumble of black lava rocks, with a plank and cycad-frond roof thrown on to keep out the frequent rains. At which it met indifferent success, Rob noticed, watching residual drips from an afternoon shower fall to the tramped-earth floor.

Surprisingly, it didn't stink inside. The busker kept body and clothing clean, anyway. He didn't object when Rob, having followed him here, followed him inside.

"You *are* Karyl Bogomirskiy, aren't you?" Rob asked.

The man was sorting through his few possessions by faint volcanic light through the open door. He stuffed even fewer of them into an oiled-canvas ruck-sack. He didn't answer.

"Be kind, man," Rob said, speaking Spañol now. "My name's Rob Korrigan. I have a proposition for you."

"The answer's no." The other's Spañol was excellent, as befitted the highly educated man Rob knew the former Voyvod of the Misty March to be.

"Ah, but I can't hear that," Rob said, digging in an

ear with a fingertip. "I'm only looking after your interests, amigo. You'll see."

Karyl looked up with eyebrow hooked. "If you're so solicitous of my welfare, why didn't you lend a hand back there?"

"You were doing quite well for yourself. I've seldom seen a man lay out three foes so slickly. Never, to put none too fine a point on it."

Bearded lips twitched. "If you'd helped, I wouldn't have had to kill any of them."

"That troubles you?"

"Taking life's a serious thing, because it's irrevocable."

He straightened, experimentally slinging a strap over one shoulder. For all his hatred of nobles, it pained Rob to see this one reduced to such a state.

"You balk at killing?" Rob asked.

"I kill when I must. I don't enjoy it."

"Why do it, then?"

"Because though my life's a small and miserable thing, it is my own, and not to be stolen from me by the likes of them."

He stood a moment, frowning pensively at Rob by weak pink light. Out beyond the hills and woods, Vieux Charlot rumbled like a treetopper's gizzard stones. He sighed.

"Obviously I have to leave town now," he said. "So I may as well hear your proposition."

Chapter 8

Gancho, **Hook-horn**—*Einiosaurus procurvicornis.* A
hornface (ceratopsian dinosaur) of Anglaterra, where
they are a popular dray beast, quadrupedal and herbivorous; 6 meters long, 2 meters high, 2 tonnes.
Named for their massive forward-hooking nasal armament. Two longer, thinner horns project from the tops
of their neck-frills. Placid unless provoked.

—THE BOOK OF TRUE NAMES

ou're a terrible musician," Rob Korrigan said.
He led his companion across Pot de Feu by
alley—briskly, because he was nervous about
Entertainers Guild spies.

Karyl, as Rob had decided to think of him, followed silently. After his spirited display of defensive
skill, he had lapsed into silent apathy.

To Rob's surprise his gibe brought a response: "I
know."

"You do? Then why d'you play?"

"I needed accompaniment. Since I didn't speak, I

found that music—even bad music—brought me larger audiences, and excited them more."

"You've the entertainer's gift. Why didn't you learn to play better? I thought you were a man who, if he did a thing at all, would see he did it well."

He expected a stinging rebuke for speaking like that to a noble. To a man who, no matter how reduced his current state, was accustomed to wielding such power as to frighten the very Empire. Part of Rob even felt he deserved a slapping down.

Instead he got a peevish complaint: "It's not as if I had money to take lessons. Faugh. It's truly said, the least reasonable of men are the Irlandés."

"So you recognized the accent, did you?"

"Forgive my poor manners, please. I needed the music. I tried to provide it as best I could, and learn by doing."

Rob almost stumbled. *A lord apologizing to a commoner?* It felt almost scandalous.

"What I've always insisted on from myself," Karyl said, "is to do as well as I could, and keep doing better until I'm at least competent. Long ago I learned that to achieve anything, one must start where one stands. Or spend eternity waiting for the right moment. Which never comes."

"Brother," Rob said, with feeling, "I hear that."

The hanging wooden sign showed a hand dipping orange lava from a volcano in a heavy earthenware mug as a miniature treetopper titan looked on apprehensively. *Pot of Fire*, it read.

"For a fact, the locals seem obsessed with this

fire-mountain of theirs," Rob said, standing with beard tipped up and arms akimbo.

"It's by the volcano's light we're reading the sign," Karyl said. "Its presence isn't exactly subdued. One day it will destroy them. If not them, their children."

Rob flipped his hand toward the open door, from which a yellower, more congenial radiance spilled, along with raucous voices and chinking crockery. "And yet the party goes on."

"There's a perfect metaphor for life on Paradise," Karyl said.

"A sentiment worthy of myself," said Rob. Feeling expansive, he went to clap his companion on the shoulder. Then he thought better of it. "You've a touch of the poet in you."

"Perish the thought," said Karyl.

Their host was a short, pasty man with a face like a bag of damp vegetables. He led them down a hall away from the common room, which was packed and roistering in a way that made Rob's fingers itch to play, his jaws to sing, and mostly his tongue to plead for ale. Mirror-backed candles in niches chiseled in the walls lit their way.

The innkeeper knocked the hairy backs of his knuckles on a door. Though Rob heard no reply, the innkeeper turned the latch. He pushed open the door and gestured the two inside.

Rob in turn waved his companion forward. Karyl just looked at him. Rob shrugged and went in first. Their host shut the door behind them.

It was a small room. Crude raptor-feather hangings covered the walls, of the sort featuring peasants with bottle bodies and bubble heads outside cottages noticeably shorter than they.

The window was closed, shutters drawn. The room smelled of sea-monster oil lamps; cinnamon, cedar, and fern potpourri in pierced-brass vessels that hung from the lantern-holders; and, like everything in Pot de Feu, sulfur. The two lamps remained unlit, creating a shadow pool in which sat a hooded figure, head down, behind a table set with a ceramic wine pitcher and two glazed mugs. Two chairs waited on the table's near side.

At the door-latch click, the hooded figure raised its head and stood. Karyl stiffened.

It swept back its cowl to reveal a short cap of curly hair, gold touched with fire, above a lovely female face. The woman regarded her guests with wide green eyes.

Karyl relaxed.

"Welcome back, Rob Korrigan," the woman said in perfect La Fuerza Spañol. She put the fingertips of her right hand against her sternum and bowed. Her left hand held a grey wooden staff as tall as she was. She looked quite young, certainly not yet fifty. She turned and bowed again.

"Welcome, Voyvod Karyl Vladevich Bogomirskiy."

"Karyl Bogomirskiy is dead," the cloaked man said.

She smiled. "But you live."

He smiled back without mirth. "Apparently."

She said something Rob couldn't understand. He gathered it was Slavo. He scowled, feeling slighted.

His companion frowned briefly too. Then he sighed.

"*Muy bien*," he said. "I was at one time known as Karyl Bogomirskiy. How do you know me?"

At that admission Rob let out a long breath. *And*

the Fae's own long time coming that has been, he thought, mentally rubbing hands in satisfaction. *That's a reward coming to Ma Korrigan's son, sure.*

This had been far from the most arduous commission of his life, but it was definitely among the strangest.

The woman's smile widened.

"All Nuevaropa knows the legends of Lord Karyl," she said. "And I know many things most do not. Please forgive my manners: I am Aphrodite. I am a sorceress."

Karyl laughed. Rob stared at him.

"There's no such thing as sorcery," Karyl said.

"If you're wrong," Rob said from the side of his mouth, "antagonizing the lady's not the happiest way to find out."

Karyl bowed his head. His hair fell forward to flank his ascetic's face.

"I apologize, my lady. I meant no offense. But if there's one thing I've learned in my lives, it's that there's no magic on this wretched little world of ours."

Rob raised a brow at "my lives." Aphrodite came around the table. She extended her staff.

"Hold out your left hand, Lord Karyl."

His eyes and mouth hardened. "As you see, lady, I have no left hand."

"Would you like it back?"

"Ah, and it's ungracious to play with him, Lady Aphrodite," Rob felt moved to say.

He found it hard to speak. He feared the woman's powers. But . . . good gold hung in the balance. His employer baiting the once-feared grande and mercenary captain, however fallen, struck him as singularly unlikely to help tip it into his pocket.

"Please, Lord Karyl," Aphrodite said. "I mean no mockery."

If only so exquisite a woman would look that way at me, Rob allowed himself to think. *If only this one weren't a sorceress. And yes, if hook-horns only had wings, I could fly Little Nell to the Moon Invisible and claim a piss-pot filled with gold.*

Karyl frowned. But he raised his left arm. Its end was smooth and rounded, without visible scarring, as if he had been born without a hand.

Aphrodite brought the tip of her staff almost into contact with the pink skin. Golden radiance sprang out to surround the staff's end and Karyl's stump. He raised a brow but didn't flinch.

The light went out.

"Is that all?" Karyl demanded, voice ragged. He held the stump up under his nose as if to sniff it. "I don't see a difference. The Irlandés was right. It's unkind to toy with me, lady."

"You need not call me 'lady,'" she said. "What did you feel?"

"Heat," he said reluctantly. "A prickling. Which persists."

He frowned and scratched the stump. "Now it itches. What did you do to me?"

"I gave you back your hand."

"If this is an attempt at stage magic, you've failed, woman. I am not duped into seeing an imaginary hand on the end of my own arm. Just the same lack I've seen for . . . weeks."

"How long exactly, Lord Karyl?"

"I'm not sure."

"No matter. You will see. The magic takes time. Your hand will grow back over the next few weeks.

It will itch far worse, I fear, before the process is complete."

He stared at her. Rob sought to read his thoughts in those intense dark eyes. He failed. He'd never had any success with that sort of thing, though his mother told him he was touched by the Fae. Then again, she'd told him plenty of lies. He never doubted that one, though.

"And the pains in my head," Karyl said. "Can your spells cure those as well?"

The woman had retreated behind her table. For a sorceress, she struck Rob as rather tentative. Perhaps she was wary of having two men alone in the room with her. *Still, shouldn't her magic protect her?*

"For those, herbs will serve as well as anything I might do," she said.

"I've some skill at herbs," Rob said. For a dinosaur master it was necessary lore. Rob had observed that cures that worked on monsters often served as well with people, in somewhat smaller doses. "I can help with that."

To his intense annoyance both ignored him. "But it's not the physical pains that torment you worst, is it?" Aphrodite asked.

Karyl's eyes narrowed to a killer's glare. "How did you know that?"

"I've had you watched, Lord Karyl."

"To what end?"

She smiled. "In part to assure myself that you were indeed the former Voyvod of the Misty March, and commander of the White River Legion."

"There's something you aren't telling me."

"Many things, señor. Will you sit and refresh yourselves?"

She indicated the pitcher and mugs. She made no

move to pour. Rob stepped up to serve himself and Karyl. They sat.

Karyl's eyes were fixed on the woman like a hunting horror's. "Why me?"

"You can ask that in response to any answer I give. To any answer you're ever given. Will it suffice you to know that I consider the Voyvod Karyl the foremost field captain of Nuevaropa?"

Rob sat down. Karyl sipped wine. Rob found it a little sweet, as the local vintages tended to be. *Still, The Books of the Law tell us it's a sin to waste,* he reminded himself.

"And yet he lost," Karyl said.

"Through treachery."

He shrugged and set his mug down with exaggerated care.

"Treachery there was," he said. "My people were murdered, my wonderful animals destroyed. But we were already defeated when the coward Jaume struck from behind."

"Through the actions of the man who sits beside you."

Horrified, Rob raised his hands to forestall the revelation. Too late. Karyl turned to look at him in surprise.

"That was a keen stroke, those mace-tails. You're a dinosaur master, then?"

"I am," Rob said proudly. If he was about to be struck dead with a bloody great hidden knife, he wouldn't bow his neck to it.

"So," Karyl said to the witch. "Perhaps the captain you want is the man you sent to fetch me instead."

Aphrodite smiled radiantly. "I wish to hire you both. I pay well."

Rob blinked, astonished.

Karyl sat back. "If you have need for a street performer, my services are available. My continued presence in this town appears no longer to be desired."

The self-proclaimed sorceress peered at him in confusion.

"But I have no need for a performer. Although the people of Providence may appreciate your skills in that regard. I need a war captain."

"For Providence, you say?" Rob said, reaming an ear with a pinky. "Isn't that where the Garden of Beauty and Truth holds sway? I thought they were all pacifists, so."

Karyl looked at him. He shrugged. "It's all the talk now, what with the Church suspecting them of heresy and all."

"It may be they will soon amend their doctrines," Aphrodite said. "In any event I propose to engage you myself. And pay you."

"What relationship do you have with this Garden?" Karyl asked.

"I am friend to their leader, Bogardus. Aggressive and brutal neighbors afflict them. I believe you will relieve their suffering."

"How? If they're pacifists, whom would I command?"

"Those you recruit."

"So that's what you want me to do? To raise and train an army from a province of peace-loving poets?"

"Exactly, Lord Karyl."

He dropped chin to clavicle and sat silent for a time. Aphrodite gazed at him calmly. Rob tried not to fidget.

Karyl laughed softly.

"If you're willing to pay good gold to a failed captain and a sacked dinosaur master to perform the impossible, who am I to argue?"

"What's that you're playing?" Karyl asked. "It isn't very interesting."

They sat in a little clearing in thick hardwood forest not far from Pot de Feu beside a discreet campfire.

"Scales," Rob said. "Just exercises. So my fingers don't forget their art. Not meant to entertain. And who's a critic here, Montador Toots-the-Flute-like-a-Half-Wit-Child? If I'd known you were going to asperse my playing, I'd've let the Guild bravos have their way with you."

"You did."

"Details," Rob grunted.

He switched to playing a melody lightly, with lost-kitten plaintiveness. Night insects sang accompaniment. The Firepot mountain drummed bass. The woods' green smell and the brushwood-fire tang almost took the brimstone from the air. Overhead the clouds had gone to rags, baring stars.

A few meters away, Little Nell browsed contentedly at thick, low ferns at the little clearing's edge, tethered by a hind foot to a stout tree trunk. Rob, with Karyl behind him, had ridden her to this secluded spot in Telar's Wood a few kilometers outside Pot de Feu. A patient, placid, amiable beast, the hook-horn had faithfully carried Rob and his gear for years. She was perhaps the only friend who had remained true to him all that time. Perhaps because she was the only one he remained true to.

"I doubt the Entertainer's Guild will pursue us,"

said Karyl, who sat with his back against his pack and his stick held against his shoulder. "Though some of them moonlight as bravos, they don't strike me as trackers."

"I don't think anybody saw us leave town, even mounted on a six-meter dinosaur," Rob said. Still, he felt unease.

Karyl rubbed at the stump of his left hand. "It itches like mosquito bites," he complained.

"Of course. It's the witch-woman's magic. You were there."

Karyl stopped rubbing. "There's no such thing as magic."

"Suit yourself."

For a span Karyl sat listening to Rob play his lute. In the firelight he looked mostly tired when Rob glanced at him.

"Is that a dirge?" Karyl asked.

"We'd call it a lament," Rob said. "Are you a lover of music, then, for all your crimes against her?"

A corner of Karyl's mouth quirked up. "My piping's scarcely the worst of my crimes."

"And what worse could you do, pray tell?"

"I banned music from the court of the Misty March, and discouraged it in the countryside. As I did the playing of games, and the wearing of bright colors, and anything else I deemed frivolous. Things I thought distracted the people from work."

"Bella! How could you *do* something like that?"

"It seemed right. At this remove, it looks like the most frivolous thing of all."

"So now you've the sack to sit here and justify such outrages?"

"No. I neither apologize for nor justify anything I did in my . . . prior lives."

"Why do you keep saying 'lives'?"

"I've died twice, by my count," Karyl said. "Once at the Battle of Gunters Moll under Duke Falk's axe. And again . . . soon after."

Rob awaited further explanation. Karyl resumed silence.

Rob plucked his strings savagely with scarred, blunt fingers. They produced plangent, dissatisfied sounds.

"I hope you've not misplaced your skill for war there in the mists of your mind."

Karyl set his sword-staff down beside him and stretched out on warm, moist grass. "We'll see."

"You're going to sleep?" Rob exclaimed. "What about watches?"

"What about them?"

Rob waved a big broad hand around at the night. "This is wild land. Anyone could fall on us here if we're not keeping lookout."

"Let them. I don't carry anything worth staying awake to defend."

"But what of your life—a 'small and miserable thing,' and I quote?" demanded Rob. "You fought for it in Pot de Feu!"

"If they steal it from me as I sleep," said Karyl, rolling over, "my pride will never know."

But hours later, in the belly of night, terrifying screams jerked Rob from deep slumber.

He scrambled from his bedroll to find Karyl sitting up in a jumble of his own bedding. His hair hung sodden to his shoulders. Sweat streamed between fingers covering his face.

He dropped both hand and stump to his lap like broken tools.

"The dreams," he said without looking at Rob. "Every night, they come."

"Mother Maia!" Rob exclaimed. "What happens in these dreams?"

Slowly Karyl shook his head. "I never remember. Just beauty. Terrible beauty. And fear beyond enduring."

Chapter 9

Titán trueno, **Thunder-titan**—*Apatosaurus louisae*.
Giant quadrupedal plant-eating dinosaur; 23 meters,
23 tonnes. Nuevaropan native. Placid and oblivious like
all titans, Apatosaurus's sheer size renders it a danger
to life and property, especially in herds.

—THE BOOK OF TRUE NAMES

With a decisive *tunk* the javelin struck the target-stand.

"Shit!" Princess Melodía said.

"Can you believe it?" Fina said. "Someone was actually murdered in His Majesty's apartments. It's so terrible."

Melodía scowled. She'd missed the matador's-eye by a full half meter. At twenty meters, she expected better of herself.

To one side of the exercise yard a nosehorn pulled a windlass arm, crunching away at a wheeled basket full of grain as it plodded endlessly around a circular track, pumping water from a stream deep beneath the Firefly Palace. She might have blamed the infernal off-kilter creaking for distracting her. She knew better.

"It's not as if he was found in my father's bed-room," she said irritably.

"My maidservant, Mitzi, is friend to the chamber-maid who found the body," Lupe said, not without a certain ghoulish relish. "She said it was horrible. All black and bloated."

"You make us *so* sorry we missed it," Llurdis said. It got her a glare from Lupe.

"But whoever would send an assassin after the Emperor?" asked Princess Fanny, hefting a feathered dart from a basket.

"No one," Melodía said crisply as she stalked downrange. "There's some mistake."

"*Someone's* gone and gotten himself assassinated," Abi Thélème said.

"But that someone was not my father," Melodía said, wrenching loose her javelin with unnecessary force.

The morning was early-hot, the sun bright through thin clouds. A long-crested dragon wheeled hopefully overhead. Ballista crews and arbalesters waited on the ramparts to dissuade the monster from trying its luck on the palace grounds.

"It must have been the Trebizons," Lupe declared with conviction.

Returning to the line, Melodía frowned and angled her head to one side. "The Trebs? Why?"

"It stands to reason," Lupe announced, as if it did. The Spañola Princess loved intrigues and conspira-cies. Which were in no short supply in the Corte Im-perial, of course. But the real ones, numerous as they were, were usually too trivial to satisfy her. She was beside herself at having an actual murder on hand.

"All right," Melodía said, curious despite herself. She wiped sweat from her forehead with the back of her hand. "How does it stand to reason?"

"The Trebizons have come to La Merced to petition for your hand in marriage to their Crown Prince Mikael."

"Who they say weighs two hundred kilos," said Llurdis. "And never bathes."

"Eww," said Fina and Fanny at once.

"Thanks so much for reminding me," Melodía said. "What's that got to do with dead men in our apartments?"

"Everyone knows the Trebizons are mad plotters," Lupe said, "just brimming with stratagems and treacheries. So they sent an assassin to eliminate whoever it is they blame for your father not giving them what they want. ¿Hola? Obvious."

"That would be me," Melodía said.

"Well, of course. You're what they came for."

"No," Melodía said with terrible precision. "I mean, the one who stands in their way is me. I am not going to some fever swamp on the Tahmina Sea. Especially not to wed an obese, unwashed Apatosaurus of a Crown Prince."

"But your father's the Emperor," Fina said.

"Did you all drink a potion of grasping the obvious this morning?"

"But, don't you have to do what he says?"

"You mean you haven't learned to get your father to say what you want him to?" asked Abi.

Waiting her turn for her next cast, Melodía cocked

an eyebrow at her. Clever and cool as Abi was, Melodía would never guess her father was easy for anyone to manipulate. Roger the Spider was Nuevaropa's most infamous intriguer.

"Papá won't make me marry anyone I don't want to," Melodía said confidently. The Emperor was highly indulgent of his daughters.

When he could be bothered to remember their existence.

Nonetheless she could see why the Trebs persisted in their suit long after its hopelessness should've been obvious even to foreigners. Although the Fangèd Throne wasn't hereditary, an Emperor's elder daughter held powerful potential to influence policy.

If only, Melodía thought. In any event, she doubted even Nuevaropa's long-term rival empire was mad enough to imagine assassination could help their suit.

"Perhaps you should set your cap for that new Northerner," said Lupe. "Terrible form."

The latter was directed at Llurdis, who had just thrown her dart into the wood post beneath the butt.

"Bitch," Llurdis said.

"*Puta.*"

Melodía rolled her eyes.

The Princesa Imperial and her retinue were dressed for exercise, in loincloths with silken bands wound tightly around their breasts for support. Brown or pale, their bodies glistened with sweat from exercise and humid heat.

War was the duty and main occupation of the noble classes. Highborn ladies learned martial arts to be ready to defend their families and themselves. Though the profession of arms was not closed to women in Nuevaropa, it was considered beneath a noblewoman's station to take the field except in dire necessity. A few women commanded mercenary companies, but almost none commanded household forces.

Naturally quick and strong of body as well as mind, Melodía excelled at most of the combat arts she and her retine practiced, which didn't penalize a woman's relative lack of muscle. She was lethal with javelin and twist-dart, a fine shot with the shortbow, adept with spear, dagger, and short sword and buckler.

At wrestling she could seldom beat Lupe's snaky wiriness or Llurdis's power, but both were skilled grapplers who not infrequently defeated boys of similar weight. The pair practiced a lot on each other, usually with little prior notice. They reminded Melodía of cats.

"But why would our Princess even take notice of that new Duke's strapping muscles and blue eyes?" said Abi archly. "She has her own Jaume, back from the wars."

"Why should that blind her?" asked Fina. "She's known *him* ages and ages."

Melodía's throw sailed half a meter over the top of the post that supported the straw-bale butt, to stick in packed white dirt ten meters beyond. "Hold!" cried Fanny, who was taking her turn at range-mistress today.

When Melodía, still fuming, came back with her javelin, her retine had found a new topic: speculating about a certain dowager countess at court and a handsome page. She shook her head in disgust.

"Oh, don't be such a wet-mop, Día," Llurdis said.

"I just don't understand how you girls can be so preoccupied with such *trivia*," she said, "with all these crises besetting the Empire."

Abi tilted her head so that her long silver-blond hair spilled down a bare shoulder, and gave Melodía a cool blue look.

"Crises always beset the Empire," she said. "Always have and always will. The Creators set it up that way, my father says."

"The Creators," Melodía said with a sniff.

Fashionably agnostic herself, she doubted the Spider said any such thing. Though widely presumed to be a complete atheist, not even Sansamour's powerful Archduke-Elector would ever dare admit it. *The Books of the Law* decreed that all forms of worshipping the Eight Creators were righteous. What they didn't countenance was *disbelief*.

Roger was also rumored to be a diabolist, having secret commerce with the duende or hada. Or as some called them, the Fae: rogue spirits of the Underworld. Histories recorded a High Holy War between the Eight and their faithful against the hada and their human allies more than half a millennium before; Melodía dismissed them as legends to glorify her family, which had raised the Empire from the War's ashes. She didn't believe in devils at all, and didn't for a heartbeat credit that Abi's father did.

"I have to learn to rule someday," she said. "I've got to be ready when the time comes to inherit our Duchy. Much as I wish he would, my father can't live forever."

"Your multiply-great-grandma Rosamaría has," Fanny said cheerfully.

La Madrota, Great Mother of the Imperial Delgao family, was approaching her three hundredth birthday. That was remarkable even in a world where, if nothing killed you, you might go on living indefinitely, like a carp.

"What's the point in fretting over politics, Día?" asked Abi. "You father will never let you near them."

"I can't talk to you," Melodía said. She turned away.

Miffed at having had center stage so long denied them, Lupe and Llurdis started pummeling each other. They fell to the ground, pulling hair and screeching like a pair of tröodons dancing on hot coals.

Huffing annoyance, Melodía looked over to the shade of a cycad-frond lean-to, where Doña Carlota, her watch-raptor, and her fellow dueñas sat sewing colorful feathers together into cloaks and skirts. The dueñas affected not to notice the scuffle. Llurdis and Lupe were just that way.

Doña Meg, Fanny's dueña, looked up and smiled. "Why, Count Jaume," she said, "what a delightful surprise to see you."

As many of her gente did, although not her charge, she spoke the Imperial tongue with a defiant Anglés accent.

"And you as well, Doña Margarita," said that familiar liquid-amber baritone, whose words were lyrics, whose sound, music.

The Anglesa twinkled. She normally disliked having her given name rendered into Spañol. But she could scarcely take exception when it came from the lips of the Empire's most renowned poet.

"And all of you ladies. Such a bouquet you create, sitting there."

Melodía clamped her lips. The deft Count Jaume had not specified what *kind* of bouquet. Melodía had in mind thornbushes, herself.

The dueñas cooed and fluttered themselves with feather fans. Except for Doña Carlota, who affected to disapprove of her charge's dashing cousin. She sat like a stump, grumping and sewing determinedly.

"And you, gentle ladies," Jaume said, bowing to Melodía's retinue.

Melodía still hadn't turned to face him. She could almost *feel* his gaze sweep the bare skin of her back, like a rare sunbeam slanting down through a rift in the clouds. She felt her cheeks take fire, knew she was blushing like a jungle-rose, and silently cursed herself.

Jaume greeted each of the ladies-in-waiting in turn. Lupe and Llurdis had even ceased their homoerotic wrestling match and jumped to their feet, where they stood blushing and shuffling in a way that Melodía could not decide whether she found more ridiculous or disgusting. Her Catalan kinswomen put Melodía in mind of a bull nosehorn pawing the ground before a charge.

Melodía still didn't turn. She wasn't sure whether she was enjoying the delicious self-torture or was simply embarrassed beyond words by her own transparent emotions. Probably both.

She felt his hands on her bare shoulders then. Her knees sagged.

"Ahem!" Doña Carlota said.

The twin touches rose from Melodía's skin. Though not without lingering a heartbeat, maddening and delightful.

"And with all due regard to this garden of unparalleled loveliness," Jaume said, "no flower pleases my eye so much as our Princesa Melodía."

She turned then, eyes downcast to the dark russet toes of his soft felt boots. She feared that if she looked into that dear and dearly missed face, she'd be unable to keep from throwing herself straightaway into his arms. Or wrapping herself around him like a drowning cat.

And I'd never hear the end of that from the retinue, would I? she thought. *Plus the choice words Doña Carlota would have to say. . . .*

A forefinger pressed gently upward beneath her chin. "Something in your eye, cousin dear?"

Her gaze climbed. Jaume's long-muscled legs were tightly wrapped in gold hose, signifying he was about court business. He wore a fine strider-leather skirt the same russet as his boots, and a loose blouse of cream silk, slashed for ventilation and incidentally revealing glimpses of his ribbed and muscle-corded torso.

Some who saw Jaume only in his finery, or focused overmuch on his renown as poet, minstrel, and philosopher of beauty, thought him soft. She knew from personal experience how mistaken that was.

She tried not to think how badly she wanted to renew that experience. *Duty*, she reminded herself. *Desire has to wait. Again.*

At last she let herself look into his face. He winked. Then, gravely, he raised her hand to his lips.

As he kissed it, she heard a scuffle of sandaled feet and an apologetic throat-clearing from somewhere behind him.

With a quirk of a smile and shrug for her alone, Jaume turned to face a youth wearing a harness that bore the Imperial badge: the stylized skull of a Tyrannosaurus imperator, gold on red.

"How may I help you, young sir?" Jaume asked.

"My lord Count," the lad piped, self-important as a songbird at dawn, "His Imperial Majesty respectfully requests you to wait upon him in his apartment at your earliest pleasure."

"Indeed," Jaume said. Even for the Imperial Champion, that meant *now*.

"Ladies, I must depart." He pressed Melodía's hands in both of his. They were long and fine, yet she could feel the swordsman's calluses upon them. "Doña Carlota, I leave this blossom in your capable hands."

Carlota mumbled something. Her slab cheeks flushed and she busied herself with her featherwork. She was a bluff countrywoman from Felipe's Duchy of Los Almendros. She would have sniffed at compliments to her notional beauty; those words had hit their mark.

Jaume gave Melodía another wink and followed the page away into the palace.

From above and behind she heard a terrible descending shriek. It ended in a colossal twang and strangled squawk.

Melodía spun to see the dragon plummeting, great wings trailing limply above. A two-meter bolt transfixed its short, furred body. On the outer wall an engine crew hooted and danced and pumped fists in triumph beside their upraised ballista.

"*A la máquina,*" breathed Lupe, wide-eyed.

The monster landed with a thump beside an empty cart.

"Take heart, Día," murmured Abigail Thélème. "You're not the only one to get shot down diving on your prey."

Chapter 10

Saltador, Springer—*Orodromeus makelai.* (In Anglaterra, the smaller *Hypsophilodon foxii.*) Swift, bipedal herbivorous dinosaur; 2.5 meters long, 45 kilograms. Usually brown spotted white, with white bellies. Timid; adept at hiding. Common farm pests in Nuevaropa. A favored quarry of hunters both human and dinosaurian.

—THE BOOK OF TRUE NAMES

D on't call me your lord," Karyl said.

Puffing more than he cared for, Rob Korrigan led Little Nell up a steep ridge near the eastern border of County Bonnechance. A wide-brimmed hat shaded his eyes from early-afternoon sun. His companion walked ahead of him with hood thrown back and head high, stabbing the white-dirt road with his stick as he walked and generally behaving as if he were alone.

"Why not?" Rob said. "What else should I call you? 'Hey, you' seems less than suitable."

"I've been called worse."

"Be that as it may."

At the crest Rob paused and took off his hat to wipe his brow. Before them the country swept down and away in short grass and cultivated fields, dotted with small hills. In the distance tiny figures trudged behind toylike nosehorns, tilling pale soil. To left and right the ridgeline glowed with yellow and red wildflowers. In the ditchside weeds, a small green-backed bouncer sat on its tail, forelimbs tucked against its yellow breast, regarding them with wide yellow eyes as it munched blossoms in its curved beak. Crested fliers rode thermals overhead.

"In any event," Karyl said, "I'm certainly not *your* lord. You're not a Slavo."

"I've been accused of most known vices and some scarcely imaginable," Rob said with a laugh. "Justly, for the most part. But never that."

"I'm not the lord of anyone anymore," Karyl said. "Not even myself, perhaps."

He walked on, down the far slope, which was gentler than what they'd just come up. Clucking to Little Nell, Rob followed. *He seems devilish composed*, he thought, *for a man who spent half the night in screaming nightmares*. Rob himself was a bit shaky on his pins for want of sleep.

"Now, how can that be?" he asked. "You're not lord of your own *self*?"

"I told you. I was killed twice."

"I saw Hornberg blindside you. What about the other?"

"I fell off the Eye Cliffs with my sword hand bitten off."

"You're joking."

But Karyl clearly wasn't. His shoulders slumped.

His voice dropped so low Rob could barely hear it for the breeze.

"I remember feeling my blood pumping from my veins," he said, as if to himself. "I felt anger, and frustration. But also anticipation, almost joy. For I knew that soon I could rest."

"Well? So then what happened?"

"I died."

"How can that be? I see you walking before me. I hear your sandals on the roadway. I smell your sweat. And those Guild bravos felt your solidity, to say nothing of your edge. You're no phantom. How can you have died?"

"How can I not have? I should have bled to death, or been killed by the fall to the Eye. But instead— nothing."

"Nothing?"

"Something resurrected me. Some*one*."

"Who?"

"I've no idea. When I came back to myself, if that's really where I am, I was walking a road in Francia on a bright winter's day. Already a vagabond jongleur, it seems."

"There're worse fates, inasmuch as that's what I am too, at the moment." Rob said. "Truly a strange tale, my—Karyl. Might the Fae have saved you, then?"

Karyl made a surprisingly vulgar noise for a blue blood.

"Don't be so fast to dismiss them!" Rob said. "I've seen and known things few mortals have. The Faerie Folk are real. Whether good, or evil as the Church tells us, I can't say. But trickish as their reputation makes them, and tenfold more."

"There's no such thing as the Fae."

"That's what you said about magic. Now it's giving you back the hand you lost—and I must have that story from you before the sun escapes the sky again. How can you still believe so strongly in your disbelief?"

"It's not giving my hand back."

"What were those little pink buds I saw on the end of your arm, then, when you changed the dressing?" Karyl's stump had grown so sensitive he had taken to bandaging it.

"Inflammations. Nothing more."

"Five of them, so?"

Karyl spat in the dirt. "This discussion grows tiresome."

Since his companion couldn't see it, Rob grinned. "All right. Who caught you when you fell, then?"

"Someone," Karyl repeated. "I can't shake the feeling that whoever it was who saved me and nursed me back to health—of the body, at least—now regards himself as holding rights of ownership in me. My greatest dread is the moment he chooses to assert them."

"Why, then, we'll fight him together, whoever he is!" Rob exclaimed.

Karyl snorted. "Bravado," he said. "I appreciate it, just the same. But be warned: those who've fought beside me in the past have not fared well."

"Fair enough," Rob said. "So now: you must tell me how it was you misplaced your hand, and found yourself falling off a cliff into the Tyrant's Eye."

Karyl walked on. Rob ran after, yanking Little Nell into a thumping lope. At which she blew through her big, fleshy nostrils altogether more theatrically than was necessary in protest.

"Wait!" Rob shouted. "You can't just walk away and not tell me."

Clearly Karyl could. "Fae take you!" Rob exclaimed.

Karyl spun. His face was bone white, his eyes bleak and black.

"Don't ever say that to me again," he said.

Rob stopped dead. Little Nell barely pulled up in time to avoid trampling him.

"But I thought you didn't believe in the Fae!"

Karyl's eyes became slits. "Don't say it again."

He turned and continued down the road into the broad green valley.

Rob sighed. "Ah well, that's the price of dealing with genius," he told Little Nell as he urged her to a placid plod. "It's contrary and cantankerous. As well you know from keeping company with me!"

It was just coincidence that the hook-horn farted loudly. So he told himself.

"Jaume! Come in, my boy. Come in!"

Smiling, Jaume advanced to meet his uncle, who rose from a purple velvet chair and came forward with arms spread to enfold him. The young Count's step faltered slightly as he saw another man seated in the room by dim sunlight through the window.

Somewhere a woman sang a haunting melody, with decent voice and a feeling Jaume admired.

Felipe hugged his nephew warmly. In the privacy of his apartments the Emperor wore loose linen trunks and a green silken vest that left his capacious, ginger-furred belly bare.

"You've met Duke Falk?" he asked.

"Not formally," Jaume said.

"Not even on the field of battle," the Duke said, rising. He came forward, extending a big square hand.

Jaume clasped it. Falk gave him an honest grip, strong and dry, with no silly games about trying to crush his hand.

"I am honored," Falk said, stepping back with a brief bow. He wore a long loose silken gown in his colors: blue, black, white.

"The pleasure's mine," Jaume said. He gave the Emperador a searching look as he took the chair Felipe indicated, though.

The door opened again. Quickly, almost surreptitiously, Chief Minister Mondragón entered. He was a tall man, lean in robes of black and brown, with black hair worn close to either side of a narrow head, a neat beard, and a nose like a blade. His eyes were large and dark.

He stopped short. "Duke Falk? *Here?*"

"Now, Don Pablo," Felipe said, "the Duke has made his submission. And I of course decreed a general amnesty for participants in the . . . late unpleasantness up North."

"Yes, but—" The minister's lips pressed to a thin line. "To be sure, Majesty."

He bowed tightly toward Falk. "Please forgive me, your Grace."

"Of course," Falk said. But the teeth at the edges of his smile seemed very sharp indeed.

"What have you learned about our mysterious visitor?" Felipe asked. He sat back and took a handful of Ruybrasil nuts mixed with candied mango and orange from a bowl on a table with a varnished nosehorn foreleg for a pedestal.

Raptor features pinched tighter. Jaume wondered how the Chief Minister might look if he *approved* of something. If he ever did.

"A member of the Brotherhood of Reconciliation," Mondragón said. "As we suspected."

"The cult of assassins?" Falk said. "Absurd. They aren't real."

Mondragón produced a dagger wrapped in reed paper. He set it on the table next to the Emperor and carefully unwrapped it. Its blade was wavy.

"Apparently they are," he said. "You recognize the pattern, surely—mind that, Majesty. Sometimes there's contact poison smeared on the blade, away from the edge to catch the unwary."

With fingertips Felipe picked up the dagger by its pommel. "The Brotherhood indeed," he said. "Who was their target, d'you think?"

"Who else but your Majesty?" Falk said hoarsely.

"Surely not," said Mondragón. "They know the consequences."

"What do you mean?" Falk said.

"The Brotherhood of Reconciliation is a chartered order of the Creator Maia," Jaume said. He smiled. "A charitable order, as it happens."

"You mean the Empire countenances assassination?" Falk's face had gone purple.

"Not as such," Mondragón said. "It remains, of course, illegal. However, as a practical matter, such things—deplorable as we may find them—will occur. Over the decades, the Imperio has discovered the most judicious course is that they be handled as . . . regularly as possible. We do not condone acts of murder, nor do we look the other way."

"But if this sect exists only *to* murder—"

"Ah, but it doesn't, your Grace," said Jaume. "It conducts a full schedule of devotions and benevolent works. Just as my own Companions do."

Falk looked puzzled. "Your Companions? Your company of Dinosaur Knights?"

"They are an Order Militant of la Iglesia Santa," Mondragón said, "like the Knights of the Yellow Tower and the Sisters of the Wind. As the Companions' Captain-General, Don Jaume holds ecclesiastical rank equivalent to a Cardinal."

"Indeed? An order? I hadn't realized."

"Certain parties within Creators' House and at court find our existence as scandalous as you seem to find the Brotherhood's," Jaume said with a smile.

Falk shook his head as if to clear water from his ears. "I don't understand. They're assassins. But they aren't."

"*Some* are assassins," Jaume said. "A messy situation and not particularly pleasing."

"But surely you punish assassins!"

"We hunt them down assiduously," Mondragón said. "And kill them. The Brotherhood disclaims responsibility for any unlawful acts its adherents perform. As for those we succeed in capturing and putting to death—one gets the impression the order's elders believe we're doing them a service by weeding out the unfit."

"Outrageous!" Falk said. "Such corruption should never be tolerated."

"Some might say the same of rebellion, your Grace."

Jaume had tossed the words out carelessly. But the Alemán turned a burning blue glare on him.

"Your Grace, I apologize," he said hastily. "I spoke without thinking. Whatever the past, you've stepped forward and made honest submission to our Emperor."

For a moment Falk's eyes bored into Jaume's like sapphire drills. Then Felipe chuckled. He had an easy laugh.

"Ah, that's my dear nephew," he said. "Always hot-blooded! Youth and enthusiasm can overwhelm the coolest head, ¿qué no? Maybe that's the reason governing is commonly left to the old. Isn't that so, Pablito?"

"Indubitably," the minister murmured. "But I wouldn't call your Majesty old."

Felipe flicked air with the fingers of his right hand. "My young lord Falk is quite the eager harrier too, according to reports. And later, Jaumet, you'll give me your full personal account of the *affair del Norte* in private."

Jaume steepled his hands before him and bowed in his chair, as was correct for his station and situation. He enjoyed a certain amount of court rigmarole—in moderation. It reminded him of an ancient ritual dance, with the grace and beauty that implied.

"The truth is, Falk my boy," the Emperor said, "the Brotherhood would never dare lift a finger against a seated Emperor, or any member of his family. That would quite cross the line, now, wouldn't it?"

He chuckled again. "They know perfectly well that if they ever did anything remotely like that, I, or whoever sat the Fangèd Throne, would have no choice but to nip right 'round to his Holiness the Pope, and see their charter revoked right smartly. And then dig them out, root and branch."

Nipping around to his Holiness was convenient too, inasmuch as the Holy Church of Nuevaropa's

headquarters were right below in La Merced, around
the north edge of circular Bahía Alegre.

Falk's eyes gleamed with a different light than the
cold fire he'd directed at Jaume. "Put me in charge,
your Majesty! I pray you." His guttural accent lent
fervor to his Spañol. "I'll root out the hada for you
in no time."

Felipe laughed aloud in delight, and his hazel eyes
gleamed. But he shook his head.

"Not unless they cross that line, my fine young
dragon! To upset our arrangement with the Brotherhood would cause chaos. And what's the use of having an Emperor, then? In fact, what's the use of an
Empire, if not to provide order?"

Felipe's vehemence made Falk sit spear-upright.
"Of course, your Majesty! Order. That is a sovereign's first duty."

Mondragón cleared his throat. "If we might return
to the issue of our intruder's intended target, my
lords—"

Falk scowled. His heavy blue-black brows were
well suited for it.

"It must have been someone close to your Majesty," Falk declared.

"One takes that more or less for granted," Mondragón said with some asperity, "given where we
found him."

Falk shot him a quick glare. Then, too heartily, he
said, "As you say, Chief Minister."

He recovers quickly, Jaume thought. It was certainly to the Duke's credit. In Spaña, Northerners had
a reputation for brick-headed stubbornness. Which
during his recent mission Jaume had not exactly found
unwarranted.

Then again he could say as much of far too many Nuevaropan grandes. The Duke of Hornberg displayed a flexibility of mind more frequently associated with the allegedly subtle South.

"Our most urgent question is: Who sent him?" Falk said.

Mondragón cocked a brow at Jaume. "What do you think?"

Crossing one leg over the other, Jaume waved an easy hand. "Our Alemán friend is doing quite well on his own. Let's hear what he has to say."

He savored the irony. Ordinarily Mondragón regarded *him* with dour suspicion, as a lightweight and possible subversive. Perhaps even a heretic. Some at high levels of both Church and Empire regarded Jaume as such, for preaching that hedonism served the Creators' will, and that the aristocracy had a duty to serve the common folk, not just be served by them.

But now Mondragón clearly looked upon Jaume as an ally against this bumptious Alemán.

"Could it be those Providence devils I've heard so much about since I got here?" Falk asked. "They sound like a nest of heretics in dire need of purging. Who knows what they might be capable of?"

Mondragón smiled. "The Garden of Beauty and Truth, as this new sect in East Francia styles itself, draws heavily upon the teachings of our own Count Jaume for their doctrines," he said with acerbic relish.

"No one's more faithful than my Jaumet!" the Emperor exclaimed. "Mind you, these Providence types do seem to take things to extremes. But they've given never a whiff of disloyalty, Falk, dear boy."

"Who's most at odds with your Majesty, then?" Falk asked.

"That rogue of a Count of Terraroja," Felipe replied at once. "Don Leopoldo. He's nothing but a damned brigand. He loots trade caravans on the Imperial High Road, calls it tariffs, and claims some musty privilege from the Spañol crown as justification. He defies the Fangèd Throne!"

Jaume's lips and brow compressed. He couldn't much fault his uncle's characterization of Leopoldo, whose Redland County lay eighty kilometers inland of La Merced, up on the arid central Spañol plateau called La Meseta. But even Jaume, whose interest in history ran mostly to phases and fancies of the Imperial arts (including the martial ones), suspected the dispute amounted to no more than the sort of squabbling over prerogatives hidalgos were forever indulging in, from the meanest hedge-knights to kings.

Falk nodded as if Felipe had delivered a revelation straight from the Eight Themselves. "Then it's obvious, is it not? This upstart hired the assassin to kill—no, no, let me speak!—not your Majesty, but someone near to you. A clear attempt at intimidation!"

Mondragón, whose attempted interjections Falk had overridden, frowned. "He'd never have the wit, surely."

"Or he has too much," Jaume said, "to try anything that rash. Attack on any member of the Imperial family is lèse-majesté—a crime worse than treason."

It was Mondragón's turn to shoot Jaume a furious look. Falk nodded triumphantly. "Exactly!" he said.

"You really think so?" Obsessed though the Emperor was, he sounded doubtful.

"Of course," Falk declared, as if that were as certain as Creation itself. Jaume doubted Falk had so much as heard of Leopoldo before a few minutes ago.

Have you already spotted my uncle's regrettable tendency, he wondered, *that when you sing a song he likes, he seldom hears false notes?*

"If he's wicked enough to defy your Majesty," Falk said, "what limit is there to his evil?"

A gusty sigh escaped from Mondragón. Falk turned to him.

"I know what you're thinking, my lord," he said.

To Jaume's surprise he sounded earnest—and somewhat wounded. *If this is acting, he's got a gift for it.*

"Please understand: we of what was once the Princes' Party never wavered in our loyalty to our Emperor. Nor did we ever raise a voice, far less a blade, against him. We sought only to call attention to the actions of counselors we believed had given him evil advice. In this we acted wrongly. But his Majesty, in his wisdom and mercy, has seen fit to forgive us, earning our devotion anew!"

Jaume really wanted to hear what Mondragón had to say to *that,* inasmuch as he was Felipe's main counselor. Although some said that role had been usurped by the Emperor's disconcertingly mysterious confessor, Fray Jerónimo. But by reflex both Jaume and Mondragón looked to their master for reaction.

Felipe beamed. "Splendid, boy, splendid," he said. "Such spirit! Was there ever an Emperor so blessed in his servants?"

In the belly of the clock that stood in the corner, a miniature portcullis opened. A silver sackbut with gilded crest emerged to mark the hour with a mournful hoot. Mondragón's face twitched in irritation.

"Blast. I'm late to another meeting with those confounded Trebs. Forgive me, Majesty—"

Felipe waved a plump hand. "We know how sticky

these Griegos are about protocol. Go, and feel free to blame me for delaying you. It'll annoy them more, and that's always worthwhile."

Mondragón bowed to the others. Then he departed with a brisk black and brown swirl.

Jaume rose as well. "I beg your leave as well, Majesty."

"To be sure, to be sure. On your way, nephew. And thanks for your counsel, as always."

"My duty and my pleasure."

As Jaume left, Felipe was turning to Duke Falk with eagerness sculpted in every contour of his face. Jaume felt a pang. *Is it wise to leave them alone together like this?*

But a duty no less pressing for being far more pleasant summoned him. And after all, nothing he could do could keep Falk from speaking to the Emperor in private, should the Emperor wish.

For all his soft appearance and mild manner, Jaume knew Felipe Delgao Ramírez possessed an iron whim.

Chapter 11

Bocaterrible, **Terrible Mouth**—*Pliosaurus funkei*. Short-necked, large-headed, predatory marine reptile; 13 meters long, 40 tonnes. Nuevaropa's most feared sea monster, a menace to small boats and even prey ashore.

—THE BOOK OF TRUE NAMES

"My Princess."

Heart in throat, Melodía spun. He stood behind her, smiling.

Surrounded by trellised honeysuckles rioting with yellow and white blooms, a table sat in a courtyard garden inside the palace itself. A modest collation awaited on it: petite roasted scratchers, a cold haunch of red-tailed springer, goat cheese, flat bread, and bowls of fruit.

"I wondered why Pilar brought me here," Melodía said. She had bathed away the dust and sweat of the morning's exercise and was dressed in a skirt of purple and yellow tröodon feathers with a matching gorget hung around her neck.

"I arranged it," Jaume said as they embraced. To her frustration he quickly pulled away. "A little cuatralas told me your guardian tyrant might be indisposed for a while."

"Doña Carlota? Yes. She came down with a toothache during morning practice, and had to rush to the apothecary to have a tooth pulled. Wait—surely you didn't arrange *that*?"

"I'm not that clever. I merely saw my chance, and took it."

"She's so *unreasonable*. Abigail's dueña makes sure she has a stock of contraceptive herbs. I have to sneak around like a thief."

"We're lucky she doesn't supply the girl with poisons too."

"I don't think Abi needs help with that. They play for serious stakes in Sansamour's court."

"They do everywhere," he said. "Even here in the pleasure dome of La Merced."

She laughed. "You can't mean that! Intrigues here are harmless. They're all about which duchess is sleeping with whose hadrosaur-groom. Or which duke is."

"No court has only harmless intrigues," Jaume said. "Ask the man found in your apartments last night."

Her face stiffened. She turned away.

"I'm sorry," Jaume said.

She made herself smile and turn back. "You taught me the truth is always beautiful, no matter what it is. So I shouldn't be afraid to face it."

They sat across from one another. During her lover's half-year absence, Melodía had at times felt as if she was going to become the first person in history to actually die of lust. With him here before her, smelling of clean, warm male flesh, sounding like music, and looking like a dream, she found herself reluctant to spoil the delicious anticipation. Now she wanted to draw this out, allow the tension to build, slowly, slowly.

She poured golden wine from a silver ewer. She handed him the goblet. His turquoise eyes met hers.

"You seem troubled," she said, feeling miffed at the fact.

He smiled sadly. "You're most perceptive."

"Jaumet, I've known you since I was a child! What makes you think you can hide things from me?"

He laughed. "Folly. But I didn't want to distress you. I just . . . wanted to delay the inevitable. Cowardice, I admit."

Not deigning to dignify *that* absurdity with a rebuttal, Melodía said, "What kind of bad news are you trying to shield me from?"

"Pere's dead."

"Oh, no." She set a forkful of ensalada back on her plate. "I'm so sorry! How did it happen?"

He sat a moment before answering, "In a way that still haunts me."

"Tell me," she said.

Jaume set down his scratcher leg and dabbed his mouth with a linen napkin. He paused a moment to collect his thoughts.

"After the fighting ended, your father ordered me to stay and straighten matters up in Alemania. When that was done, he commanded I return as quickly as possible and report in person. So, leaving most of my Companions and our dinosaurs to follow in a carraca, Pere, Luc, Dieter, and I took passage down the Channel on the Imperial war-dromon *Melisandre*."

"Montador Dieter?" Melodía asked. "I don't know him."

"Our newest Brother, accepted as a full Companion after the . . . after the War ended. Still has a bit of the egg stuck to him, but a good and talented boy. He earned his tabard."

"Sorry for interrupting," she said. "Go on."

"We were crossing the Great Bend, the wide water off the jut of Anglaterra called the Hinge. It's where the northern Canal, the Tyrant's Stripe, veers southwest to become the Maw."

"I've seen a map," she said dryly. Like most people, Jaume thought Nuevaropa—the peninsula at the western end of Aphrodite Terra—resembled the head of a Tyrannosaurus. The continental part formed its head and lower jaw, Anglaterra the face.

"A ship appeared from a squall northwest of us. A larger one, a cog with red sails."

"Corsairs?"

"Yes."

"I can't believe they dared!"

"Piracy's still a lively occupation in the islands. It's not unknown for certain coastal grandes to sponsor corsairs, even now."

Melodía's nose wrinkled. "I know. They catch them sometimes, and execute them publicly. Mercedes are usually easygoing, sweet even. But they're so bloodthirsty about pirates. It's awful!"

"Can you blame them? Anglés corsairs killed tens of thousands of their ancestors during the Rape of La

Merced in 370. And their attacks on shipping hurt commerce."

"Ah, *sí*. Mercedes hold their purses very near their hearts. But aside from the idiocy of taking on the Sea Dragons, why bother with a skinny little war-galley, instead of a poorly defended merchantman with a hull full of plunder?"

"Captain Gaspard said they could tell the *Melisandre* carried important cargo by the course she plied. Dispatches they could sell to the highest bidder, or important persons they could hold to ransom."

"If only they'd known the cargo was you and three Companions! They'd have turned right around and run."

"Maybe. There were a lot of them, and they seemed intent. And there was no way we could evade them."

"But aren't galleys supposed to be agile? How could a lumbering cog catch you?"

"I know nothing of the sea," he said, "and if it were possible, I'd know less about naval warfare. Our hosts told us the pirates held something called the 'weather gage,' meaning they were upwind of us, and could run us down with all those sails no matter where we turned. They overtook us quite rapidly. For all their skill, the Sea Dragons only got a single flaming pitchball into them from the stern catapult before they started arrowing us. Then they grappled, and we had some hot work.

"My Brothers and I barely had time to buckle on breasts and backs before the pirates started swinging aboard. Only half the Dragons wore armor. They can't row in it, so the oarsmen were unprotected. It didn't keep them from turning to with a will. They can fight, those marines."

He wet his throat with wine. "Big as she was, the cog seemed to overflow with pirates. They showed no fear of marines or us. Luc took an arrow in the eye early on."

Melodía winced.

"He kept fighting, but was quickly swarmed and killed. They were overwhelming us."

"But Maestro Sunzi's book says numbers mean nothing in war!"

Jaume smiled. His true love was fierce as a matadora—in her untried way. He prayed she'd never have to put her book knowledge to the test of real battle.

"Indeed," he said. "In a way that's the reason my Companions exist: to master quantity with quality. But . . . sometimes numbers *do* matter, when the disparity's great enough. We killed them like ants, and still they came.

"But Pere had noticed how panicky *fire* made the pirates, even though our pitch-ball barely glanced off their stern rail and didn't set anything alight. So we left Dieter to command Bartomeu and our other arming-squires and servants, fighting alongside the Sea Dragons, and clambered across to the cog.

"The corsairs gave us a brisk welcome-aboard. But we cut down enough of them to make them stand back, and put fire to their rigging and their bloodred sails."

"That sounds like you two," Melodía said, smiling.

"When they saw the merry blaze we set, with the *Melisandre* still not captured, the corsairs panicked. The fear of having their retreat cut off brought them scuttling back like handroaches."

"So you two saved the day. Again."

"Our bonfire turned the trick. Pere and I grabbed ropes to swing back home."

He stopped. The pain was like a dagger in his guts.

She reached across their forgotten meal to take his right hand in both of hers. She lifted it, kissed it, pressed it to her cheek.

"Tell me, Jaumet. It'll take some of the sting away."

"Maybe. You deserve to know, in any event. During our fight on the cog, Pere was wounded in the arm. I didn't even know. The bleeding weakened him—and made his hands slick. He slipped from the rope and fell into the sea."

"Oh, Maia," Melodía said. "Was his armor too heavy to swim in?"

"I doubt it. He always was a strong swimmer. And it wasn't as if we had full twenty-kilo suits of plate weighing us down. But—we'd been followed for several days by a bocaterrible."

Melodía's dark-amber eyes went wide. That breed of sea lizard grew to thirteen meters or more, with jaws bigger and more powerful even than a tyrant's. Everyone who lived near a coast or even a sufficiently deep river feared the monster called "terrible mouth." It more than pirates or invaders was the reason stout nets guarded the mouth of Bahía Alegre.

"Pere went under," Jaume said. "He looked up through the water. Our eyes met. He reached out to me. Then a great shadow engulfed him from below, and whirled him away into the depths."

Melodía began to cry. He moved around to hold her. Her cinnamon skin was dear remembered warmth. He stroked her dark-wine hair.

As she sobbed into his chest, he thought, *To think the last words Pere and I exchanged as friend to*

friend—instead of in the midst of battle—were a bit-
ter argument over whether I was betraying and aban-
doning him. For you, Princesa.

May you never learn it, love. That burden cannot
be lightened by sharing.

When Melodía had cried herself out, Jaume slid his
arm from around her and returned to his chair. They
ate awhile in silence.

Eventually Jaume found voice again, and asked how
things went with her. Awful as she felt over Pere's
fate, she did her best to lighten the mood with trifling anecdotes of goings-on at court: how Lupe had
caught Llurdis in the dinosaur stables with Lupe's
favorite page, and chased them both out naked into
the yard with a whip. Of a hidalgo visiting from
King Telemarco's court in La Fuerza, who made a
fool of himself over a priceless ring he'd given Abi
Thélème for favors she never got around to bestow-
ing on him. Of the suit by the importunate Trebizons
for Melodía's own hand, on behalf of their obese
and unwashed Prince.

Jaume smiled, and nodded, and laughed where appropriate. She wasn't fooled. He was holding something back. Something that ached like a wound.

It hurt that he wouldn't tell her. *Maybe he thinks*
he's sparing me further pain. Give him time.

Besides, the nearness of him, after so long and all
alone, awakened sensations that made it hard to stay
angry at him.

When they finished eating, he came around the table. Smiling, he took her hand and drew her to her
feet.

"What do you have in mind, Señor Conde?" she asked. Her eyes were turned down to the wide-leaved plants that sprawled between her feet, encased in gilt sandals, and his in soft russet boots.

"Let's dance."

She looked up at him. "But there's no music!"

He put an arm around her waist and began to lead her through a galliard. His hand seemed to scorch her bare hip. She tried to concentrate on the *cinco pasos*, the Five Steps of this particular dance. Her breath came in chops.

"Where you are, *mi amor*," he said, "is music. Isn't that your name?"

She laughed. They danced.

He turned her to face him, clasped her close. She gasped. He raised her off the ground and spun her three-quarters of a circle in a scandalous *vuelta*.

When he set her down he kissed her. She felt as if hot honey filled her veins. She kissed him back with adolescent fervor.

The flat muscles of his chest crushed her bare breasts. She clutched his lower rib cage. Strong, long-fingered hands molded her buttocks as if Jaume were a blind artist and meant to sculpt them.

He bore her back to the table. Reached to sweep spent dishes from the way.

A tiny throat was cleared.

In the act of sliding a hand down his body to the firmness that pressed against her belly through his trunks, Melodía froze. Her racing heart stumbled painfully. She knew that sound.

"*Montse,*" she hissed.

"Good afternoon, Count Jaume," the little girl said, with formal deference that was utterly unlike her.

Giving a last kiss to Melodía's sweat-streaming forehead, Jaume straightened, then turned and bowed. "A pleasure as always to see you, Infanta Montserrat," he said gravely.

Melodía glared at her sister. Montse's dark-blond dreadlocks dangled over the shoulders of a smock as grubby and grey-mottled as any garment she'd worn more than five minutes. She had wide cheekbones, a snub nose, great green eyes whose dancing mischief gave the lie to the innocence she was faking.

She curtsied. "I like you, Count Cousin. You don't treat me like a little girl."

"You *are* a little girl," Melodía said, pulling herself reluctantly and with a certain difficulty to a sitting position on the table's edge. "A nosy little brat, to be precise."

"I like to take people at their own evaluation," Jaume said. "Life plays much more harmoniously that way."

"You spoil her," Melodía said sulkily. "She oughtn't spy on people."

"I'm not spying," Montse said. "I hate spies. I want to build things. You know that."

"Yes, yes," Melodía said. Exasperating as Montse was, she found it hard to stay mad at her. "And I want to serve the Empire in a way that *matters*. And both of us are Imperial Princesses, and will doubtless never get what we want."

Jaume winked at her and silently said, "*Not so.*" She had to fight down a giggle.

"We know you weren't spying on us, Montserrat," Jaume said. "So what errand brought you here?"

"I was sent to fetch my sister to begin her preparations," she declared importantly.

"For what?" Melodía asked.

"Father's decreed a *huge* banquet tonight, to celebrate Jaume's return. All kinds of boring people will be there. I'm glad *I'm* too young to have to go."

Chapter 12

Cuellolargo, Long-Neck—*Elasmosaurus platyurus*. A kind of plesiosaur or long-necked sea monster; 14 meters, 2 tonnes. Eats fish and smaller marine lizards. Rarely attacks humans, sea-stories notwithstanding, and only when provoked.

—THE BOOK OF TRUE NAMES

Something's got to be done," declared the Conde Montañazul.

Melodía, a forkful of a salad halfway to her lips, exerted considerable will not to roll her eyes. *How many bad ideas get prefaced with that phrase?* she wondered.

Count Bluemountain was a tall man, still strongly built in middle age, with a pointy black beard striped silver down the sides. He wore a gown of scarlet silk with a blue mountain on gold shield sewn on the front. His fief was large, prosperous from mines and fine cloths, if not necessarily from wise rule. He was influential, popular among his fellow grandes.

Melodía held her tongue. For now.

The feasting hall was lively as a skimmer rookery with conversation and the companionable clatter of tableware. A small army of servants swarmed around bearing pitchers and trays. The smells of meats roasting and pastries baking competed with myriad essences the diners had doused themselves in, which fortunately blended into a mélange Melodía found pleasant. The twenty-five-meter-long blueheart table teemed with those whose estimates of their own importance accorded closely enough with the Imperial Chamberlain's to get them a place at it.

Melodía sat on her father's left, seven chairs down. Despite her rank, it was a standard placement for her at state dinners. As always she resented being excluded from the only conversation that mattered.

"Something must be done about what, Don Roberto?" the Condesa Rincón asked.

A countess in her own right, Teresa de Rincón was a widow of late middle age, silver haired and still trim. She sat across from Melodía, nestled closer to Herzog Falk von Hornberg than protocol required.

"Why, this Garden of Beauty and Truth in Providence, of course," Montañazul said. "They're a scandal. Their nonsense is likely to attract the sort of attention no one wants from the Grey Angels themselves! It wouldn't surprise me if they sent that assassin after our beloved Emperor."

Melodía swallowed anger at the implied slur against her beloved Jaume. "Wouldn't a more obvious culprit be the Princes' Party?" she made herself ask blandly. "They're the ones who made war on my father, not the Gardeners. Who are pacifists anyway."

She turned to look at the *norteño* Duke. So did everyone else in earshot. His presence at court provided such delicious controversy.

"A reasonable conjecture, Princess," he said with a blandness that made her want to kick him. He wiped his full lips on a linen napkin. "On the surface. But I ask, why? We never intended harm to our Emperor, or his family. Also, His Majesty has convinced me that no assassins would accept such a commission in the first place. So against whom would we dispatch them?"

Melodía's mouth tightened. Falk looked like just another big muscle-bound dolt, epitome of the buckethead, as wags called the Empire's warrior-aristocrats. But he was showing a most unbucketheadlike turn of both wit and forbearance.

"Might your Party try to assassinate the evil advisors the Princes claimed they fought against?" she asked.

"To what end, Highness? We lost our war and admitted our fault."

"Really, you shouldn't bullyrag our guest," Countess Rincón said, giving a squeeze of solidarity to Falk's thick biceps. "He's done his penance, and received absolution."

"Don't let Señorita Melodía fool you, your Grace," called a nasal and unwelcome voice from farther down the table.

The immaculately coiffed, bearded, and outsized head of Melodía's cousin Gonzalo Delgao sat on a white ruff as if it were a plate. Which was very much where Melodía would have liked to see it. She noticed that the diminutive, black-velvet-clad man had arranged his silver salad dish and utensils with his customary precision after finishing the course.

Across from him sat his younger brother Benedicto, big as a titan and just as swift, his great handsome brown block of a face creased by the effort of following the conversation.

"How do you mean?" Falk asked Gonzalo.

"Our Princess opposed her father's waging war on you and your comrades in the North," Gonzalo said. A beat later his brother nodded accord.

The brothers' usual partners in undermining Melodía's father, their supercilious brother-in-law René Alarcón and Augusto Manorquín, from a cadet family of Torre Ramírez, were blessedly absent. They might be elsewhere brewing mischief; Melodía suspected they were patronizing one of La Merced's justly famous brothels.

Again Falk's blue eyes fixed on Melodía. She found their intensity unsettling. It was already *quite* warm enough in here, thank you.

"Why, your Highness?" Falk asked.

"She's against war," Gonzalo said. "She's full of novel notions, my cousin."

"But doesn't war ultimately maintain that very order which supports you in your position of privilege?" Falk asked.

"I don't oppose all war," she said, shooting a ruffled-harrier look Gonzalo's way. "Only unnecessary ones. I've studied military history extensively. And before you ask, yes, I think my father should have tried harder to resolve his dispute with your Princes' Party through negotiation before opting for war."

Falk lifted a brow. "Reading about war is not the same as experiencing it, Highness."

"I know that," she said. "You fought with distinction

in that war, your Grace. Can you name me any activity *less* orderly?"

"An interesting point, Princess. Battle, at least, is the most chaotic activity imaginable."

"*Regardless* of who sent the assassin and why," Montañazul said, loudly trying to win back center stage, "I still say the Emperor has to act against this Garden of Beauty and Truth, so-called. Bring them to heel like disobedient vexers."

"Why?" Falk asked, sipping wine. "What threat can a pack of pacifists pose?"

"They teach sedition! Pacifism, to begin. Worse, far worse, is this notion that nobles owe a *duty* to their peasants: absurd! If that idea gets out, it will cause chaos. Anarchy!"

His wife, Condesa María, smiled and patted his bloodred arm. "Roberto knows how dangerous it is for peasants to get above themselves. Other hidalgos admire how efficiently he crushes their every unrest."

"One wonders that he gets so many of them," Melodía said sweetly.

"*Sí*," Countess María said, nodding. "It is a great mystery. It just goes to show how little serfs differ from the savage horrors of the woods."

To keep from laughing in her face, Melodía sipped wine. It was a fine vintage from La Meseta, the highland where both La Majestad, the Imperial capital, and Spaña's capital, La Fuerza, lay. *Something* good came out of the dusty place, anyway.

Felipe couldn't stand La Majestad or the Imperial Palace. Melodía liked them less. It was why they'd lived here since Melodía's mother had died bearing Montse.

"The Gardeners are heretics," Montañazul declared. "His Holiness has intimated as much himself."

The Pope sat at Felipe's left hand. Fearfully old, with a titan's egg of a head perched on a body scrawny as a half-starved flier's, swaddled in layers of gold-embroidered white cloth despite the heat, Pío was a great enthusiast of all the Emperor's worst impulses toward centralizing power. He was one reason for Melodía to be glad she wasn't allowed a nearer place at table: she had a hard time behaving with the Pope in earshot. Also he smelled.

That Pío never seemed entirely clean lent currency to whispers that he was a secret devotee of the Life-to-Come sect Melodía's dueña was so devoted to. If true, it *had* to be secret: La Vida-que-Viene held that the precepts of the Creators' own *Books of the Law*, which mandated things like sanitation and sensuous enjoyment of the world the Creators had given their children, were metaphors that were sinful to follow literally. Cleanliness and pleasure, believers taught, were meant to be enjoyed solely in the afterlife.

Melodía wasn't alone in wondering how they got any followers at all, much less a growing number of them.

Grinning openly now, she said, "You believe the Gardeners teach heresy, Count Roberto? How fascinating. Perhaps you'd like to take up the matter with the man whose writings they base their beliefs on."

She nodded to Jaume, who sat listening politely on Felipe's right. She felt sorry for him. The Pope-Metropolitan openly disapproved of Jaume's hedonistic philosophy. He considered his predecessor's recognition of the Companions as a holy order a mistake.

Jaume noticed Melodía looking his way and returned a quick, tight smile.

Montañazul became suddenly engrossed in the sizzling slices of nosehorn roast that had just been served him. He was an accomplished duelist, and fancied himself a jouster of the first rank. Jaume was a legendary fighter. *He's not a* total *fool,* Melodía thought.

The rest of the meal passed uneventfully. Montañazul fell to discussing war-duckbills, always a safe and welcome subject to the aristocracy, with the Duke of Alba, which was the large island down-Canal from La Merced. A ferocious old matador, Duke Luis was a former Imperial Constable with only one eye on one side and one leg on the other.

Countess Rincón monopolized Duke Falk. Melodía ate with her usual voracity, which helped her pretend not to notice how the young Alemán's eyes kept straying her way.

As she finished she became aware of a shadow hanging over her head. For no readily intelligible reason, some ancestor of Prince Heriberto's had chosen to hang a stuffed cuellolargo above the banquet board by black iron chains. Though only a small one, ten meters long or so, the long-necked sea monster had scared Melodía into fits the first time she'd seen it as a child. Montserrat, on the other hand, had even as a toddler regarded it as the most wonderful thing *ever*.

Melodía had long gotten over her terror of the toothy beast. She had a harder time shaking off a foreboding that one of La Merced's frequent earthquakes would drop the wretched thing on her head one day while she drank her soup.

Felipe stood. Silence fell like the plesiosaur unchained. The Pope squinted up at his friend in keen interest. Jaume leaned back in his chair, empty-faced.

"Your Holiness," Felipe said with a bow to the Pope. "My lords and ladies. I should like to announce a most momentous decision at which I, after much prayer to our Creators and consultations with my wise counselors, have just arrived.

"I hereby decree an Imperial Army of Correction, to march upon the Condado de Terraroja and restore that realm proper obedience, to the Empire and to the Holy Church!"

Applause and cheers flew up. Melodía squeezed her eyes shut.

She opened them to look at Jaume. His face was rigid. Out of loyalty to his lord and kinsman, Jaume was swallowing his misgivings, though she knew they burned his belly.

Wouldn't you serve Father better by speaking out against this lunacy? she wanted to shout at him. Yet, twisted this way and that by her own loyalties and convictions, she couldn't find voice either.

Felipe stood beaming brighter than the dozens of torches, hundreds of lamps, and thousands of candles that lit the banquet. He looked transported, as if, against everyone's expectations including his own, he had achieved something great in his own right. A deed to match those of Manuel the Great—progenitor of Torre Delgao, who killed the fabled Tyrannosaurus imperator, made its skull into the Fangèd Throne, and founded the Empire to rule from it.

Melodía could only shake her head. *My father makes war on his own people, and thinks it's the grandest thing he could ever do.*

Chief Minister Mondragón sat beside Jaume. His hands applauded, but his face looked as if he had had just bitten into a medicinal root. Melodía and Jaume weren't the only ones to disapprove the Emperor's latest fancy.

"Preparations will begin at once," Felipe piped. The hall fell silent. "The army will march five weeks from now. As for its commander"—he swept his smile like a beacon to his right—"I can conceive of none more fitting than Count Jaume, Knight-Commander of the Companions of Our Lady of the Mirror, Champion of the Empire, and my own strong and trusted right hand!"

"No."

The single syllable echoed like a trumpet blast. The diners turned to stare.

Duke Falk von Hornberg had risen. He was the tallest man in the hall.

"I mean no disrespect, your Majesty," he said. "Neither to yourself, nor to His Holiness, nor to noble Count Jaume. Yet I must humbly claim consideration for command of your army. By right of precedence as a duke, if not my deeds."

Old Alba slammed a big fist down on the table, making cutlery jump for a meter in either direction. "A rebel vexer-whelp commanding an Imperial army? Intolerable!"

Pío turned him a pinched look. "Might I remind your Grace that Duke Falk has received plenary pardon from both the Emperor's hand and our own?"

Conversation commenced to sizzle like grease on a stove. Falk stood unspeaking, head high, no more moved than a monolith by mist. Jaume looked pained, but still said nothing.

At length Felipe raised a hand. The babble stopped.

"We honor our kinsman Count Jaume as a great and proven champion," he said. "Yet we have also heard a great deal about the battlefield prowess of this strong young Alemán. I can see but one course of action."

He grinned as if to split his head in half. "We shall have a Grand Tourney, and the winner will command the Ejército Corregir!"

Mondragón recoiled in his chair. Jaume pressed two fingers to his brow.

Duke Falk smirked as if he'd won already.

I hate him, Melodía thought.

Chapter 13

Brincador, **Bouncer**—*Psittacosaurus ordosensis.* Bipedal plant-eating dinosaur with a short, powerful beak; 1.5 meters, 14 kilograms. Distinguished by quill-like plumes. Common Nuevaropan garden pest.

—THE BOOK OF TRUE NAMES

O nce we're married," Melodía said, "I should join you."

With barely a flinch at that, her lover, in theory if not recent fact, finished raising his right arm. His left hand, gloved in fine springer suede, pulled a release. A half-meter-long dragonfly, red from bulbous eyes to the vein lacework of transparent wings, took off from the leather bracer on Jaume's forearm and shot forward.

Jaume turned startled turquoise eyes to Melodía. "Beg your pardon, *mi amor?*"

Seeing doom arrowing toward it across the clearing, a green-and-yellow brincador the size of a small dog jumped up from behind the fern sprig that had proven so inadequate to hide it. It bounced frantically away with tall powder-blue tail plumes bobbing.

The dragonfly hit the bouncer like a crossbow bolt. The little creature screamed as the insect sank spike-tipped legs into its body. Ruby mandibles bit deep into its neck.

Blood sprayed in arcs the color of the killer's body. The bouncer kicked a final time and went limp.

"Are you all right, Melodía?" Jaume asked. "Your cheeks are flushed."

She shook herself like a wet dog. Her racing pulse made her fluttery.

"Sorry to leave you hanging, *querido*," she said breathlessly. "I said that once we're married, I should join you."

He looked at her as if she had grown a colorful crest like the one his morion, Camellia, sported.

"How do you mean?" he asked mildly.

She nudged her adored silver-grey mare, Meravellosa, to a walk toward where the giant dragonfly ripped audibly at its victim's feathered skin. A beat later Jaume's white mare followed, perforce. Around them on the hillside inland of the palace rose a mixed forest of broadleafs and evergreens.

Discussion, even of their married future, wasn't really what she wanted right now. But with four gamekeepers in Prince Heriberto's livery converging on the kill, she wasn't going to get a shot at *that*. Despite what Northerners thought, South Nuevaropans had some sexual propriety.

That the lovers got even this tease of time together resulted purely from Jaume's ability to talk his way out of the main event. The Emperor was hunting today.

"You're always off on missions," she said when she heard his horse chuff up alongside hers. "Now that you're finally home, you work around the clock readying the army for this ridiculous war."

And my role as a dutiful little Imperial daughter is to keep meekly out of the way and do nothing useful.

"We never *see* each other!"

He sighed. "I feel that as keenly as you do. You know that. But—that's my duty."

"I'd never ask you to give that up," she said brightly. The tips of the topknot that sprouted from Melodía's headpiece rasped quietly on the yellow silk stretched over bamboo frames to protect her shoulders from the sun's sting. "I know it's your joy as well as your duty. So I was thinking I could join you."

"You mean, join the Companions?"

"Exactly!"

The gamekeepers approached the kill. The dragonfly flapped its wings and hissed a warning: *Stay away! Mine!*

The three keepers hung back. They knew too well what those jaws and claws could do. The huge insect couldn't kill a fit adult human. But like an angry house cat, it could rip up a person's face pretty well.

Halting twenty meters upwind, Jaume took a small strider-leather bag from his belt. Pinching up powder ground from certain dried glands of the dragonfly's kin, he brushed fingertips together, wafting it to the rising breeze. Its appetite suppressed by the dust, the dragonfly at once let go of its prey and thrummed into the air, following the scent-trail docilely back to its master's wrist.

Melodía and Jaume rode forward. The dragonfly settled with a buzz and a clatter on Jaume's forearm.

He looped a thong noose around the junction of abdomen and thorax and drew it tight, tying the creature to his bracer. Ignoring the proceedings, it began burnishing ruby mouthparts with its forelegs.

Melodía boiled in lidded frustration. But her father had taught her that nobles owed their people certain dues, and such rituals as this one were among them, and had to be rigorously observed.

As they approached, the chief keeper, with a gaptoothed grin, held the dead bouncer up for Jaume's approval. Melodía fidgeted in her saddle and tried to distract herself by gazing out through the thinning trees downslope across a panoramic view of La Merced.

She truly loved the city, where she had grown to young adulthood in Felipe's court. In her heart it could never match her birthplace, Castillo Golondrina, nor her father's duchy Los Almendros, the Almond Plantation. But it beat La Majestad hands down.

Two great headlands enveloped the meteor-dug Bahía Alegre like arms, defining and protecting the finest anchorage on La Canal. La Merced crowded the southern and eastern rim in colorful tile roofs and soaring cone-topped towers of white limestone, dominated by the Pope's palace, Creators' House. The docks teemed with ships of every size. Its streets, from capillary alleys to boulevard arteries, pulsed with traffic, human, dinosaur, and vehicular.

The eastern headland was mostly occupied by the enormous main base of the Imperial Navy, the Sea Dragons who protected the Channel commerce that fueled La Merced's famed wealth and hedonism. Closer to hand at the bay's west end, Melodía could just see Adelina's Frown, the high chalk bluff crowned by the Firefly Palace. From here the white stone pentagon looked a lot more like the impregnable fortress it was built to be than it did from inside.

The city sang to Melodía of vitality, industry, a positive greed for the joys life offered. It offered many contradictions: respectable yet volatile, such that the Civic Guard frequently turned out for riots in cobalt-blue enameled three-quarter plate; spectacle-loving and bourgeois; tolerant and kindhearted, yet relentless and even cruel in its treatments of its ancient nemesis, pirates.

She loved La Merced. Even when it appalled her.

"Excellent, Lorenzo," Jaume said at last. "A clean kill. Keep the meat for yourself and your crew."

That won smiling thanks from the gamekeepers. They bagged the carcass and transferred the hunting-dragonfly to the lead gamekeeper's wrist. Then they trotted off toward the clamor that indicated where the bulk of the hunt was going on.

As they vanished into the undergrowth, Jaume blew out a long breath. "That's done."

Thank the Creators! Melodía thought. "You don't enjoy the hunt?"

He shrugged. "Part of me enjoys killing—or I wouldn't do what I do. There's a certain terrible beauty to it. But only if it's needful."

He fell silent, his beautiful features set in a look of pain. Once again Melodía saw evidence that something troubled him. It hurt her that he wouldn't share. But she was too sensible of his feelings to ask. Or perhaps, she admitted to herself, too proud.

She ground her teeth against what she *really* wanted to say.

"You really want to join the Companions?" he asked.

"Why shouldn't I?"

"Well, it's, it's—it's dangerous."

"Of course it's dangerous! You've got more Brothers in the ground than active, and as many more retired by wounds. It cost us Pere. But at least it's *active*. I can just sit on my *culo* in the palace and still be stalked by assassins, as it turns out."

"I don't think the assassin was sent for you."

She slumped. "Of course, you're too kind to point out the Parasaurolophus in the parlor: that I'm merely an Imperial Princess, so why would anyone bother to send the Brotherhood after me?"

Jaume looked grim.

"So why *shouldn't* I become a Companion?" she asked, her heartbeat quickening. "It would give me a chance to do something real."

They rode at a walk through glorious sunlight obscured by just the thinnest scrim of cloud, down toward the dinosaur hunt. The air was almost cool, fragrant with winter flowers and green growth moist from predawn rain. Birds trilled and chased bright lizards among soft-spined boughs.

"It's not all songs and glory," he said. "Being a Companion is arduous, sometimes boring, often terrifying. It can grind like a millstone."

"Don't you think I know that? I know you don't like to talk about it, but I hear the ballads. It's hard not to."

He laughed. "*That's* unimpeachable testimony."

"But Pe—your Brothers tell me stories. I know what it's like."

Jaume frowned. Melodía felt an urge to kiss it away.

But no. That would hardly be *decorous*. Their inferiors might see.

"I hardly know how to say this, love," he said. "I know you're brave and strong. You're well trained in combat, and show a gift for it. But becoming a Companion isn't easy. You have to qualify. You've got the character and spirit, as much as any Brother. That's part of why I love you as I do. But it demands great physical prowess as well as endurance. And—you'd have to win admission by deeds."

"And you don't you think I can?"

"When would you have the opportunity?"

"I can be your squire! Your page! Whatever you call that boy who follows you around making calf eyes at you."

"I call him Bartomeu. He's my arming-squire, which is why he follows me. And—our rules forbid us taking lovers among juniors. It's unjust. Would you want to live in enforced celibacy?"

"How am I living now? Like a Life-to-Come cenobite who hasn't bathed since last Qian! I could sign on as a mercenary—become an Ordinary, carve my way into the Companions with my blade!"

Her hand made sword slashes in the air. Meravellosa tossed her head and snorted. In eagerness, Melodía reckoned.

"Like that pretty French boy Florian! He was common-born, wasn't he?"

"Yes," Jaume said. "But they're all pretty boys."

"Is that the problem? That your Companions are just a boy's club? No *concha* allowed?"

Jaume opened and closed his mouth repeatedly without actually emitting sound.

"Your father would never let you join," he managed at last. "Especially not with us due to lead the Army of Correction to war."

She drew in a huge breath and sighed mountainously. "This stupid war! Half la Familia's aroused against my father over it, afraid that if he stirs up too much trouble, we Delgaos will lose our precious monopoly on the Fangèd Throne."

"I've tried to talk him out of it."

"He's good at not hearing what he doesn't want to hear."

"Expert."

"I wonder if this allegedly reformed rebel Falk isn't a bad influence."

Jaume shook his head. "He does tell your father what he wants to hear, no question. But I don't really think he's much to blame. He's just a boy, really—not much older than you. He is a redoubtable fighter, and shows promise as a field captain. I think his loyalty's sincere, new as it is."

"Well . . . he seems to play quite the lad with the more hotheaded court hangers-on."

"Few of whom are stepping up to volunteer for the Terraroja campaign."

She laughed. "No. They're just straw-stuffed silk doublets with sticks up their butts. But I do blame this confessor of his, Jerónimo. My father's changed since he turned up. I'm sure this current *guiso de caca* is his idea."

"How did he come into your father's service?"

"Will it get you in trouble if I say he was recommended by that horrid old corpse-tearer the Pope?"

Jaume laughed. "Only if I repeat your description," he said, "and then, only if His Holiness hears of it.

Fortunately, my men are discreet. And they can use a good laugh themselves, after their own trip home from Alemania."

He'd spent the last two days overseeing the unloading of his Companions, their war-dinosaurs—including his beloved Camellia—and their five hundred Ordinary auxiliaries with their horses from a fleet of round-bottomed cogs. They would form the spine of the Ejército Corregir, whoever won her father's ridiculous tournament.

"What's he like, this mystery monk?" Jaume asked.

"I've no idea. I've never laid eyes on him. I've only ever been in the same room with him twice, and both times he was behind a screen."

She paused. When she'd encountered Jerónimo, she had felt a strange unease, in the pit of her stomach and beneath her skin, as if sensing *wrongness* somehow.

"Pilar tells me none of the servants have seen him," she said. "I don't think my father has, even."

"Curious indeed."

An agonized scream pealed over the hills. As it died out, a nosehorn bellowed triumphant rage. Barking and deinonychus-screeches rose to an uproar. Men shouted confusion.

Melodía and Jaume looked at each other, and kneed their horses to a fast trot downslope.

"You know," Rob said, through the veil of rain sluicing off his slouch hat brim, "you were a perfect romantic hero." *Maybe even more than Jaume*, he thought, but with rare discretion chose not to say.

It was your typical Nuevaropa thunderstorm. The

sky warred with itself and the land, volleying rain, hurling howling wave-attacks of wind and jagged blue-white lightning spears, beating thunder war-drums. Despite having to punch through many layers of leaf-laden branches in the old oak forest, raindrops stung Rob's bare skin.

"Not my fault," said Karyl.

Holding his paisley parasol gamely aloft, Rob rode swaying atop the luggage piled on his hook-horn's back. Rob could feel his friend muttering disconsolately to herself. Normally stoic, Little Nell didn't like when weather got *on* her. Which, sadly, it often did.

Karyl walked point. His lack of class-consciousness sometimes truly exasperated Rob: despise nobles he might, but they by-Torre should *act* like nobles. Karyl's most recent outrage to Rob's propriety was buying a conical woven-straw peasant hat for a few copper centavos from one of the vendors who sprouted like toadstools along the better-traveled roads.

He wore it now, its string tied beneath his chin, his head bowed as he trudged into the storm. It made him look more than a little like an ambulatory mushroom himself, to Rob's admittedly fanciful eye.

"How do you know what I was, anyway?" Karyl said.

"The songs!" Rob said. "I've heard the songs for years—cut my teeth on 'em. Read the romances. Now I'm dying to hear the truth from you. You know how balladeers lie."

"Present company excluded?"

"By no means! I worst of all!"

Karyl seemed to mull that over for a bit. "Keep talking. I'll let you know when you stray too far from truth."

"What could be a lovelier tale?" Rob asked. "You defeated a rampaging matadora before you were twenty, a mere stripling without so much as fuzz on your chin. Its offspring hatched before your eyes and bonded to you. Which happens to be the only way to get a wild meat-eating dinosaur to serve as a mount. And they're far better than captivity-bred ones.

"You won knighthood from your Archduke, fair and square. But more important, you won Shiraa, nearly as fabled as you are yourself!"

Karyl produced a sound like a siege-engine stone rolling down a rain gutter.

"Ah, forgive me!" Rob exclaimed, flash-contrite. "I didn't mean to prod a sore spot, surely I did not. You still mourn her."

"She was my friend," Karyl said. "The only one to survive *being* my friend. Until the Hassling."

Rob shook his head sorrowfully. It was a song so sad it would be years before he could bring himself to sing it.

Little Nell's strong toes thumped logs sawn in half lengthwise and buried round-side down. The local grande kept his road well corduroyed. Hardwood logs came as cheap as dinosaur power hereabouts.

If the lord charged for passage, Rob had seen no sign. Rob had a dragon's eye for toll stations; he refused to pay on principle, as an Irlandés and a Traveler. Some nobles, though, were actually smart enough to be content with the proceeds from the commerce good roads brought.

"A conspiracy of barons treacherously murdered your father," Rob went on, since Karyl hadn't told him not to. "And shouldn't that be the collective phrase for them, then? 'A conspiracy of barons.' Like *a murder of crows* or *a rending of horrors*. They supplanted you with your bastard half brother and chased you into exile with no more than Shiraa and the shirt on your back."

"Breeches and barefoot. No shirt. It was raining then too."

"For years you wandered. Decades. If the legends are true, you traveled the length and breadth of Aphrodite Terra, studying the arts of war and personal combat, gathering your strength."

"The legends aren't all wrong," Karyl said, "so far as they go. Surprising."

Rob chuckled. "And then—ah, what could be finer?"

"Not this, surely."

"You returned from exile with an army," Rob said, undeterred. "Oppressed by the usurper, the peasants rallied to your flag."

"By the usurper's mother, actually," Karyl said. "Alžběta Alexandrovna, Baroness Stechkina. My half brother Yan-Paulus the Bastard isn't such a bad sort. But he was utterly under her thumb."

Rob waved an airy hand through the rain. "*Detail.* Legend cares naught for quibbles. The fact is, no tale's taller nor grander nor more beloved than that of the displaced nobleman seeking to recover the throne that was foully and unjustly stolen from him. And what did you do? Exactly that!"

He shook his head in admiration, flinging water in all directions from his hat. "That's what makes your story so compelling, Voyvod. You actually *lived* the storybook ending."

"It was the worst thing that ever happened to me."

"What?" Rob said in horror. "You broke the barons' petty, cruel rule and made men equal! Such a thing as has never been known before. And you raised the finest fighting force we'll see in all our lifetimes, the White River Legion!"

"Which you destroyed."

"Much good it did me. It's sacked I was, for up-staging the bucketheads and their precious scheme to do you down themselves! So here I am, wet, vaga-bond, and penniless."

"And I find myself in the same state, for much the same reasons. What do you think of my 'storybook ending' now?"

"But you brought years of enlightened rule!"

Karyl glanced back at Rob. Beneath the sweep of his hat, his eyes appeared so dark and deep, Rob half imagined if he looked closer he'd see the stars.

"So you believe," Karyl said.

"Isn't it true? The whole Empire still buzzes with it. It's why your own employers turned on you! They feared the example you set their own downtrodden serfs."

"Perhaps. I suspect they mostly feared I was get-ting too powerful." He shrugged. "They may've been right. If not the way the Emperor believed."

"That makes no sense," Rob said. "Are you saying you weren't a wise, enlightened ruler?"

"Yes."

Rob threw up his hands theatrically. The gesture caused his parasol, momentarily forgotten, to brush a hanging branch and dump pent-up rainwater on him. His hat brim collapsed around his head.

"I don't understand," he said, not deigning to ac-knowledge the mishap.

"Maybe someday I'll explain it to you," Karyl said.

"How about now?" asked Rob. "I hate waiting for a story's end."

Raindrops exploded on Karyl's hat and ran off the back like pale streamers. He said nothing.

"Faugh!" Rob exclaimed. "You're no easier to reason with than a cat."

That got him a laugh.

"Of course," Karyl said. "I'm a nobleman."

Chapter 14

Nariz Cornuda, **Nosehorn, One-horn**—*Centrosaurus apertus*. Quadrupedal herbivore with a toothed beak and a single large nasal horn; 6 meters long, 1.8 meters tall, 3 tonnes. Nuevaropa's most common hornface (ceratopsian dinosaur); predominant dray and meatbeast. Wild herds can be destructive and aggressive; popular (if extremely dangerous) to hunt.

—THE BOOK OF TRUE NAMES

Melodía and Jaume rode their horses downslope through the undergrowth as fast as they dared. Her heart hammered. The sharp scent of crushed ferns filled her head.

They emerged onto an outcrop of limestone boulders. As they drew rein, something big came crashing and snorting toward the clearing below.

Bellowing fury, a monster plunged forth: a wild nosehorn, a mighty patriarch seven meters long, black and green, with a bristle of hairlike feathers above mountainous shoulders. He swung his huge head left and right, looking for foes.

Melodía's breath caught in her throat. He had been raiding *estancias*, killing herd bulls and stealing the cows for his harem. He'd killed two peasants and a house-archer who'd made the mistake of trying to stop him, and a herd-girl who hadn't gotten out of his way fast enough.

Now her father was hunting him.

"Jaume!" Melodía exclaimed. "His horn."

The dinosaur's neck-frill and bony face were strikingly patterned, indigo on yellow. The horn on its massive snout was curved, a meter and a half long. Half its length gleamed wetly red.

"Probably a horror's blood, or tracking-dog's," Jaume said.

Melodía searched for a quick way down. She was terrified of what was to come. Her only thought was to help her father. *Somehow.*

From a cycad thicket near the base of the outcrop sprang half a dozen scarlet-feathered horrors with black eye-stripes. Squalling, they spread their taloned arms like wings, showing golden bellies.

Tossing her black-and-silver mane in alarm, Meravellosa sidestepped and whickered. Everything on Nuevaropa feared deinonychus, except matadors and titans.

The bull dug blunt-toed feet into the springy turf and bellowed. The horrors hopped and sidled, chattering angrily in reply. Wild ones might hesitate to attack a full-grown nosehorn, especially such a huge one, but not a human-trained pack. Some of the horrors might be gored or trampled, but once one or two got on the nosehorn's back, their killing-claws could cut through its tough hide. Even if they didn't manage to eviscerate the bull, it would rapidly bleed to death.

"I don't like those things," Melodía said. These horrors were a specially prized breed known as los Cardenales de la Muerte: Death's Cardinals. Prince Harry had gifted her father with the pack the year before. "They're cruel."

"It's their nature," Jaume said. "That said, its beauty isn't easy to see."

Cudgel-armed gamekeepers kept the horrors from closing in. The kill wasn't meant for them. To the baying of hounds and trumpets and hoarse halloos, Felipe himself burst from some saplings behind the nosehorn, mounted on a green-and-yellow great strider and carrying a hunting spear. He wore a splendid silver casque cast to resemble a horror skull, trailing long yellow and scarlet plumes, and a short red hunting cape.

As usual, the Emperor rode like a grain sack, pumping his elbows to the sides like stubby wings. Despite that, Melodía thought to see a curious touch of dignity along with a childlike joy that turned his cheeks red.

Behind Felipe came two of his favored hunting cronies. Count Esmond, the castellan, rode a big cream-colored mule, his long face even in the heat of the chase looking as if he suspected someone of dipping into palace accounts. Prince Harry, Heriberto himself, flanked him, looking as dashing as a portly man could on a black marchador. Around them a pack of hounds came quickly to a halt, prudently out of range of trampling feet and slashing raptor-claws.

Uttering a wild whoop, Felipe couched his spear like a lance and booted his unhappy strider to a charge. Melodía's first thought was that Felipe's cry was a misplaced act of chivalry—warning his target of his attack. But the instant the Centrosaurus began spinning in place with frightening alacrity, she saw the cunning behind it.

The monster's turn allowed the Emperor to drive his leaf-shaped spearhead in behind its right shoulder with a butcher-shop *thunk*, rather than into its rump.

"A heart shot," Jaume said. "Well struck."

Letting go the reins, Felipe waved off his noble companions. A mule-mounted flock of Scarlet Tyrants pounded into the clearing, faces understandably grim beneath horsehair-crested gilt helmets at their charge's complete incaution. They dismounted speedily to Felipe's either side, unlimbering cocked and loaded arbalests slung over their scarlet-caped backs.

The nosehorn squalled. Yellow eyes as broad as Melodía's palm rolled beneath bony flanges not unlike a matador's. Bloody froth bubbled from its nostrils. The powerful beak snapped futilely toward the spear's stout ash shaft.

Smelling blood, Death's Cardinals shrieked and lunged. Harry's keepers whistled them back, by the authority of meter-and-a-half staffs tipped with lead bulbs. These they used sparingly. Raptors tamed and trained to the hunt were costly. Peasants, on the other hand, came cheap.

The nosehorn kept turning. Though it inexorably drove the spear deeper into its own chest, it ignored the pain. It saw its attacker clearly now. It was determined to return the favor with its own horn.

The crossbar behind the hunting spear's head kept the bull from pushing its body all the way up the shaft to get at the hunter. Felipe clung with both hands. His mount was about the same length as the Centrosaurus, but weighed a fraction as much. Four-leg force drove two-legs back.

The bull torqued the Emperor right out of his saddle.

Melodía screamed. Whipping out her falchion, she made to nudge Meravellosa into a risky plunge down to the clearing. The mare recoiled as Jaume's hand snaked out to catch her reins.

"Let me go!" Melodía shouted. "I have to help him."

"We can't," Jaume said sharply. "It's too late. We'd just get in the way."

She snarled at him, feeling a raptorish urge to take a bite out of his face.

"Besides," he said, more gently, "don't underestimate your father. Watch."

He dropped the reins. Melodía let her sword arm fall. Sheepishly she realized the most she could do with the short, heavy blade would be to distract the nosehorn long enough for it to gore her before finishing off her father.

Although he'd landed on his broad bottom, the Emperor had immediately sprung to his feet. Now he had the spear haft clamped under his right armpit and gripped in both gloved hands. His round face showed no fear, only utter absorption.

Inevitably the gigantic hornface pushed Felipe back and around. He shifted his boots just enough to keep leaning into the spear without falling. A beat late, Melodía remembered that in his youth her father had fought Northman sea raiders and Slavos as a common pikeman in the army of his cousin the King of Alemania.

The monster groaned. It kept straining to get his huge, bloody horn into Felipe. The Emperor kept shooting quick glances over his shoulder. He worked the spear up and down, twisting the deeply driven blade to do more damage inside the vast, sweat-streaming body.

He sidestepped. With a grunt of effort, he swung the spear haft to plant its brass-shod butt against the bole of a stout bloodwood tree. His weapon thus braced, he leaned forward and held on hard.

The nosehorn uttered a vast wheezing gasp that wrenched Melodía's heart despite the eagerness and filial fear that hummed in her blood. Pink froth jetted from beak and nose. It fell onto its side.

The Emperor just managed to let go the shaft and dance aside in time to avoid being flipped into the trees. The fallen dinosaur thrashed three times and then, with a final seismic sigh, lay still.

While Emperor fought monster, more mounted courtiers had arrived. Now they flocked around him, chattering congratulations. Muttering darkly, the Scarlet Tyrants reslung their crossbows. Felipe stood smiling in quiet satisfaction, half-surreptitiously massaging his right elbow where the spear haft had given it a good crack as it was torn free.

Jaume nodded. "Now we can let your marvelous mare find us a gentle way down to join the rest," he said with a smile.

She grinned back in mad relief.

A thought struck her. He'd made a pun: "Meravellosa" *meant* "marvelous" in Catalan, her mother's birth tongue as well as his. Jaume had taken the trouble to remember the name of Melodía's mount because he knew how much she doted on the dark-silver mare with the black-and-silver mane and tail. She'd wager her fancy headpiece that he never thought of asking the name of his own lovely bay mare, on loan from Heriberto's well-stocked stables.

Melodía had always loved horses. She and the young Araba were devoted to each other. And as Melodía felt about horses, Jaume felt about dinosaurs.

To Melodía, Camellia was a large, admittedly gorgeous and friendly, but ultimately rather ungainly beast. Jaume, who would never speak or pen a word in praise of himself, had written an entire volume (albeit a slim one) on the beauties and excellencies of his Corythosaurus. He treated horses kindly—he found kindness beautiful—but to him they were simply *animals*.

Instead of following his suggestion she turned Meravellosa and let her pick her way back up the ridge they'd ridden over.

"Where are we going?" Jaume asked, though he followed her at once and was elbow to elbow with Melodía by the time he finished the sentence.

"We're slipping away," she said firmly. "Just you and me."

Considering the look he sent her, she was half exasperated and half amused to see that for all his justly famous lightning wit, he didn't get it.

"I've missed you," she said.

"And I you."

"I mean, I've *really missed* you."

"Oh." His answering smile made warmth trickle all down the center of her. "Lead on, my lady."

But no sooner had they returned to the clearing where the ruby dragonfly had killed the bouncer than Melodía heard a drumroll of hard-driven hooves approaching. She scowled. Then sighed.

"Your page, Bartomeu, is coming," she said. "To call you away to the apportioning, no doubt."

For downing the wild nosehorn the Emperador would claim the best meat for his kitchen. He had earned the frilled, horned head for a trophy as well. But Felipe didn't care much about such outward trappings of power. He loved the real thing too well.

The best of the remaining meat would go to Prince Harry's gamekeepers to feed their families. What fair amount remained Heriberto would distribute among the needy. While under normal circumstances only the wretchedest urban poor—or serfs of exceptionally cruel lords—went hungry amidst Nuevaropa's bounty, fresh flesh was always a welcome visitor to lower-class tables.

"And once again I'm being robbed of the meat I want most," she muttered.

"Pardon, my love?"

"Nothing."

Bartomeu came loping from the woods on his white mule with his golden hair blowing behind him like a pennon.

"He's smitten with you, you know," said Melodía.

"He's a beautiful boy and a dutiful squire," Jaume said. "But remember what I told you. We only permit love between those of the same rank in our order."

"So long as he's not getting anything *I'm* not."

"*¡Mi amor!*" Jaume exclaimed. "Don't even *think* that. If I had a spare moment, a spare breath, I'd share it with you."

"I know," she said sulkily. "Preparing for this war you don't even believe in consumes your every moment and all your energy. I know."

She held up a palm to his protest. "I know. Duty

comes before mere personal desire. How well I know that."

Before more could be said—which was probably for the best—Bartomeu reined in the mule with a gratuitously showy curvet.

Show-off, she thought. *I could ride rings around you on any mount you care to try.*

"My lord," the boy proclaimed, cheeks flushed and voice bronzed with importance. "His Imperial Majesty sends his fondest regards."

He reeled in the saddle and had to suck air then. He was so worked up he kept forgetting to breathe.

"He requests your presence at the ceremony of apportionment."

Melodía wondered if Bartomeu could see, as clearly as she, the rueful twist to her lover's smile.

"My sword is ever at His Majesty's service," Jaume said. He turned in the saddle and bowed to Melodía. "And yours as well, Highness."

"If only," Melodía said.

Chapter 15

Cinco Amigos, **Five Friends**—We have five domestic mammals unlike any others in the world: the horse, the goat, the dog, the cat, and the ferret. Because all are listed in *The Bestiary of Old Home,* most believe that the Creators brought them to Paradise to serve us.

—A PRIMER TO PARADISE FOR THE IMPROVEMENT
OF YOUNG MINDS

I don't even know why you're *doing* this," Melodía said to Jaume's back as he led her down into cool, companionable dimness. "You don't even believe in this war."

He glanced back over his shoulder at her. He smiled, but his brows were compressed. "If I don't get the army ready," he said, "nobody will."

"That's what I'm saying!" she exclaimed. "If you just quit, maybe the whole foolish thing will fall apart."

"You know I can't do that, *mi amor.*"

She made a frustrated sound. *I feel like a smitten*

schoolgirl, trailing foolishly after a handsome knight, she thought. *Maybe because I am?*

One of the few fleeting moments Jaume had been able to snatch to spend with her in the increasingly frenetic weeks since his return, and all she could do was *argue* with him. Yet she couldn't seem to stop herself. Which made her even madder.

She also couldn't help thinking, with a dash of added bitterness, that she was getting long in the tooth for a *schoolgirl. Most grandes my age are taking their places in the world, starting families or assuming important places in familial enterprises.*

And here I am, no practical use to anyone, another gaudy bangle in the Imperial crown.

Up the broad cement ramp from the armory storehouse, a pair of fatties trudged, a pair of casks strapped across each back, containing the Oldest Daughter knew what metal oddments. Two urchins, sexless and bare-legged in rough smocks, switched them toward the bright but cloud-filtered sunlight of a late-winter morning.

The Firefly Palace grounds were vast, but they showed only part of the picture. Following the Rape of La Merced in 376 AP, the Iron Duchess Adelina had finished her fortress before she rebuilt her city. Intending that it serve as refuge for the great port's inhabitants against future onslaughts by Anglaterrano and Gallego corsairs as well as a stronghold, she dug a network of passageways and chambers deep into the white limestone of the bluffs at Bahía Alegre's east end. Cisterns, storerooms, even stables and dormitories supposedly extended clear to natural caverns beneath the promontory's roots. Palace servants whispered breathless tales of people who had lost themselves deep in the Duchess's Anthill, never to be seen again.

The ramp ended in a great bay with oak doors flung wide. The air from inside smelled of cool stone, oil, and nose-wrinkling turpentine. A gaggle of apprentices clad in scorched and scarred nosehorn-hide aprons and little else labored at stout worktables by the shine of a light-shaft above and lanterns on the walls. Using spirits of resin, they cleaned metal objects of the hornface tallow in which they'd been packed to preserve them from damp. Brass goggles with lenses of glass ground thick to keep sparks and metal splinters away from vulnerable eyeballs turned their faces into weird human-insect hybrids.

Beyond what she could see and smell, Melodía knew nothing about what they were up to. And cared rather less.

Several journeymen stood by supervising. One harrumphed loudly as Jaume strode in. The armory workers looked up, then bowed. Aside from his being a high noble and great hero, anyplace Jaume set foot became a stage belonging to him alone. Taking note of the Princesa a step behind, they bowed again deeper.

He smiled and nodded acknowledgment. With a happy squeal a small ballista bolt hit him midthigh and clung with both arms.

"Cousin Jaume!"

"Montserrat!" Laughing, he tousled the girl's dark-gold dreadlocks. He knelt to pick her up with both hands. Straightening, he tucked her into the crook of an arm as if she were an infant.

Which was no minor feat. Though not fat by any means, Melodía's baby sister was a sturdy little nose-horn calf. She was heavier than she looked, as Melodía well knew from the odd sisterly wrestling match. Stronger, too—like Melodía herself.

"Montse," Melodía said, in a cooler tone. "What are you doing down here?—¡ay, chingao!"

The last was an involuntary exclamation squeezed out of her by a cold nose poking one ankle where the gilt buskin-thongs winding up her calves left it bare. She knelt to scoop up the creature that had greeted her so.

Montserrat's familiar curled into a soft fur pool in Melodía's palms. Obsidian-bead eyes peered at Melodía from a pointed silver face.

"Silver Mistral," Melodía said, bringing own her face near the ferret's black bandit-mask. "I suppose the question is what *you're* doing here, other than getting underfoot and making it difficult for these people to work."

Mistral stretched out to bump the Princess's nose with her own. Laughing despite herself, Melodía kissed the ferret back and set her on the stone floor. She scampered promptly over to hop and beep for Jaume's attention.

"I'm here watching Maestro Rubbio *do* stuff," Montse explained solemnly from the crook of Jaume's arm. "Mistral's helping me."

"Mistress Montse!" a voice roared. "I told you not to let that beast run around loose."

A curious figure emerged from a passage leading deeper into the palace netherworld. He had the face of an angry god, red and handsome, with goggles pushed up onto red-gold curls crowning his large head. He was powerfully built, but the bare muscle-knotted arms and legs that emerged from a thick leather tunic dotted with burn spots were half the length of a normal person's, and the top of his head barely came to Melodía's breastbone. He was an *enano*, born with a rare condition.

The dwarf stamped bare feet theatrically at Mistral, who arched her long back into a hoop and bounced sideways, beeping furiously. His behavior alarmed Melodía. The ferret could be an awful pill, but though full of mischief, she had no malice in her. She and Montse doted on each other.

But Montse only laughed. "Don't mind Maestro Rubbio," she said. "He won't really hurt her. He's just a big phony."

"Do not take me for granted, Infanta!" the Master blustered.

He spoke with the accent of Talia, a nation subject to Trebizon. Though she'd never met him before, Melodía knew his reputation. He was an internationally renowned armorer whom her father had imported to his service when he moved full-time to La Merced, after Melodía and Montse's mother, Marisol, died.

"I'm sorry, Maestro," Montse said as Jaume lowered her to the floor. "I got so excited when I saw Jaume, I forgot and put her down."

She gathered up the still-hopping ferret and tucked the animal against the front of her oil-stained smock.

"You must be the Princesa Melodía," Rubbio said, sticking out a stubby, black-nailed hand. After the briefest hesitation Melodía took it. To her surprise he raised her hand to his lips and kissed it reverently. "It is an honor to meet you at last. Great songs have been written of your beauty, but they still do you no justice."

She laughed. "I never thought I'd find a courtier in surroundings such as these."

"Never underestimate an artisan, Princess! We are men and women of parts."

He turned. "And this is the fine Count Jaume, at last deigning to visit us humble metalworkers! You are overdue, my lord. Metal is strength. Metal gives the Empire its bones, its spine. Metal encases your blue-blooded body when you ride to battle. Yet you take it for granted, and those who shape it to your needs, you nobles, you!"

Jaume smiled. "I assure you, Maestro, I don't take it for granted at all. My order celebrates skill in all kinds of making. I have nothing but admiration for you and the work you do."

The armorer raised his brows. His eyes were gold-amber and large, with long lashes. "You do?"

"My Companions Mor Ayaks and Mor Pedro Luna practice smithing and armoring as their excellences, as well as for the most practical purposes." The boyish enthusiasm in his voice thrilled Melodía. "Mor Florian is a goldsmith and metal-sculptor of great skill. They would all be honored to visit and make your acquaintance." He frowned. "If only our war preparations didn't eat up all our time."

"So, what is it I owe the honor of your presence to?" asked Rubbio.

"I'm told you're readying our siege train, Maestro. I wanted to see what we'll need to transport."

"You are in luck, my lord and ladies!" Rubbio turned and, putting two fingers in his mouth, emitted a piercing whistle. "We are just now bringing forth key pieces of your great engines of war."

Melodía didn't feel lucky. She was only here because it gave her a pretext to steal a few moments with her love. Still, she found herself intrigued by the leather bag that two pairs of apprentices carried in, hanging from a long pole held between them like a trophy from the hunt. The first two apprentices maneuvered around a large vacant table, and all four squatted. The bag settled onto the wood with a stifled *clank*.

While their master stood by watching critically, a big-shouldered journeywoman stepped forward to open the bag. It revealed a double green-metal triangle with sides almost as long as Rubbio himself was tall, and rounded points. A thirty-centimeter hole pierced the middle. Melodía realized it was an enormous bracket.

"Green?" she said.

"Bronze, Princess," the master smith declared. "It resists our wet coastal climate far better than iron or steel. The color's mere verdigris; it'll polish away nicely."

He walked up to pat the bracket paternally. "Bronze is a stout metal. It will serve you well, Imperial Champion, and never let you down, never the once!"

"So," Jaume said, "what *is* it, exactly?"

"Part of a trebuchet," Montse announced.

Rubbio nodded and smiled at her as if she were a favorite pupil. "Precisely so! It is the pivot that serves as fulcrum for the counterweighted throwing arm."

"So this is part of an engine like the ones on the palace's seaward ramparts?" Melodía asked.

"Correct! You are perhaps an aficionada of siege equipment, Highness?"

"Not really."

The big wall-mounted trebuchets had attracted her notice because they were, after all, instruments of war, a subject that fascinated her. But she lacked interest in siegecraft. She craved *action*.

"So what does the army need to carry to Terraroja?" Jaume asked.

"Mainly these beauties," Rubbio said, patting the bracket like a pet vexer. "Also the various bolts and nuts needed to hold the machines together. Once you reach your objective, lord, you need merely set your pioneers to fell and dress the appropriate trees, and fit it all together. With your great nosehorn dinosaurs to fetch and carry, a matter of hours, days at the most. And then, *ché meraviglia*, you shall batter down the evildoer's walls."

Frowning, Melodía turned to Jaume. "Why do you need to do that?"

"To pry Redland out of his castle, of course."

Rubbio laughed. "This will crack his shell for him, no matter how stout he thinks it is!"

"But why bother?" Melodía said. "It's not as if he won't come out of his own free will."

"What do you mean?" Jaume asked. He had his chin down and was frowning at the big green bracket, as if trying to compose a sonnet about it and not finding the proper words.

"I met him a few years ago when he visited La Merced," she said. "He's middle-aged, but still your basic buckethead who's never grown up."

Her cheeks went hot. "Oh! Sorry for calling them that."

Jaume laughed. "Don't worry. We use the word ourselves, though not where our fellow nobles can hear. I promise you, we have no bucketheads among my Companions."

"You know that when your army turns up in his domain, Terraroja's going to feel his honor's been challenged. He's going to call up all his allies and vassals and rush right out to fight with you. You won't *need* your big clanking metal bits."

Jaume didn't bother to reply. He just stood staring at the great ugly green thing.

He was ignoring her. As if her words were nothing more than housefly buzz. She felt warmth spread throughout her body. Not a comforting kind.

She spun and walked quickly out of the shop, toward the hot light of day.

Jaume was lost in his own head again. He wasn't wandering familiar pleasant bowers of poetry and song, nor the flame-lit pathways of military plans. Instead it was a labyrinth of grey: organization, detail, paperwork, dispiriting as it was confusing. Recent weeks had forced him to spend more and more time trying to negotiate it. It defied his best efforts to reduce it to comprehension.

Decidedly not helping was a mounting lack of sleep. So many things clamored for his attention, his energy, his time. . . .

As if awakening he blinked to the realization there was a hole in the cool underground air where the dear, bright warmth of Melodía had been a moment before.

"Omm," Montserrat said. "*Someone's* in trouble."

At first her words struck him as a complete non sequitur. Belatedly it came to him to ask, "Did I do something wrong?"

A long and echoing silence answered him. The apprentices and journeyfolk, who had been standing by watching the unusual highborn visitors with fascination, suddenly turned away and got busy again.

Montse squinted at the green-patinaed bracket. "There's something written on it," she said. "What's it say?"

Jaume walked close and bent over the bracket. "*El último razonamiento del Imperio*," he read the raised inscription aloud. "The Empire's final argument."

Montse wrinkled her snub nose. "That's *disgusting*," she said.

"Little Mistress," Rubbio said, "the truth so often is."

Vague disquiet accompanied Jaume the rest of his day. But endless demands on his attention kept it at the back of his mind. Now that most of his Companions had rejoined him, he had Mor Jacques, the order's chief administrator, to help with the unaccustomed task of organizing and provisioning a large, disparate army.

But the worries of his duty had prematurely aged the Francés knight, greyed his hair and made it retreat up his narrow forehead. He was stretched too thin already.

Mondragón and his staff provided such aid as they could. But the Chief Minister and his helpers were also overloaded by responsibilities. Not least of which was keeping an eye on the brash former rebel Duke Falk, who was acquiring a substantial following among the unattached young knights and nobles at court, and even among the ranks of the Scarlet Tyrants.

So the main burden landed crushingly on Jaume's shoulders.

Yet somehow, long after the sun had sunk into the deep forests east of the palace, Jaume found himself at loose ends.

As he wandered between the gorgeous lamplit portraits and tapestries that adorned the palace corridors he found himself wondering what to do with the unfamiliar leisure. As he did the memory came flooding back that he had somehow, in his distraction, managed to offend his beloved Melodía that afternoon.

He felt guilty and alarmed. And horny. It was time to make up with his beloved. For more things than one.

The two Scarlet Tyrants guarding the stairs on the top floor of the Imperial Wing passed him with a broad-jawed nod apiece. He knocked on the door to Melodía's personal chambers. Her maidservant, Pilar, answered.

"Count Jaume," she said, her dark and quietly lovely gitana face unreadable. "Sadly, my mistress is indisposed."

She stepped demurely back. Through the closing door Jaume glimpsed several of Melodía's ladies-in-waiting, who sat tatting together bright feathers.

"Isn't that the handsome Count Jaume?" he heard his fellow Catalana and distant cousin Llurdis say.

"Why does he look so peaked?" asked Abigail Thélème of Sansamour.

"I understand he suffers some indisposition,"

Princess Guadalupe said, "which, some say, removes the spring from his steel."

"How sad for him," Llurdis said with mock solicitude.

"But sadder still for the Princesa," said Lupe.

The door shut in his face.

Chapter 16

Sacabuche, Sackbut—*Parasaurolophus walkeri.* Bipedal herbivore; 9.5 meters, 2.5 meters tall at the shoulder, 3 tonnes. Named because its long, tubular head-crest produces a range of sounds like the sackbut, a trumpetlike musical instrument with a movable slide. One of the most popular war-hadrosaurs.

—THE BOOK OF TRUE NAMES

You're late, Día," Fanny said reprovingly. She may have been the most easygoing among Melodía's ladies-in-waiting, as well as her closest friend, but she did love her punctilio.

"I am," Melodía said.

She took her place among her retinue in the shaded viewing stand. She might have sat with her father in the Imperial box, next to it and slightly higher. But she preferred not to suffer through being ignored.

Her little sister sat in the box beside Felipe. Her minders had clearly made her attend; Montserrat would have far rather been back in their apartments reading a book, or watching her friends the servants at their work. She had her arms firmly crossed and her chin down on her red-and-gold silk robe. Her expression suggested she was determined not to enjoy herself. The tiara set with large raptor feathers in the Imperial colors that was clamped to her head like a sort of lateral crest clearly didn't soften her disposition.

As usual, the Emperor was talking animatedly with his crony and counselor Mondragón, seated on his other side, and ignoring the fact that he had daughters. He waved a half-eaten roasted scratcher drumstick for emphasis. As usual, he was also clearly enjoying the spectacle.

"What did I miss?" Melodía asked her friends.

"The monster's entrance, for one thing!" Josefina said excitedly. "So big and so white, with blood-colored eyes!"

"I saw Snowflake during the cavalcade before the whole thing begin."

"Surely you must have heard him roar," said Lupe, "even in the palace."

"It was amply loud," Melodía agreed.

"It quite terrified the crowd," Fanny said. She smiled sheepishly. "Me too, I have to confess."

"I've *seen* a king tyrant."

"Oh, Día," Fina said, sighing theatrically. "The Verdugo Imperial doesn't count."

Don Rodrigo had been imported from far Vareta decades before to serve as Imperial Executioner. He was displayed in the Plaza del Alcalde once a week, on Kingsday, the day reserved for religious observance, and such rest as the city's *burguesía* permitted themselves.

"Nobody's been beheaded by Imperial warrant for

over a generation," said Lupe, sounding vaguely let down by the fact.

"And old Don Rodrigo's toothless as a baby anyway," Fanny said, "and fat and tame as an old tabby cat from having children climb all over him and feed him sweetmeats. He hardly inspires terror. Snowflake does."

Melodía twitched her bare shoulders in irritation. Talk of dinosaurs bored her at the best of times.

"He's *beautiful*," Lupe said.

"Well," Princess Fanny said, a little breathlessly, "yes. In a thoroughly scary way. The fact that he's albino makes him more terrifying, somehow."

"Not the *monster*," Lupe said. "The man."

"You missed a great bout, Día," Fina burbled. "The Duke was magnificent!"

"Dominant," Lupe murmured. Her eyes shone. A bit glassily, Melodía thought.

"You can leave off lusting for his sturdy Alemán haunches anytime, Guadalupe," Abigail Thélème said. "He has eyes only for the Princesa Imperial."

Melodía felt her lips tighten. "Lupe's quite welcome to him." The dust and smells were already starting to oppress her. She was sure the noise would give her a headache.

"Don't forget, Melodía's betrothed," Fanny said.

Melodía shot her a slit look. Her cheeks flushed pink.

"Well, almost," the Anglesa said. "As good as. Only a formality, surely."

"You should loosen the lock on your knees, cousin," Llurdis said, biting into a pear. "You haven't gotten any in much too long. You're starting to look haggard."

"The Duke *did* see off his opponent quite handily," Fanny said firmly.

"I heard the crowd go crazy," Melodía said. "Did he win that handily?"

"Oh, yes!" Fina said.

"He didn't just win," Fanny said. "He beat poor Dom Xurxo de Viseu half to death before Duval found an excuse to step in and stop the combat. The poor young fool was too proud to yield."

"That doesn't sound chivalrous," Melodía said. "Mercedes pride themselves on their sense of fair play. I'm amazed they didn't turn on the Duke for it."

"His opponent was a Gallego, Día," Fina said.

"I got that from the name," Melodía said. "I know the Mercedes haven't forgiven their part in the Rape of La Merced, even if it was four hundred years ago. But isn't this a bit extreme?"

"Three hundred sixty-four," corrected Josefina Serena. "If you'd gotten here on *time*, Día, you'd know why the crowd's so hostile."

No tournament fan at the best of times, and horribly ambivalent about the outcome of this one, Melodía had exercised her prerogative to be fashionably late. She had purposefully avoided Falk's first bout. He and Jaume were the clear favorites to win, and anyway she was pretty sure Mondragón had jiggered the matchups to maximize the chances the beloved Campeón Imperial and the charismatic ex-rebel from the North would face each other for command of the correcting army.

That was the joust she dreaded to watch, for a rainbow of reasons. And the one she couldn't stay away from.

"Go ahead and tell me," she said resignedly.

"Well," Fina said, eyes glittering for once with something other than tears, "Mor Xurxo's first opponent was the Barón del Valle Azufre."

"Who is—?"

"He was a famous warrior in his youth."

"Which was considerably behind him," Abi said.

"Xurxo unseated the Baron on the first pass," Fina said. "Then he pranced around on his morion waving his lance as if he'd just destroyed an imperial tyrant, like your ancestor Manuel."

"All right," Melodía said. "So he's crass."

"That's not the best part," Lupe said. "When he dismounted to let Sulfur Valley get up and face him hand to hand, the old man was dead as a rock."

Fina glared at Lupe for horning in. "His heart gave out, the chirurgeons said."

"So the Mercedes naturally put the worst complexion possible on de Viseu's demeanor," Melodía said.

Fina shrugged. "He's a Gallego."

"It *was* shockingly unchivalrous," Fanny said.

Melodía shot her a narrow-eyed look. She was never sure to what extent her friend was playing a role, and to what extent she was actually that naïve.

An open wagon creaked slowly down one side of the jousting field. Laughing, a pack of sun-browned urchins dashed back and forth from it, gleefully splashing out buckets of water to lay the acrid limestone dust and keep it from obscuring the show and choking the grandes. Firefly Palace dinosaur grooms followed, dabbing the ground smooth with various tools. Another prime match was coming up directly— Jaume's long-awaited debut in the tournament.

"Have you heard the latest rumor?" Josefina Serena asked. "The court is all aflutter with it."

"You know I don't pay attention to gossip," Melodía said.

"You really ought to, Día," said Fanny. "It can play an important role in statecraft."

Melodía shook her head. She didn't like to hear that things that didn't interest her might be important.

Once Fina got started she was as difficult to stop or even deflect as a thunder-titan absentmindedly trampling a village to ruin as it strolled to new graze. Whether it was in a sudden outburst of enthusiasm or one of her more usual crying jags.

"They're saying someone else saw a Grey Angel in Providence," she said, eyes wide. "In the eastern foothills, near the mountains. Some people are afraid a Grey Angel Crusade might be coming!"

"Nonsense!" Melodía snapped. "Grey Angels and their crusades are nothing more than stories made up to frighten children."

Fina blinked her lids rapidly over eyes awash in sudden tears. "Impolitic to say that out loud," Fanny said, with a sideways nod of her head toward the Imperial box.

Lupe scowled. Her single heavy brow equipped her well to do so.

"You're saying you don't believe in the Demon War? But it's in all those history books you're so attached to."

"Historians get paid to write," Melodía said. "In this case, by my family. They have every reason to . . . make up stirring legends instead of retelling dry facts. Some of which might prove highly inconvenient for my Torre. The whole presentation of the Demon War is no doubt intended mostly to mythologize our ascension to the Fangèd Throne."

She paused to accept a goblet of wine from Pilar, who stood behind her. Absently she noted the girl had a strange smile on her face, as if she knew something her Princess didn't. But Melodía felt no more inclined to be deflected than Fina did.

"Your skinny butt could be planted on that throne someday," Llurdis said. "You might not want to be so flip about the whole thing."

"Not bloody likely, as the Angleses say. You know as well as I do that a child can't directly succeed a parent on the throne. And my father's antics are making our branch of la Familia unpopular enough that I'll never get Elected to follow whoever his successor turns out to be. It's back to Los Almendros for me. Unless I decide to let Father marry me off to that fat Treb Prince after all."

"Let's not do anything rash, dear," Fanny said.

"It *would* be entertaining to watch, though," Abi murmured. "If not from any closer than Laventura."

"Ladies and gentlemen," the Imperial Herald bellowed from the lists. "I now call your attention to our next contender, the champion of many mighty contests before: the great and puissant Don Roberto, Conde Montañazul!"

That was something that could change Fina's course. She clutched at Melodía's arm, her tears forgotten even as they still shone on her cheeks. "Jaume's up next!"

Abigail Thélème sniffed through her fine nose. "He's a fool."

"Jaume?" Melodía asked sharply. She seldom looked for a fight, and least of all with the Sansamour scion, who might well poison her pudding. But her emotions were boiling, pressed for release.

Fortunately Abi was enough her father's daughter to keep her own passions tightly reined. Or possibly just hidden beneath that cool, perfect porcelain mask of a face of hers.

"Bluemountain," she said. "He's convinced he'll command the Army of Correction. He's been strutting around like a young cock-horror for the last week, crowing about it to anyone who'd listen."

"He won his first bout handily enough," said Fina. Briskly, for her. Pink shone on her olive cheeks. Her eyes, usually sunk in dark despairing pits, glittered like obsidian buttons. "He's a great lover of tournaments. He fights frequently, and almost always wins."

"That doesn't mean he can beat that magnificent Alemán beast," Lupe said.

"Or Count Jaume," Fanny added pointedly.

"Sure," Lupe said. "Him too."

Abi Thélème looked thoughtful. "A wealthy fool, though—now, that has possibilities."

"You mustn't mock him!" Fina said, starting to cloud up. "He's a great champion!"

"So much the greater fool," Abi said, "for fighting where there's no need. But I'm not mocking, child. He may need . . . consolation . . . once Melodía's lover trounces him."

"Isn't Montador Fournier carrying your favor on his lance?" Fina asked, naming one of the younger and more vacuous of the stray knights who had flocked to the palace in the wake of Felipe decreeing his tourney and its remarkable stakes.

"A girl's allowed to change her mind, isn't she?"

The herald's tabard swelled to an extra-deep breath. *"Comes now the Imperial Champion, the Knight-*

Commander of the Order of the Companions of Our Lady Bella, el Conde dels Flors, JAUME!" he bellowed.

The crowd erupted in ecstasy as Jaume rode onto the field from between the gaudy silk banners that screened the waiting contestants. It thrilled Melodía to think that her lover might be the most popular man in all Nuevaropa. Certainly the Mercedes adored him.

And why not? He was young and beautiful, his orange hair streaming, his armor and his glorious orange-brindled morion, Camellia, gleaming white. Even better, his philosophy exalted as high virtues the very sorts of pleasures the Mercedes most loved to indulge in, as pleasing to his Lady and productive of moral good.

Melodía saw no reason *not* to adore her handsome knight. Her heart beat a quick march on her ribs, and she found it hard to breathe.

Scowling, Montañazul stroked his moustache with a thumb. He seemed to find plenty not to adore about Jaume.

Tournament Knight-Marshal Duval, his head bare, the gold-trimmed red feather cape signifying his command of the Scarlet Tyrants draped over broad shoulders, stepped out onto the thirty meters of bare ground separating the combatants. He held out his staff and in a trumpet voice ordered both to make ready.

From the *historias* Melodía had always loved to read, she knew the Iron Duchess hadn't indulged in fripperies like tourney grounds when she raised her great fortress on its white stone headland to watch over the city she was rebuilding after its destruction by the pirate fleet. Felipe had ordered his lists set up

in the middle of a kilometer of ground kept clear between the Firefly Palace's white stone walls and the
green wall of forest inland. Wooden stands rose on
either side of a field fifty meters long and thirty
wide. Panels of red and blue and yellow and green
fabric shaded dignitaries on the north side—nearer
the palace—and the less elegant but no less festive
common crowd on the south. Bright pennons bearing the contestants' insignia flapped to a moderate
breeze from staffs around the yard.

It was a grand sight, surely. Melodía could see none
of it now. She could only switch the narrow window
her vision had become between the man she had been
in love with her whole life, and the man intent on doing him all the harm he could.

The onlookers quieted. Jaume took his scoop-
shaped sallet helmet from the crook of his arm and
put it over his head. He clamped it to the bevor, bolted
to his armor that obscured the lower half of his face.
With a final sneer, Montañazul donned his own great
helm, quartered blue and gold.

"That great helmet's safer," Fina said. "But the
small eye-slits will be like trying to fight with a box
on his head. He obviously intends to win this fight
without dismounting."

"I know that!" Melodía snapped. Normally that
tone would have caused Fina to drown in her own
tears. Now she didn't blink.

Both knights took the five-meter-long lances
from the holders beside their saddles, tucked the butts
under their arms, and raised their shields.

"Go!" the knight-marshal shouted.

Melodía's heart momentarily forgot to beat.

The two duckbills dropped onto all fours and rolled into gallops that made the stands rattle and the plank seat vibrate through Melodía's cushion and up her tailbone. Camellia and her opponent were well matched in size: Camellia slightly bulkier, the sackbut longer.

They met in the middle, almost directly in front of Melodía. Montañazul's lance struck Jaume's white-enameled shield right on its red Lady's Mirror and shattered. Jaume's hit where his opponent's breastplate met the flared steel pauldron guarding his right shoulder. His lance broke too. But the impact lifted Montañazul over his saddle's tall back and sent him rolling down the sackbut's cruppers.

Despite her lack of sympathy for Montañazul, Melodía winced at the sound of his impact.

"So much for his plan to lead the Army of Correction," Abi said, languidly waving a fan of blue and white feathers at her face.

"Oh, dear," said Fina.

Jaume let Camellia ease out of her gallop, then turned her around. He grounded her, swung a leg over his saddle, and dropped two meters to hard dirt as gracefully as if dressed in a loincloth rather than forty-odd kilos of steel.

He'd told Melodía that a full suit of plate, though it could get brutally hot, felt neither heavy nor cumbersome. Not even jousting armor, fully half again as heavy as war gear.

Drawing his longsword—a tourney blunt, of course, not his famous Lady's Mirror—Jaume approached his fallen foe with gliding raptor grace. Montañazul stirred feebly, like a beetle on its back. When Jaume politely asked him to yield he spat back evident curses, though Melodía couldn't hear the actual words for the crowd's raucous joy.

Montañazul struggled to rise, failed. He kept trying, ignoring Jaume's second call for surrender.

Jaume put his rounded sword-tip against the mail gorget around Montañazul's throat. Montañazul slapped it away with a clang. The onlookers rumbled like far thunder at that breach of decorum.

Sneaking a sideways look, Melodía saw a rare frown crease her father's features at seeing his beloved nephew and champion treated so discourteously. Even Montserrat was watching now. But she didn't look happy. In fact she looked as if she were about to be sick.

Jaume put his sword to Montañazul's throat again. The Count batted it away again.

Jaume poked the sword point into the left eye-slit of Montañazul's helmet. The audience gasped. Mor Duval stepped briskly in as if to knock the blade away.

With a quick wrist-turn, Jaume twisted Montañazul's great helm sideways on his head so he couldn't see out. Then he tapped his blade twice on the helmet's side, which now faced the sky. Duval grabbed Jaume's sword hand and thrust it at the clouds it, proclaiming him victor.

Beneath a tempest of applause, Fina said earnestly, "He would've been within his rights to strike home, since Bluemountain twice refused to yield."

"I wish he had," Melodía said. "Jaume will too someday, I'll bet."

Chapter 17

top!" the archer cried. "Hand over the hook-horn and your purses, and we'll let you leave with your lives."

Little Nell sighed resignedly as she came to a halt. Walking at her side, Rob Korrigan concurred.

The afternoon light dappled the leaf corpses that mostly hid the ruts in the indifferently maintained road, and filled Rob's nostrils with a rich, dry smell as they slowly turned into humus. A cuatralas, black as a baron's heart, glided from branch to branch, chasing a purple-and-yellow butterfly. Tiny birds twittered to one another among the leaves of tall gingkoes and false plane trees, which grew far enough apart to allow enough sunlight to filter down to sustain a thriving undergrowth of barberry, ferns, and scrub oak.

Which was in turn enough to hide brigands. Like the one who'd just stepped into the road ahead, drawing a shortbow to his chest. And the pair who emerged from the bushes five or six meters to either side.

"You take care of these two," Karyl said, nodding toward the man with the spear and the one with the short sword who hovered menacingly on their flanks. "I'll deal with the archer."

"And isn't that you all over, then?" Rob murmured as his companion walked calmly forward. He neither saw how Karyl Bogomirskiy, armed solely with his sword-staff, could possibly deal with a bowman twenty-five meters off, nor doubted that he somehow would. Rob was a man who believed in fate and the Fae, and he doubted either intended such a man as Karyl to die like a stunted vexer chick in such a crappy, random way.

Nonetheless he moved to interpose the patient grey-and-blue bulk of Nell's butt between himself and the readied arrow as he pulled axe and round shield off her back.

He slid his arm through a broad swath of nose-horn leather fixed to the back of his shield to grip the narrower hand strap. He loosened the lacings of his axehead cover with his teeth and ditched it with a wrist flip.

The two brigands to either side of him seemed suddenly less eager for the encounter to proceed. His calm, crisp actions clearly took them aback. They seemed astonished that the threat of a drawn bow hadn't frozen him in place.

Rob knew the type too well. They weren't fighters,

but bushwhackers, whose primary weapons were surprise and intimidation, not the implements they were suddenly holding in oddly tentative ways, as if trying to remember what they were there for. Most of their combat seasoning came from putting the boot in on a cowed or fallen foe.

Like house-shields, Rob thought—the noble class's hired, armored bullyboys, and occasionally girls. The comparison filled him with such righteous fury it pushed all trepidation right out of him.

"What's the matter?" he demanded, turning left and right to flourish Wanda at each in turn. A showman through, he made sure to let shafts of sunlight glance off her bearded grey head. "Aren't you eager to take what I've got, then?"

Nell snorted, twitched her big tail, and stamped a hind foot. It occurred to him that he might have just given the hook-horn a swat in the fanny and sent her charging straight at the archer. It would take more skill and stone than he probably possessed to get an arrow in her eye—the only way that puny shortbow could hurt her—before she knocked him down with her horn and trampled his ribs to porridge.

Too late now. He stepped right, toward the spearman, just enough to look past the hook-horn to see how his friend was doing.

Karyl carried his staff as if it was all stick and no sword. He advanced steadily toward the arrowhead aimed for his chest. He'd already made up half the distance.

"Wh-what are you doing?" the bowman said. "I'll shoot! I will!"

Karyl kept walking.

Rob saw the spearman's eyes go wide beneath a

lank hank of black hair. He had already heard the rustle of a boot on fallen, crunchy leaves. He thrust his axe toward the spearman, shouted "Boo!" and wheeled smartly clockwise, swinging the axe horizontally and bringing up his shield.

The man with the short sword emitted a yelp through a surprisingly neat yellow beard and sat down hard on his loincloth, just in time to prevent Rob's axe from biting his guts out. Though the smell that wafted from him indicated that he cut fairly close to the Creators' strict laws of cleanliness, for a forest bandit, his breath suggested he subsisted solely on raw garlic, onions, and the sort of wine that to Rob's mind represented a waste of good turpentine.

Rob had already checked his turn. He quickly pivoted back the other way.

The spearhead scraped along the shield's Centrosaurus-hide front. Rob guided the weapon safely past and thrust hard with Wanda. The axehead took that bandit right in the mouth with a crackle of teeth smashing.

The black-haired man dropped his spear to clutch his ruined mouth. He fell down to roll about among fragrant low ferns and dainty shade-loving purple flowers. Him it could only make smell better.

This time Rob continued his widdershins wheel, in case the swordsman had found his courage and his feet again. He had. He was closing in with his arm cocked well back over his shoulder for a slash at the vulnerable back of Rob's head. Rob slammed the shield-rim into his face. He staggered back. Rob stepped up and gave him his right shin hard in the balls.

"If you drop your bow and go," he heard Karyl say, "I'll let you live."

He'd have sworn the man spoke no louder than a whisper. Yet he heard him clearly as if the dark-bearded lips were almost brushing his own ear.

His opponents having opted to drop their weapons to hold on to their violated parts and moan about their sorry state, Rob risked a look down the road.

Karyl was no more than the span of his own out-stretched arms from the head of the drawn arrow. Which was now describing increasingly wild figures of eight in the air.

Karyl advanced another inexorable step. The bow-man shrieked like a frightened child and threw down his bow. The nocked arrow tumbled, to go notch-first into the roadside weeds. The brigand turned and ran as fast as his spindly brown legs would carry him.

"The quiver too," Karyl called after him.

Without breaking stride the bandit shucked the strap off his shoulder and let the half-full pouch of arrows fall. He kept running until he vanished around a bend in the track.

Karyl had never drawn blade.

"Right," Rob said to the men he'd downed. He gave the one with the bloody mouth a boot in the ribs. "Help your friend and be off. Unless you'd like some more?"

The man scrambled up. He circled wide of Rob to the aid of his partner. His hand left a broad smear of blood on the other's forearm as he dragged him to his feet. Supporting each other, the pair staggered off into the bushes and were gone.

The quiver retrieved and slung over one shoulder,

Karyl bent over to lay the staff down and pick up the bow. He used his right hand; his left was swaddled to a sort of club. But Rob had glimpsed what lay beneath the stream-washed linen bandages Karyl rewrapped it with each night. He wondered if Karyl thought to hide the wrinkled pink worms of half-grown fingers from Rob, or from himself.

"Can you use this?" he asked, brandishing the bow at Rob. "It can bring some meat for the pot, and help resolve similar adventures in future."

Rob drew the corners of his mouth down toward his jaw. "Not well. I stick what I'm pointing at rather more often than I do my own foot, I suppose."

"It'll have to do."

Rob expected him to walk the bow back to him. Instead Karyl slung it over his left shoulder, recovered his staff, and simply stood by the road. After a moment Rob realized Karyl was waiting for him to get Little Nell under way and move forward to catch him up.

He finished hanging his shield back with the baggage piled on his dinosaur's back and collected the cover for Wanda's head.

"That was dead brave," Rob said as he fitted it back in place. "As brave as anything I've seen, perhaps."

Karyl grunted. "Physical valor is the most overvalued commodity on Paradise."

The shock hit Rob like a plunge in an icy mountain stream. Such a statement was practically heresy. More to the point, Rob was a bard—and celebrating physical courage was a primary stock-in-trade.

Karyl might just as well have pissed all over the ideal of Beauty. Or gold, or honor, or power—or the intrigue, fucking, and rampant bloodletting those things tended to engender. And did, in any self-respecting song or story.

Worst of all, Rob more than half-suspected the thing himself.

"How can you say that?" he blustered.

"Courage is as common as young men with more sperm in their sacks than sense in their skulls," Karyl said. "The willingness of men and women to die without question is a virtue primarily for the unworthy, who use it for their gain."

"But you were a mercenary leader! A mercenary *lord*. Wouldn't getting others to die for your gain *define* the job?"

Karyl nodded. "Precisely."

"And yet without so much as lifting your hand you chased off a man with arrow nocked, drawn, and aimed," Rob said, hanging his axe behind the shield. "How do you even explain such a thing?"

"In the East they say there's nothing more dangerous than one who lives as if already dead."

Rob rubbed his beard. The stresses and strains of the encounter, brief as it was, had made the sweat run briskly down his face for a spell despite the cool forest air.

"There's a thing that's easier said than done, I think."

Karyl laughed softly. "It's not hard when you've done it as often as I have."

"Done what?"

"Died." His mouth tightened inside his neat beard. "It would come as something of a relief, I think. If it *took* this time."

Shaking his head, Rob grasped the lead attached to the complicated bridle fitted over Nell's head and fringe and clucked her into amiable motion.

"All good and well," he said. "But if he had loosed at you, you'd have just knocked the arrow out of the air, right? Or snatched it with your hand like those ninja blokes in Zipangu, I shouldn't wonder."

Karyl shrugged.

"Or died," he said.

Chapter 18

Tirán Rey, **King Tyrant, Tyrant**—*Tyrannosaurus rex.* Large bipedal meat-eating dinosaur; 13 meters long, 7 tonnes. Aphrodite Terra's largest known and most feared predator; notorious even in Nuevaropa, to which it is not native. Sturdier than Allosaurus. Like the matador, encountered rarely as a war-mount.

—THE BOOK OF TRUE NAMES

The knight-marshal bellowed, "*Go!*"

Count Jaume lowered his lance, couched it, and booted his gigantic mount into a charge.

Facing him across the well-beaten lists, Duke Falk von Hornberg did likewise.

Melodía drew a deep breath. Princess Fanny took her right hand. Another hand gripped her left. She glanced that way and was amazed to see Abigail Thélème's eyes fixed on hers.

"Courage, Día," she said.

It was late in the day. The light slanting in across

the forest had taken on a buttery hue. The contest everyone expected had finally come to pass.

The two pale-skinned monsters met. Though hers was the most terrifying possible antagonist, Camellia never flinched. Jaume aimed true.

Two lances splintered on shields.

Jaume and Falk rode on to the end of the field, stopped their mounts, and turned them. Their arming-squires ran out to give their masters fresh lances.

"Tourney rules allow three lances each," Fina said. Her eyes were bright. She leaned far forward, like a starving woman toward a platter of smoking roast nosehorn.

Like living avalanches, the great dinosaurs charged each other. Again both lances shattered, with much noise and no visible effect.

By now the crowd had cheered itself hoarse. Everyone was on their feet. Melodía's father and even the ancient, feeble Pope were standing up in the Imperial box. Almost lost amid the grown-ups, she saw Montse, her feather crest gone, her dark-gold dreadlocks spilling over the hands that covered her eyes. *Is she peeking between her fingers?* Melodía wondered.

Once more the dinosaur knights swapped ends. Once more they accepted fresh lances from their squires. The black-armored rider and the white-armored one wheeled their monsters, leveled lances, charged.

The stands shook beneath Melodía's feet to the monsters' hammering footfalls. Camellia rolled forward in her rocking four-footed lope. Snowflake ran with oddly mincing steps, his tiny two-clawed hands cradled daintily to his chest.

They met. Jaume's rounded lance-tip hit the Duke's

armet above the right eye-slit. Falk's head snapped back. He reeled in his high-cantled saddle as the monsters thundered past each other. His own lance broke ineffectually on Jaume's white-and-orange shield.

Camellia's sides heaved with exertion when Jaume brought her about. Sweat glistened on her pebble-scaled skin. At the field's far end Snowflake panted, his jaws opened slightly inside the silver muzzle.

Jaume drew his longsword from its sheath behind his right shoulder. Falk took his axe from the sheath hung from his saddle where it rode before his right thigh.

Melodía had pulled her friends' hands up to her breastbone. She shook with fear and nausea. She longed for this to just *be over*. For her cousin, her lover, her best friend to be safe and well away from here.

Crying "*For the Lady!*" and "*Hornberg!*," the knights spurred their mounts directly toward each other. The passages with lances were pure formalities of the joust: in real battle a dinosaur knight's main weapon was his multi-tonne mount.

Sackbut and king tyrant met with an impact like Chián the Father, King of the Creators, pounding His fists together.

Nose to tail, the dinosaurs went around and around. Their riders belabored each other with a smithy clangor of steel on steel. White dust swirled up like smoke to obscure the fight.

Through a break in the cloud, Melodía saw Falk's axe smash into Jaume's shield. Then Camellia was squatting protectively as her master rolled backward down her rump.

Melodía screamed. Sour vomit flooded her mouth.

Fanny and Abi held her tight, kept her from toppling forward over the rail onto the field.

She heard clapping from close by. "Fina!" Llurdis snapped.

"Oh! I'm sorry! Melodía, I didn't mean—" Fina broke into sobs.

Prying herself upright, Melodía made herself look. Jaume was already on his feet, shield high, sword held out and down by his side. He gazed up at his rival—into the jagged teeth of the tyrant, dripping saliva a scant four meters from Jaume's face.

The cage of silver bars that confined those teeth seemed no more substantial than the honey-crystal straws the vendors peddled in the bazaar.

"Don't give up, Melodía," Fina sniffled. "Remember how Count Jaume climbed up behind Baron Sándoval, threw him from the saddle of his morion, and broke his wicked neck!"

Possibly in response to a signal from Falk, Snowflake thrust his head forward and roared. That he couldn't fully open his mouth didn't seem to hamper his volume.

The audience shrieked. Women fainted. Men fainted. The war-hadrosaurs penned nearby drowned out the crowd's ecstatic fear with a fanfare of terror.

Though his sallet and bevor hid his face, Jaume alone seemed unmoved. He stood erect, defying the fury and blast and charnel stink of the Tyrannosaurus's roar. The tip of his tourney sword began to tap the ground.

Melodía had to stifle a giggle she feared would turn to a fully mad laugh. It seemed as if her lover was saying, *Is that the best you have? That mindless noise?*

The crowd sensed it too. Slowly they took up the chant: "*Jau-me! Jau-me!*"

"It seems Duke Falk remembers Sándoval's unfortunate example too," remarked Abi Thélème, letting go of Melodía's arm now Melodía seemed able to stand by herself. "Look."

The Alemán had backed his mount several steps away from his foe. He gestured with his axe. Falk's arming-squire, Albrecht, pale as Snowflake's hide, scuttled out to hold the reins while Falk dismounted.

"The boy's dead brave, anyway," Fanny said. "I wouldn't fancy getting that close to that head, muzzle or not!"

Duke Falk fumed silently as he swung his armored leg over his saddle and easily dropped the final meter to the ground. Attendants ran out to throw a blanket over Snowflake's head, rendering the monster docile.

Listen to them chant his name! he thought furiously. *As if I hadn't just unseated him!*

Technically Falk had won a point. Should the fight end in mutual exhaustion or incapacitation—as two bouts already had—it would give him the match, this tourney, and command of the Army of Correction.

And here the mob was chanting for the man he'd bested.

Jaume's almost inhuman defiance of Snowflake's roar had won them, of course. It simply didn't seem *possible* not to quail when a tyrant challenged a mere man. Not when it could put to flight even three-tonne war-trained hadrosaurs.

Falk drew in a deep breath. Even with the cooling breezes off the Canal, the afternoon heat made his dark-enameled plate a furnace. Sweat slicked his body inside the formed steel and sopping-wet padding. His breathing roared like surf in his ears. Each exhalation's smell was stronger than the reek of dust and dinosaur dung.

Despite himself, Falk grinned inside his visor. *He is a hero, and no mistake,* he thought.

As if to counter that he spotted Bergdahl, standing at the shady end of the commoners' seats. He had his arms folded, head tipped to one side, and a particularly pointed expression on his goblin face. Hada, they'd call it here.

Falk could hear his servant's sardonic voice in his head: *Remember the plan.*

Yes. He remembered.

But he would see what this living legend was truly made of. And then—who knew?

Could my mother really cavil at victory? he asked himself.

Of course she could. Somehow Dowager Duchess Margrethe could always twist whatever he did, however triumphant, into failure of some kind.

Simmering, twitching his two-kilo axe in his right gauntlet like a willow withe, he began to stalk the waiting Conde dels Flors.

Warily Jaume watched his foe approach. His right kidney and hip hurt from his landing. He'd wrenched his right knee. It would soon swell, he knew. But he trusted it to carry him long enough.

He frequently practiced falling off Camellia in full armor. Unfortunately, mere practice never fully matched real combat. Despite his acrobatic skills and Camellia's well-trained help, he'd hurt himself. If not badly enough to slow him down.

He felt chagrin. No enemy had ever unseated him from Camellia before. *He's good*, he thought. *But I knew that already.*

He grinned inside his bevor. *This will keep me from getting complacent, at least.*

It was neither the young Duke's size nor strength that most impressed Jaume as Falk closed in. It was the easy, fluid way he moved despite the way his armor constrained the play of his joints. It reminded Jaume of a stalking matador.

Just out of weapon's reach Falk stopped. He let his axe hang from its thong, which he had wound around his vambrace, while he undid the straps of his falcon shield. He threw the shield aside and raised his head to meet Jaume's gaze.

Seen through the visor-slits, Falk's eyes were calm as sapphire chips. Jaume began to remove his own shield.

"Breathe, Día," Fanny urged.

Jaume sprang back away from yet another axe-stroke that looked as if it could take his head off.

"*Ohh,*" Melodía moaned.

The crowd cheered Jaume's escape. They'd sat down again, to Melodía's relief, since her legs didn't want to support her. But it sounded as if the applause was getting fainter.

"He keeps running away," Llurdis grumbled.

"Don't be an idiot," Lupe said.

Llurdis rounded on her, face clouding. "Ladies," Fanny said warningly.

"Don't you see?" asked fight fan Fina. "Jaume's trying to tire him out."

"Also that big Northern brute will smash him in half if he ever connects," Lupe said, with perhaps unnecessary fervor.

Fanny gave her a look. "Sorry," Lupe said.

Melodía forced herself not to look away. Jaume did move with phenomenal agility and speed. But his armor was heavy, and hot, although the sun had fallen so low that attenuated shadow-warriors acted out the duel against the garish screens at the lists' western end. From her own martial training Melodía knew how rapidly just *being* in a fight drained a person.

And despite his bulk Falk was no mere lumbering titan. The first time she saw him, Melodía thought the Duke thick around the middle. Having seen more of him around court, she realized the reason he didn't have a wedge-shaped back like Jaume was that he had wide hips. His torso was a slab of muscle that gave him strength to maneuver almost as quickly as his slighter foe.

And the crowd, inclined as it was to love the handsome young Imperial Champion, was getting impatient with his delaying tactics.

As was the young Duke. He lunged, swinging a two-handed blow. Jaume danced back. This time he leaned forward to tap Falk's breastplate with his sword before he could recover.

Falk roared. He swung backhand. The Catalan took a skip-step back, leaned his upper body away. The axe swished harmlessly past. Jaume closed again.

This time he tapped the top of Falk's round armet with the end of his longsword.

Bellowing like Snowflake in full fury, Falk cocked his axe over his right shoulder. Rocking his weight onto his rear foot he made ready to bull-rush his foe.

Jaume charged him first. Grasping his sword hilt with one hand and the unsharpened ricasso above the cross guard with the other, he used the leverage that added to slam Falk across the visor. The blow toppled the already off-balance Falk.

He fell with a sound like a chest full of pots and pans thrown off a castle wall.

The crowd fell silent. Then it surged to its feet like a cresting wave, shrieking adulation.

Melodía's ladies were dancing in place, hugging each other, cheering. Melodía still sat huddled around the knot of misery in her belly. It felt as if she'd taken a quarterstaff thrust.

Falk seemed genuinely stunned. He might have shaken off a much greater fall from tyrant-back. But Jaume had given him no chance to prepare. He'd landed flat on his back and driven the air from his lungs.

Jaume stood over him. "Do you yield, your Grace?" he shouted above the din.

The Alemán stirred as if trying to sit up. Jaume's coal-scoop sallet turned toward the knight-marshal, who ran up with a brace of assistants.

Sieur Duval's square, hard face was stern. He was known to disapprove of Jaume as a frivolous fop. But his exchange with Falk over the cocksure Gallego de Viseu had clearly soured his blood toward the Duke. Still, Duval was famed for ironbound, if not iron-*headed*, probity; otherwise he would never have endured two decades in command of the Imperial bodyguard.

"He does not yield," Duval bellowed in his parade-ground voice. Even the poor folk away high up in the cheap seats must have heard him clearly. "Fight on!"

At last Falk sat up. Jaume raised his sword high, brought it whistling down toward the heavily reinforced crown of Falk's helmet.

And Falk threw up his left arm, shouting hoarsely, "*I yield me!*"

Too late. The longsword hit his forearm. The steel vambrace buckled loudly. Though not as loudly as his forearm breaking.

For a moment it was as if everyone had turned to stone. Then the bubbling began: "*He yielded! He had yielded! Foul, foul! The Imperial Champion struck a yielded man!*"

Duval hesitated. Then he stepped up to seize Jaume's sword wrist.

"His Grace waited too long to yield," he cried. "There was no foul."

He flung Jaume's arm skyward. The Count's sword stood up against the sky.

"Bravo!" Princess Fanny shouted in her loudest voice. It had a nice edge of brass to it. "Bravo!"

"Bravo!" the crowd echoed. "Bravo!"

Melodía jumped to her feet. She was screaming now too. She was proud of Jaume. He had fought brilliantly, triumphed despite the desperate setback of being unseated. But mostly she was wild with joy that he *survived*.

But still she heard—was it really in her ears, or just

her mind?—the invidious whispering: *Dishonor. He struck a yielded foe.*

It was a lie. But somehow she knew it would cling to her lover like a foul smell, and haunt him like the memory of loss.

Chapter 19

La Vida-que-Viene, **Life-to-Come**—A radical sect of the Church of Nuevaropa that preached self-denial, holding that the Creators' mandates in *The Books of the Law* were metaphorical, and sometimes even meant the opposite of what they said. Despite its heterodoxy, which crossed the line into heresy when some sectaries claimed that sin could lead to eternal damnation, the Life-to-Come enjoyed a substantial following in the early eighth century.

—LA GRAN HISTORIA DEL IMPERIO
DEL TRONO COLMILLADO

She heard him knock, late that night. Heard the clatter of the latch and the hinge-creak as Pilar admitted him. With a silent smile at her mistress, the maid withdrew to her own room and softly shut the door.

Her lips suddenly dry, Melodía looked up from the window table where she read by the glow of a brass lamp. He wore a loose robe, and his orange hair hung unbound about his shoulders. Lamplight from the corridor outside surrounded him with a golden nimbus until he pulled the door to behind him.

Laying down her book, she rose to meet him. "Jaume," she said, feeling her voice vibrate low in her throat.

He smiled. "My love," he said.

She drew her long white gown up her body. She felt the slight breeze through the window, faintly cool on the fine coating of sweat on her skin.

Jaume helped her pull the gown off over her head. Beneath she wore nothing but the fine silver and polished-coral ankle chain he had given her when first they lay together. She had asked him for a token. . . .

As he tossed the gown over the back of her chair, she unbound her hair. It slid down over her shoulders in a dark cascade.

He caught her in a powerful embrace. Kissing her deeply, he ran a hand down her ribs. At the point of her hip it changed course. His fingertips tracked across her lower belly and down to her bush.

He cupped his hand over her and began to tease his finger through the dense, curly hair. Melodía shivered when its tip brushed her inner lips. The finger pressed in and up. It found the pearl of flesh in its folds at the upper juncture, pressed, began to revolve.

She moaned around his tongue and began to rotate her hips in time with his manipulations.

He slid the finger down, thrust it inside her. It hooked and began to press upward.

She uttered a small scream into his mouth. The pleasure exploded inside her. His fingertips exerted such delicious pressure as to almost become pain.

She went up on the balls of her feet. Keeping the pressure on, he leaned into her and began to walk her backward.

The hard table edge caught her just below the fold of her ass. Holding her by a hand across her shoulder blades he guided her down onto it. She barely noticed when she bumped her head on the whitewashed wall beside the window. The smell of night flowers blooming in the yard below flowed across her face like cool ointment. Fireflies as long as her hand winked at her through the fine netting over the open window.

His right hand never relenting, he urged her thighs apart with his left. She eagerly complied. He dropped to his knees. He smiled almost mischievously up the naked length of her, his dear face framed by her breasts and bearded by her pubic fur.

He buried his face in her and began to lick with long, powerful strokes. She moaned and grasped the sides of his head.

After Melodía's long drought, her champion knew exactly what she needed. She came quickly and loudly. He kept licking her as she screamed and climaxed again and again.

When she could take no more, and pleasure reached the verge of pain, he stopped. Pulling away from her, he rose to his feet—with only a twinge from the stiffness in his joints—and quickly undressed.

When he was nude, she smiled and tried to sit up, reaching for his hard cock. He intercepted her face with his. His weight bore her back down.

She uttered a shuddering groan as he plunged deep inside her.

He fucked her hard and fast. His philosophy of art allowed for embellishment, but prized directness. . . .

Her months of anxious waiting spent themselves in shuddering waves. Then he was gripping her hard with his wiry-strong arms, crushing her with his chest as he drove himself into her again and again.

He roared like a tyrant bull as his release joined hers.

Afterward they lay gently tangled on her bed, barely conscious of moving to it, in the shared soft glow of pleasure and amber lamplight.

"I'm surprised your guardian matadora allowed us this time alone," he said.

"She's sleeping soundly in her chambers down the hall," Melodía said. "I'm surprised you don't hear. She snores like an old nosehorn bull."

"Is that what that sound is? I thought it *was* an old nosehorn on the palace grounds somewhere. Maybe dozing at his capstan."

He raised a questioning brow. Her eyes tried to drink him all in. She actually blessed the dimness in the room: it made it easier for her mind to gloss over the bruises, already turning a dark rainbow of blue and green and yellow and black, that mottled his hip and thigh and arm as merely shadows.

"She's got a taste for wine," Melodía said. "Maybe too much. She resists it with her usual steel will. Mostly. Tonight her fellow dueñas encouraged her to drink as freely as she wished."

"Did they, now?" He grinned like a schoolboy to her earlier schoolgirl. "So we've got them to thank?"

Melodía nodded. "Uh-huh. They tease her, mercilessly sometimes, that if everyone believed as she does, the race would die off from failure to reproduce."

"Ah. So she's a follower of La Vida-que-Viene, then?"

"I'm afraid so. It's a frightful bore."

"How sad for her. I can't see the attraction of the Life-to-Come sect's doctrines, myself. I'd never deny their right to believe what they wish: there's nothing uglier than trying to punish people for their thoughts. Still—I can't help but see the irony that they whisper the loudest that the Garden of Beauty and Truth in Providence is heretical, when it's their beliefs that contradict *The Books of the Law*."

"They also criticize you. Old Pío is one of them, though he can't admit the heterodoxy."

"I know too well. He hates my order. He'd revoke our charter in a heartbeat if your father would let him."

"I'm glad Daddy won't. I don't know why my father pays attention to him, Pope or not."

"Because Pío tells him what he wants to hear. If you'll forgive my talking that way about your father."

"It's only true. An understatement, really."

She peered intently into his face. "Is that what's been bothering you?"

"What do you mean?"

"Since you've been back—it's as if there's some kind of barrier between us. We've always talked freely. It's why I fell in love with you. Well—one reason among many."

His brow furrowed. She pressed a finger to his lips. "No. Please don't try to tell me it's just how preoccupied you've been with readying the army to march out. Please."

"Forgive me, my love. There are things I've been reluctant to burden you with."

"Do you think not trusting me hurts less than hearing what you don't want to tell me would? Aren't we betrothed? Well—nearly?"

He took her hand in both of his. "Of course I trust you, my love. And of course we're betrothed—in spirit at least. I wanted to spare you pain."

"If I wanted to be spared pain," she said, "would I have let myself fall in love with the Imperial Champion?"

He laughed. "I never could outflank you mentally. Very well. You remember my glorious victory that capped the Princes' War? My defeat of the renegade mercenary?"

"Karyl Bogomirskiy? The Slavo who commanded the White River Legion? The servants tell me people are still singing about that in every tavern in the city."

"It's all a lie. Down to the punctuation."

It felt as if a ball of cold wet ash had materialized inside her stomach. "What do you mean?"

"In the months I spent in Alemania after the war," he said, "I investigated Voyvod Karyl as thoroughly as I could. I found many things not to admire about him. He was a harsh man. I heard reports, well attested, that he was trying to squeeze pleasure itself out of his domain."

"You're joking!"

"I'm not. Crazy as it seems, he hated all passion with a passion. He blamed *emotion* for the sum of human misery. So he tried to enforce a grey uniformity on the Misty March, and force all its energy toward creating and sustaining his mercenary war machine."

"But that's monstrous. Shouldn't you have destroyed him for that alone?"

"I've fought monsters my whole life, *mi amor*. But so far as I could ascertain, ruthless though Karyl was, he was never cruel. The mother of the man who usurped his throne, now, she was a monster, by all accounts. She murdered Karyl's father and his friends, and tortured people for sport. But when he reconquered his March, he simply had her beheaded. The usurper himself, his own half brother, he allowed to go unharmed into exile. No, in his own way, Karyl was forbearing. Even merciful."

Melodía made a skeptical sound deep in her throat.

"He was a remarkable field captain," Jaume said. "Probably the best in Nuevaropa."

She frowned. "But that's you!"

"No. I have some grasp of tactics, which is more than most of my brother and sister nobles can boast. They think there's nothing more to war than charging straight ahead and striking hard blows. Our victories are really won by the courage of my men, my Knights-Brother and Ordinaries. They're the heroes the bards should sing about."

"You are too! I won't let you deny yourself credit."

"Well—maybe. But while we Companions have a gift for derring-do, Voyvod Karyl mastered war in every aspect. He took good care of his troops, and gave good value to his employers. In short: he won battles."

He grimaced.

"Until the last. When we attacked his already-disordered Legion from behind."

"But if he was a traitor—"

"He wasn't."

Jaume sat up. He smoothed his hair back from his face and did not look at her.

"That's what I'm trying to tell you," he said. "Before his Legion crossed the frontier from Slavia into Alemania, the war was lost. *We'd* lost. His living fortresses' horns turned the Wheel toward us."

"*Three-horns*," Melodía breathed.

Even in one as indifferent to dinosaurs as she normally was, Triceratops horridus awoke awe. She knew the giant hornfaces existed, on the Ovdan plateau and eastward across vast Aphrodite Terra. Yet to Nueva-ropa they seemed to belong in Faerie tales—as wonderful and terrifying as the hada themselves.

"Yes," Jaume said. "With them, Karyl won us time to bolster Prinz Eugen's army with the Companions and a regiment of Nodosaur infantry. We were poised to crush the Princes' forces on the Hassling."

"But what about Karyl plotting to betray the Empire? Didn't he mean to seize the Fangèd Throne itself?"

"As hard as I looked," Jaume said, "I never found the slightest scrap of evidence he intended anything but perfect faith. And believe me, I wanted to."

"Then why did you attack him?" she asked.

"Orders. When the White River Legion rode into the midst of the stream and was fully engaged with von Augenfelsen's men, we couched our lances and charged Karyl's monsters. From behind. Fearsome as they are, those horns and the neck-frills face forward. They never had a chance."

"So it was Prinz Eugen?" she asked, eager to believe ill of a distant cousin she had never met, rather than . . . anyone she knew and cared for. "He ordered this, this treacherous attack?"

"No," Jaume said relentlessly. "Him I might have disobeyed. And taken the consequences, however stark."

She stared at him. The strange separation was back, stronger than before. They might as well have been fully clothed; there was no longer intimacy between them. She mourned that loss.

But she couldn't let go. "Why *didn't* you disobey? The Creators themselves tell us to defy wicked or unlawful commands. Not that I believe in them, of course. But it's in the Books, plain as day."

He raised an eyebrow at her. They had few arguments, and her determined atheism had caused most of them. She knew she was right. But as the head of a religious order and a Prince of the Church, he had no choice but to disagree.

"You're right," he said. "I'm bound by law and honor alike to disobey wrongful orders. But I've sworn loyalty to the Fangèd Throne. And to the man who occupies it, my Emperor and my uncle."

She felt sick. "You can't be saying—"

"Yes. The scroll the Prince-Marshal sent was addressed to me personally, quite explicit, and sealed with the Tyrant's Head."

"But why?"

"The Princes offered peace. With a price: Karyl's head. Many in our camp would have happily paid. Some out of jealousy at his success, some fearful of the power he was amassing, with this terrifying new means of waging war and the wealth it showered on his little March. It seems the same sentiments found voice at court. And were whispered again and again in the palace corridors until someone with your father's ear—poured poison in it."

She buried her face in her hands. Hot tears streamed between her fingers.

"It may sound like the same justification the Princes' Party used to cover treason. But it's true: someone gave your father bad advice. And this same person or persons might be leading His Majesty toward disaster. I'm terribly afraid the war we're about to begin will have the opposite effect from what Felipe intends: that far from dousing the flames of rebellion, it will spread them across Nuevaropa."

Melodía jumped to her feet, unthinkingly snatching her hand from his.

"But this is just awful," she said, pacing around the room.

"I agree," he said.

"I wish I could doubt what you're telling me. But I can't. My father would never do anything but what he deeply felt was right. The trouble is, once he *feels* something, he doesn't think about it anymore. He doesn't question himself."

Jaume smiled without joy. "Not to second-guess oneself can be a gift."

"But now it may curse us all."

She drew a deep breath.

"One thing's clear," she said. "You mustn't lead the expeditionary force out the gates tomorrow."

He blinked as if she'd slapped him. "How do you reckon that?"

"Isn't it obvious? You don't believe in it. We both know it will cause political instability—not to mention the suffering and loss of life. It's *war*. And now you tell me my father compromised your honor and your conscience. How can you serve him in this, when you know it's wrong?"

"Because he's my Emperor."

She whirled on him. "But what about your duty to the Lady? To truth? Of course my father's been led astray. He always listens to the last person to tell him what he wants to hear. And this new confessor of his, this Fray Jerónimo no one knows anything about, even the Church—I'll bet he's behind it all!"

She came back to the bed and knelt before her lover. She took his right hand. She felt its strength, and the calluses of countless hours plying lute, sword, and lance.

"You can stop this, Jaume," she said. She felt as if she was a little girl again, begging a favor from her dashing older cousin. "Please."

"But I can't."

"But you *can*. You're not just the marshal leading the expedition. You're Condestable Imperial now, ruler of all Nuevaropa's forces. My father declared you both, right there on the lists."

"That's true," he said.

"So order the army to stand down. Send the glory seekers and greedy grandes packing. March the Nodosaurs back to their barracks in the Barrelmakers' District. Put an end to the madness."

"If I gave such orders, your father would simply sack me."

"He wouldn't dare! You're his champion!"

Jaume shook his head. "We both know Felipe better than that. He's stubborn as an old nosehorn bull when he's set his heart to something."

"Then let him sack you! So what?"

She was truly angry now. *How can he keep arguing with me, when his heart knows I'm right?*

"Then the Ejército Corregir will march out of the Firefly Palace's Imperial Gate with a different *mariscal* at its head. Tomorrow, or at the latest, the day after."

"Then let it. At least you'll spare yourself having to . . . to do more evil on my father's account."

Jaume put his free hand over hers.

"Would you rather see the Duke von Hornberg command the expedition?"

She might have pointed out that Falk's broken arm had led the Emperor to release him from his oath, and even forbid him outright to ride with the army. But she had spun beyond *objection*. Fury rose up to possess her as completely as lust had so short a time before. The sense of betrayal burned like hot oil on her skin. *How does he dare? I don't want him doing this!*

"Yes!" she shouted through tears. "Anything but see you do it!"

"I must. It's my duty."

She jumped from the bed and turned away. Snatching her gown from the chair back where he had tossed it, she swept it imperiously around her shoulders.

"Then we are done here," she said to the wall. "I see that my efforts are wasted. I trust my lord Count will see himself out."

She stood, not moving, not seeing, now scarcely even feeling as he rose, gathered his clothes, and walked naked into the hall.

He closed the door as softly as he might kiss her closed eyelids.

Melodía threw herself facedown on the bed and cried until it felt as if her ribs had cracked.

Chapter 20

Titán espinoso, **Spine-Backed Titan**—*Diplodocus longus.* Quadrupedal herbivore, Nuevaropa's longest titan; grows to 30 meters and 20 tonnes. Exceedingly long neck tipped with a small head; whiplike tail. Distinguished by a row of dorsal spines.

—THE BOOK OF TRUE NAMES

A m I talking to myself here?" Rob asked, puffing slightly as he approached the hilltop. All he saw before him was white sky and his companion's cloaked back.

Having grown tired of trying to elicit details about Karyl's past, he'd been imparting his own autobiography. Or trying to. Karyl vanished over the rise.

Nothing. Just the wind whistling among the thorny weeds of the ditch. Rob scowled and grunted and tugged on Nell's lead to make the hook-horn step it up.

"My mother told me never to ask questions I wouldn't like the answer to," Rob muttered. Then, louder: "Is your heart made of stone, then, man? Don't the sad tales of my youth at least make it twinge?"

On the far slope Karyl stood by the track with the air of a man who had waited patiently for many minutes.

"If the details didn't change quite so randomly," he said, "my heart might twinge a little, perhaps."

"I'm a poet, not a historian," Rob said. "Everything I tell you is true, considered metaphorically."

"Consider my sympathy metaphorical too, then."

Karyl set off into a broad valley of tilled fields. Through it ran the river that formed the border of the province they were crossing, Métairie Brulée—Burned Farm—and Providence. Beyond stood the mixed conifer and hardwood forest known as Telar's Wood, which ran across the Tyrant's Head from Slavia to Spaña. The map said it covered much of the western, narrow end of wedge-shaped County Providence. They had already passed through a kilometer-wide spur of it.

Far beyond the forest, the mighty Shield Mountains climbed the sky. The breeze that blew from them felt cool. To Rob's admittedly fanciful perceptions it seemed to smell of never-melting snow as well as pine, cedar, and oak.

In the course of three weeks on the road, Rob had often enough found Karyl a trying companion. Along with the nightmares that frequently jolted Rob from sleep, Karyl suffered sporadic blinding headaches. When those struck, he was prone to becoming querulous, and sometimes had to ride atop Little Nell with a wet rag tied around his eyes.

But Rob found himself strangely drawn to the

man. The rare story that escaped his bearded lips was a rich reward to a man of Rob's temperament. Not to mention what such reminiscences might be worth to a professional minstrel, cast into song.

And . . . there were the bandits. Just the occasional singleton or pair, seemingly driven by greed or meanness to prey on their fellow men, since this seemed no hard land to live on. Fortunately Rob and Karyl had encountered no substantial bands. Or the larger groups hadn't thought the pair worth bothering with.

Rob knew already that, for a man who professed himself reluctant to use his sword, Karyl was alarmingly efficient with it. Accordingly they found themselves in possession of a few extra coins, for when they felt an urge to slake their thirst with something other than water, or pass a night at a country inn, out of the sometimes-chilly upland weather. Which at least got drier the closer they came to the jagged blue mountains.

Thanks to their earlier brush with bandits, they now possessed a shortbow and quiver of arrows. Rob's skill with these proving greater than he let on to, if only just, they brought a steadier and readier supply of fresh meat to the pot than his snares alone could.

Today both men walked. Little Nell ambled amiably behind, her gizzard stones rumbling as she digested a purple-leaf thornbush she had uprooted in passing. As usual, Rob let his companion keep a slight lead. Not out of deference—or so he told himself— but to keep an eye on him. The nearer they came to their destination, the more focused Karyl became. But along with the dreams and headaches, he was given to brooding, to such an extent that he appeared to lose the outside world entirely. Rob was far from certain Karyl wouldn't simply wander off and be seen no more.

Without warning, Karyl stopped and stood looking to his left.

"What is it?" Rob asked, running a thumb for reassurance beneath the springer-hide strap that held his axe across his back. The Empire's roads were dangerous places—if mostly to the bandits unlucky enough to brace Karyl and Rob. Their whole point in coming here was that Providence was beset by predatory neighbors. And Métairie Brulée was one of them.

Karyl pointed with his sword-staff. Around a ridge half a kilometer to the north lumbered a herd of a dozen spine-backed titans. Long, narrow creatures, green with pink undersides, the largest adults reached thirty meters and perhaps twenty tonnes. Calves a mere ten meters long frolicked between their columnar legs. The giants proceeded at their customary slow, oblivious pace, stripping leaves from the scrub with peg-shaped teeth.

They had no voices: they couldn't force cries down the tremendous length of their necks. From the books of ancient lore, allegedly passed down by the Creators themselves, Rob knew they needed a system of air-tubes along their neck-bones even to move the dog-sized heads at the ends of them. But when they whuffed and chuffed and farted, it carried as far as a shout. You could hear them coming.

Karyl took off his woven-straw hat and wiped sweat from his forehead with the back of his hand. His *left* hand, its fingers mostly grown out but still weak, wrapped in a bandage to protect the soft, pink skin from sunburn. Rob let Nell's lead drop so she could munch the roadside foliage, and joined Karyl to watch the monsters.

Rob knew dinosaurs. Better in some ways than he knew men—and far better, sadly, than he knew women, to go by his record. He'd spent his life around them. Still, the size and majesty of these animals struck Rob Korrigan speechless. He felt as if his flesh and the blood in his veins had chilled beneath his sun-warmed skin.

A sound like a whipcrack magnified a thousand-fold split the air. That was what it *was*. A calf had strayed too close to the woods, which might hide a matador or a horror pack. The herd bull had snapped his fifteen-meter-long tail like Paradise's biggest whip. The sound, which stung Rob's ears even at this distance, brought the young one hustling back, obediently bobbing its head.

"They may not have voices," Rob said, "but they can still talk to each other."

"Indeed," Karyl said. His eyes shone.

"You feel it too?" Rob asked.

"How could I not?"

"Ask that of most of the world, my friend."

The majority of folk viewed dinosaurs as nothing more than tools, toys, or terrors, depending on circumstance. They regarded the beasts as simply *there*, like rocks and trees, and paid them no particular mind unless they were about to be trampled or ripped to pieces by them. But no man or woman became a dinosaur master who ever saw a dinosaur, no matter how small, without a sense of affection that was almost proprietary.

And none could behold one of the titans without a sense of awe verging on religious.

Rob unstopped a water bottle, drank, wiped its mouth with a palm, passed it to Karyl. Karyl held it without looking at it, as if he didn't know what to do with it. Sometimes he needed reminding to perform basic self-maintenance; Rob cleared his throat. Karyl drank.

"Let's move on," Rob said. "They'll always be here. Whether we humans are or not, the dinosaurs endure."

Karyl nodded. He put his hat back on. Clucking to his hook-horn, Rob picked up her tether, and together the three of them made their way onward into Providence.

It was the kind of morning that made it seem as if the Creators themselves smiled on the great enterprise about to begin. The sky for once was clear over Montserrat's head, a canopy of brilliant blue. In the naked light of the sun rising in the west, the Imperial colors and Heriberto's blue, gold, and green almost glowed from the flags on the palace walls. The air was fresh and clean and redolent of the smells of the forest, thanks to the rains that had fallen overnight and then considerately stopped.

All but bursting inside her skin with anticipation, Montse stood by the road leading north from the Firefly Palace's Imperial Gate. Beside her, her father stood barefoot in the simple brown hemp robes of a mendicant of the Sect of All Creators. Montse vaguely understood that was his way of displaying humility and gratitude to those marching out to fight. Not just for him, but for the greater cause of the majesty and authority of the Fangèd Throne, and blah, blah, blah.

She wondered just how humble he thought he could look with her right there beside him in her horribly uncomfortable red-and-gold princess suit, and Chief Minister Mondragón looking important and grave. To say nothing of a whole century of Scarlet Tyrants, red-dyed horsehair crests waving in the breeze, arrayed behind and to both sides of the Imperial party.

Near the Emperor in his ceremonial sackcloth stood the other grandes. Courtiers not bound to go on the expedition tried visibly not to look too relieved. Falk glowered in his beard with his arm in a showy sling. Montse's cousins Lupe and Llurdis blinked out of deep, dark puffy sockets at the sunlight, as if unsure what it was. Josefina Serena wept; nothing unusual there.

Fanny of Anglaterra caught Montse's eye and winked. Montse gave her back a big grin, which she shifted to Abigail Thélème. Abi gave her a quick thin smile. Montse liked them both. Fanny treated her like a little sister. The skinny girl from Sansamour talked to her like an adult. Montse didn't at all understand why everybody thought she was so sinister.

It was a Day of Two Swords: Swordsday, the first Día de Lanza of the month likewise named for the Creator most identified with war. It was the most propitious possible date for a campaign to begin.

Despite the loss of productivity yesterday's tourney caused, multitudes of Mercedes had roused themselves from sleep to trudge through the murk before dawn up the promontory west of the city. Some had never gone to bed at all but roistered the night away in anticipation of this final extravaganza. Efficiency, the Mercedes would call that.

Trumpets blared from the battlements above the

immense bronze-bound gates. The crowd cheered wildly. With a seismic groan, the gates swung open.

Out rode the newly minted Constable on his beautiful dinosaur Camellia. The crowd went mad. The other Companions followed Jaume, no less resplendent than their Captain-General in their white-enameled armor with the Lady's Mirror blazing red from their breastplates.

Jumping up and down, Montse screamed, "Cousin Jaume! Camellia! I love you!"

Turning his bare head ever so slightly, the Constable caught Montse's eye. He winked. Camellia bobbed her round-crested head and snorted greeting.

The Ejército Corregir had spent the night noisily mustering in the palace grounds. Behind the Companions came the Conde Montañazul, his face like thunder above his breastplate, leading his own knights. After them rode the other nobles and knights who had sworn to carry the Imperial banner against the obdurate Count Terraroja. Then came the Companion auxiliaries, the Brothers-Ordinary: five hundred mercenaries and aspirants to Companion with white tabards over their armor, led by the veteran Coronel Alma. In a clearing half a kilometer into the woods, Montse knew, they'd swap their heavy coursers for simple, durable marchadors, as the dinosaur knights would do with their war-duckbills.

Last out the gate tramped the Ninth Legion of the Imperial Nodosaurs. First came the skirmishers and arbalesters in nosehorn-leather jerkins and steel caps, followed by artillerists with heavy gauntlets and shovels. Bringing up the rear of the whole great procession marched the main body of pikemen and women, at once stern and almost defiant in their browned sallet helmets and breastplates, their pikes trailed over their shoulders. Consigned to the rear as lowly foot soldiers, they treated that position as a place of honor, reflecting their status as the last to leave the battlefield.

Montse loved a good show like the Merced she was at heart. She hopped and waved and yelled herself hoarse. But exhilarated as she was by the spectacle, she couldn't quite forget the one figure who was missing from the great event.

Falk's arm ached like lost hopes.

He ignored it. He was accustomed to ignoring pain. He had a lifetime's practice at it.

But he couldn't ignore the emotions warring inside him: frustration, anger, disappointment. Fear that his trick might be found out.

Not that he'd heard a breath of that happening. Instead, his so-called servant Bergdahl had told him, when he came to wake his master with his usual unconcealed glee, that La Merced buzzed with the rumor that Jaume's victory was soiled: that he had performed a foul deed, striking and injuring a foe who had yielded.

Bergdahl, of course, had spent the night assiduously spreading the rumor himself.

Falk caught sight of the man now, a gallows figure looming above the mob of Mercedes on the far side of the road. Instead of watching the gorgeous cavalcade, he was watching Falk with a goblin grin.

Bastard, thought Falk. For a moment resentment of the man—and, yes, of Falk's mother, who pulled Bergdahl's strings—threatened to overwhelm him.

As if reading his master's thoughts, Bergdahl grinned

wider. Once more Falk could hear the words he had spoken as Albrecht helped prepare the Duke for his appearance.

Don't be a fool, Bergdahl had told him. *Enjoy it. You've got free rein, just as we intended. With the Emperor—and his cock-teasing daughter.*

Despite himself, Falk felt his lips extending in a smile. *Yes,* he thought, *I should enjoy those things. I've sacrificed so much for them.*

Alone in a tower that flanked the Imperial Gate, the Princess Melodía stood watching through the pointy-arched window until Count Jaume and his great cream-and-orange mount vanished among the trees.

Turning away, she collapsed onto a stool and wept.

PART THREE

El Jardín de la Belleza y la Verdad

(The Garden of Beauty and Truth)

Chapter 21

Raptor irritante, Irritante, Vexer—*Velociraptor mongoliensis*. Nuevaropan raptor; 2 meters long, 50 centimeters high, 15 kilograms. Commonly kept as a pet, though prone to be quarrelsome. Wild vexer-packs are often pests but pose little threat to humans.

—THE BOOK OF TRUE NAMES

FRANCIA, COUNTY PROVIDENCE

thought this Garden of Beauty and Truth was supposed to be a new thing under the clouds."

The morning air was cool and still, enriched by the smells of moist soil and fresh growth. A pair of robins flew across La Rue Impériale, the Imperial High Road that led from the distant Channel coast to the not-at-all distant Shield Mountains with their peaks still white with snow. Beside it flowed a wide stream called the River Bonté, or Bounty.

The travelers had left Telar's Wood for easy hills and wide fields green with early-season crops. Ahead waited Providence town, the county's seat and principal settlement. Rob Korrigan rode Little Nell, holding his tattered paisley parasol over his head. Trudging alongside, Karyl failed to respond to his leading statement. Nothing new in that.

Rob forged on regardless. "I see that peasants still sweat in the fields," he said, waving at mostly bare brown bodies, shaded by wide woven-grass hats, bent over a field of stakes twined with bean plants. "Doubtless to feed the nobles who stroll in their gardens and philosophize at their ease. It's all still the same."

"You've tilled the soil yourself, have you?" Karyl asked.

"What difference does that make? I too am a son of Paradise. Her soil made my flesh, her rock my bones."

"The nobles could say the same."

Rob scoffed. "The difference is, they're born high, I low. I'm one with the toilers in the fields."

"If you say so."

Rob retreated into a slightly sullen silence. He knew he'd come off second best.

Nothing new in that either.

The pumice metaling the Imperial High Road crunched and squeaked beneath Nell's feet. Even for Nuevaropa, the way was wide and well maintained. Rob said as much.

"Providence is a wealthy province, even if it's a small one," Karyl said. "They do well from trade across the mountains."

"Not all of it licit, I warrant!"

Karyl laughed a rare, soft laugh. "I'd be shocked if it were."

"But you're a nobleman! I'm shocked that you're not shocked."

"Ex-ruler of a March, don't forget—as close to the Shields as Providence. And I was thrown on my own resources at an early age. I'm no more a stranger to smuggling than I suspect you are."

Rob chose to let that pass in dignified silence.

"If it makes you feel better, as voyvod I did do my best to stamp out smuggling."

"Whatever for?"

"It conduced to disorder."

"And how do you feel about it now?"

"That if this current job falls through," Karyl said, "running the border pays better than juggling begging bowls."

A wagon appeared over the hill in front of them. It was tall and narrow, piled high with crates and bails precariously fastened with a drunken spiderweb of hemp rope, swaying behind a single gaunt nosehorn with a forward-curving horn. An old woman and a much younger man, perhaps a boy, sat in the box.

As they passed, both wagoneers scanned the travelers closely, with looks of suspicion on faces shadowed beneath their conical hats. The youth clutched a pitchfork across his washboard chest like a talisman.

"These people must be deeply frightened," Karyl said when the wagon was well behind them, "if they're made that nervous by a pair of ragtag wayfarers."

"You noticed," Rob said.

It was a cheap shot. And utterly unjustified: Rob knew those dark raptor eyes missed very little. He wasn't even sure why he was trying to provoke his companion just now. It wasn't a particularly good idea, for a multitude of reasons. *But ah, when has that stopped me before?*

In any event, as usual, Karyl ignored the bait.

"Our services might actually be needed here," he said. "A good sign, I suppose."

"Just take this street that leads southeast from the square," the laborer said.

He rested his brick hod beside him on the main square's cobbles. His hair was spiked and his face, well seamed and cured by the sun, streamed from a ducking in the water that spewed into the central fountain from the mouth of a fancifully carven fish. Between the stone fish stood figures of naked people, who appeared to be representing allegories that Rob had no clue of. A circle of life-sized statues of the Eight Creators stood at the fountain's center, at the focus of all the piscine water sprays and nude adorations.

The fountain struck Rob as redundant, given that the Bonté ran right along the northwest edge of the square. Nell just stuck her big beaked face into the water.

"It's not half a kilometer out of town," the hod-carrier said over the dinosaur's cheerful slurping. "Can't miss it: it's Count Étienne's old château. He gave it to the Garden when he became a convert."

Rob thanked him. He and Karyl set off down the broad avenue, away from the stall vendors' clamor. Chuckling placidly to herself, Nell trailed after at her rope-lead's length.

Providence town's buildings were tall, narrow, and whitewashed, crowned with steep roofs of ceramic tiles that glistened blue, yellow, red, orange, purple, green, white. Music tinkled from a dozen directions. Between them folk bustled along about their lives.

Children darted everywhere, laughing and yelling. Dogs chased scratchers under carts and between the legs of the nosehorns who drew them; in turn the smaller dogs were chased by domesticated vexers, squalling, toothy bundles of bright feathers and fury. Wafts of local herbs, exotic spices, and hot olive oil announced a thousand suppers cooking.

"It's all so *ordinary*," Rob said. "Masons pile stones on one another. Carpenters hammer. Merchants and customers haggle. The idle gossip on corners. Housewives shout to each other across window boxes filled with insipidly pretty flowers. It's as if nothing out of the ordinary were happening."

"Life goes on," Karyl said. "Even in the midst of war. Although I suspect this Count Guillaume's depredations have yet to reach this far."

A cat with long white fur slouched atop a garden wall. It paused in its toilet to regard the pair with green suspicious eyes. Rob favored it with a ferocious scowl, which it ignored.

"And that damned insouciant beast's the only one to pay us the least attention!"

"Providence sits astride a major trade route," Karyl said. "It's used to outsiders. Far stranger sorts than we wander down out of Ovda, my friend."

"Shouldn't a patrol have stopped us by now? Or at least given us the hard eye? The bastards can't resist leaning on outlanders. Especially ones as trail-worn as we."

"You sound disappointed," Karyl said.

Rob grimaced. "Well—at the very least the Providencers strike me as over-casual for people suffering regular raids."

They passed a stall where an elderly man selling

dried fruit was arguing with a middle-aged woman with short tawny hair and a carpenter's apron of many pockets.

"You can have your strict representationalism," the vendor said. "Give me a painting with allegory. Beauty to the eye and a moral to match."

Rob cocked a brow. "Pardon me," he said, "but are you adherents of the Garden of Truth and Beauty?"

"Beauty and Truth," the woman corrected.

"Whichever."

The Providentials laughed. "Of course not!" the man exclaimed. "We're working folk. Do we look like we have time for such frivolity?"

As he and Karyl went on, Rob let his breath slip out between pursed lips. "I begin to see why the Garden found Providence such fertile soil."

A swath of worn granite slabs, with grass sprouting between them, marked the edge of town. They were evidently remnants of an ancient wall, anciently torn down.

As the hod-carrier had said, there was no missing the villa housing the Garden of Beauty and Truth. The setting sun, a red ball through the clouds, cast diffuse shadows of the great house, with its three stories, multiple gables, walls, and outbuildings, in the travelers' faces. Farther east stretched cultivated fields, flowering fruit-orchards, a rumpling of gentle tree-crowned hills.

Outside a sun-faded blue wood gate, a meter-high stone hitching post stood beside a blooming fig tree and a mossy watering tank. Little Nell rubbed her brow affectionately against Rob's ribs as he tied her tether to the tarnished brass ring. He scratched the skin stretched drum-tight over her frill. She clucked appreciatively. He hung a nose bag over her horn and she settled into munching oats and millet.

"What about your belongings?" Karyl asked, nodding at the baggage piled on the hook-horn's back.

"People are trusting here, my friend," said Rob. "They left valuables unattended all over town. Didn't you notice?"

"And you're just the man to disabuse them of their naïveté?"

Rob laughed. "If you can restrain your impulse to revert to smuggling until necessary, I can keep my light fingers on a leash."

Karyl leaned his own pack against the post. Rob drummed his fingers thoughtfully on his lute case, slung behind Nell's saddle. He took up his axe instead, and unsheathed its head.

"I'm surprised," Karyl said. "They're art lovers here. What if they'd prefer you to play for them?"

"What?" Rob scoffed. "These Gardeners have famously refined tastes. They'd never fancy the likes of my ribaldry and thick-fingered fumbling."

He brandished the axe. "No, it's necks they pay us to strum with steel, not strings."

Slinging Wanda over his shoulder, he knocked on the gate. A young woman in a straw hat and a linen smock with green and soil stains by the knees answered. She showed neither surprise nor reluctance at their request to see the sect's leader. Instead she led them around the villa to a handsomely carved side gate. She opened it and went back to her weeds.

Inside, the head of the Garden of Beauty and Truth strolled among profuse greenery and blossoms and the buzzing of bees. Even without Aphrodite's description, there would have been no mistaking Bogardus.

The erstwhile priest of Maia was a tall man, dressed in a simple grey silk gown trimmed with dark purple. He had a large, fine head, brow high and wide beneath hair the color of unpolished iron. His eyes were grey, his nose straight, his mouth wide, with lips thick enough to be sensuous without being coarse. Despite his professed pacifism, he moved with a grace that to Rob suggested a trained warrior.

As he walked he spoke in a mellifluous baritone, cradling an orange rose in his hands. After him, rapt as scratcher chicks following their mother, half a dozen young male and female acolytes trooped along an aisle with roses on one side and lilac fountains on the other. Their garments were as simple as their leader's—and like his, Rob couldn't help noticing, made of expensive material. No grubby sackcloth here.

In the normal course of life, Rob Korrigan was not a diffident man. Yet he stood by the gate shifting weight from boot to boot, uncertain how to proceed. Karyl gave him no help. He stood holding his grounded staff, a distant look on his face. Rob felt a flash of concern that he might be straying from the here-and-now.

Bogardus noticed them. "Gentlemen," he called. "Welcome to my garden. How may I serve you?"

He let his right hand drop from the rose. A thorn caught at the palm heel. Crimson welled against pale skin.

Chapter 22

Maris, La Dama Fortuna, **Lady Fortune**—Baroness of the Creators: *Dui* ☱ (Lake)—The Youngest Daughter. Represents Fortune and the Sea; justice, fate, mariners, gambling; balance and imbalance; Equilibrium; and Wild Water. Also fish and swimming reptiles. Known for her caprice. Aspect: a slight albino woman with blue eyes and long, windblown white hair, dressed in a white robe, with the *taiji-tu* in her raised left palm. Sacred Animal: terrible mouth sea dragon (often shown devouring a man). Color: white. Symbol: a silver eight-spoked ship's wheel.

—A PRIMER TO PARADISE FOR THE IMPROVEMENT
OF YOUNG MINDS

"Eldest Brother," gasped the brown-haired young man who stood nearest Bogardus, "you've hurt yourself."

"It's nothing," Bogardus said with a smile, "except for a reminder of a truth. Here, lend me a kerchief, if you will." Several were thrust immediately toward him. He accepted one with a nod and thanks and began to wrap it around the wound.

"It's a rare rose," he said, handing it to a young woman with chestnut hair bound up in a silver fillet. Her green eyes lingered on Rob in a way he liked. "A variety developed by the former Comte Carles dels Flors, father of our own dear preceptor, Mor Jaume."

"Imagine that," said Rob, impressed and trying not to show it.

Recalling his mission, he puffed himself up and took a step forward.

"I am Rob Korrigan, and this is my lord the Voyvod Karyl Bogomirskiy."

Bogardus's followers looked at him with handsome faces as blank as fresh writing scrolls. Rob raised a brow. Karyl was a celebrated captain, his exploits widely sung. Even here in the South, only his nemesis Jaume's fame surpassed his.

"So I reckon you don't spend much time in taverns," Rob muttered under his breath.

But Bogardus nodded and smiled. "Your arrival is warmly anticipated, gentlemen," he said, stepping up with forthright stride and hand extended.

"No gentleman I," said Rob, abruptly feeling even more contrary than usual.

"The Eldest is just being courteous," piped up the youth who'd pointed out the wound to Bogardus's hand. "All are equally gentle in the Creators' eyes."

"If you say so," Rob said.

"You're most welcome, both of you," Bogardus said, shaking Karyl's hand. "Aphrodite told me she'd sent you."

Rob blinked. "Aphrodite?" Karyl said.

"Indeed. She visited us here several weeks back.

She said she'd engaged not just one but two champions to help us."

"How in Fae's name did she get here ahead of us?" Rob burst out.

He instantly covered his mouth in alarm. He knew it made him look foolish. *But question the Creators' existence as I might, I know the Faerie Folk are real. And not lightly to be invoked.*

"You know her ways," Bogardus said cheerfully. "She's a witch, you know."

Rob chuckled unkindly at Karyl's frown.

Bogardus gestured at the bandage covering Karyl's left hand. "You're injured?"

"Nothing of consequence."

"It's so good of you to come to us in our hour of need. I'm honored to meet you, my lord."

"Thank you, but I'm no lord," Karyl said, and belied it with a bow of perfect courtliness.

Bogardus smiled with what seemed warmth rather than amusement. He turned the sun of that smile on Rob.

"And you, Master Korrigan," Bogardus said, taking Rob's hand likewise in both of his own. They were surprising hands, square and strong—hands that *did* things. "An honor to meet you as well. I hadn't dared hope that we might acquire two such warriors of note. Truly the Creators smile upon us in our need."

"The pleasure and honor are mine, Lord Bogardus," said Rob.

Bogardus shook his head. "I'm no lord either, my friend. A simple philosopher, rather. And a teacher— that I consider my highest accolade."

"But I do have to say," Rob said, his tongue dragging its feet in his mouth, "I'm no mighty warrior. A dinosaur master, aye. Also a minstrel. A dab hand in a tavern brawl, I admit, but a champion never."

"He's my comrade," Karyl said. Rob looked at him in surprise. His cheeks felt unaccustomedly warm beneath his beard. "He's got more talents than he's confessing. You'll need them as well as mine."

"So Aphrodite told me," Bogardus said.

He turned to the acolytes. "Sisters, Brothers, business beckons, of a nature with which I'd rather not burden your souls. Please excuse me to speak with my guests."

With a marked lack of the graciousness that radiated from their leader, the gaggle broke up and flocked into the villa. Rob caught more than one look of startling virulence shot toward him and his companion. *Not all the Gardeners welcome our warlike gifts*, he thought.

The chestnut-haired woman paused on the marble steps. The glance she cast over her bare shoulder at Rob was not at all like her companions'.

Rob thumbed his moustache as she vanished through finely glazed doors. *It's a frightful job we're taking on*, he told himself, *but it may yet have its compensations*.

"It's hard for me to admit this," Bogardus said, "but we need help. Specifically, we need *your* help."

They sat at ease on curved marble benches surrounded by garden. Out of consideration for their host's sensitive nose, Rob resisted the temptation to take off his boots. It was a pleasant break to be off his feet after so many weary days on the road.

The setting sun shone through scarlet-flowered

vines lacing the arbor that sheltered the table, dappling Bogardus's care-seamed face. Water sang gently in a nearby marble pool, spilled from a ewer on the marble shoulder of the Creator Maris, goddess of Fortune and the Sea. Both of which, Rob knew too well, were notorious for their changeability—and capacity for sudden destruction.

"We're men of war," Karyl said. "The Garden is devoted to peace, if I've heard correctly. What help can we give you?"

"You've heard correctly. From my friend Aphrodite you've also heard how sorely beset we are."

The young woman with the chestnut hair and deep reddish-purple gown materialized from the dusk to place a silver ewer and three flagons before them on the round marble table. Rob caught her eye and grinned, leaning back and cocking one bandy leg over the other.

"A servant?" he said sidelong to Bogardus.

Bogardus smiled as he poured Rob's flagon full. "We all serve the Garden, in our ways."

"We gladly do what we can, Master Korrigan," the woman said, her voice low and thrilling. She turned and walked away. If she made an effort to subdue the movements of her buttocks beneath the thin fabric, it was not apparent to Rob.

He gulped wine. Even he recognized at once it was too good for such cavalier treatment. So he gulped a bit more and slipped a glance at Karyl.

Though the day was still warm, Karyl sat with his cloak held close about him. An arm clamped his walking stick with its concealed swordblade propped against his shoulder. His right hand held his bandaged left as if to hide it.

"We still believe in peace," Bogardus said. "But our neighbors seem bent on forcing us to choose between it and life."

"I understand your Garden follows the philosophy of Count Jaume," said Rob, helping himself to a refill. It was really excellent wine, and his throat was parched from travel. He carefully did not look at Karyl. "Who happens to be the Empire's foremost warrior. And surely no pacifist, so?"

"Indeed not. We do follow Jaume's precepts on beauty and morality. They're wise and beautiful themselves."

He reached to caress one of the woody vines. "And as we've grown our own version of them, we shape his teachings to our own needs. As gardeners do."

"And now you're reshaping them to encompass war," Karyl said.

"Purely in self-defense."

"Fair enough." He tossed back the last of his own wine and set the mug down with a *tunk*. "What's your situation?"

"As you no doubt saw on your journey, ours is a fertile land, placid and well-favored. Our people are prosperous and cosmopolitan, thanks to trade caravans passing along La Rue Impériale. Peace was the norm here for many years before our Garden's seeds were ever planted in Providence's soil."

"So why haven't your neighbors overrun you before?" Rob asked.

"Providentials may never have been warlike, but they have a tradition of standing up fiercely against invaders."

"I note you say 'they' instead of 'we.'"

Bogardus shrugged. "I'm a relatively recent arrival.

I've come to love this land and its people. A good thing, I suppose, since I now somehow seem charged with responsibility for the welfare of both."

"Does Providence still have any kind of army?" Karyl asked.

"The Counts' income has always enabled them to maintain a small but well-equipped force of house-shields."

"But no longer," Karyl said.

"No longer. Count Étienne has accepted our Garden doctrines and joined as a humble Brother, leaving a Council of Master Gardeners—the Garden Council—in charge of the province. A few of his men accepted our ways. Most sought their fortunes elsewhere. And some"—he sighed—"some have joined Count Guillaume of Crève Coeur or his allies."

"Crève Coeur," Rob said. "Broken Heart. Appropriate, if they're back of the raids."

"Knights and barons?" Karyl asked.

Bogardus sighed.

"They have to look to their own lands and castles, they claim. In truth, I don't think all of them look with favor on our experiment here. Egalitarianism is a key tenet of our beliefs. And without a seated count to compel them with oaths of fealty—" He ended with a shrug.

"Threats?" Karyl asked.

"Guillaume's the strongest and worst of our bad neighbors. The Shield Mountains protect our northeastern frontier; Grand Turan currently finds trade with the Empire more profitable than war, and the neighboring pasha suppresses raids across the passes. Which are difficult propositions at the best of times.

"Three Imperial provinces surround Providence:

Guillaume's to the north, Métairie Brulée in the west, and Castaña south across the Spañol border."

"Natural boundaries?" Karyl asked.

"If you came in by the High Road you passed over the Lisette River. It's our border with Crève Coeur as well as part of the frontier with Métairie Brulée. The other half of our Métairie Brulée border is L'Eau Riant, the Laughing Water, which also divides us from Spaña and County Castaña."

"I see."

"Since Providence is now without a ruler, as they see it, our neighboring magnates believe its wealth—and its people—are free for their taking. For now it's mostly Guillaume's knights who afflict us: raiding incessantly, plundering, burning, raping, butchering. Lately they've taken to capturing our people for slaves."

"Slaves?" Rob said. "But that's forbidden by both Creators and Imperial law!"

"Ah, but you see, my friends, no one cares. After all, we are merely heretics. We've even heard of voices being raised in the Imperial Court to wage war against us, lest our beliefs bring a Grey Angel Crusade down on the Tyrant's Head."

For a moment it was as if a breath of ice had puffed down from the high peaks. Rob made the sign of the Lady's Mirror. Not to avert *evil,* exactly: the Grey Angels were evil's polar opposite, the supernatural avengers of righteousness.

It was the zeal—and the thoroughness—with which they avenged it that made them so well feared.

He glanced at Karyl. His companion wore an unaccustomed look of discomfort behind his beard.

Rob couldn't help a certain smug satisfaction. He felt an almost malicious glee in seeing Karyl's distress.

Perhaps I owe him better, he thought, with a wisp of guilt—not the most familiar of emotions to Rob Korrigan. He knew that Karyl's skepticism, his disbelief in Creators and Grey Angels and magic and the Fae and all that mystic lot, had formed the one constant in a life full of travail and uncertainty.

With the regrowing of his severed hand, now all but complete, even that bedrock had cracked beneath his feet. Talking about Grey Angels was like running a jagged fingernail over the ultrasensitive back of his budding hand.

"What do you want us to do, Eldest Brother?" asked Rob, belatedly remembering his role as mediator.

Bogardus laughed. "First, please, just call me Bogardus. I'm trying to break the Gardeners of giving me titles I don't actually claim."

"Fair enough."

"And second—"

Bogardus leaned forward across the table, his eyes glittering like daggers.

"Teach my people how to fight."

Chapter 23

Rasguñador, **Scratcher**—Various species of *Oviraptor.* Nuevaropa breeds: 1–1.5 meters, 5–10 kilograms. Bipedal; short, powerful, toothless beaks. True omnivorous dinosaurs, named for their habit of scratching with hind legs in farmyards for insects, grubs, and seeds. Breeds vary widely in plumage and color. Kept worldwide for egg laying and meat.

—**THE BOOK OF TRUE NAMES**

The villa's banquet hall had been painted with astounding skill. It appeared to have no walls at all. Instead sunlit meadows and hedges bursting with white and purple blooms surrounded it. Vines twined up to and across square roofbeams. Behind a dais at the front of the room rose a tree so realistic Rob half expected a breeze to stir its widespread boughs. Although the wine he kept putting away at a healthy pace may have had as much to do with that as art. Almost in spite of himself he found the effect enchanting.

Rob sat at the large table on the dais. At the other

end Karyl sat next to Bogardus, with a dozen or so odd fish who constituted Providence's ruling Council eating their dinners in between. For a pack of self-proclaimed egalitarians, they looked conspicuously better bred and better fed than your common ruck of Gardner, just as Rob, the ever-cynical, had cynically expected. For some unaccountable reason, a youth who was as obvious a grounding as he was occupied the seat beside him.

The young man nudged Rob in the ribs. The wine had so mellowed Rob that he refrained from giving the lout the clout that he deserved.

"See that servant over there?" the Gardener asked over the mosquito-buzz of a hundred diners. "The grey-bearded old fellow?"

A tall, spare man, elderly but straight-backed in an unbleached hemp smock, stood decanting golden wine on a sideboard by the kitchen door.

"What about him?" Rob asked.

"That's none other than Comte Étienne, former ruler of all Providence."

The talkative young man was of medium height, a bit shorter and less sturdy than Rob, though altogether serviceable. His face was blue-eyed, open, and square-jawed beneath a shock of white-blond hair. Rob had yet to catch his name and was disinclined to make an effort to. It had been a long day.

Even if this lad wasn't playing the supercilious little prick the way the first lot had, Rob would rather have sat beside a female. The Garden grew some lovely specimens. Sadly they hadn't thawed perceptibly toward the newcomers. Except for the green-eyed lass with the chestnut hair, who was nowhere to be seen.

"Is he, now?" Rob said.

"He gave it all up," Towhead said, "to serve Beauty and Truth as a common Gardener."

"Perhaps that accounts for his somewhat sunken-eyed look." Much as he hated the nobility, Rob could scarcely conceive of any of them voluntarily giving up their status.

"Oh, he's far happier, he says. Took the notion from Mor Jaume's own father, Carles, you know. When Jaume was just a boy, all the court gossips claimed he was weak, unworthy to rule dels Flors. Then he defeated the mountain bandits, stilled all those wagging tongues, and the old Count abdicated in his favor. Now Jaume roves the Tyrant's Head as Imperial Champion and leader of the Companions, and Carles administers the county in his stead as seneschal."

"I didn't know that," Rob said. To his mind there seemed a sizable gap between scullion and viceroy. It surely didn't sound as if Jaume's dad had given up more than the title itself.

But what do I know? he thought. *I'm a Traveler, a rogue, and a dinosaur master. To say much the same thing three different ways.*

He turned his attention toward the table's head, where Bogardus spoke earnestly to Karyl.

"Oh, Guillaume's no fool. At least, not a total one. He leaves traffic on the Imperial High Road strictly alone. The Empire may wink at slave-taking among suspected heretics, especially out here on its fringes. The spice and spider-silk caravans from Ovda are another thing entirely."

"That must be why Crève Coeur raiders never troubled us on our way," called out Rob, would felt left out, loud enough to carry.

The intervening Garden Councilors shot him an assortment of disapproving glares and catfish mouths. He met them with a smirk.

Bogardus, calm as ever, simply said, "No doubt."

Heroically refraining from showing the Councilors the Upraised Finger of Triumph, Rob simply narrowed them out of his focus and concentrated on the conversation in which he'd now been tacitly included.

"Are your other neighbors attacking you?" Karyl asked.

"Not as much as Guillaume is. Comtesse Célestine of Métairie Brulée is ruthless and more than ruthless. Her father won the fief by burning the former Count in his own farmhouse, thus the name. She's his true daughter. Other people's pain acts upon her, it's said, the way poetry, painting, and song act on us. She isn't allergic to money and power, though."

"She's a hunchback," Rob's painfully blond dinner partner told him. "It might sour her outlook."

"Raúl of Castaña—" Bogardus shrugged. "He's content to follow if others lead. So long as they lead him toward profit. In fact I suspect he and Célestine both are content to wait until Guillaume commits to invading us. Then when we're engaged, they'll happily fall on us from behind."

"Are they capable?" Karyl asked.

"Count Guillaume is the ablest of the three, although he may be more clever than truly intelligent. He's ambitious. If he possesses any moral compass other than his belly and his peter, no one's yet discovered it."

Rob hoisted his wineglass. "You've the soul of a poet."

Bogardus laughed. "If only I had the poet's skill at words."

Despite his disclaimer and the softness of his tone, Rob noticed how the conversation died away around them whenever he spoke. Most of the diners leaned forward to catch his words.

"You've also got some grip on strategy," Karyl said, "which is more than most. Even those who make a profession of war. Are you sure you need us?"

"Do you like the way the hall is painted?" Bogardus asked.

Karyl shrugged. "I'm no one to ask such a question of. For all my eye and ear for art, I might as well be a lead statue of a hornface. Still, I can see it's well executed. And I like to see a thing well done."

"Fair enough," Bogardus said with a regal nod. "Our finest musicians have skilled fingers indeed. But I'd never ask Jeannette or Robert to paint the hall. Following Jaume, we encourage everyone to find their own voices in the arts; and following him we encourage excellence.

"I know which end of a sword to hold. I know what battle feels like—and sounds and smells like too, much to my sorrow. And I'm no more suited to train or lead our defense force than I am to paint the hall with my feet. That's your art, Mor Karyl."

Rob broke off another chunk of bread and tore at its tough crust with his teeth. It was good bread. Somewhat to his surprise the fare was plain, if splendidly prepared: steamed vegetables, beans with onions, and no meat grander than roast scratcher and bouncer. He ate with appetite, as befit a minstrel who never knew when he'd get the chance again. Especially inasmuch as he and Karyl were here on sufferance, not yet guaranteed so much as a roof over their heads for the night.

Bogardus acted well disposed to his guests, and seemed very much in charge no matter how much he disclaimed formal authority. But Rob reckoned strayed priests weren't much less subject to whim than any other sort of ruler. He certainly sensed ample sentiment among the other Gardeners in favor of sending the travelers off toward the border with a raptor-pack snapping at their calves.

"And speaking of art, and the wonderful painting that surrounds us," Bogardus said, "allow me to introduce the prodigy who made it: Lucas."

He smiled and nodded at the towheaded young man who sat next to Rob. The youngster's face turned pink. He hunched his head down between his thick shoulders and stammered something incoherent.

"In all Providence nobody wields a paintbrush with more skill," Bogardus said.

"Is that so?" Rob asked, turning to regard Lucas with some respect. He'd been wondering what earned the boy a seat at the important table.

"How well can your people fight?" Karyl asked.

Rob heard a joint intake of breath, as if the soft-voiced Slavo had shouted an obscenity.

"Not well enough," Bogardus said. "Not even against armored infantry, to say nothing of armored knights on horseback. Or worse, dinosaur-back. As I said, our people fight fiercely to defend their homes. But they don't have much skill. To tell the truth, our Garden's discouraged even self-defense until it became painfully, not to say bloodily, clear that words and thoughts, however beautiful, couldn't stay the hands of Guillaume's marauders."

Reaction rumbled through the hall. To Rob's well-tuned ears it hummed with something near rebellion.

Do some of these Gardeners disapprove of self-defense? He found that hard to grasp.

"All resistance does is make the intruders angrier," said the woman who sat next to Karyl. "No good can come from violence."

For the first time since Rob had clapped eyes on him, Bogardus frowned. "We've discussed this, Sister Violette."

She was a markedly handsome woman of perhaps sixty—mature, but not yet middle-aged. She was tall and slim, with silvery hair hanging down the back of a shimmery grey gown. Rob judged she'd once been Lady Violette from the softness of her fine, long hands, which clearly hadn't spent a lot of time sunk to the forearms in hot washing water, nor chopping vegetables.

Her age didn't much bother Rob; the older ones were more appreciative of his attentions, if not outright grateful for them. What put him off was the way her lean-cast features had a touch of the raptor to them.

"And we've never achieved a satisfactory resolution, Bogardus," she said. "We can't just jettison our principles because they've grown inconvenient."

Rob thought murder and slave raids a trifle more than *inconvenient*. But judging from the way Gardeners nodded and whispered to each other, that might well be a minority opinion here.

Karyl finished his meal. Laying down his utensils, he sat back and leaned his walking stick against his shoulder. He fixed his intense dark eyes on Bogardus.

"You've been a priest of Maia," he said, "and a soldier of sorts, it seems."

"The Great Mother calls on us to serve in various ways."

"But you arrived eventually at pacifism. Why forsake it now?"

"I've asked the same question," Violette said triumphantly. She looked around the hall for support. Rob reckoned she got more of it than boded well for his and Karyl's employment prospects.

"Reality intruded," Bogardus said. "Where is *beauty* in allowing my fellow Gardeners to be brutalized in the most horrific ways?"

"So you want us to train a land full of pacifists to battle dinosaur knights," Karyl said.

Bogardus sighed. "It sounds hopeless when it's so baldly put. I'll understand if you gentlemen decide it's hopeless in fact and choose to withdraw."

"It would be best for all concerned," Violette said.

Karyl smiled. "We'll need a training ground. Open, a few hectares at least, the closer to town the better. We'll also need a base of operations."

"The old Séverin farm just southwest along the High Road lies vacant, Eldest Brother," Lucas said reverently. "When the father was killed by a matador two years ago, the family moved to town. It's got fallow fields."

"That should serve," Karyl said. "You need to have somebody round up volunteers."

Sister Violette stretched and yawned ostentatiously. "This talk bores us, Bogardus," she said.

"You hired us to take care of the situation," Karyl said, "so there's no need to concern yourself with it further."

Violette's near-pretty face hardened. Rob suspected

she wasn't used to being spoken to that way. It was a new tone in his acquaintance of the man: actually imperious, as if the erstwhile voyvod and much-feared mercenary dinosaur lord was making his return.

Maybe this is good, he thought. *Maybe Karyl's coming out of his fog. So long as he doesn't annoy our employers enough that they run us off.*

"Karyl's right, Sister dear," Bogardus said. His voice was all balm and honey. His smile, though, told Rob the Master Gardener was far from sorry to see the obviously influential Violette get her long nose bumped.

Karyl rose. "Very well. If you can find us quarters for the night, we'd be most appreciative."

Rob stood up as well. It was more of an operation than he'd anticipated. *It seems I've taken more of their excellent wine on board than I realized,* he thought.

Bogardus raised a curious eyebrow. "Don't you want some token of authority?"

"If the people of Providence need to be ordered to defend themselves," Karyl said, "only the Creators can help them."

Chapter 24

Chillador, **Squaller, Great Strider**—*Gallimimus bulla-tus.* Fast, bipedal, herbivorous dinosaurs with toothless beak; 6 meters long, 1.9 meters tall at the hips, 440 kilograms. Imported to Nuevaropa as a mount. Bred for varied plumage; distinguished by a flamboyant feather neck-ruff, usually light in color. Frequently ridden in battle by light-riders, as well as occasionally by knights and nobles too poor to afford war-hadrosaurs. Extremely truculent, with lethal beaks and kicking hind claws.

—THE BOOK OF TRUE NAMES

Not bloody prepossessing," Rob Korrigan said. He sat near the abandoned farmhouse on a mostly intact stretch of fence long since weathered to grey. "I've seen a more impressive lot turned out of a tavern at closing time. Not the best tavern either."

Forty or so volunteers, all commoners, all male, peered back at him and Karyl from a grassy field. Wood and ground and foliage all smelled damp from the rain that had roused Rob from sleep in the early hours, drumming on the Garden manor's tiled roof. He'd noted the fact and returned promptly to sleep. After an arduous month on the road he didn't want to waste a second in the luxurious strider-down bed. Sleeping rough with all of Paradise for a mattress made a nice poetic fancy, which minstrel Rob appreciated. It made a shitty bed, though.

"No doubt they'd say the same about us," Karyl said. He stood next to Rob with hands folded over the top of his walking stick. He'd refused their employers' offers of rich clothes. Instead he wore a new robe of coarse sackcloth not too different from what he'd had on when Rob first found him in the village square of Pot de Feu, but without the hood.

"They've a point, so."

The Séverin farm lay just off La Rue Impériale. Perhaps four hectares of leveled land, now overgrown, it was crossed by a small stream and bounded by feral fruit orchards and a sizable oak and maple wood, both thickly undergrown with brush. The house was two stories of fieldstone and timber in the local style; beyond the windowpanes being broken out or stolen and a pervasive whiff of mildew, it seemed in decent shape. Up here the land didn't reclaim its own with the ferocity it did along the coast, or even on the central plateau.

A small flock of bipedal bouncers, drab-feathered with the season and no more than half a meter tall, browsed among vines and thornbushes that had overgrown a fallen-in outbuilding. From time to time they sat back on thick, short tails to peer curiously at the men fidgeting in the field.

"An ancient wise man of Tianchao-guo wrote that

the longest journey begins with one small step," Karyl said.

"Where?"

"Chánguo is the Spañol name. The Celestial Kingdom."

"Ah. Where they speak the Holy Language as their everyday tongue, poor bastards. Right?"

"Indeed."

The volunteers stood or sat or squatted. Some smoked long, thin clay pipes. Most were townsmen. They affected bright shapeless caps, lightweight linen smocks, either bleached or natural, and colorfully dyed dinosaur-leather shoes. The peasants mostly wore loincloths and sandals, some with straw hats or light cloth yokes to protect their shoulders from the stinging high-country sun; though it was winter, and near the Shields, the day was warm. The countrymen ran to wiry and more than a little grubby. Their urban cousins showed signs of leading easier lives. Or at any rate cleaner ones.

"I don't see any of our friends from the banquet last night," Rob said.

"Look closer," Karyl said. "Your drinking companion, young Lucas the painter, is hovering nervously in the rear."

Rob squinted. "So he is. One Gardener's willing to get his hands dirty, at least."

Karyl stepped forward.

"I am called Karyl," he called out. "My companion is Rob Korrigan. We're here to teach you to defend yourselves."

The volunteers exchanged glances and muttered comments. They didn't seem altogether approving to Rob. He had a fine sense of such things. Any jongleur had to, when even a subtle shift in audience attitude could spell the difference between an ovation and a quick sprint for the kitchen door.

"Weren't you the great mercenary captain, then?" a bare-shanked farmer asked.

"That he was," said Rob, not trusting Karyl's modesty to let him answer.

"And aren't you dead?"

The onlookers laughed. Rob scowled. Karyl showed no reaction at all.

"Who I was doesn't matter," Karyl said. "But yes, I commanded the White River Legion. And yes, I was dead. Clearly I'm not at the moment. We proceed."

Rob couldn't hold down a grin. *That quieted the rabble down,* he thought. Karyl had just secured his audience's undivided attention in a way no bluster or braggadocio could have approached.

For all the years I've spent hero-worshipping the man, he thought, *here and I still find myself underestimating the actuality.*

If he's such a fine performer, a voice from the back of Rob's head asked, *what use are you?* A familiar voice, it sounded like his, but as always reminded him of his mother.

"Ah, but I brought him here," he said into his beard. "That has to count for something."

"Has anyone here fought in battle?" Karyl asked. "Not a street brawl or a tavern fight. Real war."

The men looked uneasily at each other. Rob observed much shifting of weight and shuffling of feet. No one spoke or even looked directly at them.

One man raised his hand. "I have. I've fought Count Guilli's marauders, if that counts."

He stood at the front, a little apart from the others. He was a tall, rangy man with long, shaggy blond hair and moustaches framing his mouth. He wore low soft strider-skin shoes and leather leggings. A panache of brown and silver feathers nodded over one ear. A shortbow and quiver of arrows were slung over his back. The scuffing on the inside of the nosehorn-hide bracer around his left forearm suggested they saw a lot of use.

"More likely hid in the brush like a wood-rat," one of the peasants muttered.

Another spat on the ground. "Woods-runner."

Karyl gave them a hooded look. They didn't have the sense to cringe.

"What's your name?" he asked the woods-runner.

"Emeric."

"So, Emeric. What's a woods-runner?"

"Two-legged vermin," said the first farmer who'd disparaged Emeric. "Cowards and sneak thieves."

He was middle-aged, balding, and bearded, with a leathery belly overhanging his loincloth. Karyl narrowed his eyes at him. He paled.

Karyl returned a less alarming gaze to Emeric. After a moment the woods-runner said, "We're free folk who roam the Oldest Daughter Telar's Wood. She shelters and feeds us. We care for the forest, as best we can."

Rob noticed he didn't deny stealing from the peasants. He'd heard of the woods-runners. They had a doubtful reputation—like own his people, the Travelers. He suspected they deserved about half of it as well.

"Do you hide from Guillaume's men?" Karyl asked.

Emeric's well-weathered face worked as though he were thinking about taking offense.

"When we must," he admitted.

"And you shoot them down from cover, when you can?"

Another pause. Emeric licked his lips. "Aye. When we can."

"Good," Karyl said. "You might live."

He turned to the others. "Anybody else? Surely somebody has some experience with weapons."

A grizzled farmer with a dirty blue rag tied around his head raised a hand. "I've used a spear to keep the harriers and horrors off my beasts and children," he said. Rob noticed he had a long white scar down his right thigh, which might have been left by a raptor's killing-claw. "Most of us countryfolk have done the same."

"It's a start," Karyl said. "Let's pair you off with staves and you can show us what skills you have."

"Who put you in charge?" demanded a young man in town garb. He had a green cap arranged so its peak dangled rakishly down the left side of his face.

Karyl looked him up and down. "A fair question," he said. "Bogardus hired me."

"He doesn't rule us," the swag-bellied peasant declared.

"Watch your tongue," yelled someone from the rear. "The Council rules us all, in the name of the common good!" Only a few heads nodded agreement.

Karyl approached the contentious farmer. "What's your name?"

"I'm Guat," he said after brief hesitation. "The Town Lord Yannic is my liege."

That brought hoots and sneers from some.

"I've been hired to organize and teach you to

fight," Karyl told the group. "It doesn't really matter by whom. The reason I was hired is that I know how."

"But you lost," the green-cap youngster said.

"Name?" Karyl asked.

"Why? So you can get back at me for speaking truth?"

"His name's Reyn," a man called from behind, "a journeyman carpenter. He's Town Lord Percil's man."

"Well, Reyn," Karyl said, "it is true. "I did lose, at the last."

He waved at Rob. "And here's the man who beat me."

That rocked them back on their heels. Rob laughed.

"It was mostly luck," he said, trying to sound modest. "But now you know why to listen to us."

"Why have you all come out today?" Karyl asked.

"Fat Guilli's rangers hunt us for sport," Emeric said. "They ravage the woods and slaughter the beasts for no reason."

Karyl nodded crisply. "And the rest of you? Why are you here?"

"I—I want to learn to handle a sword!" Lucas sang out.

No one else said anything.

Karyl approached the old man with the blue head-rag and the scarred leg. The man returned a defiant glare.

"My name's Pierre," he said. "I can't speak for nobody else, but I came because my lord Melchor told me I must."

"Is that so?" Karyl said. He got back a chorus of agreement.

He told Bogardus we'd have no conscription, Rob

thought. *Some lordling's butt is in for a fine toasting.*
He grinned.

"I thought everybody was equal in the Garden of
Beauty and Truth," he called.

Pierre shrugged. "We peasants still find it better to
obey our lords."

"What about you townsmen?" Karyl asked.
"You're not entailed to any fief, surely."

The townsmen shuffled their shoes in the still-
damp grass and looked everywhere but at Karyl.

"These 'town lords,'" Rob said, "Percil, Yannic,
Melchor—any others?"

"None of consequence," Pierre said. He clearly had
decided he might as well be hanged for a fatty bull as
a calf.

"So they're barons who hold fiefs nearby, but
choose to live in town, am I right?" Rob didn't bother
awaiting a reply. "They're big employers, I'm guessing. Who strongly suggested to the Guild-masters
they should make sure we got some warm bodies."

"You seem to have it all figured out," Reyn sneered.

Rob smirked. "Can you tell me I'm wrong? Thought
not."

"If you peasants join us and fight," Karyl said,
"you won't be bound to your lords anymore."

That made their eyes go as wide as those of an old
tomcat who had just seen a full-grown matador wander into his alley.

"Do you mean that?" a farmer asked.

"Yes. And I can make it stick."

"Won't their lords have something to say about
that?" Rob burst out, astonished as any of them.

Karyl glanced back at him and smiled. "Everybody's equal in the Garden, remember."

Rob shook his head. "They're not going to like it."

In fact it offended *his* sense of the natural order of things. He chose not to mention the fact.

"If the town lords don't like it, let them defend themselves. I'll command real volunteers, or go elsewhere."

"Can we talk about this?" Rob asked, sotto voce.

"Also," Karyl declared, "you'll all be paid. Not handsomely. Your families can eat. And you can drink—off duty."

"Paid?" Rob squeaked. "By whom? We've scarcely got two centimos to clink together!"

"You'll grant I was the premier mercenary captain on Nuevaropa," Karyl said to him.

"Oh, aye."

This time Karyl grinned like a deinonychus. "Then believe me: you *can* squeeze blood from a stone. If you know whose stones to squeeze."

"And there's loot," called a townsman, an apprentice to judge by his age and shabby dress. "Plunder. And—and ransoms for rich nobles!"

"Don't rely on getting rich from this war," Karyl said. "The idea's to defend yourself and your neighbors, not beggar the people of the next province."

"They make war on us!" a peasant shouted. "Let the bastards suffer!" Many cried agreement and waved fists in the air.

"They make war on you because their lords order them to," Karyl said. "It's not peasants raiding your lands and pillaging your homes. It's nobles, and their knights, men-at-arms, and mercenaries."

"Then why should we fight them, if not for a reward?" Reyn demanded. "They haven't troubled the city yet. They wouldn't dare!"

"Why wouldn't they?" Rob said. "Who's to stop them, if not you?"

The "volunteers" looked at him in confusion.

"But they've got great nasty spears and horses," old Pierre said. "And armor."

"And war-dinosaurs," another man said. "How can we face dinosaur knights?"

"In all Nuevaropa," Rob said, "there's no one better to teach you that than Lord Karyl."

He was immediately afraid his lapse would get him yelled at. Instead Karyl said, "We can follow the example of friend Emeric, here. Strike from ambush. Never fight fair. I've . . . been a nobleman myself. We bleed and die as readily as you do. You just need to learn the chinks in our armor."

The crowd fell to squabbling with one another. Some seemed outraged at the notion of not fighting fair—which struck Rob as flat insane. Others more sensibly wondered what good a handful of defenders might do against Crève Coeur's might, however cunningly they fought. And some demanded to know why they should risk loss of limb and life while others sat home getting fat.

The woods-runner stepped up beside Karyl and Rob. "I'll fight!" he cried.

Lucas shouldered through the bickering mob. He had the shoulders for it too, Rob noted.

"I'll fight too, Lord Karyl," he said, blue eyes shining. "Just teach me how! It's all I ever wanted."

"Beware getting what you want, son," Rob said gruffly. If the boy-prodigy painter heard him over the crowd, he showed no sign.

The dispute continued as if it would never end. "They'll never come 'round at this rate," Rob told

Karyl. "Why not just order them? Force them to heel!"

"Remember what I told Bogardus? If the people here need to be commanded to defend themselves, I can't help them. Anyway, I'm done with compelling people to follow me, even if I could. I can't handle the responsibility. I doubt any man can."

Rob shook his head in disgust. "Maybe we should just cut our losses and go. We can't bloody fight Guillaume and his steel-shelled friends by ourselves!"

"We'll find the means," Karyl said. "If not these men, something else. There's always another weapon to hand, if only you look."

He's actually starting to enjoy this, Rob thought. *And they say I'm bloody mad?*

"Besides," said Karyl with an oddly gentle smile, "look to the west, my friend.

"West? Whatever are you on about?"

Rob turned. The farmhouse roof was steep. Above it a plume of smoke rose dirty brown against white clouds. It didn't seem close, which meant it sprang from a substantial blaze.

"What, you've eyes in the back of your head, now?"

"I keep my eyes moving," Karyl said. "I find it cuts down on unpleasant surprises."

Some of the crowd had noticed the smoke now too. Fingers pointed. The word *fire* began to be spoken with the customary dread.

"Ho!" a voice cried from the High Road's elevated right-of-way, beyond the neglected house. "Hey there, you men!"

A strider with its green feather ruff drooping and brown sides lathered with sweat came spraddle-legging around the stone flank of the farmhouse. A middle-aged woman in a torn, bloody smock rode it bareback. Her grey hair and eyes were wild. Soot smudged her haggard cheeks.

"Blood! Fire! Murder!" she cried. "Count Guillaume's men have burned St. Cloud! The people are scattered, slain, enslaved!"

"St. Cloud!" the carpenter Reyn exclaimed. "Impossible! That's not ten kilometers from here."

"I told you so," Rob told him. But he was staring at Karyl as if his companion of the road had just made lightning flash from his fingertips.

"We're lost!" the woman wailed. "We're helpless to stand against them!"

"Don't worry, madame," Pierre called out. "The free folk of Providence will set the bastards straight!"

The whole crowd cheered.

Chapter 25

Volador chato, Chato, Bug-chaser, Snub-nosed Flier—
Anurognathus. Common small pterosaurs; up to 9 centimeters long and wingspans of 50 centimeters. Short
tails, short muzzles with needlelike teeth; insectivo-
rous. Like almost all fliers, covered in short fur.
                    —THE BOOK OF TRUE NAMES

The road marched at an angle up one side of a
narrow, densely wooded valley. Hours after
the intense dawn rain the air still lay thick
and heavy as a feather-felt blanket. Moisture beaded
on big splayed leaves.

Steam rose from the backs of dray beasts, nose-
horns and horses, and wisped from the sodden slouch
hats and feather yokes of the drovers who kept them
trudging up toward La Meseta. The humid air muted
their whipcracks and curses. The wheels of heavy-
laden wagons crunched on the broken seashells that
covered the road. The morning's rain kept the dust
down, but on the right-of-way, the smells of sweat,
urine, and dung almost choked Jaume.

With relief, he turned the cream-colored marcha-
dora he rode at the brisk amble she was bred for off
the road into a clearing on a level stretch. But his relief was short-lived.

"Strange fruit grows in these woods," called Wouter
de Jong as Jaume rode up with several Companions.

Mor Manfredo stood with his lover Fernão the
Gallego, Wouter, and a quartet of husky Ordinaries
in mail and white surcoats at the base of a great
white-boled plane tree. He gave his head an irritated
shake. The sturdy Brabantés with the short, almost
white-blond hair seldom said much. When he did, he
didn't always choose his words as well as he might.
He and Manfredo remained best friends, though, no
matter how Wouter exasperated the Taliano.

Jaume winced as well. The two men dangling by the
necks from two stout branches still kicked spurred
heels with the final fading reflexes of broken necks.
Their white, grey, and black liveries were stained and
sticking to their faintly tinkling hauberks. The Ordinaries were shouldering the axes they'd used to break
the ladders from beneath the condemned knights,
preparing to return to their comrades.

"Ominous fruit," called Florian, swinging down
from his mule. "This'll bring trouble."

Jaume dismounted. Upslope from the clearing, two
hands of Nodosaur skirmishers in springer-leather
jerkins and browned steel hats filed along an unseen
trail. They patrolled with crossbows cocked to discourage trouble from leaping out of the undergrowth
at the vulnerable supply train. They glanced incuri-
ously at the hanged men before disappearing into the
undergrowth.

Manfredo scowled. His pride was as prickly as his rectitude was stern. Florian's sense of humor particularly chafed the Taliano knight.

"Do you object, Brother?" Manfredo asked. He didn't mention that Jaume himself had ordered the executions. Jaume doubted it occurred to him to do so.

"Not at all," Florian said. "It's trouble we were soon due in any event. Speaking of which, I do believe I see it coming down the road."

Taking a few steps back toward the causeway, Jaume saw a small party of knights trotting down the landward side of the traffic. Their colors matched the dead men's. At their head Jaume recognized Desmondo, Conde de la Estrella del Hierro himself. Even a hundred meters off, Count Ironstar's big face was visibly twisted and mottled with rage behind his imposing iron-grey moustache.

"This is a sorry affair," Jaume said. "I wish there'd been some other way of handling it."

Manfredo's long, exquisitely sculpted features showed distress. "Captain! They committed rape and murder!"

"Yes. And you've done a good thing well. I ordered them hanged with a clear heart. Our charter mandates us to punish evildoers, after all. But I can acknowledge the necessity of the thing without *liking* it."

The irate Ironstar rode up with a pair of his barons in tow. Jaume inclined his head courteously. "Count Desmondo."

The Count was a big man, with long grey-shot hair framing a face whose square jaw had begun to blur beneath the weight of years of easy living. His tunic was black, with his arms—an iron-colored falling star on white escutcheon—sewn on the breast. He had a reputation for preferring massive force to subtlety. It worked for him: an immense nickel-iron meteorite had fallen on his province centuries before, and its ore still gave him the wealth to support enough knights, dinosaur-mounted as well as horsemen, to bring it off.

In fact, Ironstar commanded the army's largest contingent of men-at-arms after Montañazul. He typified the grandes under Jaume's nominal command. An aging but formidable fighter, he wasn't actually stupid; he just exercised little control over his impulses, and saw less reason to learn the knack.

"Don Hilario!" he cried, raising black-gloved fists to the patches of sky visible through interlaced branches overhead. "Don Cecilio! What has been done to you, *mis hijos*? Creators, who can be responsible for this outrage?"

"No need to bother the gods, señor," Florian said. He waved at the slowly twisting bodies. "There you see the guilty parties. Set your mind at ease: they've gotten justice, as you can see."

Jaume's face tightened. Of all the men he had accepted into the Empire's most exclusive military order, he had felt the most misgivings about Florian. He still did. The Francés knight had a flippant attitude, and trouble controlling his tongue.

Ironstar's grey-bristled lips worked in and out. It made him look like a large, exotic fish. Even Jaume had to bite down on laughter.

"This is intolerable," the Count bellowed. "You've murdered my knights! *Madmen!*"

"These men raped and murdered a peasant woman,"

Jaume said calmly. A sluggish breeze stirred his hair around the shoulders of his white tunic. It carried the perfume of magnolia blossoms as well as less pleasing odors. "My Brothers caught them in the act. They've paid the price under law."

"A peasant woman?" Ironstar's face turned from maroon to white. "A *peasant*?"

His words came nearly voiceless, as if squeezed out by a titan stepping on him.

"How *dare* you?"

"I'm quite expansive in what I dare, my lord. Especially when it comes to enforcing my lawful writ as Condestable Imperial."

"But—" Ironstar waved his hand wildly. "To hang belted knights, *my* knights, over some peasant slut? Dishonor—"

His passion was getting the better of his elocution again; the last word emerged as a squeak that rose to inaudibility.

Jaume nodded as if concurring. "Dishonor is exactly what their actions have brought upon the Ejército Corregir and the Empire itself. I've seen what happens when an army gives into lusts and lawlessness. It won't happen in an army of mine."

"You dare prate about *lust,* you—you filthy libertine?"

Easy, Jaume told himself. He forced himself to draw a deep breath.

"Step aside with me, if you will, my lord," he said. "Let's discuss this discreetly, montador to montador."

Ironstar shied away, making his stallion toss its head and snort. "I won't go off where you can work your black sorcery on me without witnesses!"

"What?" Jaume exclaimed, taken utterly aback.

"Mind your language!" said Manfredo, shocked. "Our captain's a Prince of the Holy Church."

"Some mistakes ought be rectified," the Count growled.

"Here," Jaume said, desperate to regain control of the conversation. "There's no need for this kind of talk, *caballeros*! What I wanted to say to you, Don Desmondo, is that if we treat the people of the lands we pass through as enemies, they'll soon turn into enemies in fact. You don't want that, surely?"

"You dare to lecture me? You salacious popinjay, I'll teach you manners!"

His hand dropped to the hilt of his arming-sword. Florian interposed himself with a matador's liquid grace.

"Draw blade on your commander," he said silkily, "and you're attainted."

Ironstar went pale. *Attainder* would make him an outlaw who could be killed out of hand. It would also reduce his entire family to commoner status, and forfeit all his titles and properties to the Fangèd Throne.

"Draw sword on *me*, on the other hand," Florian went on, covering the pommel of his rapier with his palm, "and you'll have no problems at all."

Ironstar turned away. "I wouldn't sully my blade."

"Oh, don't worry, my lord," Florian said. "Small risk of that."

"Bastard!"

"Why, yes, as a matter of fact, I am. And that's the least of it. I had the basest of births: my mother was a street whore in Chanson, my father a stranger who cheated her. Yet here I am, made gentle and a montador by the hand of our Captain-General, as confirmed by His Imperial Majesty himself. A miracle of the Creators almost, no?"

Estrella del Hierro spun his horse and spurred it back up the road. His barons followed.

"We haven't heard the last of this," Wouter said. "Ironstar's gone off to cry to Bluemountain. Whose hand he licks like a dog his master's."

"It's not as if they've been subordinate so far," Florian said.

Jaume sighed. "We don't need more discord, my friend."

Several other Companions had come up to watch at a discreet distance, ready to back their Captain-General at need.

"We're passing through Noisy River," said Bernat, the stolid, slab-faced Catalan who served the Companions' as official chronicler. "We're right next door to County Ironstar. Desmondo hates his neighbor the Conde del Río Ruidoso. That's probably why he lets his men abuse the peasants."

Manfredo scowled thunderously. "When we were still in the Tyrant's Jaw, they didn't dare act up for fear of Prince Harry and the Emperor. Since we left, the whole army's acted like invading Turanians. The captain was right. At this rate we'll be lucky if we don't have to fight our way through even loyal lands."

"I don't *understand,*" Dieter wailed. Actual tears glittered in his long black eyelashes. "How can they do these things? What happened to the duty of the strong to protect the weak?"

Even Manfredo the legalist shrugged at that. "It's an ideal," he said, "more than a practical reality."

Wouter dropped a big hand on Dieter's shoulder.

"Son," the Brabanter said, "that's the reason they have *us*."

"Well, that tears it," Rob said. "Why are we lingering, anyway? With the marauders striking that close to Providence town, we'll be lucky not to have them on our necks before the sun's all gone."

He glanced back down the High Road toward their farmhouse headquarters. They were heading to the Garden villa to report to Bogardus. Sunset stretched their shadows across the River Bounty toward Telar's Wood to the west. The day had cooled quickly. The air smelled of the running water. Snub-nosed fliers skimmed a finger's width above the river, hunting insects.

"If we lit out now we might escape with our hides."

Karyl shook his head. "Relax. They won't attack the town. Not yet."

"And what makes you so sure?"

Karyl gave him a look.

"Be that way," Rob said. "Tell me how you managed that oh-so-convenient bit of business with the raid, then."

"I wish I knew," Karyl said. "The Witness did say she thought I was touched by destiny."

Rob blinked. "You made a joke!" he exclaimed. "Next thing I know you'll be turning handstands through the public square!"

"Unlikely," Karyl said. "I left that behind in Pot de Feu."

"So, d'you believe at last in destiny and magic and the touch of the Fae?"

"No." But Rob saw the uncomfortable way his

friend closed and opened the fingers of his new hand, as if stretching the still-tender skin.

They left La Rue Impériale before reaching the town, cutting across fields and through a woodlot. As they approached the Garden villa through the twilight, a figure stepped away from its shadowed western side. Rob raised his axe, Wanda, from his shoulder, ready to whip away its stout nosehorn-hide case in an instant. Karyl didn't react.

Then Rob saw the pale-yellow hair and relaxed. "Lucas, me lad," he said. "You gave me a turn."

"My lords," the painter called. "A moment of your time, please."

Rob's reflex was to disavow lordship. Out of politeness, or perversity, he deferred the task to Karyl. Instead Karyl said, "What do you want?

"Please teach me to fight."

"Isn't that what we're doing?" Rob asked.

"I mean, *really* fight. Properly, with a sword, man to man. Not just in a bunch of other men with long, pointy sticks."

Rob laughed. "Why should we?" Karyl asked.

"I'll help you! Any way I can. Anything you want me to do, just tell me. But please—teach me swordplay!"

Karyl studied him. He seemed more attentive somehow than Rob had yet seen him, even when he was taking lives. Maybe *especially* then.

"It's a lot of work," Karyl said. "It will take time away from your painting."

"I understand that. I'll find time to paint and practice both. I'm not afraid of work. I'm told I'm good with my hands, although I've never really wanted to do anything but paint. Uh, until now, that is."

"If you become more skilled than your comrades, you might find yourself asked to take more risks than they do."

"I'll happily take them. Please!"

"And you're willing to do what we tell you without question."

Lucas sighed. "Anything," he said. "I . . . I just want to show I'm not the ineffectual dauber my father always said I was. Before he disowned me, that is."

Rob grunted and scratched his chin. *Well struck, lad,* he thought, *whether you know it or not. Admitting you've a belittling prick for a father can scarcely hurt your case with our Karyl.*

"Very well," Karyl said. "I will train you in sword craft. Roust out some volunteers. Get a work gang together and clean out the farmhouse. Have it done by midmorning, when Rob and I assemble the troops again. Make it ready for us to live in."

At that point Rob expected Lucas to back away quickly. In his experience, artists lacked a taste for hard manual labor. He wasn't overfond of it himself, though as a dinosaur master he saw more than his share.

But the boy almost unhinged head from neck nodding his acceptance. "Thank you, lord! You won't regret taking me as your student. You won't!"

"See that that's true," Karyl said. And to Rob's astonishment the young man straightaway set off at a trot for the High Road.

Chapter 26

Torre, Torrey—Baron of the Creators: *Gen* ☷ (Mountain)—The Youngest Son. Represents Order (yet he's the Trickster), law, bureaucracy, priests, smiths, miners, masons, and Mountains. Also burrowing animals. Known for his authority. Aspect: a powerful blond youth with a gold mail hauberk over a brown tunic, holding a hammer and a shovel. Sacred Animal: ferret. Colors: brown and yellow. Symbol: a golden tower.

—A PRIMER TO PARADISE FOR THE IMPROVEMENT OF YOUNG MINDS

ook at this."

Jaume trailed fingertips along the ruined wall, savoring textures. Red-veined vines had suckered their way up the remnant, which in places still stood twice as tall as Jaume. Round-arched windows pierced it, long bereft of glass. Jaume recognized the style as dating from the Years of Trouble: the first two centuries of known history, before the Empire rose.

"As always, the forest reclaims its own," Florian said.

The two men walked at sunset through an abandoned temple. The ruin lay a short way down a thickly wooded valley from the clearings where the army had bivouacked for the night. The breeze rustled branches spiked with narrow leaves as cuatralas, tiny raptors, glided between them on front and hind legs that were feathered like wings. Insects trilled welcome to the coming night. The sounds of beasts bawling and men calling played faintly in Jaume's ears.

Fortunately the wind carried smells of the nobles' retinues down a valley away from this one. Too many grandes resisted both army regulations and the rather brisk words of the Creators on the subject of *hygiene*. Jaume resisted the urge to pity himself.

At least he found Florian's company congenial. Surprisingly so. The golden-haired Companion seemed to understand that *silence* could convey as much beauty as sound.

"No," Jaume told him. "Here."

Despite thick forest canopy, the day's heat still lived in the yellow sandstone. He touched a hand's-width swath where the gritty surface had turned smooth.

"It's vitrified," said Florian, leaning close to look. "Melted to glass and then reset." A skilled smith as well as painter, Florian well understood matters such as the casting of metal and glass, which were mysteries to Jaume.

"What could do that?" Jaume asked.

"A lot of heat," Florian said, straightening. He smoothed back a lock of hair sweat-glued to his forehead. "But where could it have come from?"

"Any number of sources, couldn't it?" Jaume said. "A forest fire, perhaps?"

"That wouldn't get hot enough."

"A nearby volcano? A meteor strike?"

"There's no sign of either near enough and big enough to cause this. Even after centuries, even as fast as the undergrowth returns, we'd see some evidence. Anyway, how would heat sources like those just leave streaks?"

"Lightning, then?"

"I don't think so. The path is smooth, and meters long. If you look around there are other such tracks glazed along the walls. Also . . ."

He parted jagged vine leaves to reveal a small alcove. Carved beneath it was the glyph of the Youngest Son, a solid line above two broken ones. Empty now, it must once have held a small statue or icon of Torrey: tall, blond-bearded, usually shown cradling a ferret in his hands.

Torrey was the Creator associated with order, strength, and solidity. He was also the Trickster among the Eight. Each Creator embodied both sides of the coin, as it were: Maia was goddess of death as well as life-giver, and the Lady Herself, whose element was Fire, represented both Beauty's flowering and inevitable decay.

"We're inside the old walls," Florian said. "Would lightning have struck here?"

He fingered his chin, which though somewhat long did not spoil the perfect symmetry of his features. *In ways it's a pity he never takes men for lovers,* Jaume thought. *He's probably the prettiest among my beautiful Companions.*

Not that it mattered. As Captain-General, Jaume would take no lovers from among the Companions or their auxiliaries. The rule against sex with subordinates applied to him most strongly of all. Pere, of course, had been the exception; that was a continuation of a relationship bonded tight when both were youths.

Poor Pere, Jaume thought. *I'll always love you. I'll always miss you.*

"It may be irrational," Florian said, "but this reminds me somehow of battle damage."

Jaume shook his head to clear away the vision of his friend and lover's eyes, huge and reproachful through the Channel water, and the great shadow swelling from below to carry him down and away forever.

"What weapon could score and melt stone like that?" Florian admitted there was none such. "No, my friend, you're right: your fancy's getting the better of you. Could lightning have struck after the temple collapsed?"

It occurred to Jaume that despite his misgivings, he felt comfortable calling Florian "friend." He wondered when that had happened.

"Something's preoccupying you, though, Captain," Florian said.

He kept his tone light, on the edge of bantering, as he normally did. The fact he used Jaume's title showed how serious his intent really was.

"It's the army," Jaume said. "The progress we're making—or not making. It cuts up my stomach like broken glass."

"I know what you mean. We're a week on the march, with at least as long to go to reach our goal, and here

Terraroja lies no more than a hard day and night's ride on a good mount from La Merced."

He shook his head. "And what can we expect? It took us two days to chivvy the bucketheads out of the clearing inland of the palace where the full army mustered. It's like herding cats."

Jaume laughed. "It's a mystery: if my lord Bluemountain and his peers are so eager to get at the foe, why do they drag their heels every millimeter of the way?"

"Not that mysterious. Each is as reluctant to give up the slightest scrap of prerogative as he is eager to spill blood."

"I don't understand it," Jaume said. "We've campaigned alongside nobles before. They always tend to be dense and impetuous by turns. But never like this."

"It's the Life-to-Come sect," Florian said. "Pío's Legate openly preaches it. And naturally the bucketheads love it: it turns all *The Books of the Law* on their heads, and gives free rein to their hunger for rape and blood and plunder at the expense of those they consider inferior."

"You may be too cynical," Jaume said.

"And you may not be cynical enough. No mistake, Captain: we love you for being too good for this world. But it'll bring you heartache."

Jaume's smile was bittersweet. *My heart already aches as much as it can, I think.*

"There's something else bothering you, isn't there?" Florian asked.

Jaume sighed. "I should have been there for the execution today. If I order ugly things done, I should be there to witness them."

"Ah, but you had to race off yet again to prevent Montañazul and that fearsome woman who commands the Third from having at each other with dirks over right-of-way."

"The Brown Nodosaurs are the finest infantry in the world," Jaume said. "In five hundred years, they've never run from the field of battle. Yet the grandes despise them as mere peasant 'residue'—no better than their own beaten-down levies."

Florian laughed. "And our Coronel van Damme returns their contempt with interest." The Nodosaurs prided themselves on being as prickly as their armored, spike-shouldered dinosaur namesakes.

"She's got little more use for me than Bluemountain and the rest of the nobles do," Jaume said. "She makes that clear enough. But she'll give me no trouble on her own account. The Nodosaurs pride themselves on their professionalism. I'm her commander; she doesn't have to like me to obey. It's the same rule she's lived by since she joined the ranks as a pike-pusher." Which was rare. Usually women Nodosaurs served as skirmishers.

"The Imperial infantry looks down on everyone who isn't one of them," Florian said. "Except your uncle the Emperor."

"He *is* one of them," Jaume said. "At least, he's a former pikeman. He's the only occupant of the Fangèd Throne who's ever known what it feels like to carry four meters of hardwood shaft and a meter of iron head on his shoulder all day in the heat, and the terror and exhaustion of fighting in the phalanx. They love him for it, as if he were both father and son to them."

"Eloquently put, Captain. You should be a poet. But—are you sure that's all that's eating at you?"

To cover his wince, Jaume stooped beside a cluster of white night blossoms where the broken wall stub fell away to the springy mulch of the forest floor. Because there were several, he felt no hesitation in plucking one. He rose, holding it to his nose, savoring its thick perfume and the resiliency of the stem between his fingers.

"Isn't that enough?" he said.

Melodía, he thought, *I write you every day. And all I hear back is silence. Have you really turned your back on me, my love?*

He longed to relieve the pressure of pain in his heart, to let some out. But he didn't feel close enough to this mercurial Francés yet for that much intimacy.

They left the confines of the ancient temple, moving up the game trail that led to their camp. At once the sound of rustling came through the gloomy growth ahead. Both men put hand to sword hilt.

Florian laughed.

"By the sound I thought we were about to be charged by a matador bull," he said. "Dieter, my boy, you've much to learn about stealth."

As usual, Dieter wore his emotions on his face as clearly as if portrait-master Pedro the Greater had painted them there.

"What's the bad news?" Jaume asked lightly.

"You—you have a visitor, Captain," Dieter said.

"So it's, 'when Rob and I assemble the troops,' now, is it?" Rob said on the villa's doorstep. "What's the role Rob Korrigan plays in assembling troops, then? I'd hardly know which part goes where."

"I need you to help me teach them," Karyl said.

"Teach? Teach what?"

"Everything. You taught them during weapons drills this afternoon."

"That was more by way of supervising: keeping the lads from busting each other's heads and arms. But I had to dump a few on their asses to do it. I'm not sure how fine a lesson that may be. Though I suppose they did learn Rob Korrigan was not a man to be fucked-about with."

"That sounds like teaching to me," Karyl said, without a tint of irony.

"Does it, now? You who never so much as raises his voice, much less a hand?"

"I've had more practice," Karyl said. "It's a skill, like any other: you'll learn by practice. Anyway, everyone has his own approach."

"Which might be my salvation, I suppose," Rob grumbled. He was thinking, *How do I learn your skill of looking at a body fit to freeze flames solid?*

The fact was he had felt as if he were floundering in waist-deep muck all afternoon. All he knew about teaching came from his own experience of being taught by his old master, Morrison. Which, boiled down, was: *sooner or later it all comes down to a sound thrashing.*

He caught himself asking just who he might be, to question the great Voyvod Karyl? And shook his head in self-disgust at that.

Especially since he knew he was hooked already. *Not the first time my weakness for hero-worship has sprung up to bite me on the ass, and doubtless not be the last.*

"So why'd you try so hard to dissuade the boy from dedicating himself to the sword, then?" Rob asked, mostly to change the subject. "I thought you were anti-art."

"I'm dead to it now," Karyl said, "although I wouldn't try to ban it any longer."

"Why, then?"

"I hate waste. That's all."

"Right," Rob said. "Well, I'm hungry and thirsty. So let's go in and make our report."

"Wait."

The quiet word stopped Rob with his foot raised to the step. He turned back.

"You've received the payment promised for delivering me?" Karyl asked.

A moment of silence passed, during which Rob's mouth tasted of copper and a bell seemed to ring in his head.

"Yes," he said at last, unwilling to risk trying to slip a lie past those dark raptor eyes. "Last night Bogardus took me aside privately and gave me the money Aphrodite had left."

"So will you stay?"

Frogs croaked down the darkness. Insects chirped and sang back from the trees. Terror-moths blundered about around the two men's heads, occasionally brushing cheek or brow with butter-soft wings whose backs were patterned like screaming wide-eyed faces. Tiny snub-nosed fliers flitted in pursuit, snapping at the moths with needle teeth. Detached wings and body parts fell like soft carnage rain.

Heat crept up Rob's cheeks. He didn't know what Karyl meant by that question. Instinctively he feared it.

"I suppose," Rob said with a carelessness he didn't feel. It rang false to his own ears.

Yet for a fact, where've I got to go? It's not as if anyone's clamoring for the service of a dinosaur master sacked for showing up his blue blood masters.

"Do you mean it?" Karyl asked.

"Do you want me to? And how did you know about the money, anyway?"

Karyl chuckled softly. It shocked Rob in a way, as if it came from a full-grown tyrant bull.

"It was the only way it could be. All men must eat. All women too. You performed a service in expectation of pay."

"Well—yes. Yes I did."

"I'm a mercenary. I don't share the disdain of *commerce* my class so cherishes. I was raised to look down on it, but I got that nonsense bashed from me soon enough on the exile's road. High Ovda isn't like Nuevaropa. It's drier. Living's harder. And I always had to make sure I was more valuable alive than shopped to Baroness Stechkina's assassins. So I sold my services as a caravan guard and made my way east."

Rob flinched and blinked violently as a half-eaten abdomen arced in to hit him in the eye. It dropped away at once, but he wiped furiously with his thumb at the residue he could feel wetting his cheek like an entrail tear.

Karyl cocked a brow. "Carry on," Rob said, waving his free hand at him. "I'm fine."

"Or rather, I sold *Shiraa's* services," Karyl said. "I was a kind of appurtenance, like a saddlebag, albeit admittedly useful for keeping her from eating the wrong people. I was a boy, skinny as a willow branch and not terribly skilled at arms."

Rob was rapt. It was as much as he'd ever heard Karyl say about his own past—details the legends and ballads had never covered.

If I survive this . . . whatever-it-is I find myself embroiled in, he thought, *I'll dine richly for the rest of my days spinning whole new songs into the Saga of Karyl Bogomirskiy.*

"So—you don't resent it that I took gold to deliver you like a parcel?"

"How could I? I took money for wringing labor from my own people by force. I took money for *killing*. You betrayed no confidence; you did me no harm. And to tell you the truth, you've brought me something I thought I'd never know again."

"What's that?"

"A spark of joy in my life. It's a *challenge,* preparing Providence to defeat dinosaur knights. I may not be up to it. I certainly can't do it alone. That's why I asked if you meant to stay."

Rob's breath caught in his throat. *The great captain wants me to help him?*

That other part of him, the cynical observer—or was it the realist?—observed that, despite his disinterest in and professed dislike of *passions*, Karyl knew quite well how to stir them in others.

"What do you want me to do, my lord?" he asked.

"Help me as you did today. And also, I need you to be my quartermaster."

"I'm honored beyond—wait. Quartermaster, did you say?"

"I did."

"But I know nothing about it!"

"You're a dinosaur master. You know how to get your monsters provisions and proper housing."

"Well . . . yes."

"Soldiers need those things too. The local men can live with their families for now, but the rest will need to be quartered. At that, even the locals will start to gripe if the outsiders get meal stipends and they don't."

"Sure and that's Creators' Gospel. But here, now, what about this Lucas—"

"An eager lad. But he's an artist, a Gardener in full bloom, and as practical as a paper shield. I wouldn't want to rely on him to keep me fed."

"Since you put it that way—"

"We'll also need sanitation seen to, in a hurry." Rare as disease was, in Nuevaropa at least, a lack of proper disposal of bodily wastes inevitably caused an outbreak that cut down men and beasts like an arrow storm. Even as *The Books of the Law* promised.

"Providence is rich," Karyl went on, "with its commerce and its silver mines. How long that will remain true, with so many hands turned to fighting and to . . . whatever it is the Gardeners do . . . is an open question. For now, they can afford to pay. And they're going to have to."

"You want me to tell the Council that?" Rob asked in wide-eyed terror.

"I'll tell them," Karyl said. "They dislike me already; I might as well start giving them reason. But I still need someone to do this work. I don't see Emeric in the job. And no one else has given me the least reason to trust him to pour piss from his own boot if the instructions were engraved on the heel."

"It's not the future I'd exactly envisioned for myself."

"Then hurry and train up a successor so you can move on to something else. Will you do it?"

Rob swallowed. "Yes."

Karyl clapped him on the shoulder. "Good man. Come on, then. We've lots to discuss with our employers before we can eat. If they let us."

Chapter 27

Lagarto-pescado, **fish-lizard**—*Ichthyosaur.* A common type of sea dragon, a swimming reptile resembling a fish, with long, tooth-filled jaws (or, some fancy, the fabulous *dolphins* depicted in *The Bestiary of Old Home*); 2–4 meters long; 950 kilograms. Eats fish, shellfish, cephalopods, and occasionally each other. Sailors' tales notwithstanding, rarely known to attack humans.

—THE BOOK OF TRUE NAMES

The smell met Jaume like a barrier when he entered the tent. It felt like emerging from a cool cloister into a hot and humid night. If the night blossoms outside the ruined temple down the valley had smelled like a corpse rotting in a perfume lake, the man waiting for him smelled like a corpse thrown into a cesspit, with a wheel of lamentably far-gone cheese thrown in to add body.

"My lord Bishop," he made himself say politely. He went to the end of the table opposite his guest and sat in a folding wooden chair, on a satin cushion colored cream and butterscotch. Leaning back jauntily, he cocked a leg over one arm.

It'll take days of airing-out and half a liter of rose attar to make the place livable again, he thought with bitter amusement. *Ah, Uncle, the things I do for you.*

"I will not sit," his visitor said, as if Jaume had invited him to.

"Suit yourself. May I offer you food? Drink?" Jaume gestured toward a covered plate and silver water pitcher on the table.

"Your men offered me refreshments of the flesh," the Papal Legate said. "I have no need of them."

Ever? Jaume was tempted to ask as he took a peach from a basket beside the covered dish. He was glad Florian wasn't here. He would have said what Jaume was content merely to think. Which would not, in the long run, have made matters easier on the march.

By the time Jaume and Florian got back to the Companions' camp, the night had expanded to fill every corner not occupied by separate light: of bonfires, of torches pungent with resin smoke, black and thready. Mor Jacques had intercepted him, worrying up with the latest reports of aristocratic waste and folly: three knights and some number of servants no one bothered to tally, dead in a tent fire caused by drunken roistering idiocy; a peasant's hayrick deliberately burned, for what passed among the bucketheads as fun. Jaume gave what orders he thought might do some good. For the most part all he could do was listen and commiserate.

At his pavilion waited Manfredo, looking even graver than usual. Jaume had commanded his three knights to stay outside. He'd had to be brisk about it.

"How may I serve you?" Jaume asked his guest. He

bit into the peach, savoring its flowery sweetness. He refused to give in to ugliness. And anyway, a campaigner who let bad smells spoil his appetite got awfully hungry.

"You committed what some would judge a grave offense today against Count Ironstar, my lord."

"Surely not as grave as those committed by the ones I punished," Jaume said. "I will not tolerate rape and murder. If Ironstar can't control his knights, and they won't control themselves, it falls to me to do so. As Constable I hold the High Justice. I dispensed it."

Bishop Tavares stiffened. The Legate was a deceptively slight man, younger than Jaume, with wild black hair, a stinking robe, and grime-black sandaled feet. He wore a necklace of wooden balls, each as big around as a trono, from which hung a green wooden pendant shaped like a wreath. It showed three gold lines: two broken stacked above a solid. It was the glyph of Adán, the Oldest Son, god of manhood, and of mammals, of agriculture, commerce, and wealth. As well as ruination, destruction, and impoverishment.

"When the Eight created this world, they saw fit to raise certain folk above others, as more suited to rule," Tavares said.

"So much is generally accepted."

"Those chosen to rule enjoy rights and privileges over those they rule."

"And the ruled enjoy rights in turn," said Jaume. "By Imperial law. As well as the Creators' word."

Tavares smiled thinly through a beard that consisted mostly of neglect. Jaume sized him up as extremely dangerous, in the way of one who never drew steel himself but inspired others to wield it for him.

"You refer to the words' obvious import," Tavares said. "The profane. But isn't it clear to any truly spiritual man that anything so obvious cannot really manifest divine intent? The pure truth, the holy truth of the spirit—that lies *behind* the words."

"I disagree. I trust my Creators to say what they mean."

"Certain nobles of the realm have taken up the burden of prosecuting this just war against evildoers. They must be allowed to exercise their just prerogatives. That's clearly the Creators' will, even you must admit."

"As long as they confine their prosecution to evildoers," Jaume said, "we don't have a problem. We're crossing loyal lands here, my lord Bishop. How long will they stay that way if we despoil them?"

Tavares's eyes blazed. "If they're loyal, why aren't they marching with us?"

"Because, as you point out, we've taken on the errand ourselves. I don't make Imperial policy. My task is to carry it out as best I can. Maintaining order in this army is paramount to that."

"No!" Tavares screamed. His sudden fury took Jaume aback. "You must not raise the flock above the shepherd! Your ideas will bring anarchy to the Imperio, as they have to Providence!"

"Providence?" Jaume shook his head. "I haven't followed events there closely. But what I have heard hardly smacks of disorder." In fact the Gardeners struck him as basically hobbyists, harmless and more than a little silly.

"They turn the divinely ordained order upside down!"

Putting both hands on the table, Tavares leaned forward. Jaume steeled himself not to recoil from the stink of his body and breath.

"Such impieties risk bringing a Grey Angel Crusade down on us all," Tavares said, his voice now sinuous and low. "Have a care, my Lord of the Flowers."

Jaume could hardly believe he'd heard the man right. *He must be mad,* he thought.

"Grey Angels? No one's reported them walking Paradise for centuries. Whatever transpires in some small, remote province of the Empire, I hardly expect it will bring them out."

"Don't think it won't happen just because it hasn't happened in our age. The time is coming, my lord. The reckoning approaches. Souls will be judged. Men will have to choose which side they stand on."

"Not I. I serve the Lady Bella, and the Emperor. And my men, and the innocent."

Tavares's mouth worked and he squeezed his eyes shut as if in intolerable pain. Jaume watched in fascination that felt almost voyeuristic. *His features are so bone-spare,* he thought, *you wouldn't think they'd have room to express so much passion.* He wondered what went on behind that furrowed forehead.

"And His Holiness the Pope?" Tavares finally asked, his voice still soft. "He acknowledges the truth: that the Creators' words are allegory, and that to seek salvation one must look past them to the truth. You're ordained by the Holy Church. Aren't you bound to follow where His Holiness leads?"

"If His Holiness disputes the Holy Law, that every man and woman's conscience is free so long as they acknowledge the Creators, he can tell me so himself. He has not done so." For the first time Jaume allowed his own expression to harden. "Nor has Pío seen fit to confide in me his purpose in sending you to accompany the Army of Correction."

"Saving souls, my lord. Only saving souls." The Bishop sighed. "I don't envy you, Count Jaume."

He waited enough heartbeats to realize Jaume wasn't rising to that bait. "You have eyes, but will not see the truth. Your obstinacy puts more than your own soul at risk."

Jaume didn't see that that deserved a response. So he made none.

"And the burden on your own soul must be great indeed," Tavares said, "given that so many voices within the camp are whispering that you won your baton unfairly, striking a dishonorable blow against a yielded foe. I bid you good evening, Count."

They found Bogardus sitting in the high-walled courtyard in front of the Gardeners' villa, beneath a trellis twined with trumpet vines whose orange flowers had shut up shop for the night. He sat on a silk cushion in a chair carved of limestone that showed signs of long weathering. A bevy of young Gardeners leaned forward raptly on stone benches to hear him hold forth. All were women, Rob couldn't help noticing, and decidedly comely.

Bogardus smiled when he saw the pair approach. He rose. "Ah, my blossoms, enough for today."

Blossoms, is it? Rob smoothed his moustache with a thumb. *I wonder if mine host would object if I sniffed a few?*

"But, Bogardus," whined a skinny brunette in a blue smock, "we'd barely begun."

"Of course, dear one," the Eldest Brother said. "If we talk together for a century, we'll only nick the surface of deep loam. Beauty is infinite, and so is Truth. Even our little patch we've staked out, this Garden of ours, is bigger than a single mind can hold. So contemplate what we've learned tonight. Seeds are planted. Let them grow!"

Bogardus laughed. He had a deep, infectious laugh. The women laughed with him, even the one who'd pouted. They got up and went inside, chattering excitedly about the cosmic insights the Master Gardener had shared with them.

Watching them go, Rob felt himself frown. *Nary a look for young Rob Korrigan,* he thought. *And nary a whiff of my chestnut-haired beauty, who's the only bloom I've found in this Garden that doesn't close up tight at my approach.*

Ah, well, perhaps she's avoiding me. She's hardly the first.

As soon as the door closed, their host's manner turned grave. "I've heard what happened today. We saw the smoke from here. Thirty killed or carried off to slavery. A terrible tragedy."

He caught the cocking of Rob's brow. "Does it strike you as frivolous, Master Korrigan, that we sit here in the comfort of our Garden discussing philosophy while such horrors happen nearby? I quite understand. But what can we do? We're not warriors. It's why we have you. For us . . . Paradise turns. Life goes on."

He put big hands, pale yet strong, on both men's shoulders and steered them toward benches.

"Come, friends," he said, "refresh yourselves. I'm eager to hear how your first day's training went."

"Well enough," Karyl said as Bogardus poured them light yellow wine from a silver pitcher. It was cast to resemble a mythical sea beast called a "dolphin," which much resembled a fish-lizard but possessed unnatural-looking horizontal flukes for a tail.

"The lads brightened considerably when we gave them a bit of swordplay," Rob said, emptying his cup at a draft. Bogardus refilled it without even setting the pitcher down.

"I'll want to train most of them on weapons closer to whatever tools they're used to using," Karyl said after wetting his throat with a sip. "Time's short."

Bogardus nodded. "If the raiders have gotten bold enough to attack St. Cloud, it's shorter even than we feared. Refugees streamed into town all day. They're sheltering with families there now, poor souls."

"Why haven't the Brokenhearts raided Providence town, I wonder?" Rob said. "It's the fattest target by far, even in a country as rich as this."

"Everyone fears a city fight," said Karyl. "It's all at dagger range, no room to maneuver, with every window an archer's loophole, every intersection an ambush. And of course, the roof tiles."

Rob stopped his cup halfway to his lips. "'Roof tiles'?"

"I share our dinosaur master's perplexity," Bogardus said.

"Those tiles up there," Karyl said, gesturing toward the villa roof with his fully formed but still-pink left hand. "What would you say they weigh?"

"I've never thought about it," Bogardus said. "They certainly look hefty enough, don't they? They can't weigh less than five kilos apiece, or so I'd guess."

"At least," Karyl said. "Now think of them thrown down at you."

Rob made an O of his mouth. "I see," Bogardus said.

"They'll easily smash an unprotected skull or limb," said Karyl. "I've seen such tiles dent in morions and break shields. They'll bruise a duckbill where its hide is thickest. And horses and dinosaurs alike panic when heavy things start to rain down on their heads and shatter at their feet."

"So we're protected here despite ourselves," Bogardus said.

"Until the marauders grow arrogant enough not to care anymore," Karyl said. "Or greedy enough. Both will come."

In the silence that followed Karyl's assessment, Rob heard a tenor vihuela being played somewhere inside the villa. Not without skill, he judged, but the instrument had a loose E string.

"We'll want to visit the armory tomorrow, to see what's available by way of weapons and armor," Karyl said.

"It's large and well stocked," Bogardus said with a relish that surprised Rob. "You should be pleased at what you find."

"You mean you've not yet beaten your swords into plowshares?" Rob asked.

Bogardus's long upper lip pulled longer. "From the outset I've tried to steer the Council clear of such conceits. I've long known, deep inside, we would come to this someday."

He sighed. "Perhaps my own faith in the power of our message is not as strong as it could be."

"*Nobles,*" Rob snarled. "They've little regard for

truth. Or beauty for that matter, except as a thing to rape and ravage!"

The other two men looked startled at his sudden vehemence. His cheeks hot, he took a hearty slug of wine to recover his composure.

"Was your turnout satisfactory?" Bogardus asked after a moment that went on far longer than Rob felt comfort with.

"I'll not lie to you," said Rob, feeling the excellent wine spread its warmth inside him. "It was a trifle on the meager side."

"The lords are ordering their tenants to volunteer," Karyl said.

Bogardus's grey eyes narrowed. "That's not what I told them to do. Please believe me."

"I told the men that those who volunteer will be declared free, and have their debts forgiven."

Bogardus's brows shot up. Then he grinned.

"True to the Garden's spirit, my friend. Of course, the town lords may see things differently."

"The town lords' country houses are richer targets than villages of huts with thatched roofs," Karyl said. "And no matter how well fortified, less risky than Providence town. They'd best learn to see things my way before they're forced to.

"Speaking of which, you need to send to all the county's knights and barons and ask for their help. Tell them it's in their best interest to send it straightaway."

"The town lords and country barons are proud, powerful men," Bogardus said. "What compulsion would you have me use against them?"

"None at all. Simply tell them assistance works both ways. If they don't send us men, when the raiders come to burn them in their fine homes, they may expect us to turn out to toast bread on the flames."

Bogardus laughed—a trifle shakily, Rob thought. "You are a rare man, Karyl Bogomirskiy."

"No doubt," said Karyl, "that's just as well."

Chapter 28

Your Highness," the Pope said to Melodía over a golden tureen of strider-tail and vegetable soup. "Certain rumors have reached my ears."

For Melodía the usual dinnertime hubbub in the banquet hall was abruptly overridden by ringing silence. Hearing nothing but the drumbeat of her own pulse, she showed Pío an expression that was more pulling her cheeks up under her eyes than an actual smile. The eyes of the courtiers at the great table seemed to sear her skin.

Nuevaropan culture distinguished *nudity* from *nakedness*. Being nude in public could signify ritual, exaltation, an important statement, or even social superiority. Being naked in public was humiliating.

Despite the fact that she was fully dressed, in emerald silk wound in an X across her breasts and a loose brown and cream silk skirt, Melodía felt naked.

"Holiness." The unfamiliar effort of trying to sound conciliatory made Chief Minister Mondragón's voice grate like horror claws on granite. He sat at the head of the table on Felipe's right. "One mustn't believe everything one hears."

The Emperor continued gnawing happily on his roasted bouncer haunch and conversing with Duke Falk on his left while grease rolled down his little ginger beard as if nothing untoward was happening. The Pope waved a hand like sticks bundled in a splotched and blue-veined parchment.

"Rumors persist, my child, that you speak out against your father's good and wise policy of carrying war to the vipers who nest in the Empire's bosom."

The expressions the conversation had turned on Melodía ranged from disdain through incomprehension to lust. That last came from her always-vexing cousin Gonzalo, who sat a few places down from her with his brother Benedicto hulking beside him.

The closest thing to compassion she saw gleamed in the eyes of Falk von Hornberg, which matched the royal blue of the tunic he wore tonight. She looked away quickly. She was not prepared to deal with sympathy from him.

Pío peered intently at her. The skin around his eyes

was as grey and wrinkled as the scales around a thunder-titan's.

You arrogant old reptile! she thought with a blood-hot rush of sudden anger. *You think you're going to intimidate me into backing away from the truth?* She slammed back her half-full goblet of the golden wine of Trebizon.

"You heard right, your Holiness," she said. She knew how to make her voice blare like a trumpet, and she did. "I love my father. But he's made a horrible mistake waging war against his own people. The time has come to heal the Imperio, not gash it with fresh wounds!"

Courtiers uttered theatric gasps. Pío blinked slowly. His cheeks colored.

Melodía glared at her father as if this were all his doing. He was sitting with a chunk of coarse brown bread in his hand, looking completely befuddled.

Mondragón cleared his throat. "Holy Father of us all," he said, "she's only a child. She doesn't really know what she's saying."

"I most certainly do!" Melodía shouted, jumping to her feet. She could *feel* the delicious malice in the murmur that rose with her.

Angrily she marched the length of the table. As she passed him, Gonzalo favored her with a smug little V of a smile in his obsessively trimmed goatee. She shot him the finger, and so departed her father's hall and glittering company.

"You certainly kicked over the hornet's nest with your little outburst at dinner tonight, Día." Somehow Abigail Thélème made the spike-frill mask she wore, spun together from beaded blue and silver glass rods, look delicate. "Why didn't you just spit in the Pope's eye and preach Fae-worship while you were at it?"

"I hardly think that's a tactful thing to say, under the circumstances," said Princess Fanny. Her half mask had the likeness of a regal carrack-bird, with a dark green crest and pearly cheeks.

"I'm political, not tactful," Abi drawled. "You've confused me with your mother."

"My mum's quite political, really, in her jovial, pink-cheeked Anglysh way."

Prince Harry's festival hall was every bit as huge and grand as his great hall, and considerably better lit. The better to make the costumes sparkle, and bring their million colors alive.

Or *masks*, anyway: this was *un gran baile de máscaras*, conducted in strict accordance with the latest La Merced fad. Which, Abi assured Melodía's ladies, as usual followed the Francés capital Lumière by two years, faithful as clockwork. All must wear masks, with prizes to be awarded at the end of the night for the most beautiful, the most ornate, the most amusing. Garb was supposed to be modest, so as not to detract from the masks.

Of course, *modest* was a relative term. Both skin and ostentation were on plentiful display, Melodía saw.

The chamber was packed with gaudy celebrants, although the servants, well experienced, showed no difficulty sliding among them like eels through seaweed. Looking around, Melodía saw a number of figures she recognized readily despite their hidden faces.

Not far away from the patch of wall where she and

her retinue congregated, she spotted Falk's brute bulk. The Duke wore a black tunic, hose with one leg white and the other deep blue, and a black bird-mask with open toothy beak. Melodía supposed it was intended to be his totemic falcon, but as far as she was concerned it looked like a crow.

As usual, he was attended by a flock of the young bravos, small-holding knights and second sons, who had descended on the city in the wake of Felipe's declaration of war on Terraroja. Frustrated at having arrived too late to join the Army of Correction, they continued to flutter around the court, hoping for a chance for glory or at least trouble. Falk's dark radiance drew them like moths.

Currently they orbited him at a wary distance. Falk was arguing heatedly with one of the servants, a beanpole with immense hands and lank hair of indeterminate color. By the rules of the ball, the attendants went masked as well. Whereas most contented themselves with simple dominos, this man wore one fashioned in the startlingly lifelike likeness of a dull-plumed horror.

Melodía let her eyes slide across more masks: of dinosaurs and sea serpents, of persons historical and legendary, of fabulous and no doubt mythical animals drawn from *The Bestiary of Old Home*. She spotted Mondragón's tall, gaunt form, hard to mistake even if he hadn't been wearing his usual black-and-brown robes. Even the Chief Minister's toothy plesiosaur mask, clearly modeled on the stuffed one hung in the banquet hall that once gave young Melodía nightmares, looked dour.

Where Mondragón was, Melodía's father was nearby. Sure enough, there among the dancers the somewhat portly and none-too-tall Emperor showed a brisk and not-badly turned leg alongside a much stouter Anglaterrana duchess who was visiting Prince Heriberto. Her white gown made her look like a paper lantern topped with a pale-green mask of the Creator Maris, inhumanly beautiful and maned with wild blue-green seaweed. Felipe's mask was the tan brindled with dark brown likeness of Hercules, his beloved great dinosaur-hound, fatally gored by a wild nosehorn on a hunt a few years before.

As the band struck up a brisk canario, Josefina came stumping up to protest, "But, Melodía, why aren't you wearing a mask?"

"It's the best mask of all," Melodía said brittlely.

The scion of the Principality of the Tyrant's Jaw herself had on a translucent white human mask painted with what struck Melodía as a look of hideous glee. "Fina," Abi told her, "I worry about you sometimes."

"That's not even original, Día," Guadalupe said. Her voice echoed off the hollow underside of her sackbut half mask. Jewels surrounded the eyeholes and gleamed in lines up its long back-sweeping crest. In keeping with the night's rules, she wore a plain green gown, but splashed in yellow, evidently to suggest the dinosaur's coloration. It put Melodía more in mind of a run-in with an incontinent Parasaurolophus than the animal itself, but she knew her mood was jaundiced.

Llurdis pushed up beside Lupe to jab her in the ribs with a thumb. "That's impertinent!"

Melodía stared at her Catalan kinswoman open-mouthed. Not content with a mere round-crested Corythosaurus mask in pale blue and rose, she had on an entire duckbill *costume*, complete with a meter-long padded tail that imperiled all those who happened near. Cutouts in the bulbous body let her ample bare breasts hang through. Glued-on circles of sapphires outlined the nipples. Aside from being in what Melodía found shockingly bad taste, the gemstones' color didn't suit Llurdis *at all*.

Melodía looked away to see the servant walk away from Falk, haughty as an archbishop. Falk stood glaring after him through his falcon eyes, clenching and unclenching black-gloved fists. One of his hangers-on, who wore the semblance of the ancient stage character Emphyrio, made a sly-voiced suggestion that Falk should have knocked the impertinent fellow down.

Before Melodía could catch the Duke's response, Lupe turned and gave her friend's false flank a shove. It flexed with a blooping sound. *Telar knows what it's made of,* Melodía thought.

"Leave off!" Lupe snarled.

Llurdis struck Lupe's shoulder with the heel of her palm. "Don't hit me!"

Lupe punched furiously but ineffectually at the boat-hull hadrosaur torso. It went *bloop, bloop*. Llurdis slapped at her hands.

"Bitch!" Llurdis said.

"Sow!"

"¡*Puta!*"

Melodía's stare turned from shocked disbelief to fury. The pair showed every sign of being about to launch one of their full-blown wrestling/lovemaking bouts, out here in front of Melodía's father, the gods, and everybody.

"They're like a pair of cats, really," Fanny murmured.

"Ladies," Melodía hissed, "I'm *this* far from having some husky menservants grab the both of you, spank you, and throw you out on your stinging pink asses."

"Really?" Lupe said.

"You wouldn't dare!" puffed Llurdis.

"Girls," Abi said cheerfully. That itself was a warning as loud as a temple bell rung after midnight. "You may have noticed our Imperial mistress is feeling a bit testy tonight, yes? Tread warily."

Melodía gave her a glare. Then she jumped as she felt a strong, warm pressure enfold her left biceps.

She spun to find the Duke of Hornberg looming over her like a cliff. "You look like you could use a rescue," he said.

She yanked her arm away. "I can rescue myself, thank you kindly, your Grace." She shot him a withering glare. He failed to wither.

"May I steal you for this dance, then?" he asked as lightly as his basement-baritone voice and guttural Northern accent would allow.

"Well," Melodía heard herself saying, "just this one."

Chapter 29

Hogar, **Home, Old Home**—When they were done making Paradise, and found it good, the Creators brought humans, their Five Friends, and certain useful crops and herbs here from the world we call Home. Ancient accounts teach us it is a strange place. It is cold, and we would feel heavier there, and find the air much thinner. The year is 1.6 times as long as ours. We must admire the fortitude of our ancestors in dwelling on such an inhospitable world, and always praise the Creators for bringing us to our true Paradise!

—A PRIMER TO PARADISE FOR THE IMPROVEMENT
OF YOUNG MINDS

magine those brigands, so close to our city!" Rob heard a woman say shrilly as he and Karyl entered the Garden villa's dining hall. His heart headed promptly toward his boots.

He still had no clear idea how many members—or plants, whatever you'd call them—the Garden boasted. Right now he judged there were maybe sixty dining in the big hall. On the dais sat the seven Master

Gardeners of the Council and Bogardus. Rob didn't know whether Bogardus was considered part of the Council or not.

Not that I care, he thought as he looked around for a nice inconspicuous place to sit and eat. *So long as we get paid regularly in good silver from the erstwhile Count's coffers.*

"Ah, Voyvod, Master Rob," Bogardus said in his best preacher's voice as he rose from his central place. "Come and join us, my friends."

"Yes," said Sister Violette from his right side. "Join us." She sounded less welcoming.

"Nicked again," Rob said under his breath. Karyl strode toward the front of the hall with head high, the same way he approached everything. Rob followed, all but scuffling his soles like a truant schoolboy.

At a sign from Bogardus several Gardeners vacated seats from the table nearest the dais to make room for the two. "So that's how the land lies," Rob said. "No seats at the high table for the great captain and his dinosaur master."

"We're hirelings," said Karyl, unfazed.

"I did not forget that."

As he sat, Rob polled the Council with his eyes. Violette sat smiling with her somewhat wide and thin-lipped mouth, while her namesake eyes suggested her meal would be greatly improved by the sight of Rob's and Karyl's livers roasting together on a spit. Of the rest, Rob had learned that Absolon, Longeau, and a woman named Nia were her allies. Iliane and Cuget didn't much care for Violette and didn't much care to hide it. Out of the whole bouquet arranged behind the high table, only a man named Telesphore and Bogardus didn't look at the newcomers as if they'd stepped in fresh dogshit right outside the dining room.

A Gardener on steward duty came up behind Karyl and Rob to pour them each a mug of wine. Rob smelled honeysuckle. His appreciative eyes took in the swell of a hip in a thin burgundy gown, then slid up a willowy torso.

To meet the smiling green eyes of his chestnut-haired beauty of that first evening in the garden. "I'm Jeannette," she said.

"I'm Rob."

"I know."

She sashayed away before he could utter the various gallantries that were jostling each other to escape his mouth. *I admire a girl who knows how to sashay,* he told himself, watching the fascinating interplay of her left buttock with her right. They put him in mind of two puppies in a pillowcase. *It's a lost art in our crass and caviling age, it is.*

Above them the Councilors were twittering at each other. "They'll be carrying us off to the slave markets next," Longeau declared. "It's a scandal."

"Indeed it is," Violette said, pitching her voice to carry.

Rob looked up to see her smiling down on him. Now her expression suggested the benign regard of a Black River boarcroc who'd just spied a plump fatty calf.

"Ah yes," she said. "And here sit our costly mercenaries, swilling our wine and preparing to gorge their gullets on the produce of our Garden. One might ask what they're doing to protect us?"

"What we came to do, madame," Karyl answered calmly, setting down his mug and wiping his mouth with the back of his hand. "Teaching your people to defend themselves."

"Teaching?" demanded Longeau, his voice throbbing with outrage. It throbbed a bit too much to be genuine, as Rob, a master of the spurious, was quick to detect. "*Teaching?* When marauders pillage almost within sight of our city towers?"

A tall, bulk-bodied man with dark hair cut square above a sagging oblong face, Longeau was another so-called town lord. His barony, Rob gathered, lay near the border with Castaña and the Spañol frontier.

Rob smelled honeysuckle again, and hot bread and warm spices. Jeannette was back, serving them a fresh-baked loaf in a basket and plates of roast-nosehorn slices with vegetables cooked in savory sauce. She smiled at Rob again before vanishing into the kitchen.

"In fairness," said Cuget, a middle-sized man who had a head round as a catapult ball and lank yellow hair, "you should do something to stop them."

"You overestimate what the two of us can do," Karyl said.

"You could fight for us!" Longeau said.

"I noticed you weren't present at the training grounds today, lord," Karyl said. He looked around a suddenly silent room. "In fact I don't recall seeing any of you. Except for young Lucas the painter."

Red-faced, Longeau mumbled something about his health and pressing engagements.

"You've begun training our defense forces?" asked Bogardus. He knew the answer, of course. But he wanted to make sure the rest of the Garden heard it.

"Yes," Karyl said. He knew the game, and was willing enough to play along.

"And they will be ready to protect us soon?"

"They need time to train, but yes."

Bogardus smiled broadly. "Splendid. Then let us dine, and drink, and listen to music, and speak of beautiful things."

Not all the Councilors looked best pleased at that. But Violette gave a pretty little shrug and turned to chat with Longeau. The other Councilors returned to their meals, conversing in less strident tones and not looking at the two hired champions.

Rob emptied his cup. "This won't end well," he said to Karyl.

"It's a mercenary job," Karyl said. "They don't end well. You should know that by now."

"You're a regular Sister Sunshine, you are."

Karyl ignored him.

Honeysuckle scent seemed to fill Rob's head. Jeannette had leaned down to refill his mug. He raised a brow and took the opportunity to look down the conveniently sagging front of her gown.

"When you're done here," she whispered, "meet me in the garden where we first met."

She was gone. *Elusive as a butterfly, she is,* Rob thought, picking up his mug and sipping reflectively.

Still, doomed though the job may be, the evening could well be looking up.

It was their third dance.

Elbows interlinked, Melodía and Duke Falk paced the stately steps of a pavane. Two lively dances in a row had preceded it, a galliard and a vuelta. During the latter, Falk had put both big hands around her waist and hoisted her in the air as if she were Montserrat. That took her by surprise. He was a husky lad, to be sure. But at 176 centimeters, she wasn't small, and her slender frame was well muscled.

His broken arm had healed quickly. At least, he showed no sign it still pained him.

Melodía's sides and forehead ran with sweat. She was glad she hadn't worn a mask.

Faces fanciful and fantastic were turned to watch them dance. Doña Carlota stood by a wall, radiating disapproval through her black domino. Melodía knew she'd hear all about this later.

Uncharacteristically, her ladies-in-waiting ignored the swarm of swains, mostly Falk's hangers-on, that buzzed around them like mosquitoes. Instead they stood, stared, and talked sidewise at one another.

That's not a good sign, Melodía thought. And: *Let them. Let them all scorch their eyeballs on me dancing with Jaume's rival!*

"Those two," Falk said, nodding his beautiful block of a head as he raised a knee and pointed a toe. "The nosehorn and the tyrant. They stare at you more avidly than all the rest. Do they desire you?"

She laughed. It must have sounded a bit wild. She felt him recoil slightly.

"Yes. But not the way you're thinking. And that's not just a tyrant. See? Red and gold? That's an imperial tyrant."

"Like the one slain by the esteemed progenitor of your line."

He certainly talks *like an Alemán,* she thought. "That's what the official story says. Although I doubt there was ever any such thing."

"But the Fangèd Throne is made from its skull!"

"I'm pretty sure the Fangèd Throne is made out of plaster, actually," she said. "Anyway, it's at best a major faux pas for anybody not the Emperor, his body-guards, or his family to wear the gold and scarlet. His *immediate* family. That upstart tyrant there is none other than my cousin Gonzalo. He doesn't lust after my cinnamon-skinned young body, at least so far as I know. He lusts to recruit me to his sordid little schemes to discredit my father."

"What of the other?"

"The nosehorn? That's his brother Benedicto. He follows Gonzalo's lead, is all. I don't think he's stupid, as such. But he's slow, and that makes him fear he *is* stupid. So he's afraid to think for himself."

It had come to her to ask what bloody business it was of his. What with Falk not just a relative stranger, but her father's recent enemy. But she blurted the truth anyway. It felt good to get out.

Anyway, if I'm ever going to take my proper place in politics, as Father's successor in Los Almendros if nothing else, I have to accept that yesterday's enemy can become today's close ally.

And a mischievous voice at the back of her head asked, *How close?*

The pavane ended. After a pause to allow the dancing pairs to break from the line again, the band struck up another *gallarda*. Once more Melodía found herself face-to-face—or face-to–broad chest—with the Northerner. It took some deftness to keep from pecking Melodía with his beaked mask; off to their right, servants raced to disentangle a matador who'd gotten his fangs caught in the spikes of a hornface's frill. Falk handled the task with the aplomb with which he seemed to handle everything physical.

Including me, she thought as he swept her up again and turned her effortlessly in the air. She felt herself responding to his nearness, his strength, his smell. His overwhelming *maleness.*

Her lovemaking with Jaume had been wonderful as always, despite its heartbreaking aftermath. But after so long a drought, it had only roused her appetite. The effort it took to refrain from answering Jaume's daily letters—for principle!—made her hunger worse.

Again: lift, twirl, set down. Her breasts brushed his chest. His thick muscles were so different from Jaume's lean ones. A thrill ran down her belly to her groin.

She looked up. His eyes burned like lamps behind the midnight mask. *He wants me,* she thought. *And what do I owe Jaume? We have no pact of exclusivity. And besides,* he *left* me, *on a mission I begged him not to go on.*

Her lips fell open.

Someone's shoulder jostled her from behind. "Your pardon, your Grace!" a male voice stammered from behind.

Melodía spun to see a tall, weedy figure dressed in a jeweled strider-leather loincloth, body paint, and glitter. Eyes showed white inside a false bocaterrible face.

"Oh, and Highness! Ten thousand pardons!" Belatedly Melodía recognized a local shipping magnate, a great gaming crony of Heriberto's. Occasionally they drew her father into their evenings of cards and weichi, although Felipe had little appetite for gambling. She didn't know his name.

The dance ended. The moment ended. With a last cryptic smile, Melodía spun away from Falk and lost herself quickly in the gorgeous crowd.

"Highness."

Hurrying up the back stairs to the Imperial apartments, Melodía stopped and turned back. Her heart sped up. It wasn't with anticipation.

Duke Falk's bulk blocked the narrow stairwell behind her. Melodía felt anger, and a touch of apprehension. Honored guest he might be, friend of her father even, but he didn't belong here.

"Your Grace, have you lost your way?" she asked haughtily.

He had discarded his heraldic mask. His black hair was tousled in the candlelight. His cheeks were flushed. He smelled strongly of wine.

"I've found you," he said, "so I've come the right way."

She tried to freeze him with a glare. When he failed to freeze, she hesitated, uncertain how to proceed. She wondered how she had ever found him attractive before. He seemed coarse as a dray beast now, drunk and sweating in the cramped stairwell.

Despite his size and state, he was fast. Melodía found him right beside her on the narrow way. His body pressed her back against the cool stone wall. His nearness failed to excite her as it had before.

This can't be real, she thought. She was scared. She wanted to duck under his arm and race up the steps. She knew she should.

But I am the Imperial Princess, and heir to a duchy in my own right. I am a Delgao. It isn't right to flee the likes of him in my own home!

"Don't run away so fast, Alteza." He put a hand to the wall over her shoulder as if to support himself.

"I'm not running. I'm going to my private apartments, your Grace. Good night."

"You really want to stay," he said, and leaned in close. "You want me. Don't lie."

She dodged past him. She couldn't pretend any longer that disbelief or outrage would get her out of this. She ran.

He caught her arm. She tried to jerk free, wishing she had ignored her dueña's demands and worn her dagger tonight—a noblewoman's prerogative as much as any nobleman's. She opened her mouth to scream for the Scarlet Tyrants, knowing they couldn't hear her over the music and the merriment.

"My lady."

The words, in a feminine voice with a hint of accent, came soft and deferential. Yet they rang quite loudly in the narrow stair. Falk's hand jerked away from Melodía's arm as if her skin had gone white-hot.

Both looked down the stairs. Melodía's maidservant, Pilar, stood below, in a loose white blouse and dark-green velvet skirt.

Falk's face reddened. His chest swelled as he drew breath for a bull-hornface bellow of rage.

He deflated. His massive shoulders sagged. He stepped back against the curving wall.

Smiling, eyes coyly downcast, Pilar trotted past. Melodía stood waiting, her heart still pounding. When Pilar reached the step right below her, Melodía turned and marched regally up the stairs. Her maidservant followed.

A warm rush of gratitude flooded in over Melodía's fear. *I have sorely underestimated this woman,* she thought.

Rob found her sitting on a stone bench. Candles set in stone lanterns cast a faint and fitful light. Terror-moths fluttered around them with no fliers to afflict them now.

"I thought you'd never come," Jeannette said matter-of-factly. Standing, she reached behind her shoulders to do something to her gown. It promptly fell away.

She was naked beneath.

Rob felt his eyebrows rise.

"What of my reputation, then?" he started to say. But she grabbed him behind the neck, reeled him in, and muffled his mouth with hers.

Chapter 30

Bella, *Belle*, **Lady Li**—Countess of the Creators: *Li* ䷝
(Fire)—The Middle Daughter. Represents Beauty (and
its inevitable withering), the arts, truth, lust, passion
and obsession, time, and Fire. Also cats. Known for her
passion. Aspect: a beautiful red-haired young woman
in an orange gown garlanded with white flowers, holding a flame in her right palm and a mirror with a crossbar in her left hand. Sacred Animal: cat (depicted as an
orange tabby tom). Colors: red and orange. Symbol:
Beauty's Mirror (a circle on a handle with crosspiece).

**—A PRIMER TO PARADISE FOR THE IMPROVEMENT
OF YOUNG MINDS**

Young Dom Xurxo de Viseu couched his lance
and dug long-roweled silver spurs into his
sackbut's green-and-gold flanks. Tossing its
long-crested head, the dinosaur dropped to all fours
and rolled into a gallop toward the matador that
waited, head low and dripping saliva from its fangs,
at the clearing's far side. The onlooking knights and
nobles cheered lustily.

It was all very beautiful: the gorgeous display of Bluemountain, Ironstar, and their knights; de Viseu's gold-on-green pennon flickering from his lance-head; morning light slanting in shafts through the boughs of tall red-boled conifers, dappling his plate and his mount's pebbled hide as great muscles bunched and released beneath; the musty smells of monsters, lent piquancy by pine; the footfalls of the three-tonne beast, muted to distant war-drum beats by the greyish-brown carpet of fallen needles; the sackbut's seismic grunting to the rhythm of his strides; the matador's long, sinuous body striped black over brown, shading toward a yellow belly.

As he reined in Camellia, Jaume felt his brow furrow in dismay. He himself had decreed this hunt. But he had failed yet again to account sufficiently for the strong-blooded and weak-brained valor of the nobles under his nominal command.

"This isn't good," he told his quartet of dinosaur-mounted Companions.

"No!"

Rob clacked his hardwood axe haft up between the tree limbs the two recruits were whacking each other with. A couple score more recruits stood or sat around them in the blue wildflower meadow, watching.

At least no one seemed bored by the spectacle. Some entertainments had a universal appeal.

"The object is to stop your opponent from hitting you, and *then* try to hit him," Rob said. "Not just stand there like complete gits, pounding each other's foreheads until they get mushy!"

The combatants stood back. They were naked but

for sweat and sweaty loincloths. One swiped with the back of a hand at the blood and perspiration that drew a network down his brow.

"That was getting to be something of a trial," he admitted. "It hurt."

Rob slapped his own forehead. *You think it's a trial,* he thought.

Like them he wore only a breechclout, the simplest possible linen loin wrapping. At least it had *started* the day fresh and clean. Which was more than he could say for these men's garments.

They had a shock coming, once Karyl started to really crack down on camp hygiene, as Rob knew he soon would. Rob tended to attribute their lax attitude toward cleanliness less to their possibly being followers of the loony Life-to-Come sect, which no one he'd met in Providence seemed to favor, and more to their being louts.

"A damned good thwacking's all you deserve, Dion," said the second trainee, Fredot, who'd been getting the better of it. No surprise: he was three fingers taller and a good twelve years younger. "Claiming that poseur Erasto's quatrains are better than Félix's. Pah! Erasto wouldn't know decent octameter if it bit him on his dangly—"

"Enough!" shouted Rob. "This isn't *real* fighting, you twits, it's sodding practice. If this were real battle you'd both be lying with your skulls split open and the random mud, straw, and mouse-turds that currently keep the tops of them from caving in leaking out to feed the daisies. So leave your little literary disputes at home with your clean smocks—you *own* clean smocks, don't you?—and concentrate on the bloody business at hand!"

When he and Karyl had returned to the farmhouse midmorning, they'd found it cleared of rubble and rubbish and swept out. It wasn't yet in perfect shape. But Lucas and whomever else he'd cajoled or coerced into helping him had done a surprisingly good enough job overnight to make Karyl nod and rub his chin in approbation.

It had been the equivalent of a normal man turning handsprings. Lucas had reacted like an overeager puppy, minus the wetting himself.

Karyl had reason for good spirits today despite a night rough enough that his screams had awakened Rob in his room clear down the hall. Rob was alone by then. In the morning's small hours, when he and Jeannette had spent their energies as delightfully as possible, she had kissed his nose and slipped away.

The two men enjoyed a splendid breakfast of fruit and local cheese. It had been soured for Rob only by the absence of coffee, or even tea. Not because of expense, especially of the former, but because some Council member had a bee up his butt over stimulating drinks. Or her: Rob couldn't help but suspect that rachitic old dragon Violette.

From there Rob and Karyl had gone to visit the Providence town armory, where the ancient keeper showed them a treasure trove of arms in pristine shape. What especially lit the beacons in Karyl's dark and hooded eyes was the spectacle of a whole subterranean chamber full of *crossbows,* from small ones you could cock by hand to great whacking behemoths you could almost stick cart-wheels on and call ballistas.

The weapons, it seemed, were well beyond what Karyl had hoped for. Rob had certainly never seen the man show so much delight at the prospect of *pay.*

The noonday break approached, and with it the personal swordplay-tutoring Karyl had promised Lucas. The sun shone high and hot despite the near-perpetual clouds. Rob ladled a big draft of water from a bucket and emptied what he didn't drink over his head.

He turned to watch Karyl supervising quarterstaff practice, which was intended to break the recruits in gently to pole-arm combat. Emeric helped. He looked capable enough, but even across half the field Rob could see townsmen and farmers scrunch their faces and tense their shoulders whenever the woods-runner got near them.

Karyl wore only sandals and a black kilt. Sweat sheened his rib-ridged torso, slashed across by long white scars and dotted with pink, long-healed punctures. With his constantly turning head and intent gaze, he resembled nothing so much as a bighead flier perched at the pinnacle of a lightning-killed tree, scanning for his next prey.

The hair atop Karyl's head was tied at his crown, to fall across the free-hanging hair at the back in a curious two-tiered horsetail. The unusual style gave him an exotic look, lending credence to the ballads that claimed his mother had been a princess of a wild tribe of Ovdan horse-archers.

Letting his own two overzealous if under-apt students reclaim their breaths, Rob recalled the rest of the legend of Karyl Bogomirskiy. A matador attacked a caravan in the Misty March hinterlands, scattered or killed the guards, and tore apart the maids, Karyl's mother, and his elder brother before Karyl's eyes. Then the meter-long jaws had turned to a fear-frozen

Karyl, not quite six, dripping an evil soup of spittle and his loved ones' blood onto the roadway as they came closer and closer to his face.

The songs, of course, dwelt most lovingly on the goriest and grimmest details. Bards knew what customers paid to hear.

The instant before the Allosaurus bit off Karyl's face, a patrol of mercenary horse-archers arrived and drove the monster away with a shower of arrows. Irrationally, Karyl's father always blamed Karyl for the deaths of his beloved Countess and his heir. Voyvod Vlad never forgave his son for surviving.

Small wonder the man has nightmares yet, Rob thought. But *something* beyond that childhood ordeal must drive his screaming dreams. Folk far weaker than Karyl Bogomirskiy had endured far worse without paying such a savage nightly toll decades after the fact.

Rob forced his attention back to the task. "All right," he said, grinning his wickedest, "you two sit down. Who's next in the barrel, then, you lot? *Somebody* volunteer, smart quick. Or the toe of my boot will volunteer some backsides!"

He was starting to enjoy this. From earliest childhood he had endured not just slights but tragedy at the hands of the nobly born. Now he got to spew a lifetime's fury and frustration all over his pupils and call that "motivation."

His pair of fighters eagerly ditched their stripped branches and scampered to the stream that crossed the field, where they drank and splashed like hornface calves. A wide-eyed pair of 'prentices from town stood up and faltered forward to replace them.

"Ah, victims," Rob said, "front and center, now. Sharply, sharply, that's the way to do it. For your sorry sakes I hope you show more wit than the last lot. Or I may just smarten you up with dear Wanda, here." He slapped the head of his axe, which was cased in thick, time-darkened nosehorn leather with tarnished brass rivets.

Not *quite* trembling, the youths picked up the sticks out of the dew-damp grass. They promptly began the good old hesitation-dance—two steps forward, two back—common to inexperienced fighters everywhere.

Rob was drawing in a breath preparatory to further motivational speech when a voice shot up from around the farmhouse flank: "Alert, alert! Armed men approaching down the road!"

It was no surprise the matador had found them, Jaume knew. The Ejército Corregir was a walking feast for carnivores. Pickets and angry drovers had killed dozens of the raptors, dog-sized harriers, and man-sized horrors that daily dogged their tracks or crouched in ambush. The pack-hunters still managed to leave their marks on dray horses and nosehorns, and drag the odd one down. Every couple of days they got a camp follower or scout as well. That was life on the road in Nuevaropa: the packs were like flies, to be driven off or killed as possible, and otherwise endured.

But the young bull Allosaurus posed a much more serious threat. It had stalked the great procession for several days as it ground its laborious way at last onto La Meseta in County Mariposa, next to Ter-raroja. The woods up here grew taller and sparser than in the humid coastal regions below. The ferns and scrub oaks growing between the tall, straight trees looked too small to hide a man, much less ten meters of meat-eater. But matador stealth was infamous.

Having found the army, the monster would never voluntarily leave it.

At first it had contented itself cutting out the young and the weak from the vast herds of fatties the army drove alongside to feed itself. Even the guards feared to challenge it. Jaume didn't begrudge them that; a matador could tear a lightly armed patrol to pieces.

Then the inevitable happened. A sutler's seven-year-old daughter chased a butterfly with thirty-centimeter purple-and-yellow wings across a meadow toward a stand of saplings. And the monster rose up from weeds that severely shaken witnesses swore couldn't hide a dog, and sprang.

The Gallego knight's lance-head arrowed toward the matador's yellow chest. The Allosaurus darted to its right. It struck with viper speed.

Teeth clattered on steel plate. Jaume winced as several broke with loud squeals. A terrified trumpet blast from the sackbut quickly drowned out the other sounds. The monster's flashing attack had overwhelmed the rigorous training that suppressed the duckbill's instinctive fear of big meat-eaters.

The bugling could not overwhelm the young knight's screams as the Allosaurus plucked him from the saddle.

The panicked sackbut ran into the woods, blundering into thirty-meter-tall trees and cracking their trunks. The matador reared high. It tossed Mor Xurxo skyward. As he fell back down, uselessly milling, it caught his helmet in its mouth.

Jaws clamped shut with a crunch of terrible finality. The screaming stopped. The matador whipped its head sideways. Xurxo's body came away. Trailing a gusher of blood from the stump of its neck, it cartwheeled twenty meters to slam into a tree with a sound like a barrel of cutlery dropped onto cobblestones.

Head still tipped back, the matador bit down again. Metal crumpled. Dark juices spurted out the sides of its mouth. It swallowed. Then, lowering its flanged gaze to the shocked onlookers, it roared in triumph.

The watching nobles sat their war-duckbills in horrified silence.

"And that's monster for, 'who's next,' " said Florian from Jaume's left.

From Jaume's right Manfredo cast the Francés a quelling glance. But Florian was never quelled.

"Ah well," he continued with a shrug, "at least the lad's atoned for poor old Azufre."

Jaume felt Camellia's pulse racing through his thighs clamped on her cream-colored flanks. She was afraid of the monster, but also eager. She knew that even meat-eaters fearsome enough to take her kind down could be killed. She'd helped do it.

He turned in his saddle and called to his arming-squire, who rode behind the four knights, to hand him his spear.

"You can't be serious," Manfredo said. "The Nodosaur arbalesters will be here soon. Let them do their jobs, man."

Jaume accepted the spear with a nod of thanks and a reassuring smile. From Bartomeu's pallor and the tears streaming from his eyes, he wasn't reassured.

"I must do this, my friend," Jaume said to Manfredo. "You know why."

He tested the spear's heft. It felt unfamiliar: he did little hunting, except of miscreant knights. And that took a lance.

The monster-spear's shaft was four meters long. Its head was shaped like a sword but flared at the rear into two forward-curving wings, razor-honed to cut wide wounds. Unlike a foot-hunter's spear, it had no crosspiece; once it was driven deep, the rider let it go.

"You can't!" cried Dieter, his face flushed pink above his white Companion tunic. Like their captain, and unlike the other highborn hunters, the four wore no armor. They understood what poor Mor Xurxo, now presumably awaiting his next turn on the Cosmic Wheel, had learned from today's experience: even though the mightiest meat-eater couldn't bite through plate, armor didn't offer much protection. It wasn't worth the encumbrance, much less the parboiling in the midspring heat.

"It'll kill you too!" the Alemán wailed.

Jaume smiled. "If it does, I'll die a beautiful death."

"The Gallego's wasn't!"

Jaume clamped the spear between his elbow and his rib cage and, with his knees, nudged Camellia down the slope at a trot. Like any true montador, he had no need of spurs. Nor would he torture his friend with them.

"But there's only one of you!" Dieter called after

him. In his passion his Northern accent seriously mangled his Francés.

His fellow Alemán Machtigern let the steel-shod haft of his war-hammer drop across his shoulder.

"There's only one Allosaurus," he said.

Chapter 31

Volador Crestado, Crested Flier—*Pteranodon longi-ceps*. A large, tailless pterosaur with a toothless beak and long, bony crest; 1.8 meters long, 6-meter wing-span, 16 kilograms. Piscivorous. A noted seaport and shipboard scavenger.

—THE BOOK OF TRUE NAMES

W hy did I *do* that?"

Falk turned and smashed a bare fist into a piling of the sagging, abandoned pier. The poodle-sized juvenile crested flier perched atop it half unfolded its wings and croaked complaint.

"That'll do a world of good, your Grace," his goblin-faced companion said. "Now that your arm has healed, why not break your sword hand to show how mature you are?"

He hurled another of the flat shale stones that covered this unpopular stretch of beach west of the headland that upheld the Firefly Palace. It skipped once before vanishing into grey chop that was hard to distinguish from the grey sky.

The day matched Falk's mood.

"You suggested I let Jaume break my arm," he said sullenly. Above their heads, grey and white sea-skakes spiraled as if caught in a whirlwind, noisily disputing rights of salvage with the furred fliers.

"Yes," Bergdahl said. "And I spread the rumors the blow was a foul one. I did it for the same reason I blackmailed my way into a job in the palace. And do you know what that is?"

"What?"

Another stone. This one vanished with neither skip nor visible splash.

"Because we have a *plan,*" Bergdahl said. "Your mother and I. You too, if you could be bothered to remember."

The wind turned. A stench hit Falk, one that watered his eyes and loosened his knees. Not a quarter kilometer west of here, the conjoined sewer systems of La Merced, the palace, and the great Sea Dragon base on the city's eastern side emptied into the Channel, far beneath the surface. The tiny creatures that tinged the chop there pink quickly digested the sewage, nourishing some of the richest fishing waters in the Channel. But not even the poorest fisherfolk could tolerate the stink.

"You may have heard rumors of the danger that the Grey Angels will take note of those frisky, promiscuous heretics in Providence, and might at any moment loose one of their fearful crusades to purge the Tyrant's Head from sin, as they haven't done in centuries."

Falk felt little interest in anything but his own misery. His head beat like a tercio kettledrum. His stomach had been sloshing unpleasantly even before the wind shifted.

Bergdahl showed jumbled brown teeth in satisfaction.

"My doing as well. The plan proceeds, my lord."

Falk swallowed pride and bile. "If I haven't undone it. And us."

"Stop wallowing in your self-pity like a fatty in shit. If the bitch had gone to her father, your Scarlet Tyrant chums would've dragged you to him in chains hours ago."

Falk looked at him. He felt something like hope light within him. And quickly smothered it: he knew how hope *betrayed*. He had learned as a child, often and well.

"You really think so?" he couldn't stop himself from asking.

"Likely enough. I found you readily enough in that rat's-asshole waterfront dive. You're not exactly inconspicuous, with your size and coloring and those blue eyes. Moreover, you stink, lord. Coming from me, that's almost a compliment. It's no mean achievement for a man of your station."

"Perhaps you should remember yours!" Falk snapped. Then he regretted it. It felt as if he'd clapped himself over the temples with a pair of blacksmith's hammers.

"Oh, I do, lord. Do you?"

Falk looked away out over the uneasy water.

"But you're far from in the clear," Bergdahl went on relentlessly. "The cunt will tell her trim-tail little friends. Court gossip won't undo you as rapidly as pissing off the Emp would. But it can undermine you, just as surely. Do you *want* to have suffered a broken wing for nothing?"

"No," said Falk, all sulky. "So what can I do?"

"Why, rely on your wise servant's cunning, of course. Which fortunately exists in abundant supply."

"As does your cheek," Falk grumped.

"Which also serves your Grace, no matter how it chafes your ass."

Falk hung his head. It took great effort to hold it upright, anyway. The cries of flying creatures, feathered and furred, were like needles driven into his brain.

"Attend," Bergdahl said, adopting a tutor's lecturing tones. "I've worked my skinny ass off to learn. So now it's your turn, however much your head pounds from your self-indulgent folly. Felipe's a tough nut, and that's a fact. He drinks nothing stronger than wine or beer, neither to excess. He has no interest in herbs to give him good feelings or pleasant dreams. He's practically celibate since his bitch wife died pupping another useless daughter. He has a high-priced courtesan in to visit discreetly, once a week."

That pricked Falk's interest. He wasn't stupid. He knew that very well. No matter what his mother said. And for some reason he always found himself needing desperately to show the fact before this . . . creature.

"What about her?" he asked eagerly. "Does she offer us an angle?"

Bergdahl shook his head. "Not the slightest. Mondragón's spies watch her like harriers stalking a scratcher in a dooryard. No, the truth is, our beloved Emperor has no useful vices."

"None? What about his love of comfort?"

Bergdahl cackled. "Even in Alemania, your Grace,

love of food and ease hardly rises to the level of a *vice*. Unless one takes it far higher than Felipe does. No, for weakness, we must look to his family. He has two daughters, after all, and dotes on them both. When he can be bothered to recall he has them. And the younger one, the blond-mopped guttersnipe— she's notoriously careless about her own safety."

"No! We keep our hands off Montserrat. I can't imagine anything enraging Felipe more than trying to get to him through *her*."

Almost lovingly Bergdahl reached to stroke Falk's unkempt beard. "I knew that," he said. "I was merely testing you. You passed, for once."

Falk scowled and yanked his head around. Freeing his face from Bergdahl's fingertips was like breaking an adhesion.

"Now, if we widen the circle of his family," Bergdahl said, "we see definite promise. Felipe's in far from good odor in his own Tower. Some kinsmen and women deride him behind his back as 'that bastard of a Ramírez'—even here in La Merced. Others—"

"Others are afraid his stirring up trouble inside the Empire will undermine the Delgaos' death grip on the Fangèd Throne," Falk said, actually contriving to sound bored and feeling indecently proud of the fact. "They even have allies within Torre Ramírez, who fear that if Felipe kicks over the Imperial cart, Spaña's apples will go tumbling too. No need to bug your eyes at me like a hermit crab, Bergdahl; I have eyes and ears too."

Bergdahl pulled his head back and narrowed his eyes, which had in fact been bulging. Then he gave off a laugh that set his weird little pouch of a belly jiggling vigorously against the leathery wasteland of his torso. That startled the crested flier, which stretched its wings and took off flapping low over the Canal.

It had flown no more than a hundred meters offshore when the head of a sea monster shot up from the waves at the end of a long neck and bit it from the air.

Bergdahl applauded. "That's rare! That's rich. At last you've shown me up."

Falk managed to smile.

"If only you'd kept your cock behind your codpiece, who knows what you might have learned?"

Falk's brief good feeling fled.

"Here, now, don't blame me for telling you the truth, your Grace! It's the girl. That whore of a Princess led you on. Don't you have the sense to see it? She wanted you to make a fool of yourself."

Falk felt his forehead knot and his cheeks get hot with several kinds of anger. "Why would she do that?"

"Who knows why the cunts do anything? The Creators put 'em here to torture honest men, and all the rest of us as well. I saw how she ground that round ass of hers against your wedding tackle at the dance."

Falk's frown deepened. His memories of last night were a haze at best. He felt that Bergdahl's words soiled him, somehow. *But she sure wasn't shy about rubbing up against you, was she?* a voice whispered from the back of his mind.

"Whose fault is it?" Bergdahl said, thrusting his face close to Falk's. Unlike most men, he could look his master in the eye without craning. "Look at yourself. *Smell* yourself, standing here covered in vomit and regret. You've utterly debased yourself, sucking down booze to drown your fear. And why?"

"The Princess." It was almost a question.

"The Princess. The nasty little quim had no right to lead you on like that. She doesn't understand that things have costs. Where's your Northern pride, your Grace?"

"My pride," Falk growled. He straightened a little.

"She's trifled with you. Degraded you. Shouldn't she be made to pay for that?"

Anger-flames surged higher inside Falk. He welcomed their burn.

"Yes," he said. "She should. It wasn't right what she did. And her betrothed, Count Jaume, he's a great fighter. But he's—he's a man lover. She shouldn't spurn me just for being a true man."

"Ah, but she's turned her back on her pretty boy," Bergdahl said. "As she often does in bed, no doubt. You almost beat him—would have, except for our plan. Yet she still looks at you as nothing more than a plaything. Will you lie down and let her trample your pride in shit for a lark?"

"No."

"Do as I tell you then, lord," said Bergdahl, "and you shall have everything you desire. Including the Princess Melodía—and justice!"

"I am Seigneur Yannic."

Rob and Karyl's first visitor was a tall man, thin, with squinty dark eyes and brown hair that looked as if it had been cut around a bowl placed over his head. He wore a long white gown trimmed in scarlet. He had arrived aboard a high-strung brown-and-buff great strider.

"This is Seigneur Melchor, and Seigneur Percil. We've come to take command of Providence's army."

Yannic's fellows regarded Karyl and Rob with bored hauteur. Behind them lounged the dozen mail-clad foot soldiers, house-archers, and shields who had escorted them.

The town lords had arrived at Séverin farm.

"You're doomed to disappointment, then, gentlemen," Karyl said. "One, it's not yet near an army; two, I'm already in command. This is my lieutenant, Rob Korrigan. You and your men are welcome to volunteer as simple soldiers, if you wish."

Recalling last night's terrors, Rob wondered how much of Karyl's calm certainty was a show. It was a *convincing* show, he had to admit. Perhaps when Karyl felt himself in his element—as he did here, at the head of an armed band, however motley—he might not need to pretend. Might his fears and memories only swarm to haunt him when he saw no foe or crisis to overcome?

Yannic's small, thin-lipped mouth wrinkled to a sphincter in his long, imperious face.

"What? What?" demanded Lord Percil in a high nasal voice. His big head with its receding frizz of black curly hair dwarfed his wisp of a body. His little legs had stuck straight out to the sides of his huge black courser stallion when he rode up. "What nonsense is this?"

"No nonsense," Karyl said. "Just truth."

"How can that be? We're nobles. You're—you're landless vagabonds!"

"Landless vagabonds who've been given charge of building an army from scratch, my lord," said Rob. He decided he liked this noble less than most. "Besides, isn't everyone equal in Providence?"

Percil turned red.

"Perhaps there's a misunderstanding," Melchor said. His brown slouch hat shaded plump brown-bearded features that melded at the bottom into several chins in lieu of a neck, the top couple sporting a neat goatee. His sturdy white marchador, though pretty as such creatures went, struck Rob as a greater nod toward practicality than the other town lords had in them. The hilt of the sword that hung from his belt was simple, worn, and unadorned, as was its scabbard.

"Intolerable!" Percil stammered.

"Ridiculous," snapped Yannic. "We're in charge here, and we'll brook no nonsense."

"No," Karyl said. "You're not."

His tone kept calm but the words still cracked. Yannic jerked back as though Karyl had offered to strike him.

"Why waste breath on the scum?" said Percil. "We can settle this simply enough. Men—"

Rob laughed. "Is it that eager to die you are, then?"

Percil froze and said no more. "We have guards," said Yannic. "Who's going to threaten us?"

Lucas stepped up beside Karyl. "We stand with our captain."

That's far from a unanimous sentiment, I'm sure, thought Rob, who was trying to loosen his axe-head case unobtrusively. He glanced around. To his surprise several other men had stepped up behind Karyl. The tall, blond-moustached woods-runner, Emeric, had an arrow nocked though not drawn, pinned to his shortbow by a brown finger.

"Be careful starting anything you don't know how will end," Karyl said.

"Ah, wise words," Melchor said. "Perhaps this

man's a mendicant monk, as his humble garb suggests. In any event, why put ourselves to bother, my friends, when we can simply go back and sort this out with the Garden Council?"

"Very well," Yannic said, without decompressing his lips. Percil just glowered like an angry baby vexer.

They mounted and rode away. Once they got out of easy earshot, they began to argue animatedly. Their house-troops, stone-faced, turned about and marched off behind.

Rob tipped his head near Karyl's. "Will the Council listen to them?"

"Probably."

"What if they decide those noble nitwits should lead the militia?"

"If they really wanted to do that, they'd have done it. Still, if the Garden Council does hand them command, I'll happily go on the road again."

"You'd give up without a fight?"

"It's not my fight."

Ignoring Rob's sputter of fury, he turned away and nodded to Lucas, then to Emeric and the recruits who stood with him.

"Thank you," Karyl said. "Now get back to work. We're wasting light."

Chapter 32

Terremoto, **Earthquake**—A call too low for humans to hear, employed as a weapon by crested hadrosaurs such as halberds, morions, and sackbuts. Can panic or stun; a mass terremoto, properly focused, can deal lethal damage to the largest meat-eater and instantly kill a human. Effective to thirty meters, forty en masse. Favored ranged weapon of Nuevaropan dinosaur knights, whose armor and training helps them resist its effects. As it takes a hadrosaur several minutes to recover from giving a *terremoto*, it can normally be used only once per battle, to disrupt an enemy formation during a charge.

—THE BOOK OF TRUE NAMES

Ahush had fallen over the watching grandes.
Few of Nuevaropa's nobility were physical cowards. But there was nothing glorious about Dom Xurxo's death. It was ugly. Now they watched with open admiration as their Condestable rode down the slope toward the bloody-jawed monster.

Snarling, the matador turned to face Camellia.

Smelling the meat-eater, she tossed her crested head and trilled her dismay. Jaume felt her heart beat like a bass drum inside her chest. Like their riders, warhadrosaurs could at best only learn to control their fear of such monsters, not suppress it entirely.

But the duckbills had a weapon of their own, beyond their considerable mass and strength. . . .

Jaume trusted his Companions to restrain their dinosaurs' use of their fearsome voice-weapon. A terremoto couldn't be aimed precisely enough to avoid hitting Jaume and his mount. Both had been trained to withstand the panic, nausea, and stunning effects of the ultradeep sounds. But no amount of training would protect the unarmored Jaume from burst capillaries or lesions in his lungs. He could only hope Montañazul and his friends didn't evoke their mounts' "earthquake" calls, through ignorance, heedlessness, or something darker.

Why Dom Xurxo hadn't used his sackbut's terremoto against the matador, Jaume would never know. Perhaps he thought it unchivalrous. Jaume, murmuring encouragement to his beloved beast, suspected the young Gallego knight had simply forgotten about it, in his heat-rush of fury, fear, and bravado.

The Allosaurus waited thirty meters down a shallowing slope. It roared—itself an effective terror-weapon. But it was just a scary cry; it had no further impact.

Jaume signaled Camellia with his knees. She extended her neck and opened her beak. Jaume heard a weird rumble, like Paradise playing the dulcian: the terremoto's just-audible harmonics. As the vibrations rose in power, he felt his skin creep, and his vision blurred at the edges. Pain stabbed through his skull.

But he expected those effects, and accepted them as he did the way his sword hilt stung his hand when the blade struck something solid.

The matador caught the full brunt. He reared up, bellowing in surprised pain, his scarlet eyes blinking rapidly. Camellia dropped her forelegs to the ground and charged home.

Jaume clenched his whole body to steady his spear. He aimed carefully. The leaf-shaped head sank into the monster's narrow chest.

He took the bruising impact between his arm and his ribs and hung on, allowing the full momentum of Camellia's galloping three tonnes to drive the spear deep, its flaring steel wings cutting a wide wound through muscle and the lungs working like bellows behind.

The matador uttered a wheezing scream. Its breath rolled over Jaume like steam from a volcano's vent, but reeking of carrion instead of brimstone. The shriek threatened to burst his eardrums.

The meat-eater twisted quickly to its right. The move came too late to escape the fatal thrust, but it kept the much-larger Camellia from knocking him down. The stout ash haft snapped in Jaume's hand.

The monster darted its head back to bite off Jaume's face. He leaned far over in the saddle. The jaws crashed shut. Then Jaume and Camellia were by, crunching through brush that whipped at Jaume's bare legs.

Jaume rode on between widely spaced boles to increase separation from the foe. Then he drew the Lady's Mirror from its scabbard across his shoulder and wheeled Camellia back to face the matador.

The matador had turned and stood with pink froth

bubbling from its nostrils and running from its lower jaw. It started forward, gathering speed.

Jaume nudged Camellia to charge once more. She fluted dismay, but she obeyed, plunging forward on her massive hind legs with her forelimbs tucked against her chest.

The monsters slammed together chest to chest with a mountainous impact. The matador bellowed in agony as Camellia's weight drove the spear stub deeper into its chest.

It bit at Camellia's face. She swung her head away with a glass-shattering squeal. She threw her weight into the narrowly built predator and bowled it over on its side.

Even though breath and blood gouted from mouth and nose when he hit the ground, the matador was far from finished. Sustained by rage, he immediately rolled onto his belly and started to rise.

Jaume had sprung from the saddle. As he dropped feetfirst toward the fallen-needle carpet, he gripped his longsword in both hands.

The matador's head came up. The Mirror chopped down. It took the monster on the back of the neck and wedged between vertebrae to cut the spinal cord.

The monster's body convulsed to the last impulse transmitted by its furious brain. Its tail whipped around. It caught Jaume on the right side and thigh and flung him through the air. Somehow he managed to keep his grip on the Mirror's hilt, ripping it free of the dying embrace of muscle and bone.

Jaume struck a tree trunk. White lightning shot through his body as he felt ribs crack. He fell into the undergrowth.

He lay on his back, knees up, breathing laboriously. It felt as if he were inhaling fire. He had no way of knowing if his thigh was broken. He did know that it would hurt, once the numbness went away.

He heard the matador's weakening spasms, and then more localized thrashing. "Here he is!" he heard Bernat shout in Catalan-accented Francés.

"Don't move him!" answered a deep bellow that seemed to rival a dinosaur's.

Men knelt over Jaume. Concerned faces peered down from halos of sunlight though hair. Then they went away as giant Timaeos tossed his brother Companions aside like dolls.

Timaeos was the order's healer. His hands were gentle yet professionally brisk as he examined his fallen Captain-General. The red-bearded chin sank to his breastbone, the big brows knotted in concentration. After a few moments Timaeos nodded.

"His back's not broken," he told his fellow Companions. They showed as little resentment at being manhandled by him as he had shown awareness he was manhandling them. When he set about a task, Creators help whoever or whatever got in his way. "His leg isn't either. Make a stretcher."

"Not . . . necessary," Jaume said. Talking felt like stirring glass shards around in his chest. "Help me up, please."

"Are you hurt?" It was Bartomeu, his eyes and cheeks puffy and red.

"Yes. You know—how I've always told you there's no appreciation of pleasure without pain? Well, it seems damn foolish now."

Bartomeu looked blank. The dozen Companions gathered around him now laughed, perhaps a touch more uproariously than the quip called for.

Jaume heard a loud snort. Warm breath that smelled of greenery washed over him. A broad, rounded beak nuzzled his cheek.

He laughed and scratched Camellia's muzzle affectionately in return.

"I'll live, I'm afraid, big girl," he said. "How is she?"

"F-fine," Bartomeu sniffled.

Taking Jaume by his right arm and left shoulder, Timaeos hoisted him effortlessly to his feet. That hurt a lot, but Jaume had a long acquaintanceship with pain. He could live with it.

"Mind the ribs on his left side," Timaeos said. As Florian hung Jaume's right arm over his own neck, Timaeos enfolded the injured man's left upper arm with one hand. He would steady Jaume as Florian bore as much of his weight as needed.

A couple of tentative steps and one knee-buckle dissuaded Jaume from a half-formed intention of shrugging off their help. The three gimped painfully back up the slope as Bartomeu led the cream-and-orange Corythosaurus after them by her reins.

Manfredo hovered right behind Florian, ready to catch Jaume should the Francés knight falter. There was no need to spot for Timaeos. He could have carried two Jaumes outright.

"You shouldn't have done that by yourself," Manfredo told Jaume.

From the other group of knights who had watched the fight came a clatter of gauntlet on gauntlet and hoarse *bravos*. Even Bluemountain was red-faced and pounding the pommel of his saddle in excitement. Only Ironstar sat silent on his iron-grey and forge-orange sackbut, his face as impassive as if cast from his namesake metal.

"And that, gentlemen, is how you do it," Florian told his comrades from beneath Jaume's right arm.

"At least they won't question the captain's fitness to lead anymore," said Dieter with fierce pride.

"For a week or two," said Florian.

The town lords came back next morning early. This time they brought at least thirty house-archers and spearmen.

With Rob at his side, uncased axe in hand, Karyl stood in the road to meet them as they resolved out of the mist. His silver-streaked hair hung unbound to the shoulders of his simple brown robe. His hands were folded over the top of his staff.

Lucas stood on Karyl's other side. He had an arming-sword belted on and fairly danced with eagerness to use it. *Careful what you wish for, lad,* Rob thought. *Blood's not so easy to put back in, once you let it flow. Your own no more than anybody else's.*

Emeric stood by Rob, far calmer but still alert. Rob took his demeanor as corroboration that he had seen his share of trouble, and maybe a couple of other men's as well. The woods-runner struck him as a man who neither sought out trouble nor shied away from it.

A disheartening few others came up to stand on the pumice-graveled High Road behind them. A larger number stood off the causeway near the farm-house. Apparently they wanted a safe vantage point to watch the fun.

"Maître Karyl," called Melchor, the stout, bearded Town Lord. If tones of falsity rang though his heartiness, not even a seasoned scammer's ears could hear them. Yannic on his jittery strider looked as if he were sucking on a bitter root. Persil had his outsized head hunched down between his shoulders.

"Bogardus explained to us that you're a noble from a far land, who has graciously consented to lend your considerable skill at arms to defend us from our neighbors," Melchor said. "Please forgive yesterday's misunderstanding. Naturally we shall be honored to serve under your leadership."

He bowed from the saddle of his mule, which was no easy task across a paunch like his.

Who'd've thought Bogardus could bestow a magisterial ass-chewing? The notion delighted Rob, but didn't allay his building anger.

"So if you were the greatest warrior in the land," he hissed aside to Karyl, "which of course you are, but born of a washerwoman, they wouldn't consent to learn from you?"

It sorely tried self-control not to bellow it in the noblemen's faces: "What arrogant sods!"

"Let's not make this harder than it has to be, my friend," Karyl said quietly.

To the newcomers he called, "Welcome, gentlemen. You come just in time. The morning's exercises are about to begin."

Chapter 33

The Bestiary of Old Home—A late-first-century book that describes in words and pictures over a thousand creatures claimed to be native to Home, the world from which humans and their Five Friends (horses, goats, dogs, cats, and ferrets) came to Paradise. Though superstitious people believe it was directly inspired by our Creators, educated folk think that many of the animals in it are imaginary. It does provide a rich source for art and heraldry.

—A PRIMER TO PARADISE FOR THE IMPROVEMENT
OF YOUNG MINDS

"R*íu, ríu, chíu, la guarda ribera."*
The voices rumbled like distant thunder from inside browned-iron sallet helmets. Snare drums kept time, as did the tramp of boot soles crushing tender pale-green grass into the eponymous soil of Terraroja, the Redland.

"Dios guardó el lobo de nuestra cordera."

The ominous conjoined voice repeated the second phrase. A double beat of the vast, cart-mounted kettledrums that accompanied an Imperial tercio to pound out battle signals marked the end of each measure.

A single voice, high and clear, sang a verse of the Nodosaur battle-song:

"*El lobo rabioso la quiso morder*
"*Más Dios Poderoso la supo defender—*"

Jaume guessed it was a drummer boy singing. He stood on the brow of a low ridge in the morning sun with his sixteen Brothers-Companion. All wore their full plate, simple, white-enameled, unadorned except for the orange Lady's Mirror painted boldly on each chest piece. The scents of dust, dung, and wildflowers filled the air.

By long-standing custom, the tercio's purest soprano got the honor of singing the verses. Although her face and form suggested a dray nosehorn, their commander, Lieve van Damme, possessed a strikingly beautiful coloratura voice. When she had served as a simple pikewoman, she'd sung the part for years.

"*Quizo la hacer que no pudiese pecar*
"*Ni aun original esta virgen no tuviera.*"

Mor Bernat, good Catalan that he was, had put aside the notebook in which he wrote and sketched his impressions of the coming battle to sing tenor harmony with the distant Nodosaur vocalist. Owain, his longbow strung and slung over his armored shoulder, sang baritone—a Galés would no sooner yield to a Catalan in the matter of *singing* than a Catalan would to a Galés. Ayaks added his giant-bronze-bell bass.

Jaume joined them in his own famous tenor. He was Catalan too, after all, albeit more famous as a lyricist than as a performer.

The Imperial infatry column began to split left and right, flowing outward into ranks of pikes interspersed with halberdiers and greatsword-wielders. A dozen two-horse teams pulled stingers on their light carts into position before the grim lines. Nodosaur skirmishers in springer-leather jerkins and caps trotted to the fore, carrying arbalests and javelins. Each had a brown iron buckler slung about the neck, bouncing on his or her chest. In contrast to the tercio's perfect lines, the light infantry fought in swarms like biting insects—a comparison that the Redlanders would soon find all too apt.

To either side of the Nodosaurs milled a peasant levy about a thousand strong, to use the word loosely, carrying pikes, billhooks, hunting spears, and whatnot. Even from up here Jaume could tell they were none too eager for what was to come. He couldn't blame them. Their own feudal masters despised them. And given the chance, the enemy montadors would hunt them down laughing as if they were bouncers.

The levies didn't even matter much to the outcome of the impending battle. They were there to impede the enemy, like walking caltrops. All glory would go to the men-at-arms on their gorgeous horses and war-dinosaurs. And to the extent the fight was decided on the ground, the decision belonged to the brown Imperial elite and their fearsome melody.

"What a stirring song!" Dieter exclaimed. His blue eyes shone. "What does it mean?"

"No one knows," said Bernat. "It was almost certainly ancient before the world was made. The language is a dialect of Spañol, probably a predecessor. It's about a raging river, at least. It mentions a powerful god defending a lamb from a rabid wolf—both creatures that most people consider mythical, though they're listed in *The Bestiary of Old Home*."

"Also virgins," said Florian. "Which, while not mythical, are certainly rare in Nuevaropa."

"And the 'powerful god' can only mean Chián, King of the Creators. As for the rest—"

"It's meant to scare people," Machtigern said.

"It works," said Florian.

"Why not join the song, Goldilocks?" Ayaks called to him.

Florian laughed. "Thank you, no. I have a voice like a frog in a tin bucket. It would be cruel to inflict it on your tender ears."

They watched the armies move into position from atop a red lava flow, mounded soft by grassy soil, called La Dama Rosa, the Pink Lady. Behind them their hadrosaurs grazed and drank from buckets lugged by sweaty arming-squires. The Ordinary hombres armaos waited in reserve farther back.

A road ran north up a broad, gentle slope toward Terraroja's castle on its red granite crag and its attendant town of Risco Rojo. Both armies had deployed athwart the road in conventional formation: infantry in the center, cavalry to either side, and outside of them small, powerful blocks of dinosaur knights. Estrella del Hierro commanded the Imperial left wing. The right, under Montañazul, was drawn up at the foot of the Pink Lady.

The Companions' builders and fortifications experts, Fernão, Iñigo Etchegaray, and Wouter de Jong, stood together admiring the distant keep. The usually taciturn Gallego Fernão, a master of siege warfare, was actually animated. His brown-green eyes glowed as he pointed out its various excellences—and shaped with his hands how he'd defeat them.

"It wouldn't be easy," he said, "but, Torrey and Telar, what a challenge!"

"What's Terraroja's castle called?" asked Dieter, drawn by their enthusiasm.

Wouter laughed. He was a sturdy, towheaded Flamenco from Brabant, a fiefdom of Sansamour's Archduke Roger's that straddled the border of Alemania and Francia.

"El Gallo Rojo," he said, leaning on his battle-axe. "Which means both things you think it does."

Dieter flushed. It meant "the red cock." While the Companions did not mind each other's business, especially where love and sex were concerned, in such a small group it was impossible for it not to be common knowledge that he had become the Flamenco knight's lover.

"A castle is aggression made stone, boy," Fernão declared. "Don't ever forget that."

"Still a powerful defense, though," grumbled Iñigo, scratching his beard with a thumbnail. "Leopoldo's a fool not to squat inside and dare us to pry him out. We would, of course, but it would cost us more than even a set-piece battle."

"If he was smart," Florian said, "he wouldn't be a buckethead."

Jaume pulled a rueful mouth.

"Melodía warned me we wouldn't need siege-engines," he said. "She said Count Leopoldo could never resist coming out to fight."

If only I hadn't dismissed her when she said it, he thought bitterly. *Perhaps she'd be answering my daily letters now if I'd bothered to listen to her then.*

"Terraroja sees war as a game," Florian said, "a tourney on a grander stage. So he picked a field almost as flat and clear as the lists to fight us on."

"Don't complain," said Machtigern. He began ticking the steel shanks of his war-hammer head against his pauldron. "It's one reason we consistently beat the bucketheads."

Ayaks threw up his hands and stamped off. Slight as it was, the clacking always drove him crazy.

"What?" Machtigern asked the huge Ruso's back. He always did that right before battle, just as Florian laughed louder and more. He didn't even know he was doing it.

"Count Leopoldo hasn't done so badly for himself," Manfredo said. "It wouldn't be easy to provision the castle to stand a long siege, however strong its walls. This land is arid. It's probably why banditry has such strong appeal for him and his barons."

"He's done us a bad turn," said Jacques, walking up. "He's managed to collect more men-at-arms than we have, both cavalry and dinosaur knights. Worse, to feed them all he's sucked up most of the provisions available for twenty kilometers around."

He shook his head. "It was a nightmare enough getting some of our nobles to pay for what they took when supplies were plentiful and cheap."

Jaume frowned to see just how the travails of keeping not just the Companions but the whole fractious army tight, fed, and functional had worn his friend down. His lank brown hair had gotten sparser and greyer, as had his skin. Despite his armor, his shoulders were visibly slumped.

Jacques planned to retire soon from active service and return to the order's motherhouse in central

Francia to assume direction of its ever-growing holdings from Mor Jérôme. Jérôme had lost both legs when his morion rolled onto him after taking an iron ballista bolt through both lungs. Now, health failing, Jérôme wanted to retire to his family's vineyards in Sansamour. He had done well; Jaume anticipated Jacques would do better.

But the loss of any Companion left a hole in every Brother's soul, as well as their battle-order. Even if it wasn't death that took them. And Jaume could only wonder who would care for them the way Jacques had.

Sadly, the Empire's most elite band of warrior-artist-philosophers of beauty tended to attract precious few candidates with any gift for organizing things.

"And thanks to our magnates' obsession with their feudal ties and petty honor at the expense of everything else," Florian was saying with unaccustomed venom, "our left wing's significantly weaker than the right."

Manfredo shrugged. "They'd outnumber us on both sides anyway, unless we put all our riders on one flank and left the other hanging. At least our right has a chance to hold its own against the Terrarojanos."

Manfredo was an erstwhile law student, exiled for promoting Taliano independence from Trebizon. He'd become a virtuoso of mounted tactics, as he was of musical composition and various instruments. Jaume thought him more skillful than he himself was.

Not that Jaume considered himself a master tactician. As a face-up fighter, the next man he met who could match him would be the first. He inspired men to follow him, and had a knack for clever sleights and ruses. That he won larger battles was something he attributed to bringing better tools to the task, and to being less stupid than his foes.

"I'm not happy with our position," he said. "I hate to accept battle on my enemy's terms."

"Hardly your fault, Captain," Machtigern said. "Montañazul and the rest barely listen. Tavares keeps telling them they don't have to."

"It is my fault, my friend," said Jaume. "I command."

Away to the west the Nodosaurs stopped singing.

"For a fat gob of phlegm, Melchor knows his way around a sword," Rob admitted at the noon break. He sat on an old hay bale in the shade of the house, still sweating. The day was hot and he'd been exerting himself almost as heavily as the men had. *Tough work, this teaching business.*

"I saw," said Karyl, who squatted Eastern-fashion beside him. "Yannic will be competent if he can learn to control his incipient panic. Percil barely knows which end to hold, and feels too angry and challenged by circumstances to learn."

Rob flicked eyes at him. Maybe more than at any time since he met the man, he felt like a small boy whose hero had stepped out of the ballads to become his companion. Serious about craft, if precious little else, Rob found himself awed in the presence of true mastery: the quiet mastery.

"Their house fighters could only be worth their pay among a people with a generation or two of peace under their belts. Still, they know the basics. It's better than most we've got."

"Young Lucas seems to be coming right along,"

Rob said. Karyl had spent the midmorning break, and half this lunch period, instructing the young painter privately. "He's mad avid for the blade, and that's a fact."

"He has a gift. Apparently his deftness with a brush translates to the sword as well. And it's making him overconfident. I don't like all the methods teachers use in Chánguo or Zipangu. But Lucas makes me think maybe it is a good idea, sometimes, to make an aspirant sweep the master's studio for a year before teaching him technique."

"What for?"

"To make sure he's dedicated to learning, rather than building up his ego. Eastern martial training's not about just fighting but spiritual development as well. The student needs to learn self-control most of all. Otherwise the sword- and spear-play only make him dangerous to others—and most of all himself."

"If you say so," Rob said. "But I doubt we have much time for spiritual instruction. Even if you could interest lad Lucas in same."

"You're probably right. Between the Council's fears and Guillaume's greed, we'll have to fight soon. When that happens I'll have to be more concerned with blades than the well-being of those who wield them. Which is a part of the business I never liked, even at my starkest: that caring too much for one's troops can be as fatal as caring too little."

He sighed and stood. "If nothing else, Crève Coeur's going to want to teach us a sharp lesson in how futile our efforts are."

"Whatever do you mean?"

"People come and go constantly down La Rue Impériale, in plain view of our camp. That's one of a hundred ways Count Guillaume can get all the news he needs of what we're about."

Rob frowned. "You're right."

Failing to have recognized what he now saw as plain fact chagrined him. Minstrels were famously well-placed for spying, which added to their infamy and their mystique alike. Not that he himself had ever stooped so low as to spy for some buckethead. Unless he really needed the money.

"We need scouts," Karyl said. "I think you're just the man to head them."

"I'm what, now?" Rob asked in alarm.

"It's logical. You're already quartermaster."

"Don't remind me." It was Rob's turn to sigh. "I suppose that much makes sense. Quartermasters usually have charge of foragers. Scouts forage. As well as harry enemy foragers."

"Scouts also spy. And hunt enemy spies."

"That appeals, I admit. The added responsibility, much less so."

But rather to his distress, Rob was starting to see the sense in Karyl's proposals.

"It's always pleased my noble employers to blunder blindly about the landscape until they stumbled into an enemy by chance," he said. A slow, sly smile stole across his face. "I do believe they'd regard this notion of yours as *cheating*."

"Indeed."

"If it'll piss off aristos, I'm for it. But—where do I start? I haven't a clue."

"Emeric comes to mind. His woods-runners know the country better than anybody. Especially invaders."

"Right," Rob said. "I'll just be taking Emeric aside when we finish up for the afternoon." He was enjoying even *thinking* about this new game. It appealed to his devious side.

"Just one more thing," said Karyl.

Rob frowned in instant suspicion.

"We need eyes and ears in Providence town," Karyl said. "Children should work best."

"This is no spur-of-the-moment fancy with you, is it?" *You sly bastard, taking advantage of a poor, innocent minstrel lad.*

"Their natural curiosity will cover them as well as serve us. And if they get caught, they're not likely to be punished too severely."

A lamp came on in Rob's mind "It's the Garden Council you want me to spy on, isn't it?"

Karyl only smiled. After a moment's breathless outrage, Rob found himself grinning back.

"Right, then. It's about bloody time I had some fun in this job."

Chapter 34

Armadón, **Spike-shoulder**—*Edmontonia longiceps.*
A typical breed of nodosaur: a massively armored
quadrupedal dinosaur, herbivorous, with large forward-
sweeping shoulder spikes and truculent attitude; 6.6
meters long, 2 meters high, 5 tonnes. Emblem of the
Imperial infantry, the Brown Nodosaurs.

—THE BOOK OF TRUE NAMES

The Nodosaurs stood in iron silence. It was a
favorite trick of theirs, to unnerve the opposition, Jaume knew.

They favored it because it worked.

A hundred fifty meters north of the phalanx, Redland pikes began to waver. The hapless peasant levies
knew the Imperial infantry no more gave quarter
than took it. The Nodosaurs had taken as their
mission inflicting the greatest pain possible on the
Empire's enemies. Neither Creators' Law, nor Diet
legislation, nor even decree of their Imperial master
of the moment had ever softened that attitude.

"If our left's so outmatched, then," asked Dieter,

oblivious to the drama playing out before the Companions' vantage point, "why not just shore up that side ourselves?"

Pedro the Lesser, the diminutive weapons master, was passing nearby in his customary oblivious precombat pacing.

"Strange things happen in battle," he told the Alemán. "Not even the Creators can predict them."

Then he was off again, rolling on bowed legs, bearded chin sunk to breastplate, muttering to himself. What he said no man knew. Poems? Prayers? It was inaudible, and no one cared to intrude.

At a command Jaume couldn't hear, the Nodosaur skirmishers formed a double line, front rank kneeling, rear aiming their crossbows over their comrades' shoulders. They targeted their opposite numbers, armored house-bowmen and peasant archers in light armor or none, who stood in front of the Terrarojano foot. With a single musical *tung!* of springing steel, the Imperial arbalests began to work murder among them.

Jaume heard the distant wailing wounded. Small figures fell, thrashing hideously or lying still. At this range most arrows from the light-draw Terraroja bows fell like rain in a meadow, harmless. But bolts from Imperial medium-crossbows pierced dinosaur-leather and even mail armor like wet paper. They punched right through house-archers' steel hats to trepan the skulls beneath.

The intricate dance, as those with emptied weapons moved to the rear and their comrades stepped forward to aim and loose in turn, enthralled Jaume as it always did. The smaller crossbows were cocked using a lever called a springer's-foot, the bigger ones with pulley-and-gear contrivances known as crane-quins. Jaume found the way the skirmishers kept up a steady bolt storm despite their different loading times actively beautiful. Temperamentally unsuited to the phalanx's tight formation, the Nodosaur light infantry were precise when they needed to be.

Trumpets blared across the expanse of pale-green grass and reddish soil. Drums boomed. Pennons waved vigorously. The Terrarojano army advanced. The Ejército Corregir—the silent brown pikes, the gaily caparisoned heavy horse, the dinosaur knights, unmatched in might and arrogance—marched to meet them.

Jaume turned away. "Mount up, my friends!" he called. "We'll know where we're needed soon enough."

At her master's approach, Camellia raised her head, clutching in her beak a clump of uprooted weeds with red dirt dribbling from their roots. She blew a greeting to her master through wide orange-marbled nostrils.

She wore a chamfron, a steel half mask similar to the ones used on warhorses. Overlapping plates guarded her throat, a steel boss her chest. A heavy cloth caparison and her own tough hide sufficed to protect the rest. Like their riders', the hadrosaurs' armor was white, and emblazoned with a red circle on a tilted cross: the holy Mirror of the Creator Bella, Lady of Fire and Beauty.

"Yes, it's almost time, sweetheart," Jaume called to the morion. He encircled her neck with a steel-shelled arm and hugged her crested head. She rubbed against his breastplate. He smiled and scratched her cheek behind the chamfron.

"My helmet, Bartomeu, if you please," he told his arming-squire.

The boy looked miserable. His own risk was slight. When his master was mounted, he'd join the other squires under dinosaur master Rupp von Teuzen, guarding the army's baggage train strung out south along the road. The drovers and a mercenary jinete— light rider—company Jaume had hired to scout and protect foraging parties would fight alongside them if the enemy broke through. Bartomeu didn't fear for his own safety, but for his master's.

He placed the scoop-shaped war-sallet on Jaume's head. Unlike the heavier, one-piece tourney helmet, this one had a visor that swung down to meet the bevor that guarded his neck and cupped his chin. Jaume felt Bartomeu's hands tremble as they fastened his chin strap.

He caught the back of Bartomeu's blond head with a white-enameled gauntlet and drew him close to kiss him in reward and reassurance. On the brow, so it wouldn't be misinterpreted as showing sexual interest.

"Thank you," he said.

He smiled broadly as he broke away, and showed no sign he noticed how the boy's face fell at the chaste gesture. Bartomeu strapped Jaume's escutcheon-shaped shield to his left arm. With the usual help from his squire and Camellia, Jaume mounted the saddle atop her high, humped back. His cracked ribs still pained him, but if there was one thing he was skilled at as a lifelong campaigner, it was ignoring the pangs of minor wounds. Or not-so-minor ones.

All around him Companion duckbills were rising from the grass. His was the only sallet. The others wore round armets, except Florian, who sported a bascinet whose beaked visor he had painted in the likeness of a glaring hornface. It was alarmingly realistic.

Jaume grinned at them. He enjoyed this. He lived for the thrills of battle—and embraced its horrors as gifts from the Lady too. His only fear was for Camellia and his men. When intrigue in his father's court had forced Jaume to take the field against the ferocious miquelet bandits at the ridiculously young age of nineteen, he had been forced to confront, once and for all, the fact that he would one day die.

He and his Brothers looked west, where Estrella del Hierro's mounted wing was the army's weakest point. In sheer numbers the Imperial disadvantage didn't look too bad. The Ejército Corregir had about 7,500 men, the enemy a little more than 10,000. The Terrarojanos' slight edge in missilery, and their 6,000 pikes backed by 500 spear-and-shield men facing 3,000 Nodosaurs, 2,000 peasant levies, and 400 armored foot, meant little. Van Damme would pit her tercio with its skirmishers and engineers against three times their number, even in armored household troops, and like her chances. And so would Jaume.

In all their five centuries of history, no Nodosaur tercio had ever broken. Some had died where they stood—literally, to the last man and woman, mostly during the Demon War against the Fae and their traitorous human allies, and the brutal conquest of Anglaterra. They would, if commanded, retire in good order. They seldom had to.

But knights won battles. Terraroja had twice the heavy cavalry Jaume did, and 170 dinosaur knights to his 75—which included the Companions in reserve. They outnumbered Count Ironstar's riders two to one, with a healthy advantage left over to take on Montañazul on the right. If the Redlanders could drive the Army of Correction's men-at-arms from the field, the Imperial levies would scatter like dandelion fuzz to a puff. And then Don Leopoldo could grind the Nodosaurs to blood-and-bone gruel at his leisure.

It fell to the Companions to keep that from happening.

Steel ballista bows twanged basso. Catapult arms thudded against rope-wound stops. Stone balls arced high to bounce through tightly packed formations, leaving screams and smears of deeper red on red dirt. Redlands horses shrieked piteously as iron stinger darts streaked snake-low over grass to strike through their armored flanks and bring them down in pinwheels of limbs, blood, and bodies.

"I hate this most," Machtigern said. "The beasts have no choice in being here."

"Neither do the peasants," called Florian. Machtigern frowned and flared his nostrils in dismay, but nodded assent.

The mounted masses approached collision. On the left, Estrella del Hierro himself rode in the lead with a score of barons and knights. Their star-steel armor shone like silver. Except for the personal insignia on each knight's breast, Ironstar plate was painted only with clear varnish to keep off rust.

"Why won't Ironstar order the terremoto?" Fernão demanded angrily. "What's the fool waiting for?"

"Not so foolish," said Manfredo. "Outnumbered as he is, he can't waste it at too great a range."

Uttering the devastating cries took a lot out of the war-hadrosaurs. On the move, they could deliver only one without pausing to recapture breath.

Terraroja had no such constraints. With his greater numbers he didn't have to worry about concentrating his dinosaurs' sound-weapons for maximum effect.

Jaume's teeth peeled back from his lips as he saw the Redlands monsters, rolling at a ground-eating four-legged lope, stretch their gloriously crested heads forward on their necks.

He heard nothing. But the hair rose at his nape. His stomach quivered.

Dinosaur knights and their mounts were trained against the terremoto. Their armor and shields would ward off some of its effects. But there were simply too many enemy monsters bellowing at once. The galloping Imperial dinosaurs faltered as if an invisible wall had struck them.

"That's them fucked, then," Wil Oakheart of Oakheart said conversationally. "There's where we're needed."

He clanged his visor shut.

"Pass the word to the Ordinaries," Jaume said as the Redlands duckbills rose up on huge hind legs for their final sprinting charge. "We ride west to help Ironstar!"

Tree limbs clattered in mock battle.

It was the next morning. Rob stood with Karyl by the stream to watch young Lucas fencing a house-archer in Percil's gold-and-crimson livery. To every-one's evident surprise—the archer's only slightly more than the towheaded painter's—Lucas was able almost to hold his own.

That didn't sit well with the soldier. He feinted a thrust for Lucas's belly. When Lucas swung his branch down to counter, he whipped his own club around one-handed to crack the boy nastily in the forehead.

Lucas sat down hard. The town lords and their other soldiers laughed. The recruits growled and scowled.

Lucas jumped up. He laughed too, though his blue eyes were unfocused and he swayed. Blood ran down his broad, fresh face. His opponent jabbed him hard in the belly. Retching, Lucas bent over, clutching himself with his hair falling over his eyes.

Taking a two-handed grip, the house-archer stepped up, raising his branch high over his head. He swung hard at Lucas's unprotected nape.

The limb struck the handle of Rob's axe. Rob twisted the weapon and pulled it back fast. The beard of its still-cased head caught the stick, as it was designed to do. Stepping between the two men and turning hard with his hips, Rob twisted the tree limb from the soldier's grasp and sent it spinning into the stream. Its splash made small spotted frogs croak disgust and leap into the water for safety.

"Now, that's hardly in the spirit of fair play, is it?" Rob asked pleasantly.

The archer glared at him. He had a long, dark face that hadn't seen a razor in several days. His eyes were as dark as lumps of coal.

"Fucking vagrant!" He spat at Rob's feet. "What gives you the right to boss us around?"

"The authority of Voyvod Karyl, captain of this little tea-circle, and himself a notable lord."

"He's nothing but another dirty wanderer," said the house-archer, whom Rob thought had scant call to be criticizing others' hygiene. "I'd put you in your place, if you hadn't disarmed me by treachery."

Rob tossed his axe toward Emeric. To his relief, his estimation of the woods-runner proved out. The tall, blond-moustached man caught it handily.

"Now I'm disarmed as well, by nothing but my own guileless nature. I believe you said something about showing me my place?"

"Here," called another of Percil's men. He drew his sword and threw it to his comrade. "Spit the mad dog!"

The archer looked away to catch the weapon by the hilt. When he turned back he found Rob had stepped right up to him.

Before he could react, Rob snapped his knee up between the man's legs. Impact lifted him onto his toes. He squeaked like a stepped-on mouse, his eyes bugged out, and his face went purple. He bent double, grabbing for his groin.

Rob stood him right back up by smashing his elbow upward into his face. Blood streamed from the archer's broken nose. Rob grabbed his head in both hands and dragged him face-first to make the acquaintance of Rob's rapidly rising knee.

The archer collapsed into a moaning heap.

Bending down, Rob plucked the sword from fingers limp as boiled cabbage. Then he straightened and held the point to the side of the archer's neck.

He looked to Karyl. Karyl shook his head.

The archer lay retching and whimpering on his

right side. Rob gave him two centimeters of his comrade's own steel in the side of his left buttock. He squealed.

Pulling the arming-sword out, Rob tossed it in the air and stepped back. It turned over once and plunged back, point first, a hand's-breadth into the moist ground.

Without haste, but with every wide eye on him, Rob walked over and stooped to collect his axe from Emeric. Suddenly the case was off. The oil on Wanda's head gleamed rainbows in the sun.

"Playtime's over, kiddies," he said, laying the weapon over his shoulder with elaborate casualness. "The next man to fuck with me's the next man I kill. Any questions?"

Percil was sputtering like a hot iron thrust into a blacksmith's bucket. His face glowed red. *Such hair as he has should be taking light any moment now,* thought Rob. *No wonder it's all so crispy-curly.*

Yannic looked ready to change on the spot the terms Bogardus had obviously rammed down the town lords' throats. Karyl eyed Percil with a calm intensity that suggested strongly that, should the big-headed grande order his men to make a move, the next thing to happen would be his head parting company from his neck by way of the blade concealed in Karyl's staff.

"Here, now, gentlemen," said Melchor in a soothing voice. He stepped between his peers and the mercenary captain, beaming as if this were his own surprise party. "Tempers flare even when fighting's merely practice. We all have a job to do. Let's all take a deep breath and get on with it, like civilized men."

Karyl smiled thinly, but said nothing. Fearing the

fat noble would misinterpret Karyl's silence as uncertainty and change his mind about trying to keep the peace, Rob said, "Wise words, my lord." Though his own words rasped his throat.

"Bravo," a voice called from the road.

Chapter 35

Caracorno Spinoso, Spike-frill—*Styracosaurus albertensis*. Ovdan hornface (ceratopsian dinosaur), quadrupedal herbivore with a large nasal horn and four to six large horns protruding from its neck-frill; 5.5 meters long, 1.8 meters tall, 3 tonnes. Mostly shades of yellow and brown in arresting patterns. Favored war-mount for heavy Turano and Parso riders

—THE BOOK OF TRUE NAMES

Stunned and disoriented by the mass terremoto, Ironstar's dinosaur knights stood no chance. His lead duckbills were still rearing and shrilling in panic when the Terrarojanos hit them. They slammed stunned dinosaurs to the ground with impacts Jaume could almost feel from half a kilometer away. Riders were crushed by their falling mounts or trampled by enemy monsters.

The lucky ones died at once.

Despite himself Jaume was impressed. *Don Leopoldo's using actual* tactics, he thought. He put Camellia into a two-legged trot. Behind him his Companions did likewise. The jarring did his ribs no favors. But fortunately his mind was contracting to a point, focusing on battle.

Compared to the knowledge that what he was doing would lead inevitably to great suffering and death for beasts and humans, likely even for his friends, or for himself, overlooking physical pain was a trifle.

Apparently life as a bandit lord sharpened the wits. The Count of the Redlands had not heretofore been famed for his keen mental edge. Military custom, which most of his peers followed like so many vexer hatchlings following their mother, called for heavy mounts, horses or hadrosaurs, to charge several ranks deep for mass. Students of the military arts like Jaume and his Companions knew that advantage was mostly illusion.

Instead, Terraroja had arranged his dinosaur knights in a formation much wider than it was deep, giving it more than twice the frontage of Ironstar's force. That enabled the greatest number of his duckbills to utter their subterranean war-bellows without blasting their fellows in front of them.

It also allowed them to wrap around both Imperial flanks. As the two masses of cavalry came together between monsters and infantry, Ironstar's dinosaurry shattered like a crystal goblet struck by a morning star.

Jaume's gut wound tighter. The Companions now rode at a gallop. He ached to go faster still, to stanch the disaster erupting before his eyes. *But if I push our beasts any faster, they'll be knackered before they reach the enemy. And Terraroja outnumbers us so brutally already. . . .*

Baron Sándoval and his heavy horse were holding

their own against the greater mass of Redlander men-at-arms. Jaume caught a glimpse of the Baron himself through the gorgeous scrum of knights and coursers. He was unmistakable, literally by design: unlike most, who settled for simply painting their arms on breastplate and shield, Sándoval did up his armor in his striking gold and black lozenge pattern. Jaume found that in doubtful taste. But in terms of allowing Sándoval's men to see him even in the maelstrom of combat, it worked.

From away to his right, Jaume heard a hoarse, triumphant shout of "*¡Ajúa!*" Though he couldn't see them now for the intervening mass of Imperial peasants with their long sticks, he knew the Nodosaurs had just met the enemy center. He had no doubt they would roll over the hapless Redlands levies like a thunder-titan blundering through a village's thorn fence.

He hoped their efforts weren't wasted.

"*They're running!*" he heard Owain shout from behind him. Ironstar's survivors had broken. Their dinosaurs turned tails toward the foe and raced south on two legs. Jaume frowned to see Estrella del Hierro's grey-and-orange sackbut among them, with rider in place.

Am I disappointed that he survived because he failed, Jaume wondered. *Or, ugly thought, because at least I'd be spared his nonsense if he fell?*

But that was one good thing about rushing into battle: such thoughts flew by like falling stars streaking down the night sky.

Unfortunately, *rout* was contagious. Sándoval's knights saw their bigger comrades running away as fast as their huge hind legs could pump. Badly outmanned, they saw no choice but to turn and race the hadrosaurs away from the lost field.

As he neared the panic flight, Jaume didn't glance back. He knew his sixteen Companions formed a tight wedge behind him. Canny Coronel Alma, the silver-bearded mercenary who had commanded the Ordinary hombres armaos since their inception, would follow the dinosaur knights until they could break off to intercept the pursuing Redlander horse.

Bleating duckbills, terrified beyond their riders' control, streamed across the Companions' path. Soon they'd start dropping from sheer exhaustion, dooming their riders no less certainly than if they hit the ground in the midst of a melee.

Jaume wasted no concern on that. It lay beyond his control. What did worry him was whether his men could avoid trampling the Imperial cavalry. Companion duckbills would squash the chargers like so many four-footed grapes, notwithstanding their fine barding of chain or plate. The knights who rode them would fare no better.

Worse from a tactical perspective was that riding down their own cavalry would disorder Jaume's small band. Few as they were, the Companions depended on *cohesion* for effect even more than other dinosaur knights.

With a light pressure on the reins, he angled Camellia a hair to his right. To his relief the Imperial horse thundered by to the west, eyes rolling and froth streaming from wide nostrils. But there was no way to miss the pursuing Terrarojano horse as well. While Jaume would feel far less bad about smashing *them,* it would still fatally disorder his charge.

Against an enemy who had begun the day outnumbering his Companions by better than five to one.

Karyl snarled a Slavo curse under his breath. "The sentries I posted to watch the road must be asleep."

Rob spun with his axe, Wanda, still across his shoulder. The sentries in question, a pair of 'prentice lads from Providence town, stood grinning and waving from beside an extravagant apparition. A young man clad in a green feather yoke, brown breechclout, and green boots sat astride the most flamboyant-looking hornface Rob had ever seen.

"Easy, then," he told Karyl. "I'm guessing the lads know this one." His companion still scowled. But his expression was starting to soften.

The beast was about Little Nell's size, if a bit chunkier. Its nasal horn was longer and slimmer than Nell's, with a marked upward curve. Dinosaur master Rob saw how lethal it could be hooked up into the vulnerable belly of matador or war-duckbill alike. More than sufficient to let the air out of even one of the town lords' mailed bravos. Like Nell's, its frill was surmounted by a pair of spikes. These were stronger-looking, sharper, longer, wicked in effect instead of comical. Smaller spines jutted around the frill's rim.

The big-beaked face showed stark yellow-on-brown lines. The body behind the frill was brown on top, shading to mustard below. Rob didn't know whether the facial coloring was natural, painted, or carefully bred, like the extravagant hues of a Nueva-ropan morion or sackbut.

"Handsome beast," Rob called to the rider. "A Styracosaurus, if I know my *Book of True Names*. And I do. What d'you call him?"

"Thank you, friend," the rider called back. "He's named Zhubin. Or if you meant his breed, we call that 'spike-frill.' They run wild in Ovda, and are also bred for war. I'm Gaétan, by the way. My father is Master Évrard, a merchant dealing in spices and fine cloths."

"Zhubin," Karyl said. "That's Parso for 'spear.' "

The newcomer regarded him a moment, then swung a leg over the bow of his saddle on the hornface's tall back and dropped to the road. He was a burly lad, not over-tall, with green-hazel eyes and unruly brown hair that fell onto his square, tanned face. He said something to Karyl in a language that sounded to Rob both guttural and liquid, somehow. Karyl answered in the same tongue.

"So it's true," Gaétan said. "You really are the Voyvod Karyl, famous from song and story."

"I was," Karyl said. "Welcome, Gaétan. Have you come to join us?"

"If you'll have me." He walked forward to clasp forearms with Karyl.

"Gladly," Karyl said. "This is my lieutenant, Rob Korrigan. He's a dinosaur master by trade."

"Ah. That explains why he asked about my mount before me."

"You brought weapons, I see," Rob said, nodding to the sword, round shield, and suggestively waterproof sea monster–hide case that hung from the spiky dinosaur's saddle. The case might have fit a bardic-style harp. Somehow Rob doubted it did. "Can you use them?"

The young man shrugged. "I can take care of myself. I've traveled with my father's caravans since I was a toddler. I've had to fight a time or two."

"Is that a hornbow?" Karyl asked.

Rob raised a brow. *He actually sounds eager.*

"It is indeed." Gaétan took down the case, opened it, drew out an object shaped like a huge letter C. Karyl said nothing, but his eyes lit.

Gaétan slipped a looped string over one end of the bow. Taking the other in his left hand and the string's free end in the right, he swung the C around behind his left leg. Stepping through between string and stave, he braced the bow against the back of his right knee and straightened, grunting, forcing the C back against itself. When it was bent far enough, he slipped the other loop of the bowstring on, completing its transformation to a capital D. Then he stepped out of the bow and raised it.

By now he'd acquired a large and wide-eyed audience, Rob among them. The closest he'd ever come to one of the legendary recurved bows of the Turano and Parso nomads was watching Karyl's mobile flesh-forts advance through the river mists beneath Gunters Moll, and the terrible whispering death launched in clouds from the fighting-castles on their backs.

Gaétan drew the bow. Muscles rippled in his thick, bare arms. He eased off on the string and turned to Karyl.

"Would you care to heft it, Seigneur?" he asked.

"Please. If you'd be so kind. And if you feel a need to call me by a title, 'Captain' will serve."

Rob was mildly startled. Even though he had first laid eyes on the man as a one-handed beggar, playing mute in a village square, it was the first time he'd heard Karyl sound *humble*.

Karyl turned the bow over in his hands, seeming more to be *savoring* than inspecting. "They make these of sinew and horn glued together, layer by thin layer," he explained to Rob.

"Now, *here's* a lad who seems to have some substance to him," Rob heard Guat say from behind. The chunky farmer had been a thorn from the outset. Having his liege Yannic on hand hadn't made him less of a prick.

"And what might that mean?" Rob asked.

"Merchant lad comes with weapons. And he can use 'em. Can you and your outlander friend say that?"

Rob laughed incredulously. "Have you never seen the inside of a tavern, these last ten years? All they sing of are the exploits of the great Voyvod Karyl."

The ones that didn't sing about Jaume dels Flors, anyway. He thought that unnecessary to mention.

"Tavern songs," scoffed Reyn. The townsman carpenter and Percil employee was another problem child. "Fancy fables, nothing more. Oh, this Karyl's noble-born. Fine. We bend the knee to him 'cause that's the Law. The Creators made the world with the high above the low, so the base would be wider than the top and things'd stand firm. But can he fight? All he's done since he came here is talk. And order us around."

Others began to echo the pair's words. Rob's brows had squeezed down over his eyes until he could barely see through them. *I hear the heavy hands of town lords pushing this talk to the fore,* he thought. *Right treacherous bastards, the lot of them.* Although Melchor at least seemed willing to give the foreigners an honest chance to prove themselves.

Emeric said nothing in Karyl's defense. But he had

little to say at the best of times, especially around townsmen and peasants, whom he referred to as "sitting-folk." Only Lucas raised his voice in support, and that so high it cracked, which did his case little good.

No one questioned *Rob's* prowess, he noted. He was almost sorry.

How will himself respond? he wondered.

"Might I use your bow, Master Gaétan?" Karyl asked mildly.

Gaétan grinned. "I'm master of no one and nothing except myself. Plain 'Gaétan' is fine. And sure, be my guest."

He turned back toward his spike-frill, which was pulling up a beakful of yellow daisies. He unslung a quiver of fine-grained dinosaur hide, springer or even bouncer. The arrows were fletched with black and yellow feathers.

"I'll need just four," Karyl said. Gaétan held out the quiver. Karyl drew the arrows out one at a time by the notch end and clipped them against the bow with the first two fingers of his right hand.

"Do you want me to set up a butt for you, Captain?" Lucas asked, seeming more eager than ever to make himself useful with Gaétan on the scene. "A bale of hay, maybe?"

"No need." Karyl nocked an arrow. Drawing the string smoothly to his ear he tipped back and loosed upward, just a hair off straight upward.

Everyone followed the arrow's flight. Except Rob and Gaétan. They both watched Karyl calmly yet quickly take another arrow and shoot again.

The first arrow had just reached the top of its arc. The second arrow struck it midshaft.

That made even Rob's eyes bulge. As the *tick* of impact reached his ears, another arrow struck the first one, kicking it farther away. Four meters off the ground, the final arrow hit the first.

For a moment everyone just stared. Then they started shouting at once. "I told you! I told you he was just the man for us!" Guat yelled hoarsely.

Rob looked around. No town lord was in sight. *Pity, that,* he thought.

No one dared clap Karyl on the back. He was a grande, after all. Rob reckoned, though, that even if he were the lowest peasant, people would be leery of laying hands on him after that little display. Instead they danced about like loons, slapping each other's shoulders and punching arms.

"Poor technique," Karyl told Rob, quietly aside. "They should follow because of my field skills, not skill at arms. But time presses hard."

"Great Mother Maia, man, you needn't justify yourself to me!"

Karyl showed him a fleeting smile. "I'm justifying it to myself," he said. "You, I'm trying to teach."

Lucas, his face a reverent child's, ran to fetch the arrows. Karyl handed the hornbow back to its owner.

"A fine bow," he said. "Sorry for damaging your arrow. I'll pay for it."

"You'll do no such thing!" Gaétan exclaimed. "Or rather—if you please, my lord, just give it back to me. Otherwise my family'll think I'm lying when I tell the story!"

Emeric stepped up to ask if he might try the horn-bow. The woods-runner had mightily impressed the townsmen and farmers with the prowess he showed with his own weapon. Gaétan nodded.

Karyl handed Emeric the weapon. The woods-runner tried to draw it. He could bend the string no farther than a hand's width from true, no matter how he strained or how maroon his face turned behind his long yellow moustache.

Rob nodded knowingly. *And that's your problem with these heathen mainland shortbows. They lack the range and punch of either a good Anglysh long-bow, or one of these fiendish Ovdan contraptions. They're not much use against knight or dinosaur beyond twenty paces, unless you nail an eye.*

"You found it light, didn't you?" Gaétan asked Karyl as a visibly chagrined Emeric returned the bow.

"Yes," Karyl said. "But any twenty-year-old of the Ovdan horse-nomad tribes, girl or boy, could've done what I did, horseback at full gallop."

"That's a grown-up bow," Gaétan said, "for a no-mad woman, that is. Up on the plateau I barely rate as novice, myself, although on this side of the moun-tains I'm reckoned fair."

"He's better than *fair*," Emeric said. When Rob looked at him, he added, "We have regular matches, you see. All the archers in the province know each other, whether woods-runners or sitting-folk."

"Can you get the archers to join us?" Karyl asked.

Gaétan looked at Emeric, who shrugged. "Worth a shot," Gaétan said.

Shortbowmen? Rob thought. *What good can they do us?* The question burned in his gut, but he had more sense than to ask it in front of the woods-runner.

Karyl showed him the quickest sliver of a smile. "Give it a go, then, Gaétan," he said. "We need what-ever we can get. And soon. Women too. They can shoot crossbows, if they don't know archery already."

Gaétan shrugged. "I'll pass the word around. Our family's got some adventurous womenfolk. They go on caravan just like us boys do. My older sister Jeannette used to be a pretty fair shot with a bow, but she's not likely to be interested, now that she's gotten all inward with the Garden and all their talk of peace and love. She won't go even out with the trains to Ovda anymore."

"Jeannette, then?" Rob eyed Gaétan's chest and the girth of his tan upper arms, alike impressive and left bare by his short feather cape. He swallowed hard. "Would she be tall and auburn-haired, by chance? A trifle on the willowy side?"

Gaétan grinned. "That's my sis, all right! You know her?"

"Passably," Rob said.

Gaétan punched Rob's biceps. "Well, there you go! Any friend of Jeannie's is a friend of mine."

Rob suppressed a wince.

"Honored," he said in a strangled voice.

Chapter 36

Jaume saw what to do. He waved his lance to signal for his Brothers to loose their single terremoto. As he finished the gesture, he snapped shut
his visor with the thumb knuckle of his lance hand.

His world became a tiny, echoing metal chamber
and the impacts of Camellia's two-legged trot jarring
up his spine. He poured his vision like water through
the eye-slits. His breath whooshed in his ears like a
blacksmith's bellows. He smelled the lavender-flavored

pumice-and-saleratus paste with which he'd brushed his teeth.

Obedient to his command, Camellia stretched forth her neck and silently screamed. So did his Companions' mounts behind him. Their side-blasts stabbed pain through his temples. His stomach rebelled. Dizziness spun his world. He was prepared to feel those things, and found them no more than momentary discomforts.

But unlike dinosaur knights, cavalry mounts and men-at-arms spent little time training to endure the terremoto. Dinosaurry seldom deigned to waste it on mere cavalry. War-duckbills needed little more than *mass* to destroy warhorses.

The small but intense Companion terremoto caught the Terrarojanos unexpecting. The effect almost shocked Jaume. Half a dozen chargers directly in front of the Companions went down as if shot. Others put their heads down and bolted straight ahead. Some reared, so that those racing behind slammed into them and all crashed down. Others turned and fled, back into the faces of their own comrades, or straight away from Jaume's monsters, toward the Redlands dinosaurry chasing the routed Imperials.

The path the murder-cry opened to Jaume's Companions wasn't perfectly clear, but it was clear *enough*. Jaume pulled his lance from the scabbard that held it upright beside his saddle. Turning, he brandished it.

"*For Beauty and the Lady!*" he cried. His voice rang above the drumbeat of hooves and splayed dinosaur feet, squealing horses, and screams of broken men. He shook free the white pennon tied to his lance, revealing his personal orange camellia badge and the Lady's Mirror symbol.

He swung the lance down toward the enemy. "Couch lances!"

"*For the Lady!*" his Companions echoed.

A courser in a blue-and-white caparison lay thrashing on its side in Camellia's path. Its rider struggled frantically to free the leg trapped beneath it. Jaume did not close his ears to the squelching and shrieking as he rode the morion right over them, but he didn't look down.

He dared a fast glance to his sides. On his right rode Manfredo. To the left Florian's red-and-yellow sackbut he called Here Comes Trouble slammed his breastbone against the rump of a racing bay courser and spun the half-tonne horse counterclockwise without breaking stride.

Tears flooded Jaume's eyes. He blinked them clear as they ran hot down his cheeks. He always cried in battle. Whether from sorrow at the ugliness and suffering he was causing, or from mere physical reaction, or both, he wasn't wise enough to know.

The Redlands knights rode their hadrosaurs south at a rolling four-legged gallop. Their quarry were already exhausting themselves in their desperate sprints, and dropping back to all fours. Their hunters knew they'd catch them, soon enough.

Their vision, their entire beings, had narrowed to a sort of tube focused solely on those they pursued. It was an overwhelming human impulse, Jaume knew; he and his own knights had learned to control it through training and experience.

Few other grandes saw the need. The pursuit was the *matanza*, the time of slaughter, and it was what they most enjoyed of war.

The Redlanders literally could not see the destruction

racing toward them like a stinger bolt. Until it hit them.

Now it was time to charge. Jaume signaled his Companions to draw their mounts' pawlike forelimbs off the ground, even as he did so with Camellia. A full-on sprint of those colossal hindlegs made the duckbills' power terrible.

Jaume steered Camellia in front of another morion streaked blue over green, whose rider had tastelessly caparisoned it in purple and silver. The other monster shied away from the collision, turning its head and trying to stop. It didn't hit Camellia, but Jaume cut it close enough that his lance went through its neck behind the flexible gorget that guarded its throat, just below the jaw.

The duckbill fell over to its right, spraying blood in a fan. Jaume had already let go of his lance and was reaching to draw the Lady's Mirror. A lance was as expendable as an arrow in duckbill combat. A dinosaur knight's main weapon was his mount.

He crashed Camellia's full weight into the side of a second hadrosaur, a yellow-speckled brown sackbut. His body whipped forward as Camellia stopped dead. Her breastbone knocked the other dinosaur down, trumpeting and kicking.

Jaume glanced right and turned Camellia left. She pirouetted as gracefully as a ballerina on the Lumière stage, ducking head and forequarters low and elevating her massive counterbalancing tail.

Which she swung like a log into a morion's face. The dinosaur's neck broke with a noise like rock shattering beneath a hammer. It turned into a white, grey, and black avalanche.

Using the momentum from slamming into the duckbill, Camellia spun back clockwise. The dead dinosaur and doomed rider hurtled past.

Humid and foully rich, the stench of spilled blood and vast voided herbivore intestines surrounded Jaume like swamp air. All around him men and monsters fought, with a tumult that sounded like a smithy accompanied by an orchestra of bagpipes and bugles.

He saw Machtigern's hammer dent the side-crown of a green, white, and red helmet. His victim's armor slumped as if emptied, and flopped loosely from the saddle. Roaring, Timaeos struck a black-and-white shield with his maul so hard it knocked the Redlander clean off his mount.

Amidst a wave of pink dust, its rider howling as his pinned leg was ground beneath, a downed sackbut skidded on its side into Fernão's sackbut, Lusitano. Jaume yelled as the green-and-yellow Lusitano tumbled, plunging Fernão down and out of sight.

Jaume had no chance to aid his downed Companion. A knight in a countercharged black-and-gold helmet charged him on his morion, swinging a flange-headed mace. From the way his armored body moved, Jaume could tell he was putting everything into the blow, in hopes of breaking Jaume's shield and the arm beneath.

So instead of squaring the shield to the blow, as reflex screamed for him to do, Jaume swung the shield outward from his body. The mace glanced along its face with a steel-on-steel hiss.

To strike that hard the Redland knight had to open with his own shield as well, to clear his stroke and add momentum. He also had to lean far into it.

When Jaume deflected his shot it left his enemy
wide open. Jaume thrust hard with the Lady's Mirror.
Its star-steel tip broke through the gorget with a
squeal.

Blood spurted in dainty scarlet streams through
the fine piercings where the enemy's visor covered his
mouth. The Mirror pulled free of the Redlander's
throat and armor as he fell.

Momentarily, Jaume found himself alone amid a
swirl of vast bodies. He couldn't see Fernão or Lusitano anymore. He glimpsed a terrific roil of smaller
armored bodies to the north as the Companions-
Ordinary fought the Terrarojano heavy cavalry. Like
the dinosaur knights, the Companion hombres armaos
had caught their opponents strung out, and had taken
them in the flank. Now skill, courage, and hard
blows would tell if those advantages could make up
for their lack of numbers.

Snare drums snarled. Trumpets screamed. Flags
wounded the sky with color. Great drums beat like
the heart of a frightened titan.

Death reigned.

A knight with the lower half of his unfashionably
antique great helm painted red with a series of semi-
circles for an upper border and the top enameled
white attacked Jaume at the sprint with his lance
couched. A banner with the same colors flapped from
a standard affixed to the cantle of his saddle. His
sackbut was strikingly colored: pure white, with its
limbs, tail, and beak shocking crimson, as though the
giant beast had just forded a river of blood.

Conde Terraroja had found out his chief tormentor.
Jaume turned Camellia to face the charging sack-

but. His knees nudged her into one more bipedal sprint. Her huge chest heaved like the bellows of Torrey's own forge. Saliva streamed from her beak in long white ropes. She had little left to give. But she was a fighter, and she gave it now.

"Bella and the Emperor!" Jaume shouted. He leaned forward as Terraroja's lance struck his shield with an impact that would have sent most knights sprawling backward over the cantle. But he kept his seat as if his legs were welded to Camellia's sides.

The white hadrosaurs crashed together. For a moment they strained breastbone to breastbone. The sackbut rolled its eyes wildly. Terraroja dropped his stub of broken lance and drew his arming-sword.

His Parasaurolophus wasn't as high-backed as Jaume's Corythosaurus. But the duckbills were well matched in size and strength. Rupp von Teuzen had trained the Companions' mounts in what amounted to the art of *dinosaur wrestling*. Unfortunately, the technique was no secret; Terraroja's mount held its own.

The instant Jaume realized Camellia couldn't gain him any advantage, he gave her the command to turn counterclockwise. Her opponent's own pushing helped her whip right around in place. It put Jaume and Count Redland knee to knee, Jaume's right side to his enemy's left.

Behind the slits of his great helm, Terraroja's eyes widened in triumph. Jaume had left himself wide open by giving his opponent his unshielded side.

As Camellia turned, Jaume had started his longsword stabbing for those eye-slits. Like everybody, Don Leopoldo had a powerful reflex to protect his eyes. His shield, flat at the top and tapering at the bottom, snapped up fast.

Too fast. Too high. Which increased the amount of time it blinded him.

Twisting right in his saddle, pivoting Camellia back clockwise to give him the proper angle, Jaume reached his shield toward the sackbut's rump. He caught the left rim of Terraroja's shield with the right edge of his own.

He wheeled Camellia back the other way. Her mass yanked Leopoldo half out of his saddle toward her. He roared as the two monsters slammed together, causing the steel cuisse that guarded his left thigh to flex inward with a hollow sound, putting cruel pressure on the thigh within.

Leaning into him, Jaume smashed the heavy round pommel of the Lady's Mirror into his great helm. He had Camellia sidle a fast step left. The stunned Terraroja fell right between the monsters.

Normally a war-hadrosaur would drop its torso the instant it felt its rider losing balance, to keep him in the saddle or, failing that, reduce how far he had to fall. But Camellia's sideswipe body-slam had disconcerted Redland's sackbut. It reacted too late.

Jaume directed Camellia to swat it with her tail. It vented baritone despair and fled south.

Don Leopoldo de la Terraroja lay on his back like an overturned handroach, arms and legs waving feebly. Jaume reared Camellia as close to upright as her hips and big tail would permit. Walking forward on her, he stopped just short of the step that would bring a three-toed foot and half the combined weight of dinosaur, rider, tack, and armor down on Terraroja's breastplate.

For a moment he locked eyes with Terraroja. If the Count of the Redlands harbored any notion the Count of the Flowers was bluffing about crushing him, it fled.

"Wait!" Terraroja cried. "I yield!"

"Order your men to stop fighting."

"Stop fighting!" Leopoldo called out. Still breathless from his fall, he couldn't put much volume in it. But he tried.

"Don Leopoldo yields!" Jaume shouted. *He* had plenty of breath. "Terrarojanos, your master orders you to surrender! Throw down your arms!"

Most of the action had gone elsewhere, leaving Jaume largely isolated with his vanquished enemy amidst a scatter of fallen dinosaurs and men, some moving and groaning, some not. Fortunately Timaeos was nearby. The Trebizónico added his colossus bellow, repeating the words.

The cry was echoed across the battlefield. Anyone who thought it a ruse had only to glace over and see Terraroja's distinctive sackbut running enthusiastically south, on all fours with its tail high.

Like grass swept by a sudden wind, weapons fell to the ground as the Redland army surrendered.

"There were three of them," the child said excitedly. "Two men and a montadora, their armor all bright and everything, each on a monster as big as a house."

Karyl and Rob stood listening in a shady thicket east of the Séverin farm practice field. The afternoon air was thick, and tangy from some herb unknown to Rob. Feathered gliders furiously scolded them and the child for their intrusion.

Newly minted spymaster Rob had struck gold. The luck of the Korrigans had brought him this vest-pocket virtuoso spy, a street urchin in a hemp-sack smock, who seemed to know everyone in Providence town and everything they got up to. He had a gift for getting other children—and not just the gutter-snipes—to talk to him.

Or *her*. Rob couldn't make up his mind. Beneath random black hair and a coating of urban grime, his informant had a very kidlike face, and spoke in a piping voice like everybody else that age, sixteen or so. The urchin went by the name Petit Pigeon, Little Pigeon, which gave Rob no clues either way.

"They just charged right into town down the Brokenheart Highway with their Crève Coeur badges painted on their chests, bold as you please," Little Pigeon said. "Kicked carts and kiosks to splinters, knocked ladders all flying. Dumped old Quentin Wen-Nose the housepainter on his ass so hard he cramped right up and had to scuttle for the gutter on all fours, like a bug. Everybody had to step lively to get out of the way."

Between sentences the child stuffed more of the handful of dried figs Rob had given . . . it . . . into its mouth. Rob sympathized. When your cheeks were that hollow, beneath wide cheekbones suggesting a naturally full face, eating took priority over even the most thrilling news.

Or the most horrific.

"This one kid, he's maybe five, he didn't move fast enough. The Brokenheart leader, this big guy with a shaved head and black beard, knocked him ass over elbows with his sackbut. Achille, kid's name is. Snot-nosed little bugger, but he didn't deserve nothin' like that.

"His mom, Mathilde, she's this journeyman potter in Fat Vincent's studio by the river, she was haggling with Crook-Backed Adèly the feather-monger. She's married to Igon, this Basque leatherworker from up in the mountains. She saw her child go flying and ran to help him, screaming like her hair was afire.

"So the woman knight on the green morion, she had short yellow hair and a green cross on a white shield painted on her breastplate, she runs Mathilde right through with her lance. Then the third guy, had on a cape that looked like scarlet horror feathers, his red sackbut steps on both of them and just grinds 'em into paste on the cobbles."

"Buckethead assholes," Rob said. "Pardon my Anglysh."

In went more figs. Hardened though he thought he was, Rob felt his stomach turn over at that. *You've been there yourself. Remember how real hunger feels.*

"What happened next?" Karyl asked gently. His arms were folded over his deceptively skinny bare chest. He held his staff in one hand.

"They rode right up to Town Hall," Petit Pigeon said, dribbling bits of fruit from his mouth—Rob was tired of trying to think of a child as *it*. "Black Beard hollered for the mayor. Old Ludovic came out. He's a dick; anybody *official* is gonna be one, it's just natural. But he showed some big ones, I got to tell you. He looks like this brown rat, scarcely bigger than that kid who got squashed, with hardly a hair to his head, a big old nose, and these droopy moustaches. He's quivering all over. But he faces them, up there on those giant monsters of theirs. Demands to know why they're violating his town and everything and stuff.

"So Black Beard laughs all evil and everything. 'We bring you a message from my Lord the Count Guillaume of Crève Coeur,' he says, all grand. 'The rightful Count of Providence having abandoned this fief, suzerainty lies open for any noble hand to claim.'"

Rob caught Karyl's eye and raised a brow. For an uneducated alley-runner, Little Pigeon rattled off the big words with enviable aplomb. Perhaps he was just a natural mimic.

"'The good Count Guillaume now graciously steps forward to save you from anarchy and the unnatural vice of leveling,' the guy tells Ludovic. 'In one week's time he comes. You will welcome him as your new lord.'

"'Or be crushed like the lice you are,' the woman yells.

"Then they turned around and trotted out of town like they didn't have a care in the world."

"You've done well," Karyl said.

Rob flipped the child a peso. Little Pigeon bit it skeptically and grinned. Rob grinned back. He knew the taste of silver, and the way his teeth sank ever so slightly into the true metal.

The child turned and vanished at once into the green underbrush. He might be a town rat, but he knew how to lose himself in the countryside as well.

"So that's torn it, then," Rob said. "What do we do now?"

"Fight," Karyl said. "I'll order the volunteers to get ready to march on a moment's notice. Then you and I are heading off to the villa. I suspect the Garden

Council is going to want to have its say. At considerable length."

"Aye," Rob said ruefully, rubbing the back of his neck. "They're just the sort to all want to piss in the soup to make it taste the better."

Part Four

La Cuenta

(The Reckoning)

Chapter 37

Arrancador de los Muertos, **Corpse-tearer, Bloody Bill**—*Caulkicephalus trimicrodon*. A pterandon, a crested, tailless flier, with a toothed beak that flares at the end; 5-meter wingspan, 20 kilograms. Slate-grey-to-black fur, mottled red on head, neck, and shoulders, as if blood-splashed. Which it often is. Feeds on corpses. Unwelcome but necessary habitué of battlefields.

—THE BOOK OF TRUE NAMES

Mor Manfredo knelt in the pale-green grass at the center of a circle of Companions, still in armor except for their helmets, who looked on in shared agony. Fernão lay across his lap. The Gallego had his neck arched convulsively back. Wheezing whimpers came from his wide-open mouth and his spurs kicked grooves in the tough red dirt as he fought to drag air into a chest crushed by his collapsed breastplate.

It was obvious to Jaume he would lose. It surprised

him his friend had lived so long with such a terrible injury. It saddened him as well.

A knight in full plate was largely invulnerable. It usually took consummate skill or stupid luck to hit an eyehole or a weak point at a joint and bring one down. A dinosaur knight's greatest danger was his greatest weapon: a war-dinosaur. No armor a human could carry could protect him from being crushed by a multi-tonne monster stepping on him, falling on him, or slamming him with its tail.

When that happened armor was a false friend. Instead of bursting like a full wineskin hit by a hammer and promptly dying, you got to linger with your metal carapace crumpled into you, cruelly pinching your smashed limbs and torso, as you waited to die from internal bleeding and the failure of abused organs.

As their beloved brother Fernão was experiencing now.

Manfredo looked up. He had taken off his armet and the padded coif he wore beneath. His red hair was plastered to his forehead, where blue veins stood out, and hung lank over the flared pauldrons of his armor. He looked up at Jaume with eyes full of tears. His square chin jutted with the effort of clenching back a scream.

"Help him," the Taliano gritted. "By the Lady, by the Mother, please help him."

Timaeos, kneeling beside the fallen Companion, looked at Jaume and shook his head.

"There's no point even trying to get the armor off him," the big man said. "It will only make him suffer horribly to no end. We cannot help him."

"No!" shouted Manfredo. Seeing his friend's stern

reserve torn apart by grief stung Jaume like a wasp. It sorrowed him almost as much Fernão's torment.

Which was, at least, about to come to an end.

Jaume stroked Manfredo's sodden hair. "Beloved brother. You're as battle-seasoned as any of us. You know he won't make it."

For an instant Manfredo glared up at Jaume with such glowing rage and hatred that Jaume, physically, mentally, and spiritually exhausted as he was, could barely keep from flinching. Then the Taliano squeezed his eyes shut. Tears rolled out the long, red lashes.

"I know," he whispered.

Though his losing struggle for breath had to be filling Fernão's mind, he seemed to track what was being said. A brown hand gripped Manfredo's pale one.

Manfredo drew his misericorde. Cradling his lover's head with his other hand, he bent down and kissed the darkened, sweat-coated brow.

The other Companions turned away. Not even Timaeos the healer could watch.

But Jaume did not avert his eyes as Manfredo stabbed the slim, straight dagger expertly into Fernão's ear. The Gallego stiffened. Then with a whistling sigh he fell back, and was at peace, and free of pain.

A meter-long shaft transfixed the tailless flier, whose crest and head looked as if they were splashed in blood. It snapped its toothy beak at the arrow, and fell off the chest of a helmetless Terrarojano knight who lay with blood trickling down his bearded cheeks to beat the ground with black-furred wings.

"Why did you shoot, Owain?" Manfredo asked the Galés. The Companions walked among the fallen, giving what succor they could to both sides' wounded. They had gratefully shed their armor and the sweat-sodden jupons they wore beneath as padding. "The corpse-tearer was only doing what the Creators made it to do."

The lanky Companion nocked another arrow. "That one's still alive," he said in his curious lilt, "and the flier was going for his eyes."

Florian stooped to examine the injured knight. The man's skin was sallow and beaded with sweat. He moaned as if trying to speak beneath his breath. He seemed unaware of his erstwhile enemy's nearness.

"He's done for," Florian said, straightening.

There came a whir, and a *thunk* like an axe hitting wood. Another arrow sprouted suddenly from the mortally wounded man's right temple.

Manfredo jerked and shot the Galés a mad-eyed look. After a moment he visibly reasserted self-control. Jaume relaxed.

Lover-bonding was encouraged among Companions—as had existed between Jaume and Pere before there were Companions. Jaume believed it helped inspire the Brothers to fight even more fiercely for each other. They were forbidden to take lovers among the order's lower ranks, the squires and the Ordinaries. But Companions were equals. Even Jaume, their very charter notwithstanding, who led only because the rest chose to follow.

But the loss of a lover was even more brutal than loss of a Brother. They would all carry the wound of Fernão's loss; when it healed, it would leave a scar. Manfredo's wound was deeper than anyone's. It would take longest to heal.

The bodies of men, a few women, and animals lay

strewn like storm debris over the better part of a square kilometer of the shallow flat slope. Some still moved, and the chorus of groans and cries sounded half like the moaning of the wind, half like a rookery of seabirds on a desolate, rocky shore.

The smell was . . . what you'd expect. And the bodies hadn't yet properly begun to rot in the midday heat.

Others moved about the battlefield on the same errand as the Companions. Men and women robed in Queen Maia's brown and gold, and the blue and black of Lanza, the Middle Son. Both Creators' sects emphasized training in the healing arts. For the most part they worked in pairs, one from each sect. Since they served the gentle, healing side of the Mother, rather than her complementary aspect of destroyer, the Maian sectaries preferred to leave mercy killing of humans and animals to their partners. The war-god's devotees saw delivering the final grace as little different from splinting a broken limb or suturing a wound.

Far more carrion-fliers and birds ministered to the fallen than humans. And the insects, the buzzing flies with their cobalt-blue bellies glinting in the cloud-screened sun and endless files of ants, outnumbered all. Inevitably the slaughter attracted swarms of two-legged scavengers as well, feathered and otherwise. Patrols of Nodosaur light infantry and mercenary light horse kept them away.

"Once the sun goes down," said Florian, falling into step beside Jaume, "our money-troopers will be out robbing the dead before the clouds have broken up."

With a grimace that might well be taken for a sour smile, Jaume nodded. In comparison to his own bone-aching fatigue and soul-sickness, Florian seemed almost chipper. His cheeks were pink and his step springy.

At one time Jaume would have worried once more that the lowborn Francés was shallow, or worse, lacked a conscience, and that he had made a terrible mistake by admitting him. But in the weeks since Pere died, Jaume had come to know him better. Florian replied to hardship with a smiling face and a jaunty stride. And he was genuinely resilient.

He feels as deeply as any of us. He just heals quicker. Jaume wasn't sure whether he envied him that or not.

A cry passed from throat to throat across a breeze that blew from the east, alerting Jaume that a small mounted party approached from the direction of the hidden town and the all-too-visible castle. Hands went to sword hilts.

"They fly a black flag," Florian said. "This should prove interesting."

Jaume strode toward the road. "Captain," Manfredo called, "shouldn't some of us mount up to guard you? Do you trust these unknowns?"

Jaume laughed. Almost to his surprise it was genuine, despite the pain it caused the ribs the matador had cracked for him. Now that the battle fever had subsided and the letdown begun, it was as if every wound he'd suffered came back to haunt him at once.

"No, my friend," he called back over his shoulder. "But I want them to see I'm not afraid of them."

". . . when many Imperial grandes, with the connivance if not open support of their liege lords, the kings of Alemania, Francia, and even Spaña, rebelled against Manuel's increasingly iron-fisted (and erratic) rule, and laid unprecedented siege against his capital city of La Majestad, which was still undergoing construction. But el Insurrecto came to an end when his daughter Juana, then called la Roja for her flame-colored hair, walked alone—without so much as a single house-shield to guard her—to the end of the lone bridge that ran across the abyss to the capital to announce her father's death of lingering ill health. . . ."

"Ho, my daughter dear! How are you, this fine day?"

Melodía shut the history book she'd been reading with a decisive thump. "I'm fine, Father," she said, looking up and trying not to sigh. "How are you?"

"Splendid, splendid," he said. He kept his voice muted; the library's stern guardian wouldn't hesitate to hush even an Emperor. Felipe's keen sense of justice kept that from offending him. Indeed, it amused him. Which was among the many reasons Melodía loved him more than he exasperated her.

Because it was a warm day, even here in the Firefly Palace library where immense fans powered by Centrosaurus-turned capstans kept the air flowing to minimize humidity on Prince Heriberto's vast collection of books, Emperor Felipe dressed minimally. He wore brief yellow trunks, low boots of yellow feather-felt, and a shoulder-yoke of sweeping scarlet and gold plumes. Even his shadow Mondragón, looking grim and grumpy as usual from beyond the Emperor's ginger-furred right shoulder, conceded to the heat by wearing a cloak of brown and black feathers over a brown kilt and sandals.

He nodded curtly to Melodía.

"Alteza," he said, acknowledging her only with the slightest lizard's-tongue eye-flick. *Here I spent years thinking he disapproved of me as frivolous,* she thought. *Until I realized he took far too little notice of me to approve or disapprove.*

Like most of Firefly Palace's public spaces, the library had high, rib-vaulted ceilings. Unlike altogether too many of them, it was well lit by tall windows, as well as being well kept, dusted, and continually replenished. No aficionado of recreational reading—and less of parting with good silver—the Prince of the Tyrant's Jaw nonetheless spent freely here. He approved of reading on principle, as being good for business; the library was a tradition dating from the Iron Duchess herself; the Firefly Palace was Felipe's de facto Imperial residence; and keeping La Merced's library at least a volume larger than its bitter rival Laventura's was a goal held dear by every citizen, from the lowest to the highest.

"But why are you wasting such a glorious afternoon rusticated here among musty books, my child?" Felipe asked.

"I'm trying to learn as much as I can about the history of the Empire and la Familia," she said dryly, "in order to better perform my duty toward both."

She wore emerald silk trunks and plain brown buskins. Her maid, Pilar, who stood nearby, silently helpful, had wound her hair into braids and pinned it up in an intricate arrangement with beads and a feather or two. It looked fancier than it was. It was mostly meant to keep her hair off her neck.

Felipe tutted and shook his head. "You'll get worry lines from all this studying."

"I did take on many of the duties of running Los Almendros when my mother died," she reminded him.

Instantly she regretted doing so. The loss of his adored Marisol remained an open wound for him. And the fact that Melodía's mother had died giving birth to Montse—who likewise sat nearby, poring intently over a vast open book of her own—didn't make it feel better.

But today's good mood was invincible. He only beamed.

"And a splendid job you did too, Melodía. But now we've a fine seneschal in place to take care of our home duchy. You're the Emperor's daughter, girl. You've got no worries."

She scowled. "Nor duties either."

He laughed as if that was the grandest joke he'd heard this week, and clapped her on the bare brown shoulder.

"Indeed, indeed. So why not enjoy life while you're young? Though I do regret to report that you must delay your upcoming betrothal and nuptials with Jaume for a while longer."

That made her mash her lips together till she felt them stick out like a morion's bill. It wasn't as if she had *openly* announced the rupture between her and Jaume. But it *was* as if everybody else in the bloody palace knew about it. She hadn't tried to hide it, certainly.

Then again, had she ordered her servants to paint it in red letters a third of a meter high on the wall of his bedroom, he still might not have gotten the message. The Emperor didn't take hints, even if delivered on the beak of a war-hammer. And he was especially deaf and blind to tidings he didn't care for.

Then it hit her she was being the same.

"Wait, why? What do you mean, 'delay longer'?"

"Why, only that I have hit upon the splendid notion of sending our young champion on to bring other upstart grandes into line. Once he's finished with the reduction of Terraroja, that is. But that's certain as the sun's rising in the west, and not that much further off, surely."

"You can't be serious!" she said, jumping to her feet.

He smiled fondly and patted her arm.

"So wonderful talking with you, *mi hija,*" Felipe said, patting her on the arm. "Do try to lighten up a little and enjoy your life. It's so fleeting."

Your multiple-great-grandmother Rosamaría is three hundred years old! she thought. *I have every prospect of living as long. If boredom doesn't kill me first.*

She opened her mouth to launch what she already knew was a doomed assault on the ramparts of his shiny new resolve. But he was already striding away.

"But, Majesty—" Mondragón began as he followed his master.

Felipe waved a hand at him without bothering to glance back.

"We've been down this road again and again, my friend. Why take the trouble of assembling such a splendid instrument, and placing it in the hands of an acknowledged master, only to disassemble it after first use—when there remains a world of good it might yet do for the Imperio?"

Before his Chief Minister could answer him—futilely, of course—he paused to say a few low, fond words to Montse and tousle her blond dreadlocks.

Which she hated with a passion, and only suffered now because she starved for their father's attention as greatly as her older sister did. Then he marched grandly on out the door, Mondragón still scuttling behind.

The other attendants and patrons of the library barely glanced up; he had made it redundantly clear that he wanted no undue ceremony or fuss made over him in this his own home. And he was a frequent visitor here on his own—as much as that would surprise strangers to the court, not least certain members of Torre Delgao, who saw him as nothing more than a bumptious nobody.

Melodía sighed like a thunder-titan in the rain.

"Highness," Pilar said softly, "feel gently about your father. He—"

For an instant Melodía remembered two little girls, and a different morning long ago spent braiding each other's hair and piling it into fanciful shapes— Melodía's in the likeness of the frill and horn of a Styracosaurus, Pilar's in the much more modest likeness of a tricornio—and then laughing and chasing butterflies in one of the Firefly Palace's numberless enclosed gardens. Then duty slammed over the scene like a portcullis.

Class distinctions, after all, had been handed down by the Creators themselves. Melodía might not believe in the gods. But she believed in order—and her family's primacy, which depended on it.

"You are in no position to criticize the Emperor in any way," she said brusquely. She swept past her servant toward the door her father had left by. But not quickly enough to escape the look of hurt her words stamped into those jade-green eyes, that not even the practiced immobility of the gitana's features could hide.

As Melodía passed, Montserrat didn't even look up, so quickly had she gotten engrossed in her book again. Melodía twitched a smile when she recognized it—*A Child's First Book of Sieges: Lavishly Illustrated; Feat. Eyewitness Accounts of the Most Atrocious and Lamentable Intakings*. One of Montse's favorites.

"Your Highness," a voice said from between her and the door.

As if my day wasn't spoiled enough. She recognized the remarkably deep and no less remarkably unctuous voice of the chief of the delegation from Trebizon—the one that had been pestering her father for months to promise her hand in marriage to their appalling tallow-tub of a Prince.

He stood waiting with his two fellow emissaries. His head was shaven and crowned with a splendid high cylindrical hat. His beard was black, precise, and oiled. Like the two women with him his eyes were outlined far too dramatically in kohl. Like them he dressed with no regard for the afternoon's heat, draped neck to toes in heavy flowing robes of black, or cloth so dark they appeared to be, worked through with silver threads and the occasional flash of gemstones, sapphires, emeralds, diamonds, or amethysts. Melodía didn't know whether it was because of a higher degree of prudery among the Trebs than prevailed here in their rival empire, or simply because the relatively temperate La Merced seemed cool after the Black River Delta swamps.

"May we trouble you for a moment of your time?"

"By no means," she said. "Archbishop Akakios. Megaduchess Paraskeve. Megaduchess Anastasia."

Nodding to each in turn she plowed on by, heedless to their entreaties as a treetopper strolling through a village would be to the occupants' screams as it trampled their houses. They smelled of far too much essence or incense: a cacophony of odors.

A fourth member of the embassy stood squarely blocking the point-arched doorway: a slim, elegant man of Melodía's own height, with a fine grey eyes and hair and full beard of the same shade. He wore a doublet of grey velvet, scarcely cooler than his associates' garb but marginally more fashionable, over silver hose.

"Count Dragos," she said coolly.

He clapped his hand to the jeweled but eminently serviceable hilt of the *spadataliana*, or rapier, he wore by his hip. Her heart jumped, and she briefly wished she'd permitted a pair of Scarlet Tyrants to accompany her, instead of curtly dismissing them.

But the Count, who was cut from a much different fabric from his associates, only bowed smoothly as he stepped aside to clear her path.

"The Princess looks most lovely today," he murmured in his curiously accented Spañol.

"I do," she said, and went out.

Countess Terraroja was a sturdy woman with a silvered blond braid wrapped around her head. She rode sidesaddle on a white palfrey, which had been fashionable a century before. Jaume didn't care much about fashion. The beauty he adored might change or fade. *Would* change and fade, with time and season. But not with fancy.

A similarly mounted maid and a handful of mail-armored horsemen followed Condesa Terraroja. By their seats Jaume recognized them as house-soldiers, mounted infantry rather than cavalry trained to fight on horseback. They carried neither shield nor spear, but wore swords scabbarded over tabards bearing the white and red Terraroja arms.

Their faces and postures betrayed great apprehension. But also a kind of resolution. Should Jaume intend treachery, and violate the parley-flag, they would die. Clearly they knew it. Just as clearly they were determined to exact a cost if it came to that.

The countess reined in ten meters from where Jaume stood in the road. Her maid and a soldier dismounted and bustled forward to help her. Before they got to her the Countess dismounted on her own.

She showed no fear, of Jaume, his Companions, or the army all around them. *Don Leopoldo surely doesn't live up to this one,* thought Jaume. *Which I suppose is just as well for the Empire.*

The Countess approached. For the space of a few breaths she stood gazing into Jaume's eyes. Sadness and defiance walked across her square, handsome face by turns.

She hiked up her long skirts and dropped to her knees on the crushed pumice road. "I abase myself before you, Lord Constable," she said. Her accent, like her features and coloring, suggested she was Alemanan.

"No need for that, señora," he said. "Please stand up. Our complaints lay with your husband. We have resolved them."

She rose to stand stiffly upright. She had probably never been a conventionally pretty woman. But Jaume found the strength in her face and posture beautiful in itself.

"Not altogether," she said. "I'm here to plead for his life."

The Count lay bound in a tent under guard by Ordinaries. He'd had the wit to maintain a dignified and stony silence. Which at the least spared his breath and his captors' ears.

"His ultimate fate rests in His Imperial Majesty's hands," Jaume said.

"You carry the High Justice. You could order him hanged. I beg you for the chance to plead his case before the Fangèd Throne."

"Why shouldn't Don Jaume hang him?" asked Manfredo.

Jaume's face tightened. It wasn't really the Taliano's turn to speak here. But by rule any Companion could speak his mind without penalty.

"His crimes are plain, and merit nothing better."

The Countess's blue eyes flared. After a few heartbeats of furnace glare, under which the red-haired Taliano refused to melt, she turned and gestured to the red stone castle on its red stone crag.

"If you spare Leopoldo for trial by the Emperor, I'll surrender both keep and town. Otherwise"—she shook her head haughtily and jutted her strong chin—"I will resist you as stoutly as my husband would have."

"More so, I'd guess," said Florian softly from behind Jaume.

Jaume turned and raised a reproving eyebrow. Florian held up a hand. "Sorry."

Jaume winked at him. He thought the same.

"If you surrender," he told the Countess, "I offer general amnesty, to you, your retinue, your servants, the common folk, and the common soldiers. I can't promise anything concerning your husband's vassals, however."

Her lip curled. "You can do what you like with *them*," she said, "with my blessing."

Jaume smiled. "I'm pleased to accept your offer, then, Condesa Terraroja. I give you the thanks of the Empire."

She smiled, if bleakly, and started to return to the horse her sweating soldier held. Then she stopped and turned back.

"One more thing, my lord," she said, almost shyly. "I know I've no right to ask, but . . . might I have my husband back? Until you're ready to carry him off to trial?"

The Companions protested behind him, and not just the hyper-legalistic Manfredo.

"He has to give his parole not to escape," he said.

"He will."

"And you must give yours not to permit nor aid his escape in any way. And you know what it will mean if he does."

He spoke softly, gently even. He did not reckon this woman as fool enough to mistake that for *weakness*.

She nodded. "Ban of outlawry. Attainder. We forfeit everything: land, titles, lives. I have two daughters, Lord Constable. *We* have two daughters. They're lovely girls, not a bit like their father—although I love him, scapegrace as he is. I won't have them turned to animals that every hand is free to hunt. I give you my word, as a mother as well as a countess, Leopoldo shall not escape."

"Manfredo," Jaume said, glancing back at the knight who stood behind his right shoulder, "see to releasing our captive into the Countess's custody, if you please."

Manfredo's beautiful face knotted in a decidedly unbeautiful scowl. "Captain—"

Jaume turned fully and laid a hand on Manfredo's flaring shoulder armor. The sun-hot metal stung a palm raw and bruised from haft and hilt.

He looked into the Taliano's eyes and smiled until Manfredo dropped his gaze. "Very well," Manfredo said.

"You are a good man, my friend," said Jaume.

Chapter 38

Segador chistoso, **Ridiculous Reaper**—*Therizinosaurus cheloniformis.* A large, bipedal, mostly herbivorous beaked dinosaur from Ruybrasil; 10 meters long, 5 tonnes. Possesses large, brightly colored feathers prized throughout Aphrodite Terra. Most Nuevaropans consider their usual description—short-legged, swagbellied, possessing terrifying foreclaws a meter or more long—a ludicrous invention.

—THE BOOK OF TRUE NAMES

ight though they were, hood and cloak stifled Falk, Herzog von Hornberg as he rode his rented horse through early-evening woods several kilometers inland from the Firefly Palace. Spring had come to the Principality of the Tyrant's Jaw. While seasonal variations were even less noticeable here on this tropical coast than inland, the weather had grown warmer.

He endured. Any knight was trained to do so from earliest adolescence. And of course, Falk had forced himself to learn to endure more than most. Not that it was ever enough to please his mother.

Not that anything ever was.

The locals called these el Bosque Salvaje, the Savage Woods, although they weren't a bit more savage than anyplace else on the Tyrant's Head. To be sure, you might get gored by a surly nosehorn, or rent limb from limb by a wild raptor-pack. What was special about *that*?

He suspected these decadent Mercedes, urban creatures to the core, distrusted nature and stayed as clear of it as they could. Still, he wasn't enjoying the *natural* way sweat sluiced down his broad face, stung his eyes, tickled down his sides to soak the felt-lined leather sword belt and silk loincloth beneath his cloak.

How inconspicuous can I be, with my size and noble bearing? A blue blood, a knight especially, *carried* himself differently from any other beast that walked Nuevaropa. And everyone raised on the Tyrant's Head knew the look.

He also didn't know why it had been necessary to rent a horse at a dodgy livery in town, instead of borrowing one of the fine mounts freely available in Prince Harry's—Heriberto's—stables. But Bergdahl insisted on it, as he had the hood.

Falk wasn't sure the man wasn't just toying with him. But he had done as Bergdahl insisted. As always.

In the underbrush around him, the insect choir began its preliminary voice exercises for the night to come. The setting sun pushed Falk and his mount's shadow well ahead of them along the shell-paved path as the bay trotted briskly west through a tunnel of overarching limbs. The air smelled of day-warm dust and fallen leaves.

Falk sniffed the tangy woodsmoke of the road-house's cookshack and the savory aromas of meat roasting over coals and open flames long before he turned a bend and the establishment came into sight. His stomach growled. A whole roast scratcher capon, a rack of barbecued fatty ribs with sweet-hot sauce, and to wash all down a liter mug of the house's famous beer would go a long way to setting him right.

If only something would still the butterflies in his stomach. In his mind he could hear Bergdahl sneer: *Why so timid, your Grace? You could take out these fops you're meeting with fists alone.* And his mother saying, *You're a smart boy, Falk. Why do you always act so stupid?*

He shook his head like a horse trying to chase a fly from its ear.

Of course I'm afraid, he thought by way of rebuttal. *If the wrong people spot me, I'll lose everything I've worked for.* His scarcely healed forearm twinged at the thought.

Not to mention that trifling thing, my head.

The Nosehorn Bull at Bay was a solid sprawl of fieldstone, a single story with a roof of green-painted cypress shakes. Its sign was imposing, a placard a good three meters long, hung by bronze chains from a stout tree-trunk frame. It luridly depicted the titular beast—a splendid dinosaur, with extravagant yellow-and-black eyespots on its frill, and gore dripping from its horn—confronting a quartet of mounted huntsmen with spears and a pack of snarling green horrors. The outcome seemed considerably in doubt.

Falk nodded approval to himself when he halted

his horse by a polished green-granite post and dismounted. He liked to see a thing well done.

He tethered his gelding to the greened-bronze ring hung from the post. Half a dozen horses were hitched to similar posts near the stone channel, fed from a nearby stream, that ran in front of the roadhouse. Striders pecked and clucked in a pen. You couldn't leave the ruffed riding-dinosaurs tied for any length of time. They were so highly strung they'd panic and break a leg or scrawny neck.

Stepping up onto the little stone bridge over the watering-channel, Falk tossed a few copper centimos to the skinny girl in a black smock, thong sandals, and shallow-cone hat who squatted by the door, to give his mount a handful of oats. It was a small act of rebellion: he could hear his mother and his servant deride him for his soft heart and head, coddling someone else's nag. Anyway, Falk regarded pointless cruelty as indulgence, a giving in to weakness.

Inside, the air was thick with the smoke of several kinds of pipe-stuffing, the dull reek of spilled beer, and the sounds of roistering. The publican seemed to expect him. Her manner was obsequious even though she had the face of an ancient granite statue and the proportions of a good oak gate. With his hood up he towered over her by a good sixty centimeters, but he doubted an innkeeper as seasoned as she looked to be was intimidated by mere size.

Down a stone-walled hallway, a door that clearly led to a proverbial back room opened promptly to a rap of the hostess's brawl-scarred knuckles. An aristocratic face appeared. It unwrapped itself from around a look of annoyed disdain when its owner saw Falk looming behind the woman.

Without a glance at the publican, the man who opened the door pressed a coin into her palm. He was slight of stature, carried himself like a scratcher cock, and had a head that looked the more outsized for sitting on a white ruff like an egg in a cup.

"You've come," he said. At least he had wit not to blurt out an incriminating *your Grace* into a public hallway. From the look of him it pained him not to be able to drop such an exalted title. "Excellent. Please come in."

He bowed Falk into the room. It was larger than Falk expected. Woven-feather panels lined the walls. Like the sign, they were worked with surprising skill.

Three men sat at a table set with pitchers, mugs, and bowls of fruit. One man was as bulky and oddly proportioned as the fabled Therizinosaurus, or ridiculous reaper, of distant Ruybrasil, an immense two-legged herbivorous dinosaur with a swag belly and sickle claws a meter long. Another was your standard Spañol courtier, lean, with waxed moustaches.

". . . hear how you Delgaos always call Felipe 'that bastard of a Ramírez,'" the third man at the table was saying. He was only a little larger than the man who was just now shutting the door and feverishly waving for him to shut up. "Well, let me tell you something, gentlemen: if he kicks his family off the top of the heap with his mad antics, he'll take Torre Ramírez down with it."

And he smiled insouciantly at Falk.

The first man bustled forward as if afraid he might be late to something.

"I am Gonzalo Delgao," he said to Falk, who knew it. "This is my brother Benedicto—"

The Therizinosaurus smiled shyly, despite the fact he was at least as big as Falk.

"—our brother-in-law Don René Alarcón—" The courtier. "—and our *dear* ally, Mor Augusto Manorquín, who comes of a cadet house of Tower Ramírez."

The last was the vehement and irrepressible speaker. He reminded Falk of a ferret, sleek and slender. Though clearly nowhere near as circumspect.

"Mis compañeros," Gonzalo said grandly, "allow me to present his Grace, the inestimable Duke Falk von Hornberg."

Pulling back his hood with relief, Falk nodded acknowledgment.

"Gentlemen," he said, "what can we do for each other?"

"—and so this slight, thin boy, injured and covered with blood," Rob told rapt listeners at his table near the front of the Garden Hall, "his own, and that of his dead duckbill, and the still-hot gore of the monster he had just slain, was the first thing the hatchling matador saw when she opened her bloodred eyes and screamed, 'Shiraa!' She thought he was her very mother, and in that instant bonded to him for life."

He punctuated the story's end with a gulp of the local ale. His pipes were dry again, though not for want of prior lubrication.

A masterful telling, if I do say so myself, and I do, thought Rob, gazing around at the young Gardeners. A few mouths, he saw, were tightened against skeptical titters.

I could see why a body might doubt such a wild story, if it wasn't Karyl's own, and known throughout the land.

Then again, these people were scarcely the sort to spend much time in taverns. *All my best material's fresh as a newborn babe here,* he thought smugly. *I'm going to mint coin.*

"I've heard that's the only way to get one of the great meat-eating dinosaurs as a mount," a girl with a yellow smock and flowers twined in her brown hair said. Jeannette was missing tonight. Given what Rob had learned that afternoon, it suited him just fine.

Rob drained his flagon and set it on the table with a *thump*, more loudly than he meant to. Faces at other tables turned briefly his way, then pointedly away.

"And the best ones, lass," he said, "are wild-caught. Those hatched in captivity have never the same fire."

From the head table on its dais, a bell rang for order. Tall, lank-haired Telesphore rose to call in a faint monotone for the business at hand. Rob found him a limp and pale fish for a follower of a beauty cult. *Perhaps he hides his enthusiasm well, so.*

In any event he seemed one of the better-disposed on the Council toward Karyl and Rob. Or at least, less actively hostile.

Heads turned as Karyl entered the hall. He wore his usual hooded robe and sandals, and carried his deceptive walking stick. His hair was tied back from his ascetic's face, which despite the time he spent outdoors always remained pale. His expression was calm and his manner dignified as he walked up to stand before the head table.

The contrast between his garments' rough simplic-
ity and the Councilors' expensive, faux-rustic clothes
was like a voice crying fraud.

Bogardus rose. "Voyvod," he said in his honey-rich
baritone. "Welcome. I know you're busy. We won't
keep you long. In the wake of today's atrocity, the
Council directs me to order you and your militia to
take the field immediately against the enemies of the
Garden of Beauty and Truth."

A blond girl who had taken a special fancy to Rob
put her hand on his arm and leaned in as if to whisper something intimate in his ear. He shrugged her off
like a suck fly. He leaned forward, straining to hear,
although the room had fallen silent.

"I shall, Eldest Brother," Karyl said calmly. He
bowed to the Council. If not very deeply.

"Are the soldiers ready?" asked Longeau, Violette's
best ally, in a voice that managed to mingle skepticism and contempt with a hearty helping of alarm, if
Rob was any judge.

And drunk or sober, he was. Maybe the more so
drunk. *What a good thing I'm that,* he thought.

"No army's ever ready," Karyl said. "We can take
the field."

That brought some dark looks and some confused.
People commenced to mutter, not just behind the
high table. Bogardus frowned ever so slightly around
the hall. The burbling ceased.

"How will you fight knights?" asked Sister Violette.

"A fair question," said Karyl, as if the silver witch
wasn't his greatest enemy in the vicinity not sporting
Crève Coeur green, blue, and gold. "We'll catch them
on the way home from their raids. They'll be jubilant,

off their guard, likely drunk, and loaded down with loot and captives. Which makes them ripe for ambush."

The women at Rob's table inhaled in horrified unison. Violette reared back as if the part-eaten bunch of grapes resting on the plate before her had turned into an adder poised to strike.

Longeau found his voice first. "That's unacceptable!" he gobbled. "Totally unacceptable."

"Let me see if I have this right," said Violette, who seemed more pleased than taken aback. "You're talking about allowing these marauders to rob, murder, and rape at will *before* you attack them? How is that defending us?"

"And this striking from ambush," Longeau declared. "It's barbaric! What happened to chivalry?"

"You might ask that of knights who trample children and spear distraught mothers for sport," Karyl said. "For ourselves, we can't afford it. We're outnumbered, out-armed, and out-mounted. And as for skill, we might as well be eight-year-olds matching finger-daubs in mud against young Lucas's murals all around us here. Our only hope is to use stealth and cunning. And what they can win us: surprise."

"But how does that *defend* us," Violette said again, "letting the marauders do their worst and ride away?"

"In the best way we have available. To hurt them, to teach them this lesson: that their sport shall cost them *pain*."

The hall erupted in furious gabble. "He can't be serious," the blonde who'd been trying to drape herself on Rob kept saying, red-faced and not nearly so appealing as a moment before. He wasn't sure which outraged her more: that Karyl suggested letting the raiders raid, or that he spoke of inflicting pain on them.

It's a good job they're pacifists, this lot, Rob thought, his wits no longer as dull as they had been. *Otherwise they'd be pelting him with fruit at best. And at worst, we'd be racing for the exit this very instant.*

Which was a tactic, he reflected with a certain grim satisfaction, he'd almost certainly had more experience using than the noted war captain Karyl.

Karyl simply stood and let the furor blow past him. Behind the table, Bogardus had his arms crossed and chin sunk into the square-cut neck of his yellow-trimmed green gown, looking every centimeter the ex-priest of Maia rumor made him out to be.

At last the Eldest Brother spread his arms out to his sides. It was as if he smoothed a rumpled sheet. In a moment the hall was still.

"Please, my friends," he said. "It's as good as no one having their say, if everyone speaks at once. This is a grave matter, which concerns us all. If I may presume to speak for the Council—"

He looked to Telesphore, who pressed palms together before his wishbone and bowed. *And what would Bogardus have done had that dead trout said no?* Rob thought. But he couldn't see it happening. *No more than could Bogardus, I do not doubt.*

"—those who have contributions to make may make them. Each in turn, if you please, and briefly, so that all who wish to be heard may be. And then the Council shall deliberate."

He looked to Karyl. "This may take some time, Voyvod. If you'd care to take a seat?"

Rob thought he actually might prefer to stand. But he misjudged an old campaigner.

"I thank the Council," Karyl said with another bow. He turned and walked into the thicket of hostile eyes.

Rob half stood. "Ho, Karyl," he called, making motions with his left arm as if reeling in cloth. "I saved a space for you beside me."

Actually there was none but standing room around him. But he reckoned that once he made his invitation, space would rapidly become available. Nor was he disappointed: by the time Karyl reached the table, Rob sat alone.

Karyl took a seat beside him. He propped his stick against his chest, folded his arms across it, closed his eyes, and to all appearances went instantly to sleep. Unlike at night, this slumber seemed untroubled by demons.

The speeches began. Mostly they were sheer vexer-screeches, shrill effusions of resentment and fear. Rob took to drinking with a single mind, and that mind was to tune it all out.

"Karyl, please draw near."

Bogardus's sonorous words gave Rob a jolt. He lifted chin from clavicle to see his friend rising to his feet. He shook his head, spattering droplets of mingled ale and wine from beard, eyebrows, and the tips of his hair.

"I'm not asleep!" he declared, glaring fiercely around, daring one of these mooncalf fatties to challenge him. "Just composing . . . sonnets. The right word's key—"

He let the sentence run down because no one was listening to him. Every face was fixed on Karyl as he walked up to stand serenely before the dais.

"The Council has decided that we must direct you to change your proposed methods," Bogardus said. "You must engage the foe forthrightly, not bring dishonor on the Garden by skulking in ambush. And under no circumstances can we go along with your deliberately allowing the enemy to ravage at will before striking at him. It is imperative that you do your best to prevent raids before they happen, not just avenge murdered children and burned homes."

Karyl nodded sharply.

"I resign," he said.

He turned his back on the Council and walked away.

Chapter 39

Jinete, **light rider**—Skirmishers and scouts, often women, who ride horses and striders. They wear no armor, or at most a light nosehorn-leather jerkin, with sometimes a leather or metal cap. They use javelins or feathered twist-darts, and a sword. Some also carry a light lance and a buckler. A few shoot shortbows or light crossbows, but mounted archery is very difficult, and not much practiced in Nuevaropa.

—A PRIMER TO PARADISE FOR THE IMPROVEMENT
OF YOUNG MINDS

What's this?" Longeau exclaimed. "Impertinence!"

Sitting two places down, Sister Violette smiled like the proverbial horror who'd eaten a vexer.

"Peace," Bogardus said. "Explain yourself if you please, Lord Karyl."

Halting among the tables of shocked-pale faces, Karyl turned. His own expression was one of complete surprise.

The stage lost a brilliant actor when that magnificent bastard chose to walk the warrior's road, thought Rob with honest admiration.

"Why, Eldest Brother," Karyl said, "I thought I had. Very well: if the Council wants its army led out to be butchered futilely, you've got to do it yourselves."

"Whatever do you mean?"

Rob smiled to himself. *Unused to the role as he probably is, Bogardus plays the shill well. But then you'd expect acting skills from a fallen-away priest, no?* He tried to refill his wineglass, found the bottle empty, and signaled the diligent ex-Count Étienne for another.

"All our volunteers together could scarcely stand up against just the three dinosaur knights who visited you today. Give them a handful of house-soldiers and they'd flatten us as easily as they did that poor mother and her child."

"Absurd," Longeau said. "You've got town lords."

Karyl just looked at him. Longeau flushed and looked down at the table. His fellow Councilors passed an uncomfortable glance around. Not even the fondest peace-lover, so Rob took it, could seriously imagine that Yannic, on his buffoonish great strider that weighed no more than a palfrey, stood any chance against four war-trained tonnes of monster and armored rider.

"Even with the sound arms and armor we've got from the town armory," Karyl said, "we can't hope to stop a single raiding party in open combat. Now consider what Guillaume and his friends might think to do to you if you try to thwart him and fail."

That quieted the Council right down. A sort of

sickroom whisper rippled through the hall. Bogardus's handsome face was ashen. Rob judged that likely wasn't acting.

"Have we any chance, then, whatever you do?" the Eldest Brother asked.

"A chance, and more than a chance. *If* we use the land and our wits to our advantage, and take our foe in small bites. I'd be staking my life on it.

"You need to choose which is the greater honor: to protect your homes, your loved ones, and yourselves? Or fight with your hands tied by some half-mythical code your enemies don't apply to you anyway? There seems little place for *honor* in a philosophy that preaches peace and resorts to war."

Sister Violette shot to her feet, her eyes like furnace vents. "I for one will not sit here and listen to this— this *vagabond* insult our Garden!"

"I will, Sister," Bogardus said calmly. "Or stand and listen. I'll always hear the truth, and that's what he speaks. Doesn't the divine Jaume of the Flowers himself teach that Truth and Beauty are one thing, inseparable?"

Karyl's shoulders slumped ever so slightly. *Ah, that's twisting the knife, now,* Rob thought. *But Bogardus can't know it.*

The Eldest Brother fastened a steady gaze on Violette. It seemed slowly to force her back down in her chair.

"What is to be, Sisters, Brothers?" Bogardus asked. "We have brought this man—these men—here precisely because they are highly skilled artisans. And we appreciate the craftsman as well as the artist, in this our Garden.

"Karyl has told us the only way we can fight with

a chance of winning. And after all, we're not knights, are we, hot for glory and thirsting for blood? We fight to free our people from the terror the invaders bring. We agreed to hold our principles in abeyance—largely at my urging, as I freely acknowledge—and fight, or allow others to fight in our names, to prevent a greater evil.

"Will we let this acknowledged master ply his craft as best he knows? Or shall we take the field and lead the battle ourselves?"

That got them to lower their eyes and look everywhere but at him. Bogardus fixed each Councilor in turn with dark, steady eyes and spoke his or her name, until each assented to amending their earlier decision and permitting Karyl to fight his battles his way.

"But we won't relent on his stopping the raids before they begin," Longeau said. "We can't, for our people's sake."

"It's too cynical, Bogardus," Telesphore said dolefully. "If we ambush the raiders on their way home we can recover stolen goods. But what of the lives destroyed or damaged?"

Bogardus turned to Karyl. "So the Council decides, and I concur: you may employ ambush or whatever means you see fit to defeat our tormentors. But by the Lady of the Mirror and all seven other Creators, you cannot let the reavers reave, however good a tactic that may appear to those of us who aren't being burned out of our homes."

Karyl met him eye to eye for a long breath. Then he bowed.

"I shall fight on your terms, Eldest Brother," he said.

"Wait!" Rob shouted, shooting to his feet. He

knocked the whole bench over with a bang, and upset his most recent wine-bottle, now empty. Faces
turned to gape at him with eyes and mouths like Os.

"Lord Karyl!" he roared, swaying with booze and
outrage. "Why are you giving in to these mewlers,
who aren't fit to eat the road mud off your boots?
They don't have half your birth or worth. Stand
up, man! Spit in their eyes! Defy them to the end!"

Strong arms locked his. He was hoisted bodily to
his feet. He managed to wrench an arm free and land
a knuckle in someone's eye with a mad swing of his
fist. Then he was secured again, lifted so his boot soles
swung futilely above the tile floor, and carried out of
the hall still raving.

Who knew these soft-hand Gardeners possessed
such strength? Ah, but it took a round half dozen to
handle him. One at least would be nursing a black
eye in the morning, and there'd be more than one
sore shin, or his name wasn't Rob Korrigan.

They threw him in the ditch. He sat up among the
wet weeds, still sputtering in fury as cold water seeped
up his ass crack. Little Nell, grazing nearby, saw her
master's distress. She broke her tether effortlessly,
waddled to Rob, and licked his face with her great
slobbery tongue.

"At least it's lavender you've dined on, girl," he
said, pushing the beaked snout away, "and not anything worse-smelling. And didn't my mother always
tell me to look at the bread's clean side, when I picked
it up off the floor?"

"Captain! Wake up!"

Men shouted outside Jaume's tent. As an adolescent campaigning against the miquelets, Jaume had learned the knack of coming instantly and fully awake. His dream vision of Melodía, naked with her hair unbound, spun away as he reached for her, just shy of his outstretched fingers, and vanished.

As she would have had the dream continued. As she did most every night. He grabbed his scabbarded sword from a rack near his cot and went out naked.

The stars and just-risen Eris, the Moon Visible, shone brightly in a cloudless sky. Meseta nights were cooler than on the coast, and drier. The air didn't hit him in the face like a wet blanket. Nor did it stink of mass decomposition, since he'd ordered the army to camp up the prevailing wind from the day's battle-field.

And there's my final blessing for the night, he realized as he saw flames gouting from the top of the distant red crag as if the ancient volcano that had extruded it had roared back to life. A yellow glow behind the horizon suggested fire walked the streets of the town as well.

Companions in states of dress ranging from full plate to as naked as their captain surrounded his tent, all talking at once.

"What is this?" Jaume asked, of no one in particular.

"Treachery," rumbled Ayaks.

"But whose?" asked Wouter de Jong, trying to rub the sleep from his blue eyes.

A voice called the friend-word from up the road that led toward the blaze. A moment later an Ordinary rode up escorting a leather-armored mercenary aboard a wheezing strider.

The jinete, a young man with wild hair and a scrub

of beard, hopped to the ground. Bartomeu twitched a feather cloak around Jaume's shoulders. Another squire brought a bucket of water for the winded dinosaur, which stuck its beak inside and slurped noisily.

"The bucketheads are inside the castle," the jinete announced. "They raped and plundered to their hearts' content, and fired the place for spite. While they were plucking the ripest cherry, they let their house-soldiers harvest from the village below."

"How did they get in?" Machtigern asked.

"Who knows? Some say this ruse, some another. My guess is, they claimed to bring a message from the good Count Jaume here."

Jaume winced.

"Who is responsible?" Manfredo asked. His face was a thunderhead.

"Tavares," Florian spat. He slammed his sword, which he had half drawn to examine, back into its sheath. His squire, a Spañol war-orphan named Marco he'd picked up somewhere and who always looked and acted famished no matter how much he ate, was busily doing up the latches on his breast-and-back. "Who else?"

"We can't accuse the Pope's Legate without evidence," Manfredo said sternly.

The jinete laughed wildly. "Who else but the holy man?" he said. "I heard the house-soldiers talking on the road as they made their way to the sack. The Bishop fired up the grandes. Told them they should reward themselves and punish the wicked at one and the same time."

"The wicked?" asked Jacques, his voice quavering with passion. It distressed Jaume to see how grey his friend's face looked by far flame light. "How would they tell them from the innocent? Surely the ladies and the servants had nothing to do with Leopoldo's crimes!"

"Ah, but the Lord Bishop had an answer for that too," the mercenary said. "He's a man of many answers, that one. He told them, *¡mátenlos todos, porque los Creadores reconocerán a sus propios!*"

"Kill 'em all and let the gods sort 'em out," Wil Oakheart the Anglés echoed in his own rude language. "And don't the bucketheads half love that shite?"

"Ah, that they duw, mai lord," the jinete replied in frightfully accented Anglysh. He drank deeply from a wineskin someone had handed him. Wine trickled down a gaunt cheek.

"And Montañazul and Estrella del Hierro?" Florian asked.

"They led the party that talked its way into the castle, of course."

"What about Don Leopoldo?" asked Jaume.

"They hanged him from the top of his keep. He should be roasted to a turn now."

"And the Countess?"

"As I heard it, she proved uncooperative at her own rape. So—" He pulled a forefinger across his throat.

"Let's mount and ride, Captain," Manfredo said, his eyes bright. Jaume saw the flush in his cheeks as shadow stains. "With the Ordinaries to back us we'll make short work of these vermin."

"Thank the Lady, a miracle!" Florian exclaimed. "Mor Stiff-Neck and I agree for once. We can teach our bumptious bucketheads the lesson they love to give their peasants: to fear their betters well."

"Could be tough," Machtigern said. "They outnumber us considerably. Even with the Ordinaries."

"They're disorganized," Manfredo said. "And Colonel van Damme will be only too happy to set her Nodosaurs on them."

"If they haven't joined in the plundering themselves," Wil said.

"Last I knew, the scar-faced Colonel still had them in their cantonment," the jinete said. "Once they're let loose, the Emperor Pipo himself couldn't stop them. But while they're still on the leash, they'll obey their mistress, no matter how hard they strain."

"We don't need them," Florian said. "The bastards are drunk, or distracted both. It'll be like slaughtering fatties. If rather more gratifying."

"You can't be talking about murdering knights and noblemen!" exclaimed Dieter. "Not from our own side."

"Not all of them," Wil said. "Just the ones who resist. The rest we'll thump soundly and round up. The worst actors we can hang at our leisure tomorrow."

"With Ironstar and Bluemountain swinging highest of all," Florian said with a laugh. "Think how that'll improve army morale, Dieter!"

"Brothers, gentlemen!" Jacques cried. "I beg you, listen to yourselves. You can't fight disorder with disorder."

"It's not disorder," Manfredo said. "It's bringing law. It's what we do."

"Not law, disaster!" Jacques sounded near to tears. "Attacking some of the most powerful grandes in Spaña, to say nothing of executing them—do you want to start the civil war we've all been dreading?"

"If that's what it takes to end that kind of ugliness," said Florian, "perhaps we should risk it. I don't like it either, Jacques, but there it is: soon or late, it's got to be done. And when did putting off a stable clean-ing make it smell better?"

"At your word, Captain," Manfredo said.

Jaume felt his Brothers' eyes on his skin like insect stings. He drew a deep breath. Willing down the fury that boiled his own belly, he shook his head.

"No," he said. "Stand down, my friends."

His Companions stared at him with something like horror. "It's too late to stop this evil," he said. "And Jacques is right: punishing it could bring an evil ten times worse."

"They've defied your lawful commands!" Man-fredo said.

"What about your honor, lord?" asked Pedro the Greater, as usual speaking little and to the point.

Jaume laughed, bitterly and briefly.

"There's been enough bloodshed," he said, and the effort of keeping his voice level matched his hardest exertion in battle. "I won't spill more, much less risk breaking the Empire apart, over so trivial a thing as my honor."

Chapter 40

With a groan and a crackle of branches breaking, the tall red-boled conifer fell across the trail.

From a knob overlooking the trail, just beyond the tree that blocked the raiders' forward progress, Rob Korrigan sat astride Little Nell and watched in excited satisfaction. Sweat streaming down his forehead from beneath the padding of his steel cap stung his eyes. The solidity of his axe haft in hand bolstered his morale. A round shield hung from his saddle.

Nell wagged her head and rolled her eyes. Her nervousness wasn't down to anticipation, but rather fear of the wicked creature beside her. Karyl was mounted on an Arabaya mare named Asal, whose first act on arriving at Séverin farm had been to bite a chunk out of the hook-horn's inoffensive ass. The name meant "honey" in Parso, which Rob took for typical heathen cheek: her temperament was corrosive as quicklime.

A beautiful young strawberry roan, scarcely more than a pony at a finger under fifteen hands, Asal had come as a gift from Gaétan's father, along with the fine Ovdan hornbow Karyl now held ready, and certain other tokens. Karyl and Master Évrard had made some deal Rob wasn't privy to; he reckoned it involved a hefty chunk of silver from the former Count's coffers, to make the merchant so expansive.

Around them waited half a dozen militiamen on foot, including Lucas, who wouldn't be separated from Karyl. A thornbush thicket screened them all from the marauders' view.

Around the residual rumbling and crackling as the tree bounced on its springy, sap-rich limbs, silence swelled to fill the narrow valley. The sounds that gave this forest its name, the Whispering Woods— the soft sighing of breeze in boughs and drowsy insect hum—seemed to stop. As did the intruding noises: the rough too-loud banter of men bent on joyous hatefulness, the thud of footfalls on dirt, the jingle of metal links against each other.

The leading Crève Coeur spear-and-shield man stood gaping at the tree's still-shaking boughs, stunned by the disaster that had missed him by centimeters. Belatedly apprehending the danger, he turned to flee. It saved his life, however momentarily: the green-fletched arrow aimed for his eye stuck in his temple instead. Howling and trying to yank it, out he ran stumbling back along the strung-out raiding party.

Another serial crashing announced another big tree falling behind the column. Horses reared, neighing in alarm. Men shouted. Bearded faces snapped to and fro in confusion already shading into panic.

The raid consisted of ten mailed men-at-arms on horseback and twenty or so foot soldiers, led by a dinosaur knight on an orange-and-green bull sackbut. The fallen trees had trapped them on a path scarcely two meters wide. Above them rose a steep slope. Below them it dropped twenty meters to a rocky stream.

Screams began to peal from the column's tail. Emeric had split the woods-runners he'd managed to talk into joining the militia into two groups of six, one led by him and the other by his sister Stéphanie. They raked the column with arrows from cover at either end. A hail of rocks and javelins fell on the Brokenhearts from the scrub above.

Emeric's forest phantoms and a handful of daring lads and lasses on horseback who'd joined them scouting for Rob had spotted the raiders just before they made camp last sunset. Consulting local peasants who had turned out to fight the invaders, Karyl judged the band was making for a village two kilometers west of the ambush site.

A few kilometers north lay a small yet rich silver mine. But the miners had fortified its entrance with the same skills they used to delve the meat and bones of Paradise, and defended themselves ferociously when attacked. The village, on the other hand, prospered mightily from selling the miners its produce, and was a *much* easier target.

An admirable sort of trap, thought Rob, *where the bait's been waiting years, and your quarry's already on its way to take it.*

A crossbow twanged metal music. A horse shrieked and fell as the bolt pierced its neck. Its rider jumped clear but rolled down the hill into the stream. Smelling horse blood, Asal tossed her head in agitation. But the Ovdan nomads had trained her well for war. She made no sound.

The Crève Coeur knight's longsword flashed high in sunlight filtered through clouds and branches as he reared his dinosaur and shouted to rally his men from their midst. They were blundering into each other, jostling, shouting, and waving their arms ineffectually as missiles pelted them.

Most of the missiles were no more effective than the Brokenhearts' flailing. But not all. The woodsrunners shot to deadly effect, and at a range close enough that even their shortbows had a chance of punching an arrow through mail. Rob saw figures on the ground, writhing or still, with arrows jutting from armored bodies or unprotected faces.

And now some of the militiamen, emboldened by the fact that the knight had arrogantly brought no archers of his own, emerged from the brush above the column. Rob winced as he saw a cantaloupe-sized stone strike a house-shield's helmeted forehead full on. The steel cap caved in. Whether the *crack* Rob heard a beat later was the soldier's skull breaking or his neck, the boneless way he slumped to the ground showed he was dead on the instant.

"Poor sods," Rob said, bending down to scratch Nell reassuringly on the neck behind her frill. "I pity 'em. Almost."

"How much mercy would they show you if the situation was reversed?" Karyl asked.

He wore a steel cap with a camail hanging to protect his nape, a simple nosehorn leather jerkin over an unbleached linen shirt, and jackboots to midthigh over brown linen trousers. He carried no shield. His arming-sword had been Étienne's own, a splendid weapon forged from star-metal by Aphrodite Terra's most cunning smiths, the wandering gitanos—Rob's continental kinfolk.

Karyl preferred to leave his staff sword in camp wrapped in his bedroll, like a Hanged Man card up his sleeve. *That* blade seemed to Rob to possess some dark charisma. But then, he was a susceptible lad.

"Roast me on slow fire, and the Old Hell take the Creators and their Law!" Rob cawed a corpse-tearer laugh. "So I'll waste no sympathy on the likes of them."

A man-at-arms with more presence of mind than his fellows set his horse laboring up the slope at these peasants who had the temerity to throw things at their betters. Like the others, he couched a spear in lieu of a longer, less wieldy lance. The militia scattered. A middle-aged man in a loincloth, already hobbled by some old wound, tripped and fell. He threw a futile hand in front of his face as the spearhead darted toward him.

From nearby Rob heard a *thump* and a rustling hum. The rider straightened in his saddle. The spear dropped from his hand. He looked down in amazement at what Rob could see from sixty meters off was an arrow sprouting dead center from the broken-heart emblem on his surcoat.

Startled, Rob glanced right to see Karyl pull another arrow from the quiver by his saddlebow and nock it.

"Lively now," Karyl said. "Company comes."

Four Crève Coeur riders scrambled their horses up the slope to get clear of the obstruction. Turning their frightened mounts to follow the road brought them straight at Karyl and his small group stationed to prevent just that.

Rob took up his shield as Karyl shot another raider from his saddle. Then a man-at-arms was riding straight for Rob, thrusting a spear at him underhand.

Rob turned Nell to meet the horseman and booted her into a forward spring. Her absurdly short, thick horn wasn't as lethal as a nosehorn's eponymous armament, and nothing Rob knew matched Triceratops' terrible brow-horns. But in a pinch its forward-curving tip could dig in and gut a man or beast with a downward stroke. She used it mostly as a kind of battering ram. And fair effective it was at that.

The horse veered to avoid collision, spoiling its master's attack by putting its body between spear and target. A mature hornface weighed more than all but the hugest draft horses; Little Nell, who truth to tell was on the chubby side, weighed two tonnes, and could simply bull down a courser like this one.

Ditching the spear to draw his sword as he passed, the rider aimed a desperate cross-body cut at Rob. Rob took it on his shield, then returned a whistling overhand stroke with his axe. The other arm's shield protected torso and head. Rob wasn't aiming for them. The bearded axe-head hit the horseman's thigh instead, sheering through mail legging, linen trousers, and flesh to jar against bone.

The man bellowed in pain as Rob wrenched the axe free. Rob thanked Maris, Lady of Chance and the Sea, it hadn't bit into the femur. He'd have been lucky not to be dragged from the saddle himself.

The Brokenheart fell off his horse. His left boot caught in the stirrup. The courser, now thoroughly terrified, put its head down, crashed back down onto the road, then set out at a wheezing, clattering, foam-blowing run, dragging its erstwhile rider bellowing behind.

Axe high, Rob looked for other threats. No enemies were near him. Karyl went sword to sword with a man on a chestnut. A second man-at-arms rode in from Karyl's blind side, swinging a spiked-ball flail over his head.

Rob shouted warning. As he did, Lucas rose up from the scrub right next to the flail-man. Holding his longsword hilt in both hands and yelling like a madman with pale hair flying, the painting prodigy rammed the tip into the man's side under the short ribs. Welded links popped. The horseman groaned, blood flooding down his chin. Lucas, blue eyes rolling in red face, rammed the blade all the way through him until mail hauberk and surcoat tented on the other side.

The Brokenheart fell that way. There was no way Lucas could keep hold of the blood-slick cross guard. He had to let go of the longsword.

He didn't seem to mind. Instead his success so astonished and exalted him that he whooped, threw his hands in the air, and began to dance around in triumph.

"Behind you!" Karyl yelled at him. He had finished

off his first opponent and twisted in his saddle to deal with the second, only to find that Lucas had killed him. And to see another Crève Coeur rider looming behind the youth, eyes glaring wildly past the nasal of his peaked cap and spear cocked to impale him. Agile and quick as Asal was, she had no chance of carrying Karyl close enough in time to intervene.

"Fuck," Rob said. He headed Nell that way, though she was farther than the mare, and slower. He doubted Karyl would leave much avenging of the painter for Rob to do, but the Brokenheart might be bringing friends to the party.

He heard a *clink* and a *crunch*. Just before he drove his spear home in Lucas's oblivious back, the Brokenheart stiffened and grabbed for his throat.

A chisel-tipped arrowhead stuck out of the horseman's gullet, painted bright red in the morning sun.

As the rider collapsed, Rob looked up and beyond him. At the far end of the trapped raiding party, Gaétan stood on a rocky jut above where the second tree had fallen. He was still holding his hornbow in perfect follow-through.

A good hundred meters, thought Rob. *Lad's a fair shot, for true.*

Karyl swept his sword up in a salute. Gaétan grinned and bobbed his head in acknowledgment. He was busy nocking another arrow and looking around. *He* didn't intend to get caught celebrating by a sudden enemy.

Then again, he'd likely done this before. Rob was certain Lucas hadn't. As was brought home when the boy looked from the man who'd almost spitted him, to the man he'd spitted himself to such lethal effect, and puked his guts into a berry-bush.

Rob risked a look toward the road. As a child he'd been particularly struck on a walk when he'd seen perhaps a dozen centimeter-long black and red ants near the entry to a hill of much tinier black ants. Whether the big ants had tried a raid, or merely tried the lesser ants' patience, the defenders, each perhaps a tenth the size of a single intruder, had swarmed them by the hundreds, immobilizing and slowly destroying them without regard to their own losses.

That was about the sight that greeted his eyes now. The Providentials had thrown themselves on the marauders, overmatching superior arms and training with numbers and fury. They flailed their enemies with farm implements, pounded them with rocks, and pummeled them with fists. In the midst of the mayhem, the dinosaur knight surged his long-crested mount this way and that with its tail knocking combatants of both sides sprawling, and swinging his longsword with little more discrimination.

"*Someone* fight me, Fae eat your souls!" he screamed. "There must be some man of birth to face me!"

Rob was glad to see there were few feathered darts and arrows jutting from the duckbill's green-streaked orange hide. The shortbows could only hurt the thing by hitting an eye, and Karyl had impressed upon the woods-runners how badly he *didn't* want the thing hurt. Or at least impressed Stéphanie, who harbored a savage grievance against the Brokenhearts. Which was enough: no one with his wits wanted to get crosswise of her. Meanwhile Gaétan and his arbalesters had justified Karyl's faith in them by not shooting the sackbut with weapons that could harm it.

The duckbill was a fortune walking on two big

legs. If they captured it alive, Karyl could sell it and share out a handsome prize with all. But Rob knew he had a greater gain in mind. The Empire was full of dinosaur knights who had lost their mounts and couldn't afford a replacement. They'd coming flocking for a chance to obtain a new war-hadrosaur in exchange for a year's service. Having shown he could take the beasts from Count Guillaume's vassals, Karyl could probably get some to sign on to fight as cavalry or even armored infantry in hopes of winning a new mount in battle.

Karyl rode back along the trail, keeping above the scrum. Rob followed. The knight kept thrashing about and yelling shrill challenges. The stink of blood and ripped guts beat up from the road like heat from a forge.

"Why don't you just shoot the bugger off his sackbut and be done with it?" Rob asked. "Or let Gaétan be about it. Surely you don't mean to go sword to sword with a man on dinosaur-back?"

Seeing a mounted, thus putatively noble, foeman come into view, the Crève Coeur knight pointed his sword at Karyl.

"I challenge you to meet me blade to blade as a man of honor," he cried.

"Whether I'm a man of honor or not is immaterial," Karyl replied. "You're just a bandit."

To the volunteers he called, "Get him off the monster. Use nooses or poles. Don't get hurt, and for Maris's sake don't hurt the duckbill."

"What do we do with him then?" shouted Guat, whose face was a carnival horror mask of blood. Whose, Rob didn't know.

"Whatever you wish."

The knight stared at Karyl, slack-jawed as if the Voyvod had lapsed into his native Slavo. The militiamen cheered and jeered. Someone threw a loop of rope at the knight's face. He batted it away. Others incautiously ran forward to try to pull him down by hand. He sworded one in the face and his sackbut trod another into the roadway, squeezing a last scream from bursting lungs that momentarily overrode the dinosaur's fanfares of alarm. The mob jumped back.

They started throwing sticks and head-sized rocks at the knight. These bounced harmlessly from armor or shield, or were swatted down with his sword. Emeric and his sister, who was as tall as he was, ran up behind the duckbill carrying a burly four-meter branch with a forked end. They hooked the knight smartly under his right armpit and levered him sideways out of his saddle.

He landed with a ringing *thud* that made Rob wince. The peasant army fell on him with a single feral howl of glee.

"How can you let this *happen*?" Rob demanded of Karyl as green-enameled plate armor rang to the blows of clubs and the *chink* of spear-tips. "He's a nobleman!"

"He's a criminal. He's the guiltiest of all. Whatever crimes the others committed or contemplated, they did by his command. Besides, I thought you hated blue bloods."

Rob opened his mouth. For once he could find no words to shape with it. He did hate blue bloods. He held a vengeance of his own against them. And yet, and yet—it felt wrong to stand by and let one be lynched by his lessers like this.

Face burning, feeling a strange and nameless disgust surging within, he turned Nell right about and rode her away at a trot, down to the road, and back toward the village they had saved.

But he couldn't outride the knight's screams.

Chapter 41

Telar, Laventosa, Windy, *La Tejedora de Sueños,* **Dreamweaver**—Duchess of the Creators: *Xun* ☰ (Wind)—The Oldest Daughter. Represents Fabrication and destruction, artisans, sleep and dreams, forests, and Wind. Also birds and fliers. Known for her vigor. Aspect: a woman with long, kinky gold hair in a green-trimmed white gown, working a loom as a long-crested dragon soars above her. Sacred Animal: long-crested dragon. Color: green. Symbol: a golden loom.

—A PRIMER TO PARADISE FOR THE IMPROVEMENT OF YOUNG MINDS

eeling better?" Karyl asked Rob sardonically as a beautiful, strongly curved blond woman looped a flower wreath around the dinosaur master's neck from his right. They marched side by side past the fountain in the central plaza, leading the survivors of what everyone now called the Battle of Whispering Woods on a triumphal procession through Providence town.

The woman beamed up at Rob. He could barely

help noticing she had on nothing but a colorful strand or two of blossoms, none too carefully arranged. Public nudity was less common up here by the Shields, where cold winds occasionally blew down from perpetually snow-sheathed peaks even in high summer.

"It'll do for getting along with," Rob said as a stout peasant woman, fortunately wearing more normal country garb, held her grandson up to plant a kiss on his bearded cheek. Then in Anglysh: "Faugh, the little blighter's been at the taffy! He's got it all in my beard, the little shi—yes, madame, a lovely child. May he bear you many equally lovely great-grandchildren."

Happy holidaymakers lined the Brokenheart Highway, the north road from Crève Coeur to Providence town, to welcome the returning heroes home. They cheered, banged tin drums, and blew lustily on whistles and paper horns. The noise would certainly have hurt the cultured ears of the Garden Councilors, had any of them been anywhere to be seen.

Two days after the battle, the bad taste lingered in Rob Korrigan's mouth. His dreams had not been pleasant. The Brokenheart knight, he'd learned, had died as badly as Rob's fears foretold, crushed by degrees as his steel carapace was slowly beaten in.

Rob's *mind* knew the man deserved as much, and probably worse. He'd led his merry crew toward pillage, house burning, torture, mutilation, and rape, enslavement and murder: all the filthy pleasures the rulers of this world loved to wallow in when they felt they had license. Rob's belly didn't buy it, though.

A handful of foot soldiers and two horsemen had broken through and fled toward Crève Coeur. Given how much of the way ran through Telar's Wood, and how many and vindictive were Emeric's folk, Rob was none too sure they'd gotten *away*.

The militia took six shield men prisoner, all injured. Karyl had them stripped of all but loincloths and the improvised crutches that two men needed to walk. He ordered them set free, and told them to take themselves back across the Lisette by fastest route, or die.

One made the mistake of protesting that the woods were full of raptor-packs.

"*Wild* raptors, you mean?" Stéphanie the woods-runner had asked with lye-and-honey sweetness. "Not like the tame packs you set on us, to rip us apart for sport?"

The captives cringed away in unconcealed terror. She was a good 180 centimeters tall and built like her brother, leanly muscular. She was also formidably armed, with bow and quiver slung over bare brown shoulder, a single-edged knife as long as a short sword at her hip, and a spear with a wickedly sharp leaf-shaped head, that could be used for slashing as well as thrusting. She had an alarming tendency to gesticulate with it.

The prisoners, Rob thought, feared none of those things as much as her *rage*. She seethed with elemental fury, so intense and pure that Rob felt if she sprayed it on you, it might melt your face off.

She had been a notable beauty once, he reckoned. Then Crève Coeur Rangers hunting woods-runners, whose pinprick ambushes had till now been the closest thing to effective resistance the raiders met, caught her. They raped her, carved her face up with a hunting knife, and would have tortured her to death had not Emeric led a small group of forest folk to her rescue.

The volunteers guarding the captives, or just standing and gawking, stared at Stéphanie with scarcely less horror than the Brokenhearts did. Clearly, they feared her almost as much. But shock at her words was seeping into their expressions as well.

"Oh, yes," she told them. "Guilli and his nobles love to see their pets take human prey."

And then nothing would serve but that poor Rob step in to remind the now-outraged militiamen that Karyl had ordered the prisoners be released unharmed. He always got the dirty jobs.

And in the end, it wasn't as if Lord Karyl made those unhappy lads trudge home through the forest empty-handed. He gave them the knight's head in a sack, its features frozen in a most disconcerting mask, to take home to Count Guillaume as a token of his regard.

Something bonked Rob on the forehead. It snapped him out of his uneasy rolling reverie and back to the present parade.

Brawler's reflex had already caused him to snatch the missile. "Gods damn it!" he yelped as pain pierced his palm.

He found he was holding a gorgeous purple rose. Bogardus's wasn't the only garden in Providence town, nor his acolytes the only skilled gardeners. Unfortunately whoever had grown, or at least harvested, this flower hadn't thought to strip its thorns.

"They love you so much," said a woman by his

side, "their enthusiasm gets the better of them, some-times."

He glanced at her and his eyes went wide.

I've let myself get too damned tired, if I'm oblivious of a beautiful naked woman walking right next to me.

It was the blond woman in the flower strands. Rob recognized her now from a brief meeting in the banquet hall. She was a Gardener—Nathalie, he thought her name was.

He scratched his neck. Fatigue made him uncharacteristically blunt. "What are they so worked up about? It's not as if we didn't lose anybody."

A dozen volunteers had been injured, seven killed. Losing nearly a fifth of your total force like that was usually enough to break even professional soldiers.

But it wasn't pay that moved our people, he thought, *nor the lust for futile glory. It was fear for their homes, their loved ones, and themselves—and revenge for the hurts already done them.*

"But you won," Nathalie said, her blue eyes shining. "In the past the knights have killed us and killed us, and there was nothing we could do. You've shown us they can be stopped, you and Captain Karyl and all the rest!"

And that was just how Karyl wanted it: an easy victory, to hearten the volunteers and rouse the people of Providence to the banner. It seemed cold, somehow. Even to the likes of Rob.

No one wanted to hear that. Not the militia, nor the cheering crowds. And least of all delectable nude Nathalie. So Rob held back his ever-eager tongue—as had become a terrible habit, since he linked his fate to Karyl's.

He pasted his best jongleur's smile back on and

waved to the throng. He knew the value of an audience, did Rob, and how fleeting its applause. He meant to savor it while he could.

All of it.

And her a pacifist and all. So it's true what I hear, that victory makes strange bedfellows.

The moment Karyl and Rob got the militia back to camp at Séverin farm they set to work growing and shaping it. For four days, half a week, it seemed Lady Fortune or the Fae favored them.

Rob still sweated and hated the quartermaster's duties. But Gaétan had scared up a few clerks from his family warehouses to take part of the load off Rob's shoulders. He was trying to recruit a cousin who, he said, was a wizard at provisioning as well as a master accountant. Though a small woman, and unmartial as a dormouse, she could face down the rowdiest drovers drunkenly demanding a raise, and the most supercilious blue blood sneering at the notion of paying bills due commoners, and never flinch. If she agreed, she'd take the job over completely.

Gaétan himself, experienced at recruiting and commanding caravan guards, proved a natural at training raw recruits. He got help from an unlikely source: two Gardeners who had been house-shields for Count Étienne before he converted. They confided to Rob that they'd joined mostly for the easy sex with pretty boys and girls. Yet they were truly drawn to Bogardus's philosophy—and, somewhat paradoxically, to his inspiration, Jaume, who after all had been winning campaigns when both of them were stealing apples out of orchards with their boyhood friends.

Now they were bored and itching for action. Also they chafed that, as two of the most menial-born members of the supposedly egalitarian Garden, they found themselves doing the most menial tasks. And one expressed discomfort at a dogmatic bent he claimed to see growing in the Garden, or at least the Council.

Frankly, their concerns struck Rob as uncommonly dainty for a noble's paid enforcers. But they were Providentials, and thus contrary. They did know their weapons, and were good at passing their skills along.

Karyl still hadn't found a new dinosaur knight to ride the duckbill they'd captured. But it was early days yet; word would get around, and one would turn up. Meanwhile Rob doted on his new sackbut, a biddable if slightly skittish female whom he named Brigid. He'd never admit it to the lads and lasses assigned him as grooms, much less to Karyl, but tending to a real war-hadrosaur made him feel fully a dinosaur master again.

The militia now had a leavening of trained fighters. Providence's northern barons didn't dare leave their fief for fear that bold Count Guilli would snap them up. Not wanting to miss out on any more loot or glory—and taking to heart Karyl's warning, via Bogardus, about what to expect if they didn't help defend the province—they had sent contingents of their mailed house-archers and shields, each duly commanded by a spare relation.

Better, two authentic dinosaur lords had joined the militia: Baron Travise de les Clairières and Baron Ismaël of Fond-Étang. But while each came with a duckbill and full panoply, they brought no warriors, just arming-squires and servants. Les Clairières, from western Providence near Métairie Brulée, and Fond-

Étang, from south along the Lisette, feared their neighboring magnates too much to weaken their home defenses further.

Still, war-dinosaurs were war-dinosaurs. They gave the militia much-needed muscle. They also gave Rob two new chicks to take happily beneath his wing.

And all the while recruits streamed steadily in, from town, from country, and even woods-runners—some of whom spoke with strange accents. The woods-runners lacked any regard for borders; they considered all of Telar's Wood, which spanned Nuevaropa from Slavia and Alemania to Spaña near the coast of the Océano Aino, their home. They constituted a loose, nomadic tribe, culture, or even sect.

One that traditionally didn't get along with the "sitting-folk" on the great forest's fringes, neither farmers nor townspeople. But the camaraderie among those who had fought at the Whispering Woods had done a lot to allay mistrust in both directions. Eager to help, now that Karyl had demonstrated both his intent and his ability to harm their hated enemies, the woods-runners were rapidly learning to cooperate with Rob's small but flamboyant squadron of mounted scouts. Mixed teams of woods-runners and jinetes were already starting to spoil the Crève Coeur Rangers' nasty human-hunting sport.

Curiously, only a few volunteers trickled in from the east. The locals assured Karyl that that was to be expected. Hard against the mountains, that country was higher, drier, and more sparsely settled than the rest of Providence. Its folk had a reputation for aloofness. They could afford it, Rob reckoned, having the rest of the province to buffer them from their unfriendly neighbors, and the high Shields to discourage raiders from Ovda, with whom peace had prevailed in this district for a generation anyway.

So things went. For a blissful while. But Rob of all men should have remembered how Fortune, or the Fae, were fickle.

It was a fine day they picked to remind him.

The sun was a blinding-bright spot in a white sheet of cloud as he walked across a practice field bustling with mostly purposeful activity. The midmorning heat oppressed him far less than it would have on the coast. The air was dry, though the ground, trampled almost bare by hooves and the feet of men and monsters, was still damp from last night's rain. The moisture had settled the dust, and brought the surrounding grass and midsummer flowers on so strongly that their clean sweet smells masked those of sweat, wet leather, and dinosaur farts.

Sometimes.

Rob was wearing buskins, loincloth, a short brown feather cape to shield his shoulders, and a broad cone-shaped straw peasant's hat. He'd just come from overseeing dust baths for the militia's three fine hadrosaurs. It was a tricky process, since the monsters loved it and participated with heedless enthusiasm. Now he was heading across the stream to look in on the crossbow practice taking place by the woods, and make sure the troops had enough untipped quarrels.

Rob, who thought mostly in Anglysh, was amusing himself with the very notion there might possibly be a shortage of "quarrels" when so many Providential men and women were thrown together, when someone fell into step beside him.

He tensed. *You've got little to fear in the middle of your own armed camp,* he told himself. Although with recruits and provisions coming in all the time, it would be no great feat for an assassin to slip in unnoted. Count Guilli hardly seemed the type to hire the Brotherhood of Reconciliation, if only because he enjoyed doing the dirty so much himself. After the Whispering Woods, Rob couldn't afford to grow too complacent, lest he find out how it felt to have a wavy-bladed dagger sunk to the hilt in a favorite kidney.

But it was only a boy from town, who had a random thatch of straight black hair and was grubby, gangly, dressed in a torn linen smock, barefoot, and one of his spies. His name was Timothée. He was barely twenty-one, if that, and at that painfully sprouting stage when a body grew like bamboo, seemingly centimeters a day.

"The Council's coming," Timothée said. "It's like a parade. They've got the mayor and the Town Guard and a band and everything."

Rob winced. Between Little Pigeon, the horse-scouts, and the woods-runners, little went on in Providence town or its environs that he didn't know about. But the Garden villa's stone walls so far defied all his prying. Not even Jeannette—for whom his ardor had cooled somewhat, since he found out who her brother was—nor the normally complaisant Nathalie would whisper a single tale out of school. Little Pigeon's spies could only have figured out what was afoot after the procession set out.

"You've done well," he told the boy. "Thanks. Run off to the commissary and get some food."

Rob turned right back toward the farmhouse. Off by some outbuildings, Karyl was walking Lucas through longsword counter-and-attack techniques using tree limbs as weapons. Both men were stripped to the waist.

Rob frowned, mostly at himself. For all his many duties, Karyl was devoting a lot of attention to the painter. Rob wasn't sure why that bothered him, but it did.

Karyl raised his stick to the level of his forehead, "point" forward. Sweat plastered Lucas's almost-white hair to a forehead fisted in concentration as he painstakingly mimicked every movement. The tip of his tongue stuck out of his mouth. He'd become even more fanatical about sword practice since he'd gotten a taste of battle.

"Karyl," Rob called as he approached. "Our lives are about to get interesting again."

Karyl lowered his stick. "Enough for now," he told Lucas. "Remember, spiritual development is as important to your training as physical techniques are. Skill without self-mastery is hollow. A set of clever tricks, no more."

It was as if shutters closed behind Lucas's blue eyes. As it always was when Karyl talked to him that way. And as always Rob thought to see Karyl's shoulders slump ever so slightly, and a look of pain pass over his fine, ascetic features.

The procession was nearly as grand as Timothée described it, though Rob thought it a bit of a stretch to call a pair of female Garden acolytes beating a drum and tootling a fife a "band." Bogardus strode resolutely in the lead, and close on his flanks came Ludovic with his lugubrious moustache and Sister Violette, looking surprisingly good in white silk robes and smiling in a way Rob thought couldn't possibly bode well. Bogardus's strong oblong face said neither yea nor nay. Which came as no surprise: he'd been a priest, and was now a politician.

Half a dozen Town Guards brought up the rear, slouching in breastplates-and-backs still slightly shiny from the grease they'd been packed in. An unprepossessing lot, they consisted of skinny young men and stoutish older ones. They had their morions pushed back on their heads and toted their halberds haphazardly over their shoulders. Rob had never seen them do much, and couldn't imagine what they might be meant to do here.

Behind Violette walked her crony Longeau, tall and somewhat ungainly, smirking most fatuously.

"Great news," he called. "Thanks to your notable victory, the Council has decided to order you back into the field at once, to defeat our foes for good and all. I shall join you. In a strictly advisory capacity, of course."

"We're nowhere near ready," Karyl said, drying his hands of sweat on a twist of straw.

"You said an army was never ready," Sister Violette said. "But you won."

Yannic, Melchor, and Percil came up to exchange hearty forearm-clasps with Longeau. "He's a town lord too, you know," said Gaétan at Rob's elbow. "Longeau. He's well off, though he didn't buy his patent like Percil."

"We have to wait," Karyl said, speaking straight to Bogardus. "Our numbers are increasing. The volunteers are learning rapidly. But we still can't face a real army in the field."

"Don't be ridiculous," Longeau said, with a huge smile smeared all over his face. He turned to the crowd. Most of the army had turned out to see the show, over two hundred men and women who'd flocked to the silver thistle on green banner of Providence.

"What do you say, good people?" he asked in a voice that boomed like a veering wind. "Shall we take the battle to the evil ones who have tormented us so long?"

From the back of the crowd came a hearty, "Hip—hip—*huzzah!*" Rob looked around to see knots of town lord soldiers, pumping their fists in the air in unison and shouting. *A handy claque they make,* he thought sourly.

By the third time through the chant they had the whole militia with them: "Huzzah! Huzzah! Huzzah for victory!"

Violette and Longeau grinned as if they'd just seen Count Guillaume off himself. Bogardus's face was stone, Karyl's polished bone.

All Rob could do was shake his head and mutter to himself, "This'll not end well."

The vexer trotted past, impudently close to Jaume and his two Companions on the tufa-graveled road, proudly carrying a severed human forearm in its mouth.

Florian aimed a kick at the Velociraptor. The little creature veered clear without even looking at him.

From its flashy green-and-yellow plumage Jaume guessed it was a domestic gone feral; the local tribe of wilds was streaked brown and grey.

"They have their tasks to do, as we do," Manfredo said reprovingly. "The dead belong to Paradise. Scavengers help us return."

"I don't like seeing the little bastards so smug about it."

Jaume frowned at the burned-out ruins of the town of Terraroja ahead. "Did it come from there, I wonder? I thought we'd pulled out the last of the bodies."

Though he could not bring himself to intervene, once the sack and ruin was well under way, out of what it would cost the Empire, he had led his Companions and a number of volunteer Ordinaries to the survivors' succor before the breaking of dawn. As a matter of course, they had gone armed—as a few lingering looters, who in particular had chosen to carry off liquid booty in their bellies, had found to their dismay. Briefly.

But killing a handful of straggling evildoers had been little more than their help in putting out the burning shops and houses, and escorting shocked refugees safely home from the Redland hills: palliative.

Manfredo sniffed as the town itself came into view. His nose wrinkled.

"They'll be some time yet, retrieving the last of their dead, by the smell."

Jaume's gut tightened. That was plain enough even through the thick stinks of the damage done by fire, and by the water used to put it out. But that was why he had come here: to drink in, for one last time, the results of the other night's treachery. The fire-gutted buildings. The strewn garbage, broken chairs and crockery, ripped-up feather screens and hangings, the things that had been cast aside in the hunt for valuables to steal—or simply vandalized from frustration or fun. The smaller, less stoutly constructed buildings that showed unmistakable sign of war-hadrosaurs having been ridden right into them. The wretched knots of survivors working to clear the rubble of what had been their lives.

"It looked as if the arm was scorched, anyway," Florian said. "It may well have been filched from the burn pit outside of town."

He showed a lopsided smile. "I doubt the only naked and plundered bodies being cremated belong to helpless victims."

Jaume felt bad for the flickering gratification the suggestion caused. When he'd led his relief force here, he'd brought with them a *manipulo* of Coronel van Damme's Nodosaurs to guard the town. Disgruntled at missing out on the plunder, they were more than eager to take out their frustrations on any blue bloods or their hirelings who gave them the pretext by trying to sneak through their lines. Or bluster or bully their way through.

He halted atop a low rise overlooking the ruin. Terraroja had been a fairly large and prosperous town. It was amazing how much devastation the runaway army, whipped on by Papal Legate Tavares, had managed to accomplish in so short a time. Even to a campaigner as seasoned as Jaume, who had seen the like before.

"Have you finished your penance now, Captain?" asked Manfredo. "You—we—couldn't have helped them. We were already too late."

"Thank you, my friend," Jaume said. It was never

easy for a man of the sort to qualify as a Companion to acknowledge error; as much humility as service to the Lady required, it needed that much pride. "But this happened under my command, so it is my fault. I felt the need to see and smell and *feel* what my carelessness caused, one final time."

Florian made a disgusted sound low in his throat.

"I cannot see," he said, "why the Emperor refuses to do the sensible thing, and let us march the army back home straightaway and muster it out, now that its task is done."

"Felipe has decreed that we continue our campaign, against a new target," Jaume said. "I can only obey."

"It's our job to bring law," Manfredo said. "Conde Ojonegro is no less lawless than Terraroja was."

Florian swept his arm to encompass the town. "Is this the law we bring?"

Manfredo looked pained, and found no words to say in return.

"I fear for the Empire," Jaume said. "Troubled times are coming. You all know that I think what we're doing is likelier to bring them on than head them off. And still—I have no choice."

Florian laid a hand on his shoulder. "We're with you."

Jaume gripped the hand.

"At least Melodía's safe from the chaos to come," he said.

Chapter 42

Libro de los Nombres Verdaderos, The Book of True Names—A book, said to have been given us by the Creators themselves, that tells us the true names from Old Home of the creatures of Paradise, dinosaurs, fliers, and sea monsters, along with the names we commonly call them by. However, we are not listed, nor are our domesticated Five Friends.

— A PRIMER TO PARADISE FOR THE IMPROVEMENT
OF YOUNG MINDS

The arming-sword clanged against the two-headed black falcon painted on the blue-bordered white shield. Watching the duel from her chair on the shaded loggia above the small limestone-flagged palace courtyard, Melodía winced. Duke Falk von Hornberg struck back with his axe as the two combatants charged past one another. His opponent warded off the blow with his own shield.

Both combatants wore full armor. Falk had his royal-blue plate. His opponent wore a red feather cape, a gilded breastplate figured like a muscular male chest, and a gold barbute helmet with bobbing red and yellow plumes: the armor of an officer of the Scarlet Tyrants.

Their commander, in fact.

"I think it's terrible," Princess Fanny of Anglaterra said.

It took Melodía a few rapid heartbeats to realize her friend didn't mean the duel to the death between her father's new favorite and his chief bodyguard. Her face felt as if it had been stuccoed and allowed to dry in the noonday sun.

A few meters away Felipe sat watching. He talked animatedly with Mondragón, who stood as always at his elbow.

"What's terrible about it?" Lupe asked. "Those rebels got what they had coming, didn't they?"

"But Terraroja had surrendered," Fanny said. "To hang him without trial was dishonorable. The rape and murder of his wife and servants was criminal. And the poor villagers!"

"The peasants always suffer," said Abigail Thélème dryly. "I suspect in future the Emperor's foes will think twice about surrendering to his Army of Correction."

Metal rang on metal in another rushing flurry. Most fights ended in seconds—a single quick exchange and one was down, injured or dying. Or both were.

But these two fighters were unusually skilled. And shield combat put a special premium on circling to take advantage of the fact that a shield blocked vision as well as blows. Those things protracted a duel. But as always, both fighters moved constantly, whether around each other or toward.

"And now your father's ordered the army to march on Condado Ojonegro over a tariff dispute," Fanny said. "Poor Jaume. To think he never really wanted any of this."

Melodía had to keep herself from cringing. Her heart ached for her lover. She wanted nothing more than to comfort him, by letter if not in person.

But I can't. He has to apologize first. I've taken this too far to back down.

She refused to read the letters herself. In part for fear she'd weaken: she better than any of his myriad admirers, in Nuevaropa and across all Paradise, knew the power of the poet Jaume dels Flors's words. But she had Pilar read his daily missives, each and every one, to see whether Jaume said he was sorry for what he'd done to Melodía.

And he still had not.

Falk rushed Duval. His axe hit the Riquezo's helmet but glanced down its peak.

Duval struck at Falk's leg. Falk's shield came down. But the cut was a feint; Duval spun toward the taller, younger foe and hammered his sword pommel into Falk's visor. Falk staggered. Pressing into him shield-to-shield, Duval got just far enough behind him that Falk couldn't hit him. Then he got three ringing hacks into Falk's head before Falk shoved him away.

The Scarlet Tyrant commander was built like an ankylosaur, wide and low to the ground. Though he'd just turned one hundred, the center point of middle age, Duval kept himself rigorously fit. Like all his men, he hailed from Riqueza, a mountainous fief of Sansamour whose folk were famed for their ferocity in battle—and their belligerent insistence on exercising more autonomy than Archduke Roger was willing to grant them.

Falk's round helmet showed dents. Though he kept trying to power his opponent down with nosehornbull rushes, Melodía didn't think he was stronger than Duval. And the older man had the edge in skill.

She wound a handkerchief tightly in her hands. She didn't know why she felt so unbearably tense. She didn't even know whom she wanted to win.

What she *wanted* was that the fight wasn't happening. She didn't even know why Falk had challenged Duval. What she *knew* was that nothing good could come of it.

Falk had been busy since the Ejército Corregir marched. He'd even found followers among the younger Scarlet Tyrants. Melodía didn't like the smell of that at all. But whenever she tried to mention her misgivings about a recent rebel acquiring so much influence to her father—who himself was leaning increasingly on Falk in Jaume's absence—he just smiled and said, "Of course, dear," as if she were a child.

As usual.

Another surge and clangor. Falk struck savagely at Duval's thigh. He was using an infantryman's axe, both head and haft longer and heavier than the battleaxe he carried when mounted. Many knights would've disdained it as a peasant's weapon; Falk was clearly a man who cared most for results.

Melodía didn't think he got the one he desired this time. Though the axe left a groove in the steel cuisse that guarded his opponent's thigh, the Riquezo's shield didn't twitch downward by a millimeter. Instead Falk had to snap his head aside to avoid a thrust to the eye-socket of his helmet. The tip of Duval's sword left a bright silver scratch on the blue-enameled visor.

"What do you think about all this fuss over the Garden of Beauty and Truth?" Josefina Serena asked, looking everywhere but at the brutal contest on the yellow flags a story below. In her beloved tourneys, death or even serious injury were accidents, neither intended nor desired. Here they were the *point*. Which clearly upset her. "Is Providence really full of heresy, the way everybody says? My father says all of La Merced's abuzz that they're going to bring a Grey Angel Crusade down on us."

"Curious," Abi said with a frown. "Mercedes are an easygoing lot, leaving aside the odd riot for sport. They're not normally the sorts to get worked up over doctrinal differences."

"But a Grey Angel Crusade is more terrible than anything!" Fina had a broad superstitious streak, which she hadn't gotten from her father, an all but overt agnostic. "That would scare anybody."

"Wouldn't that make Melodía's boyfriend a heretic too?" asked Llurdis, biting into a peach. "They follow his doctrines in Providence, don't they?"

She lowered the fruit and looked around at her fellow ladies-in-waiting with juice running down her chin. "What?"

"Tactful, Llurdi," Abi murmured.

"Brainless bitch," Lupe hissed. "I've a mind to—"

Melodía slammed fists down on thighs left bare by her emerald-green silk loincloth. "Enough!"

Duval had pressed Falk back until his shoulders almost touched the ivy-covered courtyard wall. As he rushed in to press his advantage, Falk thrust his axe-head at his opponent's eyes.

Reflexively Duval whipped up his shield. Even as he did Falk was casting his own aside. While Duval was blinded by his shield, Falk gripped the axe with both hands, swung it high, and brought it down in a brutal woodcutter's chop.

It caved in Duval's shield. The arm beneath broke with a loud crack.

The Anglés ambassador, Sir Hugo Hugomont, broad as a castle gate and jovial, started to step forward to thrust his staff between the men and end the fight. He was acting as knight-marshal. With Duval's obvious injury, honor was now satisfied. The Scarlet Tyrant commander could concede without disgrace.

But Duval did not yield. He stabbed at Falk's belly so hard his sword-tip broke through the Herzog's breastplate. Falk raised his axe overhead again.

It hacked through the crown of Duval's helmet. Blood squirted from his eyeholes. A scarlet plume, severed, floated gently to the ground.

He landed before it did.

Using only his alarming strength, so as not to dishonor his fallen enemy by stepping on him, Falk wrenched his axe free. Melodía heard someone vomit behind her. Maybe more than one. She held her breath; if she smelled puke, she'd throw up too.

She had not been able to watch when Jaume fought Falk. She'd made herself watch this fight to the end. Now she wondered why.

Stumbling-eager, Falk's arming-squire Albrecht brought his master a cloth to clean his blade. The Duke did a rough, quick job of it. Then, as nimble as a dancer despite heat, exertion, and twenty kilos of plate, he walked up to kneel beneath where Felipe sat, and lay his weapon symbolically at his Emperor's feet.

Melodía narrowed her eyes. Her father's face had frozen when Duval fell. The two had never been friends; the gruff Riquezo often said that if his principal felt friendly toward him, he wasn't doing his job. He served the Fangèd Throne, not its current occupant. But he had served both throne and occupants devotedly for seventy years.

Felipe was no man to ignore that fact. But he was a sucker for a gesture such as Falk's.

"It saddens me that things had to come to this," he said. "But I am pleased to welcome the new commander of my bodyguard. You've proved yourself worthy, Falk von Hornberg."

Melodía rose and turned to go. She felt as if her whole body was clenched like a fist. She didn't care if her ladies followed. She just wanted to get *away*— somewhere dark, cool, and alone.

She wasn't trying to flee the carnage so much as her reaction to it. Disgust filled her, and sadness for a good man who had never done her harm. Yet she also felt strangely stimulated. Almost aroused.

That was harder for her to confront than the reek of vomit or the sight of a bright red pool with greenbellied flies crawling on dough-colored clumps of brain. Or even the way servants hovered at the courtyard's edge with their buckets of sawdust and water, their scoops and brushes, waiting to clean the yellow flags.

"What's that noise?" asked Fina, dropping her hands and looking around.

"It sounds like some disturbance in the city," Abi said. "Must be big, if we hear it here."

Down the loggia a commotion broke out as a pair of Scarlet Tyrants tried to bar the approach of what was unmistakably a postrider, whose springer-leather jackboots and jerkin were spattered with dried road mud.

"Your Majesty!" she cried. "An urgent dispatch from Comte Guillaume de Crève Coeur!"

"Let her through," Felipe said. The Tyrants lowered their halberds and stepped back.

The messenger knelt three meters before the Emperor.

"Terrible news, your Majesty," she said, proffering a scroll bound in a scarlet ribbon and sealed with a broken-heart signet in blue wax.

Mondragón took the dispatch and handed it on to Felipe. "Tell me, please," the Emperor said.

"Count Guillaume of Crève Coeur reports that a Grey Angel has been seen Emerging in County Providence!"

"They're coming!"

Both scout and bay mare ran with sweat in the morning heat. They'd appeared at a dead run over the rise ahead of Karyl and Rob. The light, porous tufa gravel that covered the road squeaked loudly beneath flying unshod hooves.

She reined up before the two men, at the head of the marching column.

"They're only a few kilometers up the road," she reported, leaning forward to pat the shoulder of her dancing, eye-rolling mount to calm her. "A dozen dinosaur knights, thirty heavy horse, a hundred house-shields. There're forty, fifty house-bows and peasant archers, and a couple hundred levies."

"Any idea who leads them?" asked Karyl.

"They're following a gold cup on green banner."

"Baron Salvateur," said Rob. The name didn't taste good. Guillaume's top henchman, Salvateur was a scar-faced, hot-tempered man, and by all accounts a canny field captain. "I was hoping a fool commanded; they're in such rich supply. Well, no need to tell me that this is war, and we get what we get, not what we want."

Karyl had already turned away. The Providence army had begun to emerge from a dense wood of evergreen broadleaves peppered with pines. Karyl was issuing orders to deploy them at the forest's edge.

The day was beautiful. It had briefly rained the night before. Providence had kept its roads well paved and drained even after Count Étienne abdicated, so they didn't have to slog through a ribbon sea of mud. But the air was almost unbreathably thick with the smell of damp leaves and undergrowth.

Before them undulated gentle hills covered with wildflowers, blue as a lake on a thin-cloud day. These resembled tiny bells, gleaming as if jeweled with water droplets. Rob's poetic nature rebelled at the notion that through this beauty a small but powerful army approached, bent on destroying him and his friends.

Remember, he told himself, *no day's too fair to die on, nor too foul either.*

Gaétan, mounted on Zhubin, was helping Karyl's other lieutenants chivvy the militia's leading elements into the undergrowth to either side of the road. Karyl wore the same helmet and leather coat he had in the Whispering Woods. Gaétan was similarly kitted-out.

Anticipating hotter and closer action, Rob had opted for heavier: a breast-and-back of bony-scaled armadón hide; a light linen blouse beneath, with just enough sleeve to keep the arm-holes from chafing; cuisses of nosehorn hide boiled in wax strapped over the thighs of yellow silk trousers. An open-faced steel burgonet, with a crest and a bit of bill to protect his face, topped the ensemble. His round shield hung from one side of his saddle, his axe, Wanda, from the other.

"What's this nonsense?"

Rob turned in his saddle, scowling. Longeau drummed up at a brisk trot on his white gelding rouncy. His fellow town lords followed close behind, forcing foot soldiers to dive off the right-of-way into the ditch or be trampled.

"Why are we stopping?" Percil demanded in a voice as pinched and querulous as his face. "We hear the enemy's been seen. We must attack without delay!"

"We're taking up positions in the woods," Karyl said. "They're our best defenses. Neither their foot nor their mounted forces can attack us en bloc there. And they can't easily pursue us if we have to with-draw."

"What's this?" Longeau almost screamed. "De-fend? *Withdraw?*"

"We must attack!" Percil said.

"That's suicide," Karyl said.

"Enough of this defeatist scratcher-shit," Yannic said to Longeau. "What says the Council?"

Longeau drew an arming-sword and brandished it in a glittering circle over his head. "Forward, men and women of Providence!" he bellowed. "Forward to victory."

"Stop that," Karyl said. "I command here."

"Not anymore," Percil said.

Melchor puffed his fat bearded cheeks. "Enough of this make-believe. A member of the Council leads us now."

"And the serfs will obey us, as they're accustomed to," Yannic said.

"The townsmen too, if they know what's good for them," added Percil.

"In the name of the Master Gardeners of Beauty and Truth," Longeau trumpeted at the bewildered volunteers, "I command you: forward!"

To Rob's horror they obeyed. Raising a wild cheer at the urging of house-soldiers wearing the colors of Percil, Yannic, and that fat fraud Melchor, the army surged forward. They split around Nell and Asal like water around rocks, and went streaming up the road at an eager trot.

Few so much as glanced at Karyl.

"Spare no one!" Yannic cried, waving his sword. He spurred his strider to a two-legged run to take the lead. It clacked its beak anxiously, and its ruff stood out stiffly to the sides. Cuget of the Council rode after him, waving an arming-sword and hollering. Melchor on his pony, and Percil on his big black stallion, hung back to continue shouting encouragement to the militia, as if afraid *sense* might suddenly break out.

Travise and Ismaël rode by, aloof and distant atop their mountainous hadrosaurs. They steered courteously to either side of Rob and Karyl. The infantry in their path had to step lively or get trodden into the tufa, of course.

Gaétan had turned his spike-frill to face the road, and sat staring aghast as the army of Providence fled almost gaily to meet the unseen enemy.

"What's the matter with you?" Rob shouted at Karyl in sudden anger. "You're the most famous field captain in Nuevaropa! Why don't you order them to stop?"

"Never give an order you know won't be obeyed."

The human torrent began to thin. Most of the militia had already vanished over the blue-covered hill. Suddenly Lucas was by Karyl's stirrup. The painter was almost hopping from foot to sandaled foot in indecision as his comrades flowed past. He wore a light leather tunic and his new longsword with its hilt sticking up above one shoulder. His face was red and wracked beneath the pale bangs sticking out beneath the brim of his plain steel cap.

Karyl's own face was as tormented as if one of his killing headaches had struck full force. "Don't, boy," he said. "Please, don't go."

"But you don't *understand*," Lucas said. "You came; you'll go. We've always had the town lords, and we always will. We've always obeyed them. And they'll find ways to punish us if we don't now."

"We can change that," Karyl said. "Together. You know we can."

Lucas stilled. "Well—"

Guat the farmer ran past, his belly bouncing over his grimy leather loincloth. He had a spear in his hand and a leather helmet askew on his head.

"Come on, lad," he called. "Glory's this way! All you'll find here is a coward's shame."

Lucas gave Karyl a last agonized look. "I'm sorry," he said, and ran along with the rest.

Karyl lowered his head and squeezed shut his eyes.

"I failed you, boy," he said, so softly Rob could barely hear him from the cheers and the thumping of heedless feet. "I should have trained you better."

He opened his eyes and shook his head once quickly, as if clearing water from his hair.

"Right. Now let's get busy saving what we can."

Chapter 43

Eris, La Luna Visible, the Moon Visible—The moon
we see at night when the clouds usually clear. As distinct from La Luna Invisible, the Moon Invisible, where
pious girls and boys know the Creators lived when they
made Paradise out of Old Hell. It of course cannot be
seen, but nevertheless, it is there.

—A PRIMER TO PARADISE FOR THE IMPROVEMENT
OF YOUNG MINDS

Filled with dark joy and darker purpose, his
new scarlet cape of office flapping from his
shoulders, Falk von Hornberg strode the corridors of the Firefly Palace. A fist of five Scarlet Tyrants trotted behind.

The Empire was overdue for revolution. He was
bringing it. Not to overthrow the Emperor, but to
give him all the power an Emperor should wield.

Falk had worked hard and fast to consolidate his
own power once Felipe confirmed him as the new
chief of his Imperial bodyguard. Now was the time
to take the last and boldest steps.

They came to a door. Gently, Falk tried the latch. It was locked.

"What if we brought the Angel," a voice like an overgrown child's half sobbed from the door's far side, "for our sin of plotting against the Emperor? Our own kinsman!"

"If the Grey Angels went on crusade every time there was a little plotting," said a second, supercilious voice, "they'd never stop."

"How many times must I tell you, Benedicto?" came a third voice, crisply precise but touched with weariness, "Nobody's plotting against Felipe. We only want to get his attention. You're overreacting to this imaginary apparition."

"La-la-la-la! I can't hear you! It scares me when you call the Grey Angels imaginary, Gonzalo! Please don't."

Falk smiled. Then, rearranging his face in a suitable scowl, he looked to his squad.

"Break it down," he said.

Doors in the Palace of the Fireflies were well built and sturdy. They'd laugh at a mere boot. A heavy bronze ram wielded by four husky Scarlet Tyrants proved less humorous.

With a squealing groan the door blew inward.

The little man with the outsized head sprang from his chair facing the door. A rapier in a ruby-set scabbard hung from a twisted bronze lampstand. As the cabo in charge of the Tyrant squad preceded Falk inside, he yanked out the long, slim blade with a sliding ring.

"Gonzalo Delgao, you are hereby placed under arrest—"

The Tyrant corporal saw steel pointed his way,

glinting yellow in the lamplight. The Emperor's body-guards were trained to respond with bowstring speed. The cabo interrupted himself in mid-oration to ram his arming-sword through the sternum of the armed but unresisting Gonzalo.

The little man gasped and went to his knees.

"You hurt my brother!" roared Benedicto. His neck and the veins in his face engorging in fury, he picked up a heavy table of blueheart wood and slammed it down on the sidewise crest of the Tyrant's helmet.

"Benedicto, stop!" shouted Falk von Hornberg, sidestepping the cabo, who lay head-to-head with Gonzalo. His outflung fingers twitched as their blood mingled on a formerly splendid Ovdan carpet.

Fists knotted so tightly the knuckles cracked, Bene-dicto rushed the Duke. As he cocked his right arm for a blow, Falk stepped to meet him, grabbing his left forearm and right biceps. Benedicto was even bigger than Falk, and weeping mad with grief and rage. For a moment each pushed against the other, so wound around the effort they couldn't speak. Then Falk shoved the bigger man stumbling back, to fall on his broad rump on the tiled floor.

"Benedicto—" Falk said. Agile as a schoolboy, the big man scrambled up and rushed him again. He didn't charge head-lowered like a nosehorn bull, but upright, looking to smash the interloper with his fists. Tears streamed down a face the color of sun-bleached bone.

Falk's left hand whipped a broad-bladed cinque-dea, a five-finger dagger, from his belt. He planted his right palm against Benedicto's breastbone, trying to ward him off with a stiff-arm. Benedicto drove him back toward the door, one pace, two.

The dagger bit like a viper: once, twice, so many times in blinding succession Falk himself lost count. Benedicto squealed like an enraged Tyrannosaurus. Blood flew from his mouth, to splash hot across Falk's bearded face and down his gilded breastplate. He kept pushing hard against Falk's outstretched arm until he suddenly stiffened and his eyes rolled up in his head. He went limp and fell down dead.

The other four Tyrants had laid aside their ram and come into the room to help their new commander, spears at the ready. They saw their fallen cabo.

René Alarcón had been caught standing by a wall hanging that portrayed the Rape of La Merced, pouring wine from a decanter. He set it down on a cabinet beside his cup and arched a disdainful brow at Falk.

"You've a brisk way with the bereaved," said Alarcón. "If your Grace's wits were as sharp as your steel, perhaps—"

A Tyrant stuck his spear into the nobleman's open mouth. Its tip poked out the back of his skull with a crunch. Alarcón's eyes snapped wide with final surprise.

"That should hold your tongue, traitor," the guard snarled as Alarcón collapsed.

Falk frowned around at the bloody shambles the room had become in a matter of heartbeats. He hated to think what his mother would have said of this state of affairs.

I see I'm going to have to do something about the Tyrants being quite so quick to stab first and ask questions later.

Still, thinking about it, perhaps things had worked out for the best. The three dead men's silence was more useful than anything they could say. Traitors had resisted justice and died; inconvenient details could be concealed readily enough by the leader of the Emperor's bodyguards.

Public examples were needed. They would be made. That was all accounted for.

Now Falk needed something else. Still frowning, now deliberately, he swung his gaze to the surviving member of the quartet. He still held the dripping dagger in his hand.

Augusto Manorquín, as sleek as a house cat, had never so much as uncrossed his legs where he sat in a velvet chair whose green matched his doublet.

Correctly reading the question on Falk's face, Manorquín raised much-beringed hands, spread wide with pale palms forward.

"Whatever suits the needs of the State," he said, "I will happily confess to."

Falk smiled through drying blood. "Wise man," he said.

Barely pausing to wipe the blood from face and armor with a rag a Tyrant handed him, Falk handed over his prisoner and set off on his next errand. A fresh *puño* of guardsmen followed. Their corporal, rather older and more weathered than the last, kept them alert and eager as vexers on the leash. They'd *heard* what happened to the previous squad-leader.

Falk took a shortcut outside through soft sunset air, between a guest wing of the sprawling main residence and the tower that housed the Imperial apartments. The clouds were breaking apart into bands of slate underlit with orange-and-yellow forge light along the eastern sky above La Merced. The first stars glittered in indigo overhead. Fireflies danced below them like living lanterns. The wind was fresh from the Channel, smelling of salt and the greenery of Anglaterra on the far side.

Instead of the cheerful music and laughter that usually greeted day's end in the Palace of the Fireflies, Falk heard hushed conversation on every side. Somewhere someone sobbed heartbrokenly.

He smiled.

Panic had spread rapidly through the palace and the city below. News of the Angel's Emergence had taken even Falk aback. Not because he thought it was true, but rather because its timing and import so perfectly capped off Bergdahl's machinations, building suspicion against Providence and the Garden over the weeks since the army departed.

Falk knew Bergdahl and his mother communicated regularly, in a code the best cryptographers he could find in La Merced—something of a hotbed of the trade—had so far proven unable to break. Could they somehow have had advance knowledge of the Grey Angel's Emergence?

He immediately dismissed that as absurd. If the Dowager Duchess knew all this was going to happen, corroborating that the fabled Angels existed would be among its least unsettling ramifications.

Entering the tower, he led his squad up the spiraling staircase to the Imperial apartments. Precisely on schedule: a pair of Tyrants stood flanking a door that was swinging open even as Falk led his men into the corridor.

Mondragón, dressed in his usual loose robes of brown and black, halted a step outside the door. The expression on his gaunt raptor-beaked face never changed. But Falk read the knowledge in the slightest flicker in those obsidian-flake eyes.

"So this is how it goes," the tall old man said, with the slightest of aristocratic lifts of his brow. "I admit I am surprised. Well played, young man. Well played."

"This way, Señor Ministro, if you will," the cabo said, stepping to the fore as his men surrounded Mondragón. The corporal's voice was gruffer even than usual. A Scarlet Tyrant had to be no respecter of persons other than those of the Emperor and his immediate family. But it wasn't every day they were called upon to arrest the Emperor's Chief Minister and best friend for treason.

As expected Mondragón fell into step behind as the cabo led off along the corridor. Out of courtesy Falk didn't order him bound. In turn the minister made no undignified and ultimately futile resistance or attempts to escape. They were both professionals, after all.

One more arrest, thought Falk with a thrill of dread as well as anticipation. *The most important and risky of all.*

But he'd take no direct part in that. As Bergdahl had advised him not to.

Instead he followed the *puño* and their prisoner at a brisk pace through the Imperial apartments. It was appropriate that the Tyrants' commander oversee the interrogation of such an important prisoner. Even though whatever Mondragón said or did not had as little bearing on what was going to happen as it did on whether or not Eris would rise in the West tonight.

———

Melodía sat naked on the edge of the bathing pool in her quarters. Serving girls daubed her with sponges soaked in infusions of flower petals. She had opted not to take another full bath before retiring. The day's cataclysmic turn of events had drained her. She just wanted to sleep as soon as possible.

From outside came a crash, and an angry shout from Pilar. "You can't come in! These are the Princess's rooms!"

Melodía stood up, scowling as her servants shrank back. Five Imperial guardsmen burst in. As always they were gorgeous in their scarlet cloaks and golden armor. Their brash masculine presence was still a profanation.

Armed and armored, trained and strong, the five men still quailed before the Princess's wrath. Invading a hidalga's private bath was a serious matter. And when that hidalga was the Emperor's favorite daughter and heir. . . .

"What in the name of the Old Hell do you think you're doing?" she demanded.

One of them, she saw, was trying to fend off Pilar, who was kicking and punching at him like a furious horror.

"Pilar," she said, putting s snap to her voice. "Stop."

Her maidservant dropped her arms and stood back. Her black hair was a crazy tangle. Pink spots shone high on olive cheekbones. They almost matched one coming into being beneath the right eye of the guard who'd battled with her. She'd caught him a smart one with her fist.

"You can't help me, *querida*," Melodía said. "Thank you."

Pilar slumped. She sighed, hung her head, and

stepped back. Her erstwhile opponent rearranged himself, looking like a man trying to hide relief.

"Your Highness," the cabo said, "we have come to arrest you on suspicion of conspiring against the Emperor."

"Against my *father*? Are you insane?"

"Those are our orders. Which we follow to the death."

"How melodramatic."

A Tyrant approached holding a robe of white silk. She raised a hand to halt him. "If I'm fit to be arrested in this state," she said with a haughty chin lift, "I'm fit to walk to my fate in it."

The cabo's brow furrowed. He rubbed his thick jaw, causing a furtive sound like mouse claws in the wainscoting, from what she guessed was permanent stubble.

Public nudity could be used to show sincerity, and as a protest. Melodía meant both. Though he didn't seem an unduly subtle man, the Tyrant under-officer clearly understood it.

His four men could have forcibly robed the naked Princess. *Eventually*. He glanced at his man who'd grappled with Pilar, who was developing a prize black eye.

The cabo waved the robe away. "Alteza," he said, gesturing toward the door.

Melodía drew in a deep breath, well aware her captors couldn't keep their eyes off her still-moist breasts riding up her ribs. "When my father hears of this—"

She faltered. Stopped. For the first time she felt the needle of fear through her chest.

If my father didn't know, she thought in horror, *how would they dare arrest me?*

Her knees threatened to give way. Feelings of anger and betrayal and confusion—and lost, lost sorrow—engulfed her as though a star-strike in the Channel had caused a vast wave to inundate the palace.

By a wrench of will she made her face a mask. Squaring her shoulders, drawing her head up high, she swept past the men and out of the bath chamber without another word.

Chapter 44

What have I *done?*"

His despairing words chased each other through the low, torchlit passageway, part of a labyrinth of retreats and storage rooms below the Firefly Palace, like Fae voices mocking. He slammed a fist into niter-crusted stone. White powder drifted down and made him blink and sneeze.

Arms crossed over his chest, Bergdahl leaned

VICTOR MILÁN

coolly against a wall. "Why, I think your Grace has pulled off a remarkable coup, progressing from rebel scum to master of the Imperial bodyguard in a matter of months. That, and gotten dripping drunk."

Falk turned and blinked at him. His vision remained blurry though the niter-powder's sting had subsided.

It must be the wine, he thought. *I'm not weak enough to cry.*

"Easy for you to be flip about this damned game you've got me playing," he growled. "It's not your neck between the tyrant's jaws."

Bergdahl showed crooked brown teeth. "No. I'm for the wheel—all my limbs broken and braided through the spokes. When it comes to servants who displease the nobility, the Creators' rules against torture fly out the window like pretty blue little birds."

"You don't *understand,*" Falk half sobbed. "I've just arrested the Emperor's best friend and Chief Minister on false evidence. That *you* concocted, and I planted. On even worse grounds I've taken the Emperor's own daughter and heir into custody and thrown her into secret confinement. Without a scrap of authority for any of it!"

"An admirable summation," said Bergdahl. "But don't neglect the deft way you murdered those poor, inconvenient bastards you pretended to conspire with. Even I admire that one. And you came up with it all on your own."

"But what if someone finds out?"

Bergdahl sneered. "Your lady mother's right about you. Sometimes you're a dull boy indeed."

Falk raised ham-hock fists to smash that great beak of a nose and hada face past repair or recognition, to batter this impudent peasant until his eyes rolled in ruined sockets and he choked on a soup of his own blood and teeth.

Instead he dropped them to his sides. "Why am I doing this? Why do I listen to you?"

"You listen to me because your lady mother told you to. You listen to me because you know I have your best interests at heart. And you listen to me because I'm right."

He paused. "Just as your mother and I were right about your father. Remember, your Grace?"

Mention of his father brought a stab of remembered pain through his bowels. *But he can't hurt me anymore,* he reminded himself. *Not since I pushed him down the stairs.*

As Mother wanted me to. As Bergdahl showed me how.

He swayed. He blinked at Bergdahl. Not for the first time he felt as if those grey eyes could read his thoughts right through his own.

"But why was it necessary that I do these things?"

"For a higher cause. As you'd recall if you stopped wallowing in self-pity for a moment, and took control of yourself long enough to think."

"What 'higher cause,' Bergdahl? *What?*"

"The Empire," the servant who was in so many ways his master said. "The Empire needs strong hands to guide it—as you yourself helped prove, when you rose against it. Now you've chosen to serve the Fangèd Throne. For that you must serve this Emperor, in spite of himself if that must be.

"And, of course, you did these things because it is your mother's will. She only wants what's best for you. And for the Empire, of course."

Falk sighed heavily. "Of course," he said sarcastically. He was starting to return to sobriety. It wasn't a pleasant place to be.

Bergdahl's crooked half smile never flickered. He shed sarcasm like a carrack-bird's ass.

"And the Emperor's daughter?" Falk asked. "What about that little detail?"

"The whore? She's the biggest prize of all! Her arrest lends credence to the whole bag of maggots. It proves your case: if you're willing to arrest the Emperor's own daughter, how certain must you be you're right?"

"But it's not true, Bergdahl. She was never involved." For some reason Falk found it difficult to utter his star prisoner's name. "Those pathetic schemers, Gonzalo and the rest, never talked about her without complaining that she wouldn't give them the time of day."

"Nonsense. Your new pet songbird, Manorquín—won't he swear she was up to her tits in it? If you haven't persuaded him to already?"

"Yes." Sullenly.

"And there you have it, your Grace. People just have to be made to believe. If the right people believe it, it *is* true, in the only way that matters."

Falk shook his head. The crackling and spitting of the tarred-rush torches, the blood-roar in his brain, the dull throb at his temples, the slosh of wine in his stomach made him feel dizzy and disoriented.

"What about justice?" he asked.

"What's 'just' is *just* what those with power say it is. Like truth. No more, no less. Now you have the power. The Emperor trusts you, more than ever. You've uncovered a heinous plot against him, and broken its back as if you were stamping on a viper. Even though it meant imprisoning his daughter."

Bergdahl stopped, cocked his villainous round head and squinted an eye at Falk.

"Has that bitch cut your balls off, then?"

"*What?*" Falk roared. His voice seemed to raise the round stone ceiling.

"She's done nothing but dangle you by your dick. Like a toy on a string."

"How dare you—"

"She wags that apple ass of hers under your nose. I saw her do it at that dance. And if you tried for a nibble, what would've happened?"

Falk deflated into a sulk.

"Yes. The Scarlet Tyrants would've drubbed you soundly and pitched you in the dinosaur-stable dung heap."

Falk felt something stir inside him. Somewhere deep.

"Yet you can bet the bitch gives that ass up freely to that orange-haired half man of hers."

"Watch your stinking mouth!" Emotions Falk couldn't name, much less control, were slurring his speech as much as the wine was now. "Jaume's a great champion. The greatest fighter in Nuevaropa. He beat me, don't forget, little man."

Only a man as huge as Falk could call the gallows-pole peasant "little." But Bergdahl scoffed.

"You threw the fight. Or has hiding your face in wine-barrels made you forget that too?"

"He had me beaten," Falk said. "You're talking about warrior matters here. A churl like you wouldn't understand."

"As you like. But I ask you, your Grace: who commands the Scarlet Tyrants now?"

"I—" Falk paused. The conversation's quick turn had scrambled his wits again. "I do."

"So what's to prevent you taking what should be yours by right? Taking what she happily gives up to Jaume—who in turn rejoices in giving it up to those pretty boys of his?"

What had begun as a smolder within Falk was sparking into flame. Still, he scowled at his servant.

"What are you saying?"

"You have the power. Use it. Or are you unworthy? Is it possible you're afraid of the little cunt?"

"No!" Falk bellowed. The anger flamed up to embrace his brain in red.

Bergdahl smirked. "Then go. And do what you want." He chuckled. "She'll likely thank you for it, once the pain subsides."

When she paused for breath in her bawling, Montserrat heard a voice, soft but insistent, say, "Please, Highness. Listen to me."

She lay facedown on the absurdly pink silk comforter on her bed, her head buried in her arms.

"Go away, Pilar," she sniffled.

"You don't mean that, Highness. You want to help your sister."

Montse took a ragged breath. She felt a sneaking relief at having been sucked out of her crying fit. She turned her head and opened one eye.

The gitana maidservant sat on a stool beside the bed. Her face, which Montse thought was almost as pretty as her sister's, was filled with concern.

Pilar wasn't a stupid person. No matter how Melodía sometimes treated her. Sometimes even Melodía acted stupid. And by not being stupid, Pilar set herself apart from most servants and almost all the grandes of the court.

She always treated Montse with respect, instead of as if *she* were stupid. Just as cousin Jaume treated her.

Montse felt soft impacts and heard insistent beeping from her springer-down pillow, just past her head. She looked toward it. Tear-soaked dreadlocks flopped in her face like dead octopus tentacles. Through them she saw Silver Mistral doing the All-Purpose Ferret Dance, which served as war dance, celebration, and in this case commiseration: back arched and hopping up and down in place.

Montse sighed.

"All right," she said, sitting up. Though watery snot ran freely down her upper lip, she spoke in a tone whose normality surprised even her. She gathered the jumping ferret into her arms. Mistral gave off beeping at once and even allowed Montse to cradle her on her back in her arms like a human baby, which normally affronted Mistral's dignity.

Painfully Montse became aware of what un-Montserrat-like behavior she'd been indulging in. She *hated* being out of control of herself. Even though sometimes she just had to cry, it didn't *fix* anything.

Smiling, Pilar smoothed errant dreads from the girl's face. Montse usually hated having people fuss over her. Somehow this didn't bother her.

"Why do you want to help Melodía?" she asked.

Pilar pulled her head back and blinked as if the girl had slapped her. "What do you mean? I'm her maidservant."

"But she's mean to you sometimes," Montse said.

"You're blunt, Princess," Pilar said with a smile.

"Yes, I am. Please call me by my name, Pilar."

"Montse, then. It's . . . unusual for someone in your position to say 'please' to a person in mine."

"I try to be nice to everybody." Montse left unspoken the *unless they piss me off*. She took that for a given.

Pilar pressed her lips down hard on what Montse suspected was another smile. She noticed that the woman's green eyes were as puffy as her own must be.

"To answer your question," Pilar said, "I love Melodía as if she were my sister too. We were raised together, did you know? We played together constantly. Much the way you do with the servant children."

"What happened?" Montse asked.

"We grew up."

Montse scowled. That struck her as a typical adult nonanswer.

"We each found ourselves forced to . . . play our roles," Pilar said. "She's the Princesa Imperial, after all."

"But she won't inherit the Fangèd Throne. Nobody can do that."

"The title's still important. Very ceremonial. Some people put a lot of stock in that."

Some people are stupid, Montse thought.

"Melodía's very independent. But—" Pilar shrugged. "She has to act the way she's expected to. As most people do."

"I'll never understand," Montse growled. "If growing up means having to treat your friends like, like pieces of furniture, I don't ever want to do it!"

Pilar laughed. "Your sister's strong-minded," she

said, "but she can't come close to you, little one. If anybody can force the world and Torre Delgao to let her grow up on her own terms, it's you. But we've got lots to talk about, and not much time. Do you see now why I want to help Melodía?"

Montse nodded. Then she bit her lip.

"I heard servants whispering that Melodía might be put to death. Daddy wouldn't let that happen. Ever!" She felt tears threatening her eyes again. "Would he?"

Pilar took a deep breath. "He might not have a choice."

"But he's the Emperor!"

"Even the Emperor has to be obey the Empire's laws."

"But it's wrong! Melodía hasn't done anything bad!"

"You're right. But she has said things that wicked people have twisted to mean what they want them to. She's caught in a web of things she doesn't understand. Me neither, for that matter."

"So what can *we* do? I'm just a child. People always point that out. And you're just a servant."

Uncharacteristically, Montse regretted words that had left her mouth, as soon as they had. Servants were her playmates, her friends. She was the last person in the world ever to mean, *just a servant*—in the sense customary to her class, meaning, *instead of a person*.

"Don't worry," Pilar said, "I know what you mean. And that's the thing: you know how people overlook children . . . and servants?"

Guardedly, Montse nodded. It was like asking if she knew about *breathing*.

"Well, *that's* how we'll save Melodía."

Montse thought about that for a moment. She hugged Mistral up against her chin. Her friend's soft warmth reassured her.

"What's the plan?" she asked.

Chapter 45

Estólica, **Spear-thrower**—also *Atlatl,* or *Lanzadardos,* Dart-thrower. A stick, usually about half a meter in length, with a nub or cup at one end that fits against the butt of a spear or dart. It is used to launch such projectiles with greater speed and accuracy than a person can throw, and is popular among the mounted skirmishers called jinetes.

—A PRIMER TO PARADISE FOR THE IMPROVEMENT
OF YOUNG MINDS

The morning was still bright and cheerful as a traitor beneath thin, high clouds. It was warm by upland standards, enough for sweat to beset Rob's eyes from beneath his helmet's bill and tickle his ribs inside the thick nodosaur-hide cuirass in spite of leafy shade. A light breeze stirred the bell-shaped blue flowers that cloaked the hill to its crest a couple hundred meters north. It blew out of the east and smelled of the flowers' faint perfume and green growth. The fragrance was as soothing and pretty as the scene.

"That'll change, soon enough," Rob Korrigan muttered to himself.

Beside him Little Nell shifted from foot to foot. He wasn't sure whether that was because she was picking up the tension among the hundred or so men and women Karyl had spread out under cover of the shoulder-high growth at the edge of the forest between them and the derelict village, or from the fact that her archnemesis Asal stood browsing for tasty shoots just a few meters away.

Karyl and Rob stood between their saddled mounts, just inside the screen of brush. Without glancing Rob's way, Karyl nodded. He knew what Rob meant. And he knew even better than Rob how ghastly true that was.

He held his hornbow in both hands before him, and stood gazing straight ahead as if he could see what was happening.

And like enough he can, Rob thought. *He knows this song as well as I. Better.*

The Providence army's cheering had been met with first scattered cries and then a hoarse distant shout as soon as they hit the hillcrest. The Providentials' voices had merged with those of the lead Crève Coeur element into an inchoate chorus. Now the clamor rose an octave. Trumpets blared.

A muscle at the edge of Karyl's jaw twitched. Screams shot up like startled fliers.

Well away to the left, a mounted quartet appeared. They rode their three horses and tan-ruffed russet strider not at a panic run, but at an easy lope. They were some of Rob's scouts, not fleeing but doing their jobs.

He looked at Karyl. Karyl nodded.

"It won't make any difference if the Brokenhearts realize we're here," he said.

Rob put fingers in his mouth and emitted a shrill whistle. The horses' ears perked up. The four turned their mounts and clucked them into a gallop toward where the forest met the road.

On the road a single beast crossed the summit, heading their way. It was Yannic's green strider, rider-less, its golden ruff distended, running as fast as its long legs could pump. Its toothless beak was open in a cry unheard for the greater tumult of pain and fear rising behind it. Rob was interested to note it still hadn't shat itself out.

The scouts drew rein near Rob and Karyl's hiding place.

"It went like the captain said," said Gilles, a rare townsman among the light riders, whose black hair clung lankly to his skull at all times, not just in the heat. "The whole army started to falter the moment they saw the first Brokenhearts crest the next hill."

"Rangers," said the strider rider, a woodcutter's daughter named Françoise who hailed from this very region. "Guilli let them trot ahead to find the game for the lords."

"Who showed up to hunt quick enough," Gilles said. "Our own noble masters rode straight ahead, never even looking around to see they'd left the foot behind. We only saw five Brokenheart war-duckbills, and maybe twenty-five horse. But they were enough to swamp the town and country lords. Baron Ismaël was unseated promptly by a pair of knights riding morions. A sackbut rode Stalk-Neck Percil down straightaway and squashed him."

"It crushed his great black charger too," said Marie,

a farm girl who was sturdily built for a light rider. She had black hair done up in ringed pigtails to either side of her head and a gap in her top teeth. "That was terrible."

"We reckoned we'd seen enough then," Gilles said, "and came back to report."

"Any sign of Longeau?" asked Karyl, to Rob's bafflement. The scouts shook their heads.

It struck Rob that he clearly recalled seeing Councilor Cuget riding off all full of vainglory with the three town lords, and the pair of barons following on their monstrous mounts. But he could not recall seeing so much as a feather from Longeau's downy tail after he finished his spew of rousing piffle.

Ah well, he thought, *that's not a one I care to remember. Even compared to that treacherous toad Melchor. . . .*

"You've done your jobs," Rob told his riders. "Fade back into the woods and rest your mounts."

The scouts laughed. "They're just knights," said Marie. "Their beasts are fat and slow. Can't we give them a hard time?"

For emphasis she brandished a feathered twist-dart with its thong of strider hide wound around its meter-long shaft, to give it spin when cast from a spear-thrower.

"Go ahead," Rob said. Then he let his eyes slide sideways to Karyl. Karyl's neatly bearded chin dipped once, which made Rob feel warm inside like a gulp of brandy.

The scouts rode away to the right, so they could sting the pursuers' eastern flanks. The terrified strider ran right up the road past the defenders, still squalling cacophonously.

To the right—east—of the road, a lone man topped the blue-flowered hill. He ran in great ground-eating bounds the way the strider had, despite the tails of his mail hauberk slapping like lead weights at his legs. A household soldier, Yannic's man by the arms on his tunic, he had thrown away shield and weapons alike in his frenzy to escape.

Next came a few clots of men. And then the army of Providence, in one great wave of fear.

"Steady," Karyl called to his small, concealed force. They were woods-runners, dismounted scouts, volunteers who had chosen to defy their hereditary overlords. Most had bows, though some carried spears, axes, or swords and bucklers from the town armory. To Rob's surprise, even a handful of armored house-archers and house-shields had opted to remain with Karyl. Rob honestly didn't know whether cowardice or courage motivated them.

Karyl had spaced them far enough apart to allow their fleeing comrades to pass freely between them, although he expected the bulk of the routed to choose the road's quicker path.

"Stay out of sight until I give the word. All our lives depend on you."

Rob vented a long sigh. "You were right all along," he said to Karyl. "Courage *is* overvalued. It betrayed them all. They let it drag them off to die for the unworthy. Just as you said it would."

"But at least they won't let it lead them astray so easily, next time."

Rob had to bite down hard on the obvious rejoinder that *next time* appeared to be in no good prospect.

Ah, but isn't that what we're all about here, with even Ma Korrigan's son getting ready to face off with

*mounted and armored knights, contrary to all good
sense and prior practice? To make a next time?*

As the broken army swept down the slope toward
the woods, a horseman appeared, already among
them. He speared a running man through the back as
casually as he might a fallen leaf off the forest floor.
The mountainous forms of war-hadrosaurs rose over
the crest. They rolled down like a living avalanche,
crushing men like flowers.

The Brokenheart nobles' arrogance made Rob's
blood burn in his veins like lye. Most riders wore helmets without visors; those who had them didn't deign
to close them. They were prepared not for battle but
for slaughter: for an encounter that would involve at
most a short, sharp shock, and then panicked flight.
They anticipated that Providence's defenders would
have their hearts and taste for glory crushed in their
torsos at the first sight of armored men on horses,
let alone three-tonne dinosaurs, and would run before their enemies got within shortbow shot of them.

Which had happened.

As Karyl surely knew it would, if the army he had
so carefully grown and nurtured with the care of an
actual master gardener tried to fight the battle the
town lords wanted to lead it into. Even though those
who had fought with him in the ambush at Whispering Woods knew something most commoners did
not—that even a high-and-mighty dinosaur knight
could be pulled off his high-and-mighty dinosaur and
done to brutal death by the meanest hands—they were
in no way prepared for the emotional shock of facing
such knights in the middle of open ground, with nothing but air and flowers to keep their powerful mounts
from grinding them to screaming paste.

Still, Rob couldn't help but feel almost as much disgust as fear as the mobile massacre rolled toward him. *This is nothing more than Count Guilli's advance guard,* he thought. *Were any of us—even the great captain, Karyl—any less daft than Longeau and that lot to think we stood any chance against them?*

"We have to help them!" Gaétan cried. Rob could clearly see him sitting astride Zhubin, behind the screen of bushes on the other side of the road.

"Stand where you are and use your bow, and you will," Karyl said.

"But they're being slaughtered!"

Rob laughed harshly. "So why add your futile blood to theirs? Some bleed, all run; now's when all the murder's done. When men flee like bouncers but less expertly, and more easily ridden down from behind."

"Poetic," Karyl said. "But accurate, withal."

He swung aboard Asal and held up his hornbow. "So we'll cover our friends' flight with flights of our own."

Gaétan's eyes blazed. Tears gleamed on his cheeks. But he nodded, as if slamming his forehead into a wall.

It's a shocking bad idea, Rob thought, *but except for abandoning all and getting out while we can, it's the best of a bad lot. Or so I suppose, not being the great captain here.*

The first refugees reached the woods. Some crowded together onto the road, seeking the swiftest possible escape from the death that pursued them. Most just ran straight ahead, taking the most direct route away from their pursuit.

The distinctive towhead of Lucas the painter turned sword prodigy appeared over the rise to the left of the road, followed quickly by the rest of him. Though he ran with the rest, having little choice if he didn't want to be summarily ridden down, he still carried his longsword. Most of the routed men had jettisoned their arms and such armor as they could easily detach on the run, to speed them on their way.

Maybe he saw Karyl mount his mare. Maybe he simply knew the master he'd turned his back on would be just inside those woods, watching and waiting. Because just a few meters down the slope he stopped and turned to face his pursuers.

He reversed his longsword, gripping it with both hands near the tip. Rob knew the meter and a half blade wasn't honed to shaving sharpness, and that this was why: so it could be safely grasped. Though Rob wouldn't have wanted to do so barehanded as Lucas did. Any more than he'd care to stop and stand in the open with a blood-bent knight sure to bear down on him at any moment.

One did. Rob could see his bearded face laughing in his open helmet. He carried no shield, and held his spear with its bloody point to the clouds, clearly expecting to have to ride farther before he made another kill.

Lucas swung the sword like an axe and caught the knight full in the face with the cross-shaped hilt. Of all the heinous things a body could do with a longsword, that was the one that men called the "murderstroke."

The Brokenheart's face exploded in red. He flopped backward over his courser's croup. Lucas turned around to Karyl, whom he knew waited in the woods, and brandished his sword triumphantly over his head.

"You fool!" Karyl shouted. "Guard yourself!"

The head of a spear stood suddenly out from the young man's chest as another horseman loomed up behind.

Lucas stretched an agonized hand toward Rob and Karyl. He opened his mouth. All that came out was a torrent of blood, shining in the cloud-filtered sun. He fell forward among the blue flowers he'd never get the chance to paint.

The horseman let go the spear and drew an arming-sword as he rode over Lucas's prostrate form. Rob glanced at Karyl. Behind his beard Karyl's face was hard and white as bone as he drew an arrow back with his left thumb. The recurved bow of Triceratops horn droned deep as he let go.

Rob whipped his head left to see it avenge Karyl's wayward sword-apprentice. Instead it struck through both scarlet and blue cheeks of a magnificently brin-dled sackbut. The nearest of the Crève Coeur war-duckbills, it had turned its head to the side for some reason at just that instant.

Rob's astonishment that Karyl had shot something other than Lucas's killer was almost overridden by amazement that he had missed the monster's eye. Of course, it would have taken a master Anglysh long-bowman to make such a shot, and never mounted; but Rob trusted Karyl, Ovda-trained, to do it. *Has grief gotten the better of his aim?* he wondered.

Across the now-crowded roadway Gaétan's bow boomed as if to echo Karyl's. The Brokenheart who had speared Lucas was raising his sword over his shoulder to strike down another fleeing Providential. It was as if the motion carried him on backward out of his saddle—but for the fact that Rob's eye had just registered the young merchant's arrow smashing

through the center of his forehead, just below his
helmet-rim.

Blatting shrill distress, the Parasaurolophus Karyl
had shot turned and bolted back the way it had come.
Two more Crève Coeur monsters followed closely
behind to either side. The wounded sackbut slammed
keel-to-keel into the halberd-crest following to its
right. Both dinosaurs went down in a thrashing, musically discordant chaos of limbs, vast bodies, and
massive tails. Their cries could not drown out the
agonized bellow of the Lambeosaurus's rider as their
combined mass crushed him like a cherry.

Rob's eyes widened. Karyl's aim had been as true
as his mind was clear. That shot had been neither accident nor mistake.

Off to his left Melchor rode into the woods. Though
his marchador's ears were pinned and fear-foam
trailed from its mouth, it kept up the steady fast-
walking pace it was trained to that gave it its name.
The beast must be sturdy indeed to keep up its amble
despite carrying an ashen-faced Yannic as well as its
stout owner.

The farmer Guat ran toward the undergrowth to
Karyl's right, weeping as he tried to cradle his spilled
guts in his filthy blood-soaked arms and doing a
bad job of it, trampling and tripping on their shred-
ded loops that had fallen free. As Rob watched,
some woods-runner gave him the only mercy available: an arrow through the temple.

More arrows arced from the trees as strung-out
Crève Coeur horsemen came in range of short continental bows. Most stuck in mail coats or colorfully
painted nosehorn-hide breastplates. One rider fell.
A stricken horse reared screaming, and its knight

scarcely managed to throw himself clear before it crashed to the ground.

Karyl loosed again. The Brokenheart who had steered his sackbut wide of the fallen duckbills went down with the shaft through his gullet. The remaining two dinosaur knights turned about and headed back the way they'd come. They were in this chase for the joy of slaughter, not to suffer pain or death themselves.

The field was theirs in any event. Nothing Karyl could do would change that, for all his genius.

Which was why his genius meant he wouldn't bother to try.

The horsemen were too hot for the chase to notice their dinosaur-riding comrades retiring. They converged on the road. Why thrash about in the underbrush when the easy meat lay that way, packed in ahead of them?

Rob reckoned the woods-runners, scouts, and volunteers of Karyl's scratch covering force could show them plenty of reasons, and pointed ones. But Gaétan suddenly rode his spike-frill out to block the Brokenhearts' path.

He hadn't had time to set his own recurved bow aside and take up shield and sword. He loosed a final shot. Links sprang open with a chiming sound as the arrow stormed into the hauberk of the lead rider, not four meters distant, and cut his heart in two. As the knight pitched off to his right, Rob saw the arrow tenting out back of his mail for a handspan.

The next rider speared Gaétan through his chest.

Chapter 46

Gran Canal, **Grand Channel**—The body of water separating mainland Nuevaropa from Anglaterra. The top leg, running southeast, is called La Raya (the Stripe) of the Tyrant's Head for its resemblance to an eye-stripe. At the gulf called El Bocado (the Gullet or Gulp), it turns southwest into La Fauces, the Maw. Also called La Canal Corsaria, the Corsair Channel.

—A PRIMER TO PARADISE FOR THE IMPROVEMENT
OF YOUNG MINDS

*A*t least they put me in a north-facing cell, Melodía thought, *so I have the breeze off the Gran Canal to comfort me.*

She withdrew the hand she had reached between the black iron bars that were the only visible manifestations of *cage* to push open her window. Outside, the thirty-centimeter insects that gave the palace its name performed their intricate three-dimension dance, their green-yellow glow leaving bloodred streaks to linger briefly in her eyes. Eight or ten meters below, Prince Harry's house-shields trudged the ramparts between torches whose light flickered orange on their peaked helmets, and on engines pointing out to sea, ready on the instant to defend against an attack only insanity would launch.

Away far off on the white cliffs of Anglaterra, hidden by the night, a single blue light shone. The daytime clouds had unraveled, leaving the sky to black and stars. Out on the Channel, the minute orange gleams of a ship's lanterns at prow and stern crawled from east to west. From within the palace walls came the sounds of someone strumming a *guitarra,* the hot-iron smells of the unsleeping palace forges, the kitchens' steamy scents. The commonplace nature of it all almost reassured her.

And then it all turned like a knife in her belly as she remembered why she was here.

She sighed and turned back to her small, spare room, high up the northwestern tower of the Firefly Palace. They'd brought her clothes. She only bothered to wear a green silk loincloth. She'd been locked up a night and a day. Some robed men she didn't recognize had shouted questions, accusations, and threats at her. She answered the first as best she could and ignored the rest, all with simmering dignity.

Since then she'd been left alone. Downcast servants, always accompanied by Scarlet Tyrants equally disinclined to meet Melodía's gaze, brought her ample food. Despite her usual harrier appetite she ate little. Nobody responded to her demands to know why she was being held, how long she would be held, and to be allowed to send a message to her father.

She had a comfortable bed and a water closet fed by a rain cistern on the tower roof. She even had books of Nuevaropan history brought with her morning meal, stacked on a sturdy table near the window. A comfortable cage. But a cage withal.

It was when the Tyrants had first slammed the door behind her that Melodía cracked. First she went into fist-hammering rage. That only skinned the heels of her hands on the bare, buff-plastered walls. Then she slumped against the door in a paroxysm of tears.

Now, recovered, she had returned into detachment. She was resilient. Indeed, she felt something like *relief*. She had convinced herself that this was all nonsense. There was simply some misunderstanding. Everything would be cleared up soon.

So I finally get my father to notice me. . . . She shook her head ruefully.

The door opened.

She looked that way, expecting to see servants bringing her supper, with their armed and red-cloaked shadows behind. Instead she had a single visitor, dressed in a loincloth, buskins, and royal-blue cloak. Although he was certainly big enough for two.

"Duke Falk," she said. She frowned. "Did my father send you to let me go?"

Then she caught the strange gleam in his Northern sapphire eyes, and the smile, triumphant yet somehow sickly, that twisted his full lips. *Something's very wrong,* she thought.

Then it was as if her reality were a window shattering in reverse: the pieces all flew together at once, and she saw the whole with sudden clarity.

"*You're* behind this outrage?" she said. "How could you dare?"

He laughed. "I'm the man of the hour, Melodía. I'm your father's chief bodyguard."

With a small internal jolt of alarm, Melodía realized that his speech was somewhat slurred. By drink, her nose already told her. But by emotion as well. None of which boded well.

"And I've already proven my value," Falk said, "by breaking a heinous plot against the Emperor."

"What?"

He nodded. "Arrested his very Chief Minister and seen him condemned. And cut down those three arch-conspirators, your kinsmen."

"My kinsmen?" She frowned in utter incomprehension.

"Gonzalo Delgao, his brother Benedicto, their brother-in-law Barón Alarcón."

"Them?" She shook her head rapidly, like a dog clearing water from its eyes. "They, they—they're obnoxious loudmouths and total fools. But they're harmless. Poor Benedicto's dim, and Gonzalo's so clever he only outwits himself."

She ran down. It struck her belated that Gonzalo had manifestly done exactly that. For the last time, if this appalling former rebel told the truth.

And from the way Falk carried himself, managing to strut while standing still, she knew he did.

"It's all written down and attested to, you see," Falk said. "Manorquín told all."

"Manorquín? Don Augusto? And you *believed* him? Out of everybody at court, he was the most likely to mean my father harm. He's been in love forever with the notion that a full-blood Ramírez should sit the Fangèd Throne instead of a member of Torre Delgao!"

Falk smiled. "Precisely. Who better to confess the whole nasty scheme? And your own role in it, my lady."

"*My* role? Are you crazy? If I *were* conspiring against my father, which is completely and utterly absurd, those four buffoons were the very last creatures on Paradise I'd choose to do so with. Including the ridiculous reapers of Ruybrasil!"

Falk's smirk became outright fatuous in its self-congratulation. Somehow the near-imbecility of such an expression on the face of what she knew to be a most intelligent man made him far more frightening.

"That's not what Manorquín's confession says."

"But it's a lie!"

Falk laughed. "The truth's what people believe, isn't it? More to the point, your father believes it. Who'd be so disloyal as to contradict *him*?"

He frowned and cocked a theatrical brow. "Except his own daughter, perhaps? You've been most intemperate criticizing his policies, Princess. People have heard. And wondered."

"How could anybody possibly believe I'd plot to overthrow my own father? To what purpose? M-much less to, to—"

She couldn't say *kill him*. The thought of *anyone* wanting to harm her father horrified her to the pit of her stomach. That anyone could think *she* might was literally unspeakable.

"These are perilous times, Highness," the young Duke said. "The news from Providence has terrified not just the La Merced rabble but the entire court as well. Who knows what might have caused one of the Creators' Avenging Angels to Emerge, after so many centuries of sabsence? It can only be the blackest evil. Perhaps Fae-worship. Perhaps—"

He had gotten close without her being aware of

anything but that sinister smile and those scary eyes. Now she smelled not just sweat and wine but something else, as if his passion itself exuded a reek. His huge bare chest was almost touching her equally bare breasts. Her buttocks pressed against the edge of the stout table that stood by the outer wall. She could retreat no farther.

"Perhaps even a princess plotting her father's demise," he breathed. "And in such uncertain times, who could doubt even a princess can fall into evil, dabbling in questionable doctrines?"

"Questionable doctrines? You mean Jaume's teachings? They're as orthodox as can be! The Creators themselves tell us to take pleasure in the world they made us—it's right there in *The Books of the Law*. That's not *questionable* at all. It's—"

Her words ran down. *It's that damned Life-to-Come cult, with its upside-down theology. And among its adherents, rumor has it, the Pope himself. Good job defending your* novio, *there.*

She looked at the sweat that streamed down Falk's face in spite of the cool Channel air through the window, and wondered if it might be too late already.

He smiled. His pale skin was flushed. His lips, pink ever so lightly touched with blue, looked unpleasantly fleshy inside his night-black beard.

"Your father's allowed you to run wild," he said in a husky whisper. "Now it's time you learned some discipline."

He reached for her. She flinched away. Then she snapped upright and flashed her eyes.

"You don't dare touch me," she said. "My father—"

"Won't believe a word of it. I'm a man of proven loyalty. Whereas *you* are a spoiled princess caught in folly, possibly a trafficker with demons, making mad accusations out of spite." He caught her arm. "You women think nothing of men."

She shot a knee toward his groin. He turned his hips and took it on the thigh.

"You think we're nothing more than dirt beneath your pretty little feet," he said. She tried to grab his lip and twist. With bull-tyrant strength and startling speed he spun her to face the table. Bending her arm cruelly up behind her back, he forced her down until her breasts were squashed painfully against the un-yielding wood.

"You think you can do what you like with no con-sequences," he rasped. "Well, I'll *show* you conse-quences, bitch."

She screamed. She hated herself for doing it. Being slammed with the knowledge of helplessness had bro-ken her vaunted self-control.

No matter how clever she liked to think she was, she couldn't think of anything else to do.

And worse . . . she knew screams wouldn't help. The walls and doors were thick enough to muffle sound. And if the sentries on the wall heard, she knew they wouldn't intervene.

Creators' Law forbade torture. But sometimes even divine law got stretched. Especially when the terrible Grey Angels stalked the surface of Paradise once again. The guards, human, feared the Angels as much as any.

Melodía felt her loincloth wrenched away, heard it flung to the wall. A great sweaty hand clamped on her right buttock. A broad powerful thumb probed between her cheeks. She gasped as it pushed inside her.

"Jaume's a boy-lover," Falk grunted. Sweat dripped from his lank hair to scald her back. "He's used you this way. I know he has."

Like most girls her age—and in spite of Doña Carlota's best efforts—Melodía wasn't virgin in any sense. But what she'd done, she'd done *willingly*. No one had ever dared try to force her. It had never entered her head that anyone *might*. She was the Emperor's daughter. As a hidalga she'd been trained to the use of arms. As was the custom she always carried at least a dagger.

Except it had been stripped from her by rough hands, along with her dignity and freedom. Lacking a weapon, she was defeated by mere strength.

This. Can't. Be. Happening.

She screamed again in fury, frustration, and pain as he rammed himself into her.

Chapter 47

Gordito, **Fatty**—*Protoceratops andrewsi.* A small ceratopsian dinosaur with a powerful toothed beak, a
frilled, plant-eating quadruped: 2.5 meters long, 400
kilograms, 1 meter high. The only "hornface" to lack
horns. A ubiquitous domestic herd beast, not found
wild in Nuevaropa. Timid by nature.

—THE BOOK OF TRUE NAMES

These flagstones are hard on my knees, thought
Pablo Mondragón. *I'm too old for this.*

A man who seldom smiled, he smiled thinly
now. It was his age, in ways, that had brought him
here.

He wouldn't be growing older. A consolation, of
sorts.

The sun through high overcast stung the back of
his bowed neck and beat up at his bowed face from
the yellow limestone flags. He was aware of the crowd
gathering around the fringes of Creation Plaza by
their murmuring, like the sound of surf in the Channel
nearby. The onlookers were subdued. As Mercedes,

THE DINOSAUR LORDS   531

they had small taste for public cruelty, except where pirates were concerned. But being Mercedes, they couldn't resist a spectacle.

The execution of a disgraced Chief Minister to the Emperor was, by definition, spectacular.

Don Pablo had a mind attuned to irony. He recognized it in the fact that, even in the last hours of his life, locked in a small cell in the Palace of the Fireflies, he still attracted *information*. He knew that Heriberto, Prince of the Tyrant's Jaw and landlord, disapproved of the sudden spin of the Wheel in his Imperial tenant's affairs. He had refused use of the great central square, el Mercado, for the morning's proceedings.

But his Holiness had no such reservations. So it came to pass that Mondragón knelt alone in the center of Creation Plaza, nearly as vast as the Mercado, awaiting his executioner. Whoever and whatever it might be: certainly not the venerable Tyrannosaurus Don Rodrigo, fat, tame, and without a tooth in his head. El Verdugo Imperial could do no more than gum a convict's neck and drool down his back.

Mondragón felt oddly content. While it was axiomatic that the Emperor possessed too little overt power to conspire against, the Fangèd Throne's prestige and influence still drew abundant intrigue. The Chief Minister's job was to serve as lightning rod for the occupant of the Fangèd Throne. Mondragón had never expected to die peacefully in bed. Few of his predecessors had.

I wish my successor luck, whoever he may be. He was distressingly aware of the ease with which that recent rebel and upstart child Falk had outmaneuvered him. *Clearly, I lost my edge. Perhaps this turn of Maris's Wheel was overdue, for the good of the Empire.*

He was afraid that the wildest of the rumors flying in the wake of the terrible news from Providence would prove true: that Felipe's confessor might succeed him. He didn't trust the Father Sky sectary. Fray Jerónimo was unaccountable-for, thus unaccountable.

Mondragón believed that was his only fear. Then he heard the crowd gasp, looked up, and knew that *fear* had been a total stranger before.

Seeing a pure-white Tyrannosaurus bull waddling toward him, thick tail swinging, ruby eyes fixed upon him, and Duke Falk astride his back in his glittering Scarlet Tyrant armor, introduced Don Pablo to the genuine article.

An *alguacil* read loudly from a scroll of condemnations. Mondragón couldn't hear him for the pulse roaring in his ears.

There was no need for him to hear the traditional call to lift his head to ease the Executioner's task. As the great white head filled his sky like Eris falling, he could look at nothing else.

Saw-toothed jaws almost as long as Mondragón's whole body opened wide. The beast's breath washed hot and wet over him. It smelled incongruously of the spearmint-imbued grit with which Falk's hapless arming-squire had to clean the monster's teeth after every meal. Saliva ropes fell across Mondragón's upturned face.

He screamed as the tyrant's jaws enveloped his head, blotting out the light. The last thing he felt was the touch of terrible teeth on his neck.

The clack of a lock opening roused Melodía from a restless drowse of fatigue compounded by despair. As the door opened she raised her face from a pillow still sodden with her tears. She was too drained even to fear that Falk had come to use her again.

But it was neither the Duke nor hooded interrogators she saw by the grey dawn light seeping from her narrow window. A crone in a stained cloak and cowl hobbled in, stooped over a cane. A loosely woven hemp mask covered her face.

The woman coughed. Melodía recoiled in fear. Her captors' new torment shocked her right out of her sump of despair. Disease was rare—so rare that its onset was considered a curse. Legend claimed the Grey Angels favored plague as an instrument of divine retribution. Paradisiacals feared few things more than *sickness*.

"What's this?" she demanded. She aimed for hauteur, managed to avoid a terrified squeak. The words stung her raw throat.

She glimpsed a flash of red cloak in the corridor. The door slammed behind the newcomer with unusual emphasis.

Melodía's unwelcome visitor straightened. The hood slipped back from her head. She stripped the contagion-mask from her face with a relieved exhalation and stuffed it in a sleeve.

Through eyes gummy and swollen from crying Melodía saw a handsome middle-aged woman shaking out long black hair streaked with white. She had a long straight nose and a thin-lipped mouth, perhaps a touch over-wide. She looked somehow familiar. But Melodía didn't know her name.

"My name is Claudia, Princess," the woman said. "I'm here to get you out."

Heart pounding, Melodía hobbled into the corridor outside her cell. The pair of Scarlet Tyrants who had opened the door to the insistent tapping of her cane stood well clear to let her pass. One stuck a helmeted head around the doorjamb. On seeing a slim feminine form lying beneath a blanket, he yanked the door quickly shut and practically skipped back away from the stooped and masked figure.

Melodía coughed as convincingly as she could. Her savior Claudia had thoughtfully cleaned her mouth with lavender pastilles before donning the contagion-mask. But that just meant it inevitably smelled of lavender-scented spit.

It was a hardship Melodía was willing to bear.

The Tyrants didn't even tell her to be on her way. It was as if they feared just *talking* to her could infect them. Melodía had no idea what Claudia had told them to get them to admit her to the cell. It didn't really matter.

Terror of immediate discovery threatened to override even the relief flooding through her. Melodía found it almost impossible to focus on the details of the plan—short and simple as it was—that Claudia had recited as she cleaned the Princess with water from the tap in the closet.

The skin between Melodía's shoulders crawled in anticipation of the fatal shout. But when she reached the stairs, all she heard was gusty sighs of relief. She only just remembered to hobble on her cane as she began to pick her way down the winding steps.

At the bottom another tall female figure awaited. Melodía stopped and almost fled. *They found me!*

Then: *"Pilar!"* It was half sob, half prayer of thanksgiving.

She tensed to sprint down the last few steps and grab her maidservant in the tightest hug of their lives. But in the lightest, most conversational tone possible, Pilar said, "Stay in character."

Melodía froze. Emotions too many and too intense for body and mind to process filled her up. There was sodden-foolish gratitude, relief, lost-dog love. And also: *Who does she think she is, this servant daring to speak that way to a Princesa Imperial?*

That brought back Melodía's self-control. *You are a princess,* perra, she told herself. *So act like one.*

Pilar gave her hand a quick squeeze as she reached bottom.

"Follow me," she said, still as if she were simply sharing the latest gossip. "Don't hurry, but *¡muévete!* Understand?"

"Yes," Melodía said, in what she hoped was a suitable disease-victim croak. That didn't take much acting thanks to the dryness in her throat.

Covering Melodía's head with a black mantilla, Pilar led the way through the yard, around the corner of the great residency complex toward the fortress's west wall, farthest from La Merced. Around them the great living organism that was the Firefly Palace buzzed with coming dawn, everything so *everyday* it almost hurt. Melodía smelled onions and garlic frying for breakfast. Sturdy, red-faced women called cheerful banter as they carried great steaming tubs of freshly boiled laundry. Horses neighed and nose-horns bleated, expectant of their breakfast oats. A cool dawn breeze blowing up La Canal caressed her cheek—bringing with it an unfortunate brimstone tang from the sewage-bloom west of Adelina's Frown.

Tamely Melodía followed her servant under clouds consolidating into a grey ceiling as pallor reached the western sky. Her mind and spirit had become numb. She seemed to drift through mists, through phantoms, her surroundings at once familiar and bizarre. She could have believed the last few days an evil dream but for the pain that stabbed up her backside at every step.

Great yellow-brick warehouses and draft-animal stables dominated the compound's western end. Here a certain note of worry permeated the talk among stable hands, warehouse workers, and drovers. Fear of the Grey Angel's Emergence was alive and thriving. But business as usual predominated, with the usual rough humor as prevalent as dread.

Pilar led Melodía into a great, round-arched opening in a sod-covered mound. Melodía followed, even more hesitantly than her stoop and cane commanded as her eyes adjusted to relative darkness. A walkway ran above a broad ramp down a tunnel that sloped beneath the palace proper and on to the city. Its barrel-vaulted ceiling rang with the bawling of nose-horns and fatties, horse snorts and whinnies, and profanity-laced shouts from drivers and loaders. Lanterns hung along the reinforced limestone walls created everlasting amber twilight. Immense fans powered by dinosaur-driven capstans aboveground kept fresh air moving up the tunnel, but on first entry the stink of piss and shit made Melodía's eyes water.

She quickly grew accustomed to it. It reminded her to cough conspicuously, which at least was useful. Their fellow pedestrians gave them a wide and fearful berth on the footpath.

Ramp traffic, loaded wagons going up and empty ones going down, was already heavy. The rather steep grade took its toll on beasts climbing and brakes descending. But it was far quicker than going south overland and circling down from the promontory.

Pilar turned into one of the numerous wide bays cut into the walls. Still conscientiously leaning on her cane, Melodía followed. Inside a pair of women dressed in wide straw hats and what appeared to be hemp sacks tended to a brown-dappled cream Centrosaurus hitched to a dray. As one looped the strap of a wooden feed bucket over its long nasal horn, the other dumped handfuls of oats from an open bag into a second pail. Nosehorn beaks couldn't scrape all the tasty oats from the bottom; they'd occupy themselves happily for hours trying to get at every last flake with their tongues.

When the strap passed before the nosehorn's eyes, it tossed its frilled head and bleated alarm. The laborer hauled off and booted the beast in its near front shoulder with a skinny, brown-skinned leg.

"Creators light a fire in your belly, you scratcher-beaked sack of shit!" she yelled in a familiar voice.

"Lupe?" Melodía asked.

The woman wheeled around. "Who the fuck wants to know?"

Filth smeared her thin cheeks. Her eyebrows formed a solid line, which, Melodía realized, had been augmented with charcoal. As viciously sensitive as Lupe was about her tendency toward a unibrow, Melodía could think of only one person in all the walled town that was the palace brave or rash enough to do such a thing—

"¡*Puta estúpida!*" the other laborer exclaimed. "You hang the strap from the fucking side. Don't you know *anything*?"

Lupe turned ominously toward Llurdis. Before the two could launch their fisticuffs, Melodía dropped her cane and flew forward to enfold them both in a desperate hug.

"You're doing this for me?" she said, turning left and right to kiss their grime-smudged cheeks.

"Why the fuck else would we be fucking around with this nasty fucking—"

"Yes, Día," Llurdis said.

"A servant woman named Claudia took my place." The words gushed out like water from a broken jug. "I'm so worried about her."

"We know," Llurdis said, disengaging herself. "We're in on the plot, you know."

"Anyway, what do you care?" said Lupe, tugging at her arms. Melodía realized she was throttling the smaller girl and let her go. "She's only a servant."

Pilar stepped forward. Melodía frowned. *Was I ever that callow and callous?*

"She's covered, Highness," Pilar said. "*Later.*"

"We'd best move with a purpose," a feminine voice called from behind. "The longer we dither, the greater the chance Snowflake will take our heads."

Melodía spun. At the mouth of the bay, two incongruous figures stood side by side. One resembled a walking bag of grain, in a head-muffling shawl and a dress even more amorphous than Lupe's and Llurdis's. The taller was a scarecrow, draped in a smock made entirely of varicolored patches, with a ratty straw hat drooping around narrow pink cheeks and a grin that showcased an absent tooth.

After a wide-eyed moment Melodía registered that the sunburn was cunningly applied rouge, and the "missing" tooth even more cleverly painted-out with lampblack.

"Fina? *Abi?*"

"Somebody's got to drive," said the normally elegant scion of Sansamour. "My father taught me any number of useful talents."

"Mine too," Josefina Serena said.

Melodía hugged them both fervently too. "But what's that about Snowflake?" she asked.

"Don Rodrigo's not up to serving as *actual* Imperial Executioner anymore, you know," Fina said.

"Falk's albino tyrant decapitated Don Pablo in Creation Plaza an hour ago," Abigail Thélème said. "With Falk sitting astride him."

"What? Don—Mondragón?"

Abi nodded.

That was another breath-robbing blow. The Chief Minister had never been likable. Just like Sieur Duval, he always claimed that if people liked him, he wasn't doing his job. Mondragón remained aloof to anything of less import than matters of state, and had always treated Melodía as an annoying little girl. But he had worked tirelessly to keep her and her sister safe. And most of all he had served her father with unflagging loyalty.

If Papá will do that to his best friend— She let the thought go. She couldn't stand to follow it a single step more.

Pilar touched her arm. "Highness, we should go.

The Condesa is right. Eventually our trick will be found out."

It took Melodía a heartbeat to recall that Abi had a title in her own right: the Countess of Silvertree. She turned to regard the wagon dubiously.

"We put an oiled canvas down in the bed," Llurdis explained. "When we get you and Pilar inside, we'll put another over you and give you some pieces of bamboo to make sure you can breathe when we cover you up.

"Pilar?"

"I'm going with you, Princess," Pilar said firmly.

"What's *in* the wagon?" Melodía asked, sniffing and wrinkling her nose. "It smells like the whole passageway. Except, uh, more so. Like—ahh—like—"

"'Shit' would be the word you're looking for," Lupe said. "Horse and hornface both. Swept up nice and fresh off the ramp!"

"We're going out buried in—that?"

"We have to hide you somehow to get you out of the palace," Abi said. "Who's going to look twice at a dinosaur-dray full of shit?"

"Especially since a score just like it go out each and every day," said Fina.

Melodía set her lips. As a matter of fact, it wasn't that bad. Herbivore manure smelled nowhere near as vile as a meat-eater's.

"Remember what awaits us here, Alteza," Pilar murmured.

She nodded. Moistening her lips, she began, "If only—"

She found she couldn't finish that either. Tears choked her off again. *If only Fanny, my very best friend*, had bothered to come see me off. Or Mont-serrat. Whom she suddenly found herself missing as fiercely as if they'd been parted for years already. *Who knows when I'll see either again? Or even if?*

With something like a tugging at the backs of her eyes Melodía realized she'd never see Meravellosa again, nor the beauty of the palace gardens. Nor, well, everything she'd known. Her knees began to buckle.

She stiffened them sternly and shook her head as if to dislodge the traitorous thoughts. "Why are you doing this?" she asked, clutching Fina's and Abi's hands as the nearest points of contact available.

Abi quirked a smile. "I love you, Día. But the fact is, life here in the Imperial Court's pretty damn boring. Hardly any duels to speak of, and no poisonings at all. The big excitement occurs when some half-wit knights-errant take too much wine on board and get into shouting matches at a banquet. And that usually just ends with the Tyrants dragging the contestants out in the yard and drubbing them groggy. There just isn't enough at *stake* with the Fangèd Throne to draw serious intrigue."

Her blue eyes took on a bit of steel glint. "Until now. . . ."

"We're your *friends*," Llurdis said. "We have to stand by you. And also what Abi said."

"Thank you," Melodía said.

So she kissed them all, and said good-bye to Llurdis and Lupe, and climbed into the wagon. Pilar came after.

The two women lay facing each other. Pilar smiled reassurance. Lupe handed them both bamboo tubes to breathe through. She and Llurdis rolled an oiled canvas sheet over them.

And then, with what struck Melodía as completely unnecessary enthusiasm, her noble ladies-in-waiting set about burying the Princess Imperial in shit.

Chapter 48

Cosechador de Ojos, Harvester of Eyes, Eye-taker—
Several small species of *Germanodactylus.* Short-
tailed, crested pterosaurs (fliers), some marine, some
terrestrial; wingspan 1 meter, weight 1.25 kilograms.
Widely hated for their habit of perching on the heads
of wounded fighters and sailors adrift, and pecking out
their eyes. Similarly sized to gulls, their avian rivals.

—THE BOOK OF TRUE NAMES

Gaétan reeled and fell from his saddle into the
bushes west of the trail. Zhubin bleated alarm
and bolted into the woods behind Rob and
Karyl.

Drawing a sword, the knight who had speared
Gaétan plunged along the road after the routed Providentials. But others closed in as if to finish the fallen
young man off.

Roaring his furious battle cry—"*Sod this for a
game of soldiers!*"—Rob wheeled Little Nell and
booted her into motion, out of the brush and into the
road.

She didn't have much time to gather speed. But speed wasn't her strong suit at the best of times. Head down, she slammed the first rider's horse in the barrel with the thick black boss of her horn. The horse screeched and fell thrashing. The rider jumped clear. He landed in a scandal-berry bush, but was up again in an eyeblink, waving his sword but none too certain on his pins.

Rob caught a glimpse of Stéphanie dragging an unmoving Gaétan into the brush. He spun Nell right. She'd used up her forward momentum bulling down the courser. But even standing still she could turn with an alacrity startling in one so tubby.

Even then he had to swing with all the speed he could muster to knock astray the spear another rider was aiming for Nell's vulnerable belly. The rider plunged past.

And suddenly Rob found himself surrounded by enemy horsemen.

Dab hand though Rob was in a brawl, drunk or sober he was never so brash as to think he stood a chance fighting a single knight, much less a mob of heavy horsemen at once. Nuevaropa's warrior class had little to do on any given day but train to fight. Except for hunting, feasting, and raping the occasional peasant, which they did after hours.

He'd made use of his knowledge of the first principle of dinosaur combat: that the main weapon was the monster. And certain sure it was that neither training nor combat experience could adequately prepare the horse knights to face a mad Ayrish poet riding two tonnes of plump and outraged Einiosaurus.

But while bucketheads could be dumb as dirt, especially about tactics—or *unthinking,* which fell out the same way—they were nothing if not resourceful when it came down to trading hard blows. The forest road was just wide enough to allow them to circle his powerful but ungainly mount like a harrier-pack. In a flash they were doing just that.

Rob's only recourse was to keep Nell turning rapidly this way and that. He warded blows with his shield as best he could and swung his axe lustily at any Brokenheart who ventured into range. But again his main defense was Nell, fending off the pack with horn and tail. Bold as they were, the knights were less willing to risk their precious mounts' legs and bellies than their own. A dismounted montador wasn't just at a disadvantage, he was a contradiction in terms, and not untainted with disgrace, to whatever small degree.

But it was still a wasting game he played. Durable though she was, the hook-horn wasn't used to this kind of exertion. Especially not at this intensity. And he suspected the stress of having enemies trying their best to kill her might drain her as fast as it did a human—and was draining Rob, right now. Sooner or later, she would fatally tire. Or he would.

And like the savage Pyroraptors they were emulating, the riders knew how to wait and watch for the opportunity to dart in and snatch a mouthful of their prey. Rob felt an impact beneath his shoulder blade as a spear struck his tough backplate. The armadón hide held. He wheeled Nell counterclockwise in time to glance his axe off the helmet of the rider who had tagged him, briefly staggering him in the saddle of his horse.

But a sword-stroke hit the cuisse protecting Rob's right thigh, slipped off, and gashed the leg right behind the knee through his silk trousers. The slice was only skin, inflicted by the arming-sword's tip as Rob kept Nell turning; a blunter longsword would never have cut him at all.

But in a fight with blades, the moment you got cut, you started dying. Even a tiny trickle of blood would weaken a body with shocking rapidity. You wouldn't bleed to death from it, but it would slow you. And that would get you slashed again and again, until you did bleed enough to fail.

Rob knew that from observing knight fights. He himself steered clear of them as best he could, preferring to fight with a weapon that gave him some working room, like a table leg or a chair. Or best of all his weapon of choice: a clean pair of heels.

But the difference with a sword and spear fight was that those weapons could easily inflict a killing blow— which was surprisingly hard to do with a knife.

Seeing blood, the Brokenhearts pressed harder. As Rob fought with increasing desperation to keep further blades out of his body, he became aware of shouts and screams from right nearby, the whinnying of horses and the clangor of steel on steel. He could spare no attention for that right now. This fight was his all—or nothing.

That obnoxious observer who lived in his skull with him, and mocked him like an eye-taker from a gallows pole, told him those battle sounds boded badly for his prospects—of rescue, or if he miraculously escaped on his own. Those who had hidden in the woods relied primarily on their bows and ambush. Few wore armor better than their shirts. They stood even less chance in a hand-to-hand fight against mounted knights in mail than Rob did.

Pain caught Rob's breath briefly in his throat as a spear found seam between breast-and-back on his left side. He felt steel hit a rib and grate. Then he bellowed like a scorched nosehorn bull as a sword raked his right cheek.

Nell was slowing. But her master's cry revived her. She responded to his knee press as if fresh to the fight, wrenching the front half of her body right while flinging her hips and tail left to add momentum.

The knight who had cut Rob was a fresh-faced young buck with blond hair darkened and plastered against his chin by the sweat from his open burgonet, and a rampant raptor of some sort in green on a silver field on his tabard. Emboldened by drawing blood, he had kept in close to his prey. He had his longsword raised one-handed for a killing blow.

But Rob's retaliation was already humming down in furious overhand. Wanda hit the helmet just to Rob's left of its low crest, split steel and skull clear to an astonished green eye.

A shock almost as great as the physical one that traveled up his arm punched Rob from inside to out. *I killed a knight!* he realized. Exultation and revulsion alike surged in him. He felt a sense of soaring triumph—and of having committed a profanation.

But he let none of that stick him immobile. That would kill him just as dead, and just as fast. This wasn't the first man he'd slain. Just the first noble. Though he would surely see that wide eye staring at him in his dreams as blood flooded it, he knew. If he lived, of course.

But to do that he must first free his axe, which was stuck tight in the young fool's head.

Hollering wordlessly, with outright panic rumbling

like lava from his belly both ways, Rob drove Nell against the horse's shoulder. Raising a boot from his stirrup, he put it against the rider's mailed chest to brace the flaccid corpse and yanked the axe free with a spasm of effort.

Another spear hit him in the back. This one actually went through the tough, pebbled nodosaur hide to sting his left shoulder blade.

Nell's turn widdershins was perceptibly slower. The spearman opted to pull out his spear as he danced his horse back away from the big swinging head and brutal down-hooked horn. But another Brokenheart closed in from Rob's right. His arming-sword had already begun the stroke that might or might not sweep Rob's head from his short, thick neck, but would most certainly kill him.

Giving his last, best, futile effort to bring his axe around in time to knock the sword astray, Rob saw something flicker down over the rider's wide, dark eyes and sadistic grin. Then the knight whipped right backward over his saddle's high cantle. Beyond his horse's speckled white rump, Rob caught a glimpse of the Providential farm youth who had noosed the Brokenheart 'round the neck with a catchpole. He grinned even wider than the knight had as he hauled his catch thrashing down into the brush and out of sight.

No enemies remained in view to Rob's left, down the forest road. All he saw that way was the backs of the last of the routed army. He turned a now-wheezing Nell clockwise once more.

A spear darted for his face. He knocked it half a meter past his right cheek with his shield rim. Then he lowered the round shield, just enough to see over the top.

He faced a trio of horsemen, right where the trees began to close in over the road. His heart dipped momentarily as beyond them he saw still more riding strung out down the blue-clad slope toward the woods. They ignored the darts and javelins flung at them by the handful of mounted scouts who buzzed around their flanks to the left and right as thoroughly as they did their taunts.

Despite the way his vision kept trying to tighten into a tunnel, Rob caught motion in his right eye's corner. Karyl was out of the trees and riding toward him with sword drawn.

A Brokenheart veered to charge him. The flat of Karyl's blade guided his overhand sword cut safely by. As the horses passed each other, Karyl took a flawless forehand draw–stroke across the knight's throat, cutting to bone and sliding slickly out without getting bound in meat or cartilage.

As before, Karyl didn't seem to fight. He *killed*, with the efficient inevitability of watermill's grinding, and yet with a horror's unsettling liquid grace as well.

The marauder who'd speared Rob circled left, seeking an opening. A shadow dropped onto him. Above the mailed shoulder, Rob saw the cruel beauty of Stéphanie's dagger-sculpted face turned crueler by a snarl as she wrenched the knight's head sideways. His neck broke with a thick crack.

The other two Brokenhearts turned their horses smartly 'round and spurred back the way they had come.

"The lard butts have fled and left our balls to roast in the sacks!" one shouted to his comrades, speaking of the Crève Coeur dinosaur knights.

"Let's go," the second called. "There's no honor and less loot, scrapping with these savages."

Some of the approaching horsemen turned back. Others faltered, slowing their mounts to a trot.

To Rob's unalloyed horror, a dinosaur rose up from behind the hill beyond them. It was black, its chest and belly crimson shading to gold. As it stopped at the crest and dropped to all fours, Rob saw its rider wore clear-enameled armor. His shield was also black, painted with a yellow figure Rob couldn't make out at this range. A black-and-gold pennon streamed from the tip of the lance he carried upright with its butt in its leather cup by his stirrup.

"Salvateur," said Françoise, emerging from the undergrowth to Rob's right on her strider.

"And that's us right fucked, then," Rob said as trumpets blared and mailed infantry with spears and round shields spread out to either side of the enemy commander.

But instead of charging at the fanfare, the Broken-hearts who were still riding toward the forest turned back.

"That's the recall!" somebody cried from the brush. A cheer went up.

Salvateur's voice boomed out like the challenge of a rutting nosehorn bull. Rob couldn't make out the words, but he got the distinct impression the Baron was roundly ranking out his knights for riding themselves into a trap to no good end.

The basso thrum of Karyl's hornbow from Rob's right startled him. He resisted the urge to glance aside, and kept eyes fixed on Salvateur.

The Baron raised his shield. Rob could see the

quiver of motion as the arrow stuck in the middle of it.

The spearmen started downslope at a careful walk, shields high.

"Nice warning shot," Rob said.

But Karyl frowned. Rob recognized that barely visible brow-furrow signified what in a normal human being would be scowling, shouting, beard-tearing rage—that last being a thing Rob had often heard of, but never actually witnessed and would pay good gold to do so. Or at least silver.

"I shot to kill," Karyl said. "A competent captain who has Guilli's ear is as deadly to us as a hundred dinosaur knights."

Karyl's scratch defensive force was still shouting triumphantly, and even hurling catcalls at the advancing but still-distant house-shields.

Surging relief flashed over into anger inside Rob. "What are you cheering about, you gits?" he shouted. "We still lost the battle! And barely touched Guilli's army, which will be on our necks while you're still applauding your fool selves!"

"You did well," Karyl called to those who'd stood with him. "And Master Korrigan's right: we've still got a fleeing army to protect. Fall back, keep to cover, and get ready to ambush the enemy if the pursuit picks up again."

Emeric stepped out on the road. From the commotion coming from the underbrush, Rob gathered that a few Brokenheart knights were still in the process of dying, and not as expeditiously as they'd like. He didn't much care. The woods-runners were especially vindictive toward their tormentors; Emeric himself

showed little appetite for that sort of thing, preferring to leave the more protracted forms of vengeance-
taking to his sister. But few in Providence had much
love for Count Guillaume's armored reavers.

"What about the wounded?" the woods-runner
asked.

"Help those who can walk," Karyl said. "Leave the
rest."

Emeric nodded and faded into the woods.

"What?" Rob demanded in disbelief. "There must
be fifty of our people still out there! And Lanza alone
knows how many more over that hill."

"We can't retrieve them," Karyl said. "And we can't
carry them. They'd slow us down too much. Salvateur may pursue us at a more deliberate pace than
his vanguard knights did. But he will pursue."

"But the Brokenhearts will butcher them!"

"They're lost to us already. We can't afford to lose
still more in a futile attempt to recover them."

"*What kind of heartless bastard are you?*" Rob
screamed the words.

"A commander," Karyl said. "It's not my first time
to it."

He looked out across a hillside strewn with writhing bodies, crying out for the help he'd just denied
them. A few crawled toward the hopeful shelter of the
woods, leaving trails of beautiful blue flowers crushed
and stained with gore.

"And in spite of all my efforts, it seems I've yet to
see my last."

Chapter 49

Maia, La Madre, the Mother, *Madre Terra,* Mother Land—Queen of the Creators: *Kun* ▤ (Land)—The Mother. Represents Motherhood, soft power, birth (and death), healing, and Paradise. Also mammals. Known for her compassion. Aspect: beautiful grey-haired matron in brown-and-gold gown, holding a sheaf of wheat in one hand and a sickle in the other. Sacred Animal: horse. Color: brown. Symbol: a wheat sheaf.

> —A PRIMER TO PARADISE FOR THE IMPROVEMENT
> OF YOUNG MINDS

Hunger like a baby horror swallowed live, kicking at the insides of her belly with its tiny killing-claws, roused Shiraa from sleep. She knew at once what had wakened her. The sweet, sweet scent of the flesh of prey beasts roasting filled her head with intoxication at every breath she took. It was an acquired taste, taught her as a hatchling by her mother. She listened hard and sniffed, ignoring as best she could the delicious odor. She detected no danger nearby—no creature even as big as a half-grown tailless two-leg.

She rose, taking care to make as little noise as possible, and poked her snout cautiously out of the canebrake where she'd sheltered for her nap. The sun was setting to her left. The hills cast lengthy shadows out into the farmlands to the west.

A trickle of smoke, slaty in the twilight, rose above the next hill south. Somewhere unseen, fatties bleated as a herder drove them to their nighttime pens. A stream wound behind the hill, and now above the blandness of upland plants, Shiraa smelled dressed wood and metal and strangely altered animal hides, and the commingled odors of a throng of the tailless ones: all the signs of a settlement.

Training and experience alike taught Shiraa never to seek out contact with the tailless ones without her mother telling her to do so. But in the slowly thickening gloom she could just see, this side of a stand of trees atop the hill, a familiar hooded figure.

She caught, again, the faintest teasing wisp of her mother's scent.

The Hooded One was not her mother, she somehow knew. Yet it was guiding her, slowly, to where her mother awaited her. She knew that too.

She slipped out of the thicket and down toward the valley. *Eat?* she thought hopefully.

And, *Shiraa lonely.*

"All right, contraband!" Abi's indecently cheerful call was muffled by the cloth and hundreds of kilos of animal dung that covered Melodía and Pilar. "Enough lazing about. Time to be up and doing."

The two women lay pressed together tightly. Their bamboo tubes, angled up past the canvas to protrude a couple of millimeters from the excrement, had let in enough air to keep them alive. They hadn't kept crumbled dried dung, and some not so dry, from filtering in with them.

While it was true that herbivore crap didn't intrinsically smell all that bad, Melodía had forgotten some of it had been scooped up moist from the underground ramp. On the drive through La Merced and up into the hills to the south it had begun to ferment.

Melodía heard a crunching noise. A sudden flood of light made her blink.

"We'll have you out in no time, Día," Fina said brightly.

"What are you doing?"

"Digging you out," Fina said, puffing with effort. "Help is on the way."

"Help?"

A corner of the canvas was lifted. Melodía found herself looking up at a small head haloed with morning light that glowed through dark-gold dreadlocks.

"Montse?"

"You could make yourself useful too, Melodía," her sister said, "instead of lying there like a truffle waiting to be rooted out by a fatty."

"Don't mind her, Día," another female voice said. Melodía's heart jumped again at its sound. She felt dizzy, and not only from the fumes she'd been breathing. "Just sit tight and we'll have you out in half a mo'."

Melodía began to squirm free. Pilar helped, mostly by trying to keep dung from falling in their hair and faces. She wasn't terribly successful.

Lying on the hard wagon bed trying to move and even breathe as little as possible had knotted Melodía's muscles. Her joints felt solidified. Even though the ride had lasted no more than three-quarters of an hour, most of it across well-maintained city streets and corduroy roads, it had been abundantly bumpy.

Montse peeled back the canvas as weight was shifted off it. Hands pulled Melodía to her feet. Without thinking about it, she turned and bent to help Pilar up as well.

The dray stood parked in a clearing among tall hardwood trees. The nosehorn's feed bucket had been removed. It grazed on low, feathery ferns with lavender underparts, which gave off a scent of mint when crushed.

Early sunlight slanted down to the clearing through fine clouds. Plate-sized blossoms—bright yellow and streaked from the centers with crimson, orange, or pale violet—decked the undergrowth surrounding the glade. Speckle-faced bouncers peeked from among them. Forest-gliders soared between lower branches, and fliers chirped from the higher ones.

Montserrat hit Melodía and almost toppled her into the heaped shit. She clung to her elder sister with startling strength, weeping wildly. Melodía found herself sobbing almost uncontrollably as well.

"Perhaps you'd like to climb out of the crap, Día?" Abi said. "I mean, if you're happy up there . . ."

Gently Melodía disentangled her sister. Josefina Serena and Princess Frances of Anglaterra helped the two down to the turf. Pilar scrambled lithely after.

Melodía looked down at herself. "Fanny, I—" she began, ineffectually batting at clumps of mostly dried dung that clung to her coarse robe.

"Oh, don't be ridiculous." Fanny embraced her.

"I was afraid—"

"I wasn't—"

"I know."

Something nudged Melodía from behind. She heard a whicker, felt a soft exhalation of warm breath on the back of her head. She turned to find herself staring up the flared nostrils of her mare, Meravellosa.

"Maia!" she cried, hugging the horse around the neck. Looking past her she saw a pretty white mare and a strapping bay gelding with a homely bent-nosed face and its back piled high with baggage tethered nearby.

"I love you all," she told her friends with tears streaming down her cheeks. "Thank you so much for saving me. But you shouldn't have done it. What were you all *thinking*?"

Montse shook back her ropes of hair. "I ordered everybody to do it! It's all my fault. They can punish me if they want to."

"This one's a fighter, Día," Abigail Thélème said. "It isn't true, of course. We all did it because we wanted to."

"Who thought this up? Was it you, Abigail?"

"I admit I helped flesh out the plot. But I can't claim much credit. Your sister and that servant wench of yours cooked it all up between them. Amateurish, but worthy of Sansamour withal."

Melodía turned to the guilty pair in amazement. Pilar calmly met her gaze.

"Your sister's much beloved among the servants," she said. "For her they'd do almost anything."

Not for me, I notice, Melodía thought. "And you?"

Pilar smiled and reached up to pluck a twig from the hair over Melodía's forehead. "We grew up together, Princess. Remember?"

Melodía felt her lips compress. *Maybe I didn't,* she thought.

"We didn't have any trouble on the way," Abi Thélème said. She sounded almost disappointed. "But we've got no way of knowing when your disappearance will be detected. Maybe it already has been. You two need to get away from here in a hurry."

Fear for her friends, and Pilar, and Claudia, and the other servants who must have aided her escape, hit Melodía hard enough to make her sway.

"Really, Día," Fanny said encouragingly, "the fact that we're working together with your sister should give us all immunity. It'll all be written off as a lark by foolish girls who've heard too many ballads of Companions' derring-do."

"Your father better not try to punish us," Fina said, frowning fiercely. "Nor my daddy's servants either. He'd find himself out on the street right quick!"

Melodía's stomach clenched. "Don't be too sure," she said.

Do I have to go back, to save my brave foolish sister and my brave, foolish friends? Lady Bella, please spare me that!

"Día," Fanny said, "we'll be fine."

"Keep a special eye on Falk. He's dangerous. He—I believe he's behind all this."

"We figured that out on our own," Abi said dryly. "Too late to help. I—let's just say I let everybody down."

Even in her seethe of fear and hope, Melodía

couldn't help wondering if this was the first time she'd ever heard Abi sound *uncertain*.

Another thought almost drove her to her knees. "*Papá*," she whispered.

How much did he know? How much does he know? Does he know what that bastard did to me last night?

She didn't dare think about that now. Maybe ever. If she had an "ever."

Someone took her hands. "Melodía, your father loves you," Fanny said. "We don't know everything that's going on."

She drew in a deep breath and opened her eyes.

"Very well. I need to get away, if I'm going to." She frowned as the obvious question slapped her in the face. "But—where?"

"Providence," Fanny said. "Where else?"

Fina gasped theatrically. "But that's where the Grey Angel Emerged!"

"It's still best," Fanny said. "They follow Jaume's philosophies there, after all. If anyone's going to welcome her, it'll be the Garden of Beauty and Truth."

Mention of Jaume stuck another dagger in Melodía's soul. What this news would do to him she couldn't imagine. *After I was too proud to say goodbye, or even return his letters. . . .*

"Fanny's right," Abi said, sounding just the slightest bit surprised. Melodía judged the cool Sansamour scion too canny to be taken in by Fanny's fluff-head act, but she doubtless considered the Anglesa a hopeless amateur at intrigue. Which most intriguers this side of Trebizon were, next to Abi. "If the Providentials don't actively oppose Church and Throne, they're certainly not in awe of either. They might well be willing to defy the Empire by sheltering a fugitive."

She paused, scowled, and exhaled through bared teeth.

"Or maybe they'll see you as the perfect coin to buy their way back into your father's good graces. I'm afraid the only choices we have to offer you range from bad to worse, Melodía."

No, Melodía thought. *Not worst.*

"Providence it is," she said. "I'll just have to take my least-bad choice. And do the . . . the best I can to get by." Her voice faltered.

Montse hugged her again fiercely. "Don't sell yourself short, Día!" she cried. "And stop taking Pilar for granted!"

Melodía looked down at her sister in surprise. She smiled.

"I have," she said. Pilar stood nearby. Melodía reached out to take her hand. Lifting it to her lips she kissed it, then let it go.

"Be well, Pilar. I'll miss you."

"How?" her servant asked. "Inasmuch as I'm coming with you."

"You can't!"

"Try and stop me." Pilar smiled. But her tone didn't joke.

"But—"

"Be realistic, Día," Fanny said. "You can't go all the way to Providence by yourself. It'll be hard enough for the two of you."

"But—I can hire guards."

"You don't dare," Abi said. "Too much risk they'll recognize you. Your father can pay them more to drag you back than you can pay them not to. Anyway, if you don't take the girl, I'll be happy to hire her. She shows a lot of promise. I can use someone with that kind of enterprise and courage."

"No! I'll go with Melodía if I have to follow her like a lost dog."

Given Abigail Thélème's customary aristocratic chill, Melodía expected her to take offense at such summary refusal from a mere maidservant. She showed no sign of doing so. Melodía's friend—and whatever else she was, Abi had proven truly that—was a deeper pool than she'd ever realized.

Like all my little circle, she realized with a shock. *Everyone but me. Evidently I'm the shallow one.*

Still, she teetered on the edge of ordering Pilar to stay behind. And found she couldn't. To do so would be to cut herself off from everything she'd known.

"I don't have the words," she said. "I've got more and truer friends than I ever imagined—and the best sister in the world."

She tousled Montse's hair. "And now, when I finally understand that, I have to leave you all."

She turned to Pilar. "Except you. Of course you'll come with me. If you're truly willing, after the way I've treated you for so long."

"Of course, Melodía dear."

It came to her to ask why. *I don't have time,* she thought.

Then she faced the truth. *I don't have the courage. Not yet.*

Everyone cried and laughed as she hugged and kissed her sister and friends most thoroughly. Then she mounted Meravellosa. Pilar climbed aboard the white rouncy. And turning their faces away from La Merced, the Corte Imperial, and the lives they had known, the two young women rode north at the best speed their packhorse could sustain.

"Hey, minstrel-man," a voice called through the ceaseless rain.

Through mud and downpour the defeated army trudged back toward Providence town. In front of all trudged Rob Korrigan, leading Little Nell by a rope. His slouch hat had slumped until the brim was a sort of sad, sodden skirt around his head. He wore only a linen breechcloth; the downpour had already defeated his best oiled-linen rain cape. He went barefoot because the shin-deep mud would've sucked boots or buskins off his feet into oblivion.

He might have ridden the hook-horn, since his baggage was following on a cart. But he felt the need for some sort, any sort, of activity. Despite the bone weariness weighing him down like plate armor made of lead, bizarre energy filled him. It gave his mind no rest, and thus wouldn't allow his body any. He had to do *something*, he felt, or burst into flame.

He looked back. Behind Nell a female nosehorn pulled a hemp-canvas-covered wagon full of wounded. A house-soldier who'd picked the badge of allegiance from the front of his sodden tabard with his dirk walked beside it.

The big, blunt, streaming face grinned. "Give us a song."

A few paces beyond the soldier, Rob spotted Karyl aboard Asal. Karyl's headaches and nightmares had all but vanished once he began building the militia. Rob—who had forgiven him for abandoning the wounded, having simmered down enough to conceive of the alternative—had feared its shattering defeat would bring them slamming back.

Instead Karyl was more alive than Rob had seen him: constantly *here* or *there* without seeming to have moved through the space between, urging along, soothing, scathing, solving problems, and always keeping the army together and moving away from the enemy.

Which, Rob's scouts informed them, pursued. But at a leisurely pace, to allow the wagonloads of luxuries and whores that Nuevaropan nobles always insisted on dragging on campaign with them to keep up. A brisk pursuit, of course, would have meant that Karyl's brilliant fight to cover the Providence militia's retreat had done nothing but defer their destruction. Baron Salvateur, or more likely his master Count Guillaume, held the Providentials in such contempt they thought them unworthy of the exertion.

Rob wouldn't call Karyl *happy*. If nothing else the fallen voyvod was far too consummate the military professional ever to be made happy by defeat. But it had clearly energized him.

It's the very challenge of the thing keeping the man alive, Rob realized. *I only hope his craving for a task worthy of his mettle doesn't get us all killed.*

But no, that wasn't likely and he knew it. Karyl's pride was woven far too deeply into saving what the town lords' debacle had left of the army to let him fail. Rob found that altogether reassuring.

Now Karyl caught Rob's eye. Rob glimpsed a flash of teeth through beard and rain.

It's also reassuring that himself is mortal enough to descend to inviting me to admire his cleverness, he thought. *Or so I suppose.* He wondered if Karyl had picked up the sleight of using shills from the town lords, those sleek, perfidious bastards, or had known the thing himself all along.

Others, drovers and soldiers, took up the call: "A song! Give us a song."

Rob grinned back.

"Very well," he said.

To give himself a moment to gather his thoughts— and a respite from this fucking mud—he swung aboard Nell's back. She swung her heavy head, flinging water from her frill, and sighed.

Rob turned around backward. The hook-horn knew how to follow the road as well as he did. He sucked in a deep breath of cool air, from which the downpour had rinsed all smell except its own. He began:

> *"Now hear me sing,*
> *"Of a wondrous thing,*
> *"When men and women, though their birth was base,*
> *"Nevertheless still dared to face*
> *"The iron knights of Brokenheart,*
> *"That day on Blueflowers field."*

He paused. Then the ambulance driver, a woman who shared a build and apparent temperament with her stodgily sturdy dray beast, began to clap and cry, "More! More!"

"Don't stop there, man!" the erstwhile house-shield called.

Behind him, Karyl nodded once. Then was gone, trotting back along the road's edge, to find the next task that needed doing.

The refrain had come to Rob by then. He sang out lustily:

"And though the field, the knights held at last
"The blood they bled
"Like ours, was red
"That day on Blueflowers field!"

Those in earshot shouted approval. To give himself time to catch more words from Bella's grace, he used the pretext of unstoppering a water gourd and wetting his throat. Ale would have soothed him better. But so would being dry, and warm, and romping between silken sheets with a lively pair of beauties.

Ah, but *those* were the spoils of victory. Losers got rain. And mud.

"Wait!" a young man's voice called from somewhere Rob couldn't see for the wounded wagon. "Teach us those first words before you go on!"

Rob smiled.

And so, appropriately ass-foremost, Rob Korrigan led the army of Providence in retreat and defiantly singing—

"Although our blood we freely spilt
"Upon those fair blue flowers,
"The blue bloods, though they called themselves,
"Shed blood the same as ours!"

—The whole way back to the outskirts of the town.

Where a squad of Town Guards, bristling with halberds and looking as draggle-tailed in their streaming morions and rain slicks as the men and women who'd actually fought a battle and lost, promptly arrested him and Karyl for treason.

Falk came onto the tower's flat roof to find the Emperor of Nuevaropa standing alone, watching the lights of La Merced begin to sparkle like a bowl of jewels below. The twilight air was soft as a kiss. The evening meal roasted aromatically in the cookshacks. A falling star streaked across a growing rift in the clouds above; fireflies danced around the tower as if in emulation.

"They've returned, your Majesty," Falk said, marching up to him. He wore his Tyrant armor and carried his helmet in his elbow's crook. "The three ladies-in-waiting and the Infanta. I've detained them."

"Well done," Felipe said. "Now let them go."

"What do you mean?" Falk said, thunderstruck. "They helped your daughter escape!"

Felipe turned to him. The old man was smiling in his ginger beard. Moisture glistened in his pale-green eyes.

He put a fatherly hand on Falk's shoulder. "Yes, my boy. Exactly. They helped my daughter escape."

"But—"

Felipe held up a single finger. Falk shut up. Felipe turned back to the crenellated rampart, to gaze off to where the sun fell through what seemed a layer of blood, to the Channel beyond the great Sea Dragon base on its spur of land.

"I don't dare alienate the whole gente of Anglaterra," the Emperor said. "Nor Sansamour, which for all its submission to the Francés crown might as well be a kingdom in itself. Josefina Serena's father, Prince Harry, is already annoyed with me over the very policies that upset my elder daughter. He's much too important to anger further by subjecting his heir to indignities. Not to mention the fact that I like it here in the Palace of the Fireflies, and have no desire to be turned out to return to that drafty Torre Imperial in La Majestad, where every broken-tailed courtier in Nuevaropa waits to bend my ear. Along with the entire Diet.

"And then there's the small matter of Montserrat. A mere child, as well as my daughter. The only one I have left, it would appear."

He turned back to his new chief bodyguard.

"Besides, they've done us a signal service, these girls."

"I don't understand, your Majesty."

"Whatever Melodía's said or done, it all springs from a child's passionate heart—and unformed judgment. Exile would be a possible sentence, even if she were found guilty. Of crimes I know in my heart she never meant, whether she committed them or not."

He sighed. "This way, my daughter is spared the ordeal of a trial. And not just her: the Imperio and Torre Delgao. And last, and truly least, an old man who's wearing himself to a specter trying to do what's best for all. Really, my boy, this is the best outcome possible for a terrible dilemma."

To believe in power, Falk reminded himself, *is to obey the man who has it. Anything else is anarchy.*

He drew a breath down deep, tamped down the black rage in his belly, and bowed his head.

"Yes, my lord," he said.

"Once again," Felipe said, brightening visibly, "Fray Jerónimo's wisdom is approved by events. He told me it was best this way, even as my heart longed to believe."

His smile saddened. "He said I should approve allowing you to duel poor, loyal Duval for command of the Tyrants too, did you know?"

Falk's skin prickled as if it had been left too long unprotected in high mountain sun. *I thought I'd have his ear alone,* he thought. *But another's there as well.*

He felt a certain grim amusement. *Didn't count on this mystery confessor, did you, Mother? Bergdahl? You're not infallible after all.*

Yet triumph swelled inside him, displacing anger and disappointment at his most precious prey's escape. Though Jaume, absent, remained the Emperor's right hand, Falk was now undoubtedly his left. That was power.

And now change would come to Nuevaropa. Falk would see to that.

"Come on, my boy," the Emperor said. "Our dinners await. I'm famished."

Epilogue

La Conversación
(The Conversation)

Ángeles Grises, **Grey Angels, the Seven**—The Creators' supernatural servitors: Michael, Gabriel, Raphael, Uriel, Remiel, Zerachiel, and Raguel. They have the task of maintaining the Creators' Sacred Equilibrium on Paradise. They possess remarkable powers and mystic weapons, and when they walk out in the world, they often take on a terrifying appearance. They are not humane, and regard all things as straw dogs.

—A PRIMER TO PARADISE FOR THE IMPROVEMENT
OF YOUNG MINDS

LA PALACIO DE LAS LUCIÉRNAGAS. IN THE SEWERS
DEEP BENEATH THE ROOTS OF ADELINA'S FROWN,
THE SHEER LIMESTONE CLIFFS ON WHICH THE
PALACE OF THE FIREFLIES RESTS.

IT IS PITCH-BLACK. THE PLAYERS NEED NO LIGHT
TO PERCEIVE EACH OTHER PERFECTLY. LIKEWISE THEY

PERCEIVE THE FEEL AND SMELL OF THE RAW SEWAGE
FLOWING PAST THEIR BARE LEGS IN ABUNDANT
DETAIL. IT BOTHERS THEM NOT AT ALL.

RAGUEL: Equilibrium.

URIEL: Our service, in perpetuity. What have you been up to, brother?

RAGUEL: Walking to and fro in the world, and going up and down in it.

URIEL: That joke was ancient before we were Created.

RAGUEL: One seeks small amusements where one can.

URIEL: That was a deft job you did, managing the story of your Emergence. It happened almost a year ago, by surface reckoning. How'd you contrive to have it arrive here at such a useful time?

RAGUEL: The usual sleights. Shadowed some mortal minds so that the herd-boy who saw me wasn't believed—and not wholly disbelieved either. When the time came, I sent dreams to reawaken fears. Count Guillaume did the rest, in his eagerness to win approval for his depredations on his neighbors, sending a messenger off to warn the court.

URIEL: Where he's caused quite a stir.

RAGUEL: That pleases me to hear.

URIEL: I've been out of the loop for quite some time. Where is our eldest brother? What's he up to now?

RAGUEL: The usual: leading a fight to drive the damned Anomalies deeper into the depths. To the Abyss of Holofernes and down, if he can. The abominations have been active of late. Even on the surface.

URIEL: And His strong right hand?

RAGUEL: At his side, of course. Our sister was never one to hold back from a fight. Especially against the demons after they held her captive so long. I believe the plan is to drive them so far down into the Core they'll be swallowed irretrievably by the Entropy from which they sprang.

URIEL: Will it work?

RAGUEL: Probably not. If we've not extirpated the demons in five Outerworld centuries, why should we expect to do so now? Not without some brilliant new scheme, anyway. Madness, it's said, is doing the same thing over and over and expecting different results. But still, it gives the brethren something to while away the cycles.

URIEL: What of *Her*?

RAGUEL: She walks beneath the sun as well.

URIEL: She's taken Herself a body?

RAGUEL: No. That's not Her way; you know that.

URIEL: Indeed. Still, instead of wasting their time chasing mice into the cellar, I wish our eldest brother—and who is like him?—would lead the kindred in a hunt through the Core for the place She keeps Her *corpus aetherium*. While Her intention strays out under the clouds, we could put an end to Her meddling once and for all.

RAGUEL: But that would end *all*, Uriel. It would destroy the world.

URIEL: Is that so different from what you and the Command and Sister Strength intend, brother?

RAGUEL: Yes! All the difference in the world. We only intend to excise a cancer, and heal the world's hurt. Not to unmake everything we ourselves were made to preserve!

URIEL: We were made to preserve all Paradise, Raguel, my friend.

RAGUEL: Sometimes a gangrenous limb must be amputated to save the body, Uriel.

URIEL: You mix metaphors with a large spoon. Still, I grasp the argument that what you'd have us do is no more than something we've found need to do before. Only on a more ... comprehensive scale. But we are bound to preserve what we can.

RAGUEL: Then what of your mad plan to destroy the World-Soul?

URIEL: Not *plan* so much as *desire*. Or idle fancy, if you prefer. Still, we could hold things together ourselves, we Seven; we are not so different from Her.

RAGUEL: And if we could not?

URIEL: Then things would, as always, seek and find a new Equilibrium. Without us, or the need for us.

RAGUEL: Your sojourn here among the cancer cells has given you a morbid turn of mind, Fire.

URIEL: Perhaps it has, Friend. Perhaps it has. Yet it is all my aim to preserve—as much as can be preserved.

RAGUEL (*LAUGHS*): That's our aim as Purifiers as well. We simply have a different appreciation of what can be preserved.

URIEL: "Should" is not the same as "can." We were not made to make such judgments, only to carry them out.

RAGUEL: But who shall make such judgments, then?

URIEL: None, perhaps. The Eight have told us what we're to do. They made us to carry out Their Design and nothing else. If They want us to change what we do, They can tell us.

RAGUEL: A thing most unlikely to occur, as well you know.

URIEL: Then we carry on as we have, obedient to our eternal duty.

RAGUEL: Ah, Fundamentalism. As good a refuge as any, I suppose, should reasoned debate fail.

URIEL: Call me Fundamentalist if you will. And what's wrong with that? This world was Created by the Eight, and us with it. Why complicate things?

RAGUEL: Faugh. You're as bad as the Affable One. Far too forbearing. Especially of the apes.

URIEL: That is my nature. Unlike some, I'm content to follow the Path I was Created to take.

RAGUEL: Daoism warmed over! I looked for better from you.

URIEL: Then you don't know me as well as you might, ice-spirit.

RAGUEL: Judgment is also part of your nature.

URIEL: I have judged. You simply disagree.

RAGUEL: You're far away from ice and snow here, good friend.

URIEL: I will return to them when I've succeeded. I've much to do before then. I wish you all success. (pause) You know the colors of the flames of my soul, Raguel! You know I mean it. We all serve the same end.

RAGUEL: True. Mind you remember it yourself.

URIEL: Always.

RAGUEL: I'll be back to it, then. Who knows what the apes've contrived to get up to in my absence?

URIEL: Farewell to thee, God-Friend. I leave you with the sign of Equilibrium, the *taiji-tu*.

RAGUEL: And mayest thou fare also well, God's Fire. I look forward to the day when all Seven act again as one.

URIEL: I wonder, will that bring the end of humankind? Or of us?

Read on for a preview of

The Dinosaur Knights

VICTOR MILÁN

Available in July 2016
from Tom Doherty Associates

TOR A TOR BOOK

Part One

Colloquy in a Sewer

Prologue

Los Ángeles Grises, **Grey Angels,** *Los Siete,* the
Seven. . . . —The Creators' supernatural servitors: Michael, Gabriel, Raphael, Uriel, Remiel, Zerachiel, and
Raguel, who are charged with maintaining sacred Equilibrium on Paradise. They possess remarkable powers
and mystic weapons, and when they walk out in the
world, they often take on a terrifying appearance. They
are not humane, and regard all things as straw dogs.

> —A PRIMER TO PARADISE FOR THE IMPROVEMENT
> OF YOUNG MINDS

Firefly Palace—*The sewers far beneath.*

URIEL: Before you go, my friend—a moment.
Raguel: You're not going to try to change my
mind again, are you?

URIEL: No. I'll abide by the compact—until my
turn arrives. I only wonder how you plan to return to Providence?

RAGUEL: Release this body back to dust and re-
animate the one there. It's waiting for me in a
safe place, nice and dormant and ringed about

with the strongest protections. It probably won't even have decayed appreciably, in such a brief interval by Outerworld standards.

URIEL: But aren't you the least bit nervous there might someday be a duplication error—and, you will forgive my saying this, cause you to undergo the True Death?

RAGUEL: The prospect does not unduly worry me.

URIEL: Don't think it can't happen just because it hasn't happened yet.

RAGUEL: It hasn't happened to any of us. Not that way.

URIEL: The prospect chills me to the core. What about her? Might Aphrodite intervene to cause such a thing?

RAGUEL: She wouldn't dare. That would bring her the same fate.

URIEL: She dares much, though. She walks the narrowest of lines, with her meddling on behalf of the dirt people.

RAGUEL: But she's bound no less than we, by the same terrible threat that compels us all. Anyway, given the way she always prates about it, she does take seriously her role of preserving Paradise and all its creatures. Including us.

URIEL: And therein lies the problem.

RAGUEL: The one thing that concerns me is my Providence avatar getting destroyed.

URIEL: What a shame that would be.

RAGUEL: I'm sure you'd weep bitter tears that our faction lost, and had to yield to yours. You're not getting too eager, are you?

URIEL: Not enough to cheat. It's your turn, you and your fellow frothing Purifiers.

RAGUEL: And I shall yield to you and your fellow Fundamentalists. If I should fail. I just won't.

PART TWO

Rebirth

Chapter 1

Chillador, Squaller, Great Strider. . . . —*Gallimimus bullatus*. Fast, bipedal, herbivorous dinosaurs with toothless beak. 6 meters long, 1.9 meters tall at the hips, 440 kilograms. Imported to Nuevaropa as a mount. Bred for varied plumage; distinguished by a flamboyant feather neck-ruff, usually light in color. Frequently ridden in battle by light-riders, as well as occasionally by knights and nobles too poor to afford war-hadrosaurs. Extremely truculent, with lethal beaks and kicking hind-claws.

—THE BOOK OF TRUE NAMES

Somewhere in central Francia:

Unseen, the hunter crouched in dense brush, watching with scarlet eyes.

Her belly rumbled so loudly with hunger that she feared it might give her position away. Her every instinct raged at her to strike, to rush down, snap the tailless two-legs in half, kick over their wooden shell-on-wheels, sink her teeth behind the frill of one of the hornfaces tied to it and rake its belly open with her powerful hind-talons.

But she would not. Could not.

Her mother, her lost mother for whom the longing was a constant ache, had taught her well. She must not kill two-legs, no matter how hungry she was or how tasty they were. Not unless ordered to by her mother, who wasn't here to do so. Or unless they attacked her.

The Allosaurus was cunning, intelligent for her kind and in her fashion. That did not equip her to persuade herself that her mother would, if present, give her leave to eat two-legs because she was hungry. Her thoughts were simple as a blade and direct as an arrow's flight.

Besides, she had learned the hard way that if the two-legs spotted her, they were liable to turn out armed with spears and bows and torches, in numbers too great even for her to think of killing them all. They were persistent and resourceful, worse even than horrors. Like those vicious little raptors, they could endanger even a full-grown matadora if enough of them attacked.

So, breathing shallowly, the monster stayed crouched, and let the small trade-caravan wind its way out of the copse of saplings through which the narrow track ran without attacking it.

When they were gone she rose from the brush and stepped out on the road. As she looked longingly after the carts, she saw a small figure standing atop one of the wooded gentle hills that dominated the terrain: a two-legs with a strangely pointed head.

Her mother could put on different heads at will, she knew. Her mother was a great sorceress. Though she knew it was not her mother, the hunter had come to recognize this two-legs and its peculiar head. And as always happened when she saw it, a hint of her mother's long-lost scent reached her nostrils. Joyous certainty filled her, that somehow she was coming closer to her mother, day by day.

A shift in the wind brought her a whiff of fresh nose-horn. Wild ones, from the tang of ferns and berries, not the tame beasts hitched to wagons and fed on gathered fodder and grain. A small herd grazed somewhere nearby.

She was a good girl. She had not eaten the two-legs. And she wouldn't go hungry much longer.

She allowed herself a soft, happy cry: *shiraa*.

She turned. Despite her tonne and a half of weight and eleven meters' length, she flowed back into the brush like a fish among water-weeds, making little more noise.

"I can't take it anymore."

Letting the reins fall in the middle of a sun-dappled forest roadway, *La Princesa Imperial* Melodía Estrella Delgao Llobregat clutched her hair with her fists and screwed up her face in misery.

That hair was dungeon-depth black now. Pilar had slipped into a town and bought dye to hide Melodía's distinctive dark-wine hair. Her own hair, a black so deep as to seem blue in certain lights, she left as it was; she was insignificant, the only reason for anyone to identify her being that she was the fugitive princess's companion. And anyway her coloring wasn't exactly rare here in the south of the Empire of Nuevaropa. Her eyes, startling emerald green, were a problem. But not even her gitana wiles offered any means of disguising them.

Pushing their mounts as hard as they dared, the young women had quickly crossed the border from Spaña into Francia. Avoiding the major Imperial High Road they then made for County Providence as rapidly as they could. There they hoped followers of Melodía's lover Jaume's doctrines might shelter them. It was a thin strand, but the only one in reach.

Once her first flush of mad elation following her escape had faded, Melodía traveled in a state of floating numbness. The physical pain of the rape by Falk had gone away even before that. She didn't think, she didn't feel. She mechanically did what Pilar told her. It was as if her senses, her body, even her mind had been swaddled in down.

But now, without warning, the numbness had vanished.

Sudden weight crushed her like an anvil falling. It drove the breath from her, the strength. And tears.

"I miss Montse," she said in a voice like a fistful of pottery shards. "I miss Daddy. I miss my friends. I miss sleeping in a bed. I just can't stand this."

Pilar stopped her white ambler and turned back.

"Princess," she said gently. "We need to move. We don't want to be caught here in the open."

Both were dressed as hidalgas, in loose silken blouses and linen, with boots, belts, and broad-brimmed way-farers' hats. Master plotter Abigail Thélème had sug-gested that looking like young women of consequence was the least risky of bad options for their flight from the false accusations of treason that had led to Melo-día's imprisonment, violation, and desperate flight into exile.

To start with they were well mounted, suspicious for the lower orders. If they seemed affluent they admittedly risked being robbed or grabbed for ransom. But their apparent breeding would still likely win them a measure of respect for their persons, for reasons of habit as well as potential reward versus risk.

But as commoner women traveling alone they'd run terrible risks of rape, enslavement, or murder—and not just by the bandits who swarmed the Imperio's byways.

They carried a few weapons Pilar's coconspirators had provided: smallswords for each, a shortbow and ar-row quiver for Melodía. Pilar was at least a vigorous, determined young woman, while Melodía had been well trained to use weapons. But as far as Melodía was concerned right now they might have been wet blades of grass: dank, limp, useless.

"It's just so hard," she sobbed. "What's the point, anyone? We don't have a chance. Not really. Everyone's against me. They're just going to chase us down like rats. Or bandits will swoop down on us and gobble us like a flying *dragón*. I'm tired and dirty, and my legs and butt ache all the time."

"Come along, Princess," Pilar said, grasping for the reins that slung slack over Melodía's pommel. "At least let's move off the highway. Please?"

Melodía batted her hand away. "I can't take it anymore! Don't you understand? Aren't you even listening?"

Pilar pressed her lips and drew a deep breath. "Very well. Then listen to me, and listen well. You need to grow up now, Melodía. You're not a Highness anymore. You're not a princess. You're a fugitive criminal, a renegade with a price on her head. You're also a young woman on the road, with the Fae alone knowing what is following you, amidst a countryside crawling with bandits. We're in deadly, constant danger."

Melodía stopped sniffling, dropped her hands, sat up and blinked. Her serving-girl's voice, always pleasant and deferential before, now cracked like a whip.

"I know you're intelligent. Lots more than you're showing now. You've got all the strength of will you could ever need too. I know you better than anybody— even your sister; I've known you longer than she. But you need to grow some sense, and in an Old Hell of a hurry, and bend that intelligence and that will to something bloody useful. Because both of our wits and wills together won't be too much to keep us alive to reach Providence.

"So if you want to live—if you want to clear your name, reunite with your sister and your father, reconcile with Count Jaume who loves you, and get vengeance on that filthy belly-crawler Falk, you need to straighten up and you need to do it now."

At last some sensation broke through the squishy and previously impermeable layers of Melodía's self-pity. Lightning outrage flashed through her brain, down her throat to the pit of her belly.

"How dare you? How dare you speak to me that way?"

"Because I still serve you," Pilar said. "And because I'm your friend."

Meravellosa had briefly tried reaching back to reassure her mistress with a lick on the cheek. Finding no success at that, she dropped her head to crop the lush green grass that grew beside the crushed tufa, the long-frozen volcanic foam that metaled the roadbed. Now she pricked her ears and whickered low in her throat. Pilar's mount and their cranky bay pack-marchador began to snort and sidestep.

"Shit!" Pilar said. Around a bend in the forest road behind them a horse whinnied greetings to others of its kind. "Quick, now, into the brush—"

But the riders were on them before Pilar could do any more than make another grab for Meravellosa's reins.

There were seven of them: six men-at-arms on coursers, led by a splendid young knight on an extravagantly ruffed blue and yellow Great Strider. They wore dinosaur-leather jacks over light tunics, and high boots lined with felt to keep from chafing bare legs. All carried long spears and yellow shields with red nosehorn heads on them. The knight wore a morion with a poofy yellow plume nodding above the crest. His horsemen made do with peaked steel caps and less splendidly tooled boots.

Melodía and Pilar had been overtaken by your basic baronial bandit-hunting patrol.

Melodía's heart felt like a small bird trying frantically to escape through her throat. *We're caught!* she thought. Her despair of a moment ago now seemed mere childish tantrum. *Now I've got something to cry about.*

"Ladies," the young knight said courteously. His goatee and moustache and the hair that hung to his shoulders from beneath his helmet were a yellow only slightly less gaudy than that on his shield. He was handsome and slim, and his facial hair couldn't conceal the fact he was little if any older than Melodía.

Dropping the butt of his spear into a holder by his saddle he swept off his helmet and bowed low. "Mor Tristan of L'Eau Noire, at your service. I ride for Baron

Francis of La Licorne Rouge. Whom have I the honor of addressing?"

The riders were all around them. Pilar had pulled her ambler up alongside Meravellosa. Fortunately the two beasts were at peace with one another, and didn't flatten their ears and try to bite or kick.

Pilar shook back her heavy hair and sat up straighter in the saddle. "I am Lucila, la Baronesa de la Castilla Verde, off to visit my cousin Montador Cédric, who serves Comte Modeste of Tempête de Feu." Which happened to be the next county but one along the way to Providence.

"And who might this beauty be?" asked Mor Tristan, eyeing Melodía appreciatively.

"My maidservant Marta," Pilar said. She spoke Francés flawlessly but with a strong Spañola accent—such as any self-respecting Spañola noblewoman might affect, even if she could speak without the accent. All the Towers of Nuevaropa, *Mayor y Menor*, were equal before Imperial law. But the Spañoles were, as the saying went, more equal than the others, and appearances must be preserved.

"She's been weeping," Tristan said.

Even in her surprise and terror and renewed outrage—*a servant, am I?*—Melodía felt fresh discomfort. This young knight was uncommonly observant for his kind. Which could be uncommonly inconvenient. Or fatal.

"The impudent wench spoke back to me," Pilar said. "Do you believe? I let her feel the edge of my tongue. And she responds like this. The weakling! But that's the lowborn for you. They have no steel in their spines."

Tristan tipped his head to one side. "It's been beaten out of them, over time," he said.

"Say," said one of his men, bending close to Melodía. "Don't these two look like the fugitives we were told to look for?"

Melodía's outrage was suddenly sidetracked by a sensation as if her heart, that fluttering flier in her throat, had turned to lead and dropped straight to the pit of her stomach.

"Perhaps so, Donal." Tristan rooted in a saddlebag and produced a handbill printed on springer-skin parchment for durability. "The Princess Melodía of Torre Delgao, no less—the Emperor's daughter. Apparently she's been very naughty. And her own serving wench."

He looked at both of them. "But it's hard to tell anything from these damned secondhand scribblings. And anyway, the renegade princess has red hair. It says so clearly here. Whereas neither the Baronesa nor her slattern shows so much as a glimmer of red."

"Slattern?" Melodía yelped. "Why, you dirty—"

Pilar backhanded her across the face.

It was a smart blow, driven by a strength surprising in one who hadn't had the extensive physical training afforded to women of the upper class. Although perhaps it shouldn't have surprised Melodía, given a servant's life spent washing and lifting and carrying. But more than arm-strength it was the sudden pain in cheek and nose, and sheer shock that it even happened, that knocked Melodía off her saddle and into the crunchy light gravel between her horse and Tristan's dinosaur.

The strider gobbled alarm and hopped back like a startled bird. Tristan fought to control it as the horses shied away. Melodía had landed on her butt, which though padded well with muscle was already sore, and gotten a jolt to her spine, adding both insult and injury.

"What the Hell do you think you're playing at?" she shouted at her serving-girl.

Or started to. When she opened her mouth Pilar brought her riding crop down in a whistling-vicious slash. It took Melodía across the crown of her head. It hurt like fuck, despite the cushioning of hat and hair. She flung up both hands protectively.

"How dare you talk back to me?" Pilar yelled. Even in a seethe of pain and indignation it rang uncomfortably familiar in Melodía's ears. "I'll teach you to be impertinent."

And leaning from the saddle she proceeded to thrash Melodía most thoroughly on her upflung arms, and then her back and shoulders, until the Princess collapsed, sobbing helplessly, in the pumice.

"There," Pilar said in satisfaction.

Looking up through a waterfall of tears Melodía saw her servant straighten in her saddle and let her crop— which she had never used on her actual mount—dangle by a strap.

"She'll remember that lesson a while, don't you think, Mor Tristan?" she said, smoothing her hair and white blouse.

Tristan bowed low again. "I shall certainly remember it, Mademoiselle," he declared, and Melodía could hear unmistakable irony in his voice. "It would be our honor to escort you to the border of our county."

"Stop sniveling," Pilar said imperiously. It actually took Melodía a moment to realize she was talking to her. By sheer process of elimination, mostly, at that: she was the only one sniveling after all. "Pick yourself up and get back on your horse. Or I'll give you something to *really* whine about—and at the next farm I'll sell that mare, who's much too fine for the likes of you, and buy you a bony nag far more in keeping with your station."

Melodía's arms and back blazed with unaccustomed pain. Her pride hurt scarcely less. But that pitiless voice sounded as if meant what it said. Feeling older even than la Madrota, the unbelievably ancient Queen Tyrannosaurus of Tower Delgao, she picked herself up, pushed away Meravellosa who was trying to nuzzle her comfortingly, and hauled herself onto the saddle with approximately the same grace as she would have loaded on an equivalent weight of meal in a sack.

The unlikely cavalcade set out again. The "Baronesa" rode knee to knee with the handsome young knight, gossiping with cheerful malice about what Melodía realized were thinly veiled personalities from the Corte Imperial. Having never seen young Tristan's face at court, Melodía knew he'd have no way of recognizing they weren't really hangers-on of some bent-centimo magnate of La Meseta.

Young Mor Tristan restricted his contributions to agreeing gallantly with whatever had fallen most recently out of Pilar's mouth during her infrequent pauses. As Melodía's pains and passions settled back from the boil, she found her perceptions unnaturally keen: the rustle of the broad splayed leaves above them, the smell of the forest and the sweating beasts, the usual chittering debate overhead between toothy birds and furred fliers, the feathery touch of a breeze on her face. Which now felt as if a red-hot iron mask had been clamped over it.

The men riding behind her also spoke, pitching their voices low. "Did you see the rack on that Baroness? Shit-fire or not, I'd love to bury my cheeks between them."

"I'd pay to see you try, Corneille. Me, I'd rather try to screw a red-feathered horror. Safer in the long run."

"How about the wench, then?" persisted Corneille, who was manifestly hornier than was good for him. "She's almost as hot."

Almost? Melodía thought. She carefully kept her shoulders slumped and eyes downcast. But she did wish for soldier ants to bite Corneille most enthusiastically on the genitals at the next stop.

"You'd be almost as great a fool to lay a finger on her," said the other man. "Me, I'm afraid to touch anything that belongs to that she-spider. Even her shadow."